DATE DUE

DEC 03

JAN 13			
FEB 23 04			
NOV 12 04			
FEB 4 '05			
7-8-05			
JAN 31			
MAR 09			
4-8			
GAYLORD			

THE BRIGHT SILVER STAR

THE
BRIGHT SILVER STAR

DAVID HANDLER

THOMAS DUNNE BOOKS

ST. MARTIN'S MINOTAUR

NEW YORK

THOMAS DUNNE BOOKS.
An imprint of St. Martin's Press.

www.minotaurbooks.com

Library of Congress Cataloging-in-Publication Data

Handler, David, 1952–
The bright silver star / David Handler.—1st ed.
p. cm.
ISBN 0-312-30714-4
1. Berger, Mitch (Fictitious character)—Fiction. 2. Mitry, Desiree (Fictitious
character)—Fiction. 3. Motion picture actors and actresses—Crimes against—Fiction.
4. African American police—Fiction. 5. Film critics—Fiction. 6. Policewomen—
Fiction. 7. Connecticut—Fiction. I. Title.

PS3558.A4637B73 2003
813'.54—dc21   2003050619

First Edition: November 2003

10 9 8 7 6 5 4 3 2 1

FOR PAMELA BOND,
WHO WELCOMED US HOME

THE BRIGHT SILVER STAR

Prologue

July 25

ONE OF THE THINGS that almost no one knew about him was that he was an awful driver. The worst. Not only was he easily distracted from the road in front of him but his eyesight was bad. Especially at night. Especially on narrow, unlit country roads.

Especially when he was stoned off of his gourd, had his foot jammed hard to the floor, and didn't care whether he kept on living or not.

A dense river valley fog hugged low to the ground in the heavy stillness of the summer night. Whenever the twisty road dipped down into a gully the fog became so thick he could see only his headlights before him in the mist, his wipers swishing back and forth, back and forth. Briefly, he would rise back up out of it, catching occasional snapshot glimpses as he tore along—of granite ledge crowding right up against the narrow shoulder. Mountain laurel and hemlocks. A guardrail where the shoulder dropped right off, the rain-swollen Eight Mile River rushing by a hundred feet below. The distant lights of a remote, lonely farmhouse. Then he would plunge back down into the moldy, overripe fog.

And into his own nightmare.

He hurtled right down the center of the road. If anyone happened to be coming toward him it would all be over. But there was no one else out after midnight on the Devil's Hopyard Road. Just him, with Neil Young cranked up full blast on the CD player. An old album with Crazy Horse called *Everybody Knows This Is Nowhere*, which had to be the single most hopeless, painful album that had ever been recorded at any time by anyone. The man made Nirvana sound like the Cowsills.

It fit his mood much too perfectly.

He hunched low over the wheel, left hand gripping it tightly, right hand groping on the seat next to him for the pint bottle of syrupy peppermint schnapps that lay next to his cell phone. It had been his best friend back when he was in junior high school. He drank it whenever the Bad People came.

He took a deep gulp as he came tearing around a curve, tires screaming, and suddenly two of them were standing right before him in the middle of the road. He swerved to avoid them, scraping the guardrail, a harsh, grinding sideswipe that startled him and sent sparks flying through the air. He did not stop to take a look at the damage he'd done to the car. He did not care about this car or any car. He kept right on going.

He had to keep on going. He was a man on a mission.

And the knowledge of what he was about to do gripped him with such panic that neither the schnapps nor the joint he'd smoked could even begin to help. He was sweating. His hands trembled, his breathing was shallow and quick. But he had no choice. No way out. And he knew this. And it hurt. God, how it hurt.

I have at long last met my soul mate, my one and only love, only it so happens that this person is not my wife. And so tonight I must say good-bye.

Honestly, he could not even believe he had gotten himself into this. How could he fall in love with someone else? God, it was all just so pathetically middle-aged and tawdry. But none of that mattered anymore. All that mattered was that it did happen and he had to end it right now.

He drove, suddenly spotting two more Bad People ahead of him in the mist, darting for cover in the brush. He sped his way past them, knowing full well he could not lose them. Whenever he felt frightened and lost and alone, they came.

He had started calling them the Bad People when he was no more than four and he'd lay awake at night with his heart pounding, waiting for them to come. They lived inside of his bedroom wall. He could hear them rustling around in there when they were coming out, and he could see them if he flicked on his light real fast. They were tiny creatures with horns and tails and hooves that made little clip-clop noises on the wooden floor. They had slimy purple skin, eyes that were narrow yellow slits, teeth that were sharp and dripping with saliva. He did not know why they had chosen him. He only knew that they meant him grave bodily harm.

And that no one else on earth could see them. Just him.

He remembered crying out for his mother when they came. Often, she would ignore him—just leave him alone with his terror. But sometimes she would come and sit there on the edge of the bed so they couldn't get at him. Dab at his damp brow with a wadded tissue. *My good little boy*, she would call him. *My good strong boy*. But then she would leave and there would be only him and the Bad People and the fear.

They did hide during daylight hours. But his fear was with him from sunrise until sundown. Always, it was with him. If only people knew just how hard it was for him to get through each and every day without giving in to it. But they didn't know. No one did.

They see me but they don't see me. No one knows me. No one.

He drove. Somehow, he made it all of the way to the end of the deserted road, where the entrance to the falls was. The state park closed after sunset. A barrier was lowered to keep people out of the parking lot. He pulled over onto the shoulder of the road and shut off the engine and the music. His was the only car there. He was the first to arrive. He sat there for a long moment, hearing the steady roar of the waterfall, his agitation mounting. He needed to hear a sane voice. It was imperative. He lunged for his cell phone and called Mitch. They hadn't known each other for long. But Mitch actually *understood* him—who he was, who he wanted to be. Plus he wanted nothing in return. Only honesty. And this was unusual. Hell, this was unheard-of.

Although right now the voice on the other end of the phone just sounded groggy and disoriented. "H-Hello . . . Whassa? . . ."

"I'm sorry if I woke you. I just wanted you to know something."

"Okay . . . Uh, sure . . ." Mitch sounded semialert now. "Where are you?"

"I'm on Sugar Mountain, with the barkers and the colored balloons."

Long silence. "Wait, give me a second. I know what that's . . . Neil Young, right?"

"You are."

"What's that whooshing noise? Are you hanging out in a men's room somewhere?"

"Not exactly."

"What time is it anyway?"

He sat there breathing in and out, feeling much less fear now. More an overbearing sadness. "It's too late. The damage is done. The hangman says it's time to let her fly."

"*What* hangman? What the hell are you talking about?"

"Good-bye, Mitch."

"Wait, don't—!"

He flicked off the phone and hurled it out his open window, hearing it clatter to the ground. Got out of the car and staggered his way blindly down the footpath toward the falls, clutching the schnapps bottle in one hand and a book of matches in the other.

It was so dark he kept stumbling over the loose rocks and exposed tree roots. He lit a match, squinting. Ahead were the picnic tables where they'd made love that first night. It all started here. And *there* was the walkway to the top of the falls. During the day, people came from miles around to see the waterfall, to photograph it and wade in the cold, clear pools at its base, to eat their gray, greasy junk food and drink their carbonated sugar water and do the other normal, stupid things that normal, stupid people did.

He staggered on. A wooden guardrail hugged the edge of the cliff, smelling of creosote. Wire mesh was stapled to the posts to keep small children from slipping under the rail and falling to their death. He lit another match. Now he stood before the warning sign that read: *Let the Water Do the Falling. Stay Behind This Point.*

He paid no attention. Climbed right over it and out onto the flat shelf of granite ledge, directly over the falls. This was *their* place, the secret haven where they came to make feverish, forbidden love, night after night, as often as they dared. They were alone here. Just them and the water and the darkness.

The bare granite was slick from the fog and the spray. And it was a bit cooler here. But still he was sweating. He crouched here on the ledge; feeling the full power of the river as it tore right past him into the darkness of space, smashing down onto the smoothed hollows of granite a hundred feet below, swirling and foaming and cascading before it bottomed out into a river once again. He did think about hurling himself right off the ledge right now, sparing himself the pain of what was about to come. But he could not will himself to do this, no matter how much he wanted to. The words had to be spoken.

And so he waited in the fog for his one true love to come.

He didn't hear the other car arrive over the roar of the falls. Or hear the quick, sure footsteps until they were very close to him. He couldn't see the shimmer of golden hair or the shiny, trusting blue eyes. He didn't need to. He could see everything with his own eyes shut, just as his lips knew the achingly soft, sweet lips that were now kissing him, kissing him.

"Hey, baby," he said as they sat there in each other's arms. They didn't have to raise their voices as long as they stayed very close.

"God, I'm so glad you're here. I wasn't even sure you'd make it tonight."

"I said I'd be here, didn't I?" he responded lightly, hearing the quaver of insincerity in his own voice. "Want some peppermint schnapps?"

"Ugh, no."

"Why wouldn't I be here?"

"You sounded funny on the phone. Was *she* standing there?"

"Not really." He groped in the darkness for a hand, clutching it tightly, knowing that once he said the words he had to say that he would never, ever feel its caresses again. "But I do have something kind of heavy to lay on you . . . about you and me."

"What about us?"

"We can't do this anymore," he blurted out.

"W-What are you saying to me?" They were no longer holding

hands. They were apart, now and forever. "You don't want to *be* with me anymore?"

"No, I *do* want to be with you. That's not the point."

"Then what is?"

"That it's over. That it . . . it has to be over."

"Just like that? You're insane!"

"I know this," he admitted, hearing only the roar of the falls for a moment.

Until he heard a gut-wrenching sob. "My God, do you actually think that you can just snap your fingers and the love's not there anymore? Like it's some kind of a-a choice? Paper or plastic? Smooth or chunky?"

"Look, it's not *you*, okay?" he said, his own voice rising helplessly. "It's *me*. I can't keep doing this. It's not going to be easy to stop. In fact, I think this is the hardest thing I've ever had to do in my whole life. But I have to do it."

"But *how*? We'll still see each other every day. How can we pretend that nothing's happened?"

"We've been pretending that ever since we got involved."

"You mean, ever since you came after me, don't you?"

"I warned you about me from the very start," he shot back, growing defensive now. "I told you what would happen."

"You told me you'd break my poor little heart. You didn't tell me you'd stab me in the chest with a dull knife and . . . and why are you *doing* this to me?" Now he heard another sob in the darkness. "God, listen to me. I sound like a pathetic old lady."

"No, you don't. You sound great. You *are* great. And I wish we could go on like this forever. I swear, I've never been this happy in my whole life."

"Only because your whole life is a lie. You are living a lie."

"Hey, your marriage is just as dead as mine."

"This isn't about me. It's about *you*."

"I know, I know. . . ." He breathed in and out, his chest beginning to ache. "I just can't keep chancing it like this. Not in Dorset. People are bound to find out, and when they do they'll talk. It's what they live for—to talk about people like us."

"So let them. Who cares? I don't."

"Well, I can't risk it. I won't risk it."

"Every day you get out of bed there's risk. Without risk, you're as good as dead."

"Right now, I wish I was," he confessed.

"Screw you and your self-pity. You're not the one who's getting hurt here—I am. And I hate you. Do you hear me? I *hate* you!"

"Look, this doesn't have to end badly," he said soothingly. "It just has to end." He drained the schnapps bottle and set it down on the stone next to him, climbing unsteadily to his feet. He'd said what he had to say. Now all that was left was the ugliness, the words that hurt.

"Wait, where do you think you're going?"

"Home."

"What about *me*?" They were both standing now. "Don't you realize how much *I've* risked?"

"Yes, I do," he said, even though it was not nearly the same. Not even close. "And, believe me, this is better for you, too."

"God, you are so totally full of shit. Our lives were dead until we found each other. We've got something special together. How can you turn your back on that. How can you walk away?"

Now the sob was coming from his own throat. "I *have* to. You know I do."

"I don't know anything—except that I *won't* let you walk away from me. I'll . . . I'll tell her about us. I swear I will."

He stood there in choked silence, realizing that he was trapped in a love he could not get out of. No way out. No good way, anyhow. And now it began to creep into his mind—the terrible thing he had been trying not to think about. Which was that this secret place of theirs, this private, perfect perch where they made love, was also a private, perfect place to kill. And, worse, that he was totally capable of doing it.

I am one of them. I am one of the Bad People.

Maybe he had known this all along. Maybe that was why he'd been so freaked out all evening. Because he was coming here to murder the great love of his life and he damned well knew it.

He stood clenching and unclenching his fists, preparing himself for what he was about to do. "I have to think about my future," he explained.

"You say that as if you have one."

Which he didn't.

"No, don't!" he cried out as he felt himself suddenly being shoved toward the edge of the cliff.

And it was all so unexpected, so ferocious, so *unthinkable* that he had no chance to hold his ground. He did try, in that desperate last fraction of a second, to cling to the slick stone, digging at it with his fingers and his toes like a wild, desperate animal. But now he was pitching over backward into the blackness with his arms waving wildly and the roar of the falls growing louder and now the roar was coming from out of him as his head *smacked* into something hard. And everything went from black to red.

As he lay there on the rocks, he thought he heard a sob coming from somewhere far away, but that may have been his own last groans he was hearing. He felt no pain, no fear, no regret—only a powerful rush of relief.

I am free of them. I am free of the Bad People. They can go torment someone else now, because they can't have me. Not anymore. Because I am free . . . I am free . . . I am . . .

Eighteen Hours Earlier

CHAPTER 1

THERE WAS NO LOLLYGAGGING in the feathers on Big Sister Island. Not in July. Not when the sun came beaming through the skylights in Mitch's sleeping loft at five-thirty in the morning. Not a chance. These days, Mitch Berger, creature of the darkness, got up when the sun got up.

And he loved every glorious minute.

He loved the cool, fresh breezes off Long Island Sound that wafted through his antique post-and-beam carriage house no matter how hot and sticky the day was. He loved the blackberries that grew wild all over the island and the fresh vegetables that he had brought to life in his own garden. He loved mowing his little patch of lawn with an old-fashioned push mower, which had to be one of the great lost pleasures of the modern age. He loved parking his pudgy self in a shell-backed aluminum garden chair at sunset, cold beer in hand, waiting for Des to come thumping across the rickety wooden causeway in her cruiser. He loved the bracing dips in the Sound they would take together. He even—and this was the truly amazing part—loved those disgustingly healthy dinners of grilled fish, brown rice and steamed vegetables she would cook for them.

If he didn't know any better Mitch would have sworn he was turning into somebody else.

Every day he learned something new about the sun-drenched natural world around him. Goldfinches are attracted to sunflowers, hummingbirds to the color red. The male osprey stays behind to teach the fledgling how to fly while the female migrates south on her own. Many of these things he had learned from Dodge Crockett, unofficial head of the unofficial walking club Mitch had fallen in with at the beginning of the summer—four local men who hiked the three-mile stretch of beach that ringed the Peck's Point Nature Preserve every morning at seven so as to exercise, to bird watch and to chew each other's ears off.

There was no getting around this: Mitch Berger, lead film critic for the most prestigious and therefore lowest paying of the three New York city metropolitan dailies, was in a male bonding group. Or so Des called it. Mitch simply described it as four Dorseteers who liked to walk together, eat fresh-baked croissants and discuss life, love, and women—three subjects they freely admitted they knew nothing about.

Besides, today he had a serious career-related matter to discuss with Dodge.

At the sound of Mitch stirring around in the kitchen Quirt came scooting in the cat door for his breakfast. Quirt, who was Mitch's lean, sinewy hunter, liked to sleep outside during the summer on a bench under the living room bay window. Clemmie, his lap cat, still preferred the safe confines of the house, but slept downstairs in his armchair as opposed to upstairs on Mitch's bed, snuggled into his collarbone. Mitch had grown accustomed to her being there at night and missed her terribly, but he had also come to understand cats and the high priority they placed on their own comfort. When autumn blew in, and Clemmie felt the need for Mitch's considerable body warmth, she would return to his bed as if she'd never left.

Right now, she yawned at him from his chair and stretched a languid paw out toward him, which was her way of saying good morning.

Mitch was otherwise alone this morning. Des had taken to spending three or four nights a week with him, the rest at her own place overlooking Uncas Lake. Bella Tillis, her good friend and fellow rescuer, had moved in with her on a trial basis, which meant Des could stay over with him and not fret over her own furry charges.

While Quirt hungrily munched kibble Mitch squeezed himself a tall glass of grapefruit juice. As he drank it down he stood before his living room windows that overlooked the water in three different directions, savoring the quiet of early morning on his island in the

Sound. A fisherman was chugging his way out for the day. Otherwise, all was tranquil. Mitch dressed in a faded gray T-shirt and baggy khaki shorts. Shoved four blue tin coffee mugs in his knapsack, along with an eight-ounce plastic water bottle filled with that see-through low-fat milk Des had him drinking—he himself vastly preferred whole milk of the chocolate variety. But Des was absolutely determined that Mitch take off some excess poundage this summer. And a determined Des was no one to trifle with. Ever since she'd turned his kitchen into a No Fry Zone he'd gone down two whole waist sizes.

He started out the door, binoculars around his neck, and headed down the footpath lined with wild beach roses and bayberry toward the causeway that connected Big Sister with Peck's Point. The island had been in the Peck family since the 1600s. It was forty square acres of blue-blooded paradise at the mouth of the Connecticut River just off Dorset, the historic New England village. There were five houses on the island, a decommissioned lighthouse that was the second tallest in New England, a private beach, dock, tennis court. Mitch had been only too happy to rent the converted caretaker's cottage, and to eventually buy it. During the cold months he'd had the whole island to himself. Right now one other house was in use—Bitsy Peck, his garden guru, was living in the big Victorian summer cottage with her daughter, Becca.

Not a day went by when Mitch didn't tell himself how extraordinarily lucky he was to be here. He'd been a total wreck after he lost his beloved wife, Maisie, a Harvard-trained landscape architect, to ovarian cancer when she was barely thirty. He had needed somewhere to go and heal. And it turned out that somewhere was this place. Slowly, he *was* healing. Certainly, Des Mitry's arrival in his life was a huge reason why. So was his determination to plunge himself headlong into new experiences—for Mitch Berger, a socially challenged screening room rat, walking in the sunshine every morning with three men who he'd only recently met qualified as a huge leap into the unknown.

He could see them waiting for him there at the gate as he crossed the narrow quarter-mile wooden causeway—a trio of middle-aged Dorseteers in sizes small, medium, and large. Will Durslag, who towered over the other two, was the fellow who'd brought him into the group. Will and his hyperkinetic wife, Donna, ran The Works and Mitch was a huge fan of their chocolate goodies, or at least he had been until Des put him on his diet. Standing there in his tank top and baggy surf shorts, knapsack thrown carelessly over one broad shoulder, thirty-four-year-old Will looked more like a professional beach volleyball player or Nordic god than he did a jolly chef. He was a tanned, muscular six foot four with long sun-bleached blond hair that he wore in a ponytail. Early one morning, Mitch had encountered him on the bluff hiking with Dodge Crockett and Jeff Wachtell. Introductions had been made, a casual invitation extended. Next thing Mitch knew he was not only joining their little group every morning but looking forward to it.

It was a loose group. If you were there at seven, fine. If you couldn't make it, that was fine, too. No explanations required. There was only one rule: you could not take yourself too seriously. Any subject was a legitimate topic of conversation. The group had no name, though Mitch was partial to the Mesmer Club in tribute to *The Woman In Green,* one of his favorite Basil Rathbone Sherlock Holmes films. Not that he had bothered to mention this to any of them—they would not understand what he was talking about. They had not, for example, grasped the origin of the *Rocky Dies Yellow* tattoo on his bicep.

"Good morning, men," he called out to them.

"Another beautiful day in paradise," said Dodge, his face breaking into a smile.

"*Ab-so-tootly,*" piped up Jeff, an impish refugee from a major New York publishing house. Jeff ran the Book Schnook, Dorset's bookstore.

They set out, walking single file down the narrow footpath that edged the bluffs. Beach pea grew wild alongside of them. Cormorants and gulls flew overhead. Dodge set the brisk pace, his arms swinging loosely at his sides, his shoulders back, head up. Mitch fell in behind him, puffing a bit but keeping up. When he'd first joined the group, Mitch could barely cut it. He was definitely making progress, although his T-shirt was already sticking to him.

Dodge was far and away the oldest of the group. Also the wealthiest. He came from old Dorset money, had been a second-team All American lacrosse player at Princeton, and remained, at fifty-four, remarkably vigorous and fit. Dodge was also the single most rigidly disciplined person Mitch had ever met in his life. So disciplined that he never needed to wear a watch. Thanks to his strict, self-imposed regimen of daily activities Dodge always knew within two minutes what time it was. What made this especially amazing was that Dodge had never held a real job in his life. Didn't need to. And yet he was never idle. Each day he awoke at six, walked at seven, lifted weights at eight, read *The New York Times* and *Wall Street Journal* at nine, attended to personal finances at ten and practiced classical piano at eleven. After lunch, the remainder of his day was given over to meetings. Dodge was president of the local chapter of the Nature Conservancy as well as commissioner of Dorset's historic district. He served on the Wetlands Commission, the executive board of the Dorset library, and the Youth Services Bureau. Some years back, he had also put in two terms as a state senator up in Hartford. A few of the old-timers around John's barbershop still called him Senator.

And yet, Dodge was no tight-assed prig. Mitch had heard him do some pretty amazing things with "Great Balls of Fire" on that Steinway of his. Mitch enjoyed being around the man every morning. He was good company, a good listener, and somehow, he made Mitch feel as if walking with him was the highlight of his day. Dodge also possessed a childlike excitement for life that Mitch truly envied. Hell, the man's whole life was enviable. He had health, wealth, a beautiful renovated farmhouse on ten acres overlooking the Connecticut River. He had Martine, his long-legged, blond wife of twenty-six years who, as far as Mitch was concerned, was merely Grace Kelly in blue jeans. Between them Dodge and Martine had produced Esme, who happened to be one of the hottest and most talented young actresses in Hollywood.

And the reason why Mitch needed to speak to Dodge this morning. Because this was by no means a typical July for Dorset. Not since Esme Crockett and her actor husband, combustible blue-eyed Latino heartthrob Tito Molina, had rented a $3 million beachfront mansion for the summer. Tito and Esme, each of them twenty-three years old, were the biggest thing happening that summer as far the tabloids were concerned. She was a breathtakingly gorgeous Academy Award winner. He was *People* magazine's Sexiest Man Alive, not to mention a man given to uncontrollable bouts of drinking, drugs, and rage. Just within the past year Tito had served two stints in drug rehab, thirty days in a Los Angeles County jail for criminal drug possession, and been sued twice by tabloid photographers for his violent behavior toward them in the street outside of the couple's Malibu home. Their arrival in Dorset had sparked debate all over the village. Esme was one of Dorset's own and the locals were justifiably proud of her. This was a girl, after all, who'd gotten her start on stage in the Dorset High production of *Fiddler on the Roof.* From there she'd starred in a summer revival of Neil Simon's *I Ought to Be in Pictures* at the Ivoryton Playhouse, where she was spotted by a top New York casting director. He was searching for a young actress to play an underaged Roaring Twenties gun moll in the next Martin Scorsese crime epic. Esme won not only the part but an Oscar for Best Supporting Actress. Now she was one of Hollywood's top draws.

But Dorset also cherished its decidedly *un*-Hampton low profile, and Esme and Tito had brought a media army with them, along with stargazers, gawkers, and more gawkers. The village was positively overrun by outsiders, many of them rude and loud—although none ruder or louder than Chrissie Huberman, the high-profile celebrity publicist who the golden couple had imported from New York to run interference for them.

"Oystercatchers at three o'clock, Mitch!" Dodge called out, pausing to aim his binoculars at the rocks down below. Dodge had a bristly gray crewcut, tufty black eyebrows, and a round face that frequently lit up with glee. He was no more than five feet nine but powerfully built, with a thick neck, heavy shoulders, and immense hands and feet. He wore a polo shirt, khaki shorts and size-15 hiking boots. "Two of them, see? They almost always travel in pairs."

Mitch focused his own glasses on one of them. It was a big, thick-set bird with a dark back, white belly, and the longest, flattest orange bill Mitch had ever seen. "Wow, a cartoon shorebird. What a hoot."

"Not to mention a dead ringer for my uncle Heshie," said Jeff as they resumed walking. "I wonder if he cheats at cards, too." Jeff was an odd little puppy of a guy in his late thirties who had a habit of sucking in his cheeks like a fish whenever he was upset, which was pretty much all of the time lately—he was in the middle of a rather ugly divorce. Jeff had moppety red hair, crooked, geeky black-framed glasses, and freckly, undeniably weblike hands. He also happened to walk like a duck. Jeff possessed even less fashion sense than Mitch. Right now he had on a short-sleeved dress shirt of yellow polyester, madras shorts, and Teva sandals with dark brown socks.

"Raccoon poop at nine o'clock," Dodge warned them so they wouldn't step in the fresh, seed-speckled clump on the edge of the path.

The path cut down through the bluffs toward the beach now, and they started plowing their way out to the end of the Point's narrow, mile-long ribbon of sand. It was a very special ribbon of sand. At its farthest tip was one of the few sanctuaries in all of New England where the endangered piping plovers came to lay their eggs every summer. There were two chicks this season. The Nature Conservancy had erected a wire cage to protect them from predators. Also a warning fence to keep walkers and their dogs out. One of the walking group's assignments every morning was to make sure that the fence hadn't been messed with in the night. Kids liked to have beer parties and bonfires out there and sometimes got rowdy.

"You know what I was thinking about this morning?" Dodge said, waving to an early morning kayaker who was working his way along close to shore. "I've traveled all over the world, and yet I would never want to live anywhere but here. Why is that?"

"Open up your eyes, Dodger," Jeff said. No one else in the group called him Dodger—so far as Mitch knew, no one else in the world did. "It's awful damned pretty here."

"If you ask me," said Will, "it's Sheffield Wiggins."

"Old Sheff Wiggins? My God, I haven't thought of him in ages." To Mitch and Jeff, Dodge said, "He used to live in that big saltbox across from the Congregational church."

"You mean the cream-colored one?" asked Jeff.

"That's not called cream, my friend. That's called Dorset yellow."

"I've seen that same color all over New England. What do they call it if you're in, say, Brattleboro?"

"They call it Dorset yellow."

"Okay, I think we're drifting off of the subject," Will said.

"You mean this wasn't a story about paint?" Mitch said.

"Yes, what *about* Sheff? He's been dead for an honest twenty years."

A faint smile crossed Will's lean face. He was a good-looking guy with a strong jaw and clear, wide-set blue eyes. Yet he seemed totally unaware of his looks. He was very modest and soft-spoken. "Sheff's sister, Harriet, called my mom about a week after he died. This was in January and the ground was frozen, so they had to wait until spring before they could bury him. My dad used to dig the graves over at the cemetery, see." Will was a full-blooded swamp Yankee whose late father had done a variety of jobs around Dorset, including serving as Dodge's gardener and handyman. Will was only a kid when he died. Dodge gave Will odd jobs after that and became like a second father to him. The two remained very close. "Anyway, Harriet called my mom to tell her that Rudy, Sheff's parakeet, had died—"

"Honest to God, Will," Jeff interjected. "I can't imagine where this story is going."

"She wanted to know if my mom would keep Rudy in our freezer until the spring so that he and Sheff could be buried together."

"You mean in the same casket?" asked Mitch, his eyes widening.

"I do."

"And did your mom? . . ."

"She did. And, yes, they are. Buried together, that is."

"How old were you, Will?" Jeff asked.

"Ten, maybe."

Jeff shuddered. "God, having that parakeet in my freezer all winter would have given me nightmares. What color was it? Wait, don't even tell me."

"My point," Will said, "is that Harriet Wiggins thought nothing of calling up my mom to ask her. And my mom didn't bat an eyelash. *That's* Dorset."

"In other words, everyone in town is totally crazy?" asked Jeff.

"I like to think of it as totally sane," said Dodge as they trudged their way out to the point, the sun getting higher, the air warmer. The tide was going out. Dozens of semipalmated plovers were feeding at the water's edge on spindly little legs. "Martine was talking about you last night, Mitch."

"She was?"

"They desperately need tutors over at the Youth Services Bureau. All sorts of subjects—history, English, math."

For weeks, Dodge had been trying to convince Mitch to join up with some local organization or another. Already, Mitch had turned down a chance to become recording secretary of the Shellfish Commission. Not the sort of thing he could see himself doing. It seemed so Ozzie Nelson. But Mitch was coming to understand that getting involved was part of the deal when you lived in a small town. Will Durslag served on the volunteer fire department. Jeff was a literacy volunteer.

"We have a bunch of really talented kids in this town, but they're just not motivated. Would lighting a fire under one of them be your kind of deal?"

"Maybe. I mean, sure."

"Great. I'll get you an application."

This man was relentless. Still, Mitch greatly admired his commitment. Mitch could hear a helicopter zooming its way toward them now across the Sound, moving low and fast. A news chopper from New York. All part of the Esme-Tito circus. Another day, another breathless new inquiry. Here was yesterday's: Did she or didn't she just have a boob job? Inquiring, very small minds wanted to know.

Mitch sped up so as to pull alongside of Dodge, the other two falling in behind them. "I wanted to give you a head's-up," he told him, puffing. "My review of Tito's new movie is in this morning's paper. I panned it. I hope that won't be awkward for you."

"Don't worry about Tito. He's much more levelheaded than people give him credit for. Besides, I'm sure you were your usual tactful self."

"Tactful is not exactly the word I'd use."

Tito's movie, *Dark Star,* was in fact Hollywood's hugest, loudest clunker of the summer, an ill-conceived $200 million outer-space epic that the studio had held back from its Fourth of July weekend opening because preview audiences were laughing out loud in all the wrong places. It was so disastrously awful that Mitch had called it "The most unintentionally hilarious major studio bomb since *Exorcist II: The Heretic.*" He went on to say, "Tito Molina has such a pained expression on his face throughout the film that it's hard to tell whether he wants to shoot the aliens or himself."

"I really like this kid," Dodge said. "I didn't expect to, not after everything I'd read about him. But I do. And I don't just say this because he's my son-in-law. He has a broken wing is all. Can't fly straight to save his life. That doesn't make him a bad person. You'd like him, Mitch. I sure wish you'd reconsider my invitation."

Dodge wanted him to join them for dinner one evening. Mitch didn't think that socializing with performers was a good idea for someone in his position. "I'd love to, Dodge, but it wouldn't be appropriate."

"Sure, I understand. I just think you'd enjoy his company. He's one of the most intuitively brilliant young men I've ever met."

This in spite of Tito's famously troubled childhood in Bakersfield, California. Tito's father, a Mexican migrant worker, was killed in a bar fight when Tito was seven. His Anglo mother, a schizophrenic, was in and out of state mental hospitals until she committed suicide when he was thirteen. He took to living on his own after that, often in abandoned cars, and survived by dealing drugs. His big break came when a Britney Spears video was being shot at the Bakersfield high school that he'd recently dropped out of. A girl he was dating auditioned for a bit role. He tagged along with her. The video's director was looking for a bad boy from the wrong side of the tracks to play the bare-chested object of Britney's sweaty affections. One look at Tito's intense, smoldering good looks and he got the part. The video was such a hit on MTV that Tito shot straight to teen dream stardom, acting in a succession of edgy teen angst dramas—most notably the highly successful remake of the greatest teen angst drama of them all, *Rebel Without a Cause,* in which he stepped into James Dean's almost mythic shoes and, somehow, made them his own. It was Esme who was cast in the Natalie Wood role. They fell in love on the set, fueling the picture's on-screen heat, and married shortly thereafter.

Inevitably, critics were labeling Tito as his generation's James Dean. Mitch was not one of them. He believed that labels were for soup cans, not artists. He only knew that when Tito Molina appeared on-screen he could not take his eyes off him. Tito had an untamed animal quality about him, an edge of danger, and yet at the same time he was so vulnerable that he seemed to have his skin on inside out. Plus he had remarkable courage. Mitch was completely won over after he saw him conquer Broadway as Biff Loman to John Malkovich's Willy in an electrifying new production of Arthur Miller's *Death of a Salesman.* As far as Mitch was concerned, Tito Molina was simply the most gifted and daring actor of his generation—even if he had just stumbled badly with *Dark Star.*

"He and Esme are like a pair of special, golden children," Dodge said. "When I see them together, hand in hand, I think of Hansel and Gretel on their way through the woods to grandmother's house. They absolutely adore each other, and she's been able to help him some with his rage. And their publicist, Chrissie, really does try to put a smile on his public face. But it's a challenge. He's just such an intensely unhappy person."

"He's an actor," Mitch said.

"So is Esme, and she's not like that. She's a sweet, big-hearted girl.

A total innocent. I just . . . I hope he doesn't hurt her. He isn't faithful to her, you see."

"How do you know this?" Mitch asked, glancing at him.

"I just do. You can always tell—like with Martine," Dodge said, lowering his voice confidentially. "She's not faithful to me. She has a lover."

"I'm so sorry, Dodge," Mitch said, taken aback.

"These things happen over the course of a marriage," Dodge said, his jaw set with grim determination. "I sure wish I knew what to do about it. But the unvarnished truth is that I don't."

"Well, have you spoken to Martine about it?"

"Hell, no. What good would that do?"

"Communication is a positive thing, Dodge."

"No, it's not. As a matter of fact, it's highly overrated."

They were nearing the tip of Peck's Point now. The osprey stands that the Nature Conservancy had erected out in the tidal marshes were no longer occupied. The ospreys had nested and gone for the season. Mitch did spot two blue herons out there. And the two rare, precious dun-colored piping plover chicks were still in residence in their protective enclosure, tiny as field mice and nearly invisible against the sand.

He and Dodge inspected the cage and warning fence as Jeff and Will caught up with them. A fence stake had worked its way out in the night. Dodge pounded it back down with a rock as Mitch swabbed his face and neck with a bandanna, wondering why Dodge had chosen him to confide in about Martine. Why not Will? The two of them were so much closer.

Mitch opened his knapsack and got out the mugs and plastic milk bottle, his stomach growling with anticipation. From his own knapsack Will produced a thermos of his finest fresh-brewed Blue Mountain coffee and a bag of croissants he'd baked before dawn. Will was up every morning at four to oversee his extensive baking operation. The beach constituted his only break from the punishing fourteen-hour shifts he worked.

There were two driftwood logs with plenty of seating room for four. Jeff filled the tin mugs from the thermos. He and Will took their coffee black, Mitch and Dodge used milk. Dodge passed around the croissants. Then they all sat there munching and watching the killdeer and willets poke at the water's edge for their own breakfast.

Mitch chewed slowly, savoring each and every rich, flaky bite. His diet restricted him to one croissant, and he wanted to make the most of it. "Honestly, Will, you're a true artist. What's your secret, anyway?"

"Nothing to it," Will said offhandedly. "I've been making these ever since I was working in Nag's Head. My partner in those days gave me the recipe."

"You two owned a place together there?"

"No, not really," he replied.

Which Mitch had learned was typical of Will, who was perfectly friendly and polite but could be rather vague when it came to career details. Mitch knew he'd attended the Culinary Institute of America and had led the Have Knives, Will Travel life of an itinerant chef up and down the East Coast before he hooked up with Donna, who was working in the kitchen of the same Boston seafood place at the time. Donna was from Duxbury. After they married, Will brought her home to Dorset and they'd moved into the old farmhouse on Kelton City Road that he'd inherited from his mom. This spring they had pooled their considerable skills to open The Works, a gourmet food emporium that was housed in Dorset's abandoned piano works. The food hall was the biggest piece of an ambitious conversion of the old riverfront factory that included shops, offices, and luxury water-view condominiums. Dodge had helped finance the venture, and it was proving to be a huge success. Already it had attracted Jeff's Book Schnook.

Jeff could not have been more different than Will—every detail of his life was fair game for discussion, whether the others wanted to get in on it or not. The little man was a walking, talking ganglion of complaints. Inevitably, these complaints centered around his estranged wife, Abby Kaminsky, the pretty little blond who happened to be the hottest author of children's fiction in the country—America's own answer to J. K. Rowling. Abby's first two Carleton Carp books, *The Codfather* and *Return of the Codfather*, had actually rivaled the Harry Potter books in sales. Her just-released third installment, *The Codfather of Sole*—in which Carleton saves the gill world from the clutches of the evil Sturgeon General—was even threatening to outsell Harry.

Unfortunately for Jeff, Abby had dumped him for the man who'd served as her escort on her last book tour. Devastated, Jeff had moved to Dorset to start a new life, but an ugly and very public divorce settlement was looming on his personal horizon. At issue was Abby's half-boy, half-fish hero. There was a lot about Carleton that struck people who knew Jeff as *familiar*. Such as Carleton's moppety red hair, his crooked, geeky black-framed glasses, his freckly, undeniably weblike hands, the way he sucked his cheeks in and out when he was upset. Not to mention his constant use of the word "*ab-so-toot-ly.*" Though Abby vehemently denied it, it was obvious that Carleton was Jeff. As part of their divorce settlement, Jeff was insisting she compensate him for the contribution he'd made to her great success. Abby was flatly refusing, despite what was sure to be a punishing public relations disaster if their divorce went to court. To handle the publicity fallout, Abby had hired Chrissie Huberman, the very same New York publicist who was handling Esme and Tito. As for Jeff, he was so bitter that he refused to carry Abby's books in his store, even though she outsold every single author in America who wasn't named John Grisham.

"Hey, I got a shipment of your paperbacks in, Mitch," he spoke up, chewing on his croissant. Mitch was the author of three highly authoritative and entertaining reference volumes on horror, crime, and western films—*It Came from Beneath the Sink, Shoot My Wife, Please* and *They Went Thataway*. "Would you mind signing them for me—you being a local author and all?"

"Be happy to, Jeff. I can stop by around lunchtime if you'll be there."

Jeff let out a snort. "Where else would I be? That damned bookshop is my whole life. I'm there twelve hours a day, seven days a week. I even sleep right over the store in a cramped little—"

"Two-bedroom luxury condo with river views," Will said, his eyes twinkling at Mitch with amusement.

"Plus I have to drive a rusty old egg-beater of a car so the locals won't think I'm getting rich off of them," Jeff whined.

"Which, correct me if I'm wrong, you're not," Mitch pointed out, grinning at Will.

"Damned straight I'm not," Jeff said indignantly. "Listen to this, I had to give an old woman her money back yesterday. It seems I recommended a thriller to her and she hated it. Oh, she read every single word of it all right, but she pronounced it garbage. Stood there yelling at me in my own store until I paid her back. It was either that or she'd tell all of her friends that I'm a no-good bum. Barnes and Noble can afford to be so generous. Me, I'm barely hanging on. I don't know what I'll do if things don't pick up."

"But they *will* pick up," Dodge told him. "You're already building customer loyalty and good word of mouth. Start-up pains are perfectly normal. The Works felt them, too, and now it's doing great, right, Will?"

After a brief hesitation Will responded, "You bet."

Which Mitch immediately found intriguing, because if there was one thing he'd learned about Dorset it was this: Often, the truth wasn't in the words, it was in the pauses.

"Sometimes I feel like I'm not even in the book business at all," Jeff grumbled. "I'm in the *people* business. I have to be pleasant to strangers all day long. Yikes, it's hard enough being pleasant around you guys."

"Wait, who said you were pleasant?" asked Mitch.

"By the way, Dodger, Martine did me a real solid—she's so popular with the other ladies that as soon as she joined my Monday evening reading group they all wanted in. I may even add a Tuesday reading group, thanks to her. Best thing that's happened to me in weeks. You'd think with all of these media people in town I'd be selling books like crazy, but I'm not." Jeff drained his coffee, staring down into the empty mug. "Did I tell you they're trying to buy me off?"

Mitch popped the last of his croissant in his mouth. "Who, the tabloids?"

"They want me to spill the dirt on Abby. Every time I say no they raise the ante—it's up to two hundred and fifty."

"*Thousand?*" Will was incredulous.

"And I've got plenty to spill, believe me. Hell, I've known her since she was typing letters for the children's book editor and I was the little pisher in the next cubicle."

"You're still a little pisher."

"Thank you for that, Mitchell."

"My Yiddish is a little rusty," Dodge said. "Exactly what is a pisher?"

"She loathes kids, you know," Jeff said. "Calls them germ carriers, poop machines, fecal felons . . . She hates them so much she even made me get a vasectomy. I can't have children now."

"I thought those were reversible in a lot of cases," Will said.

"Not mine," Jeff said. "My God-given right to sire children has been snipped away from me—all thanks to the top children's author in America. Nice story, hunh? And how does the little skank repay me? By boning that—that glorified cab driver, that's how. I swear, every time I see a box of Cocoa Pebbles I get nauseated."

Mitch and the others exchanged an utterly bewildered look, but let it alone.

Dodge said, "Any chance you'll take them up on their offer?"

"I'm flat broke, man. I might have to if she doesn't give me what I want."

"Which is . . . ?"

"Twenty-five percent of the proceeds from the first book. My lawyer wants me to aim for the whole series, but that would be greedy. I'm not being greedy. I just . . . I deserve *something*, don't I? I nursed that book along, night after night. I read every early draft, helped her refine it and craft it months before she ever submitted it."

"Plus you *are* Carleton Carp," Mitch added. "That ought to be worth something."

"I am not a fish!" Jeff snapped, sucking his cheeks in and out.

Dodge, the human timepiece, climbed to his feet now, signifying that it was time to start back for his eight o'clock weight training. Mitch wondered if the man was ever late.

"You'll never do it, Jeff," Mitch said. "You'll never sell out Abby to the tabloids."

Jeff peered at him quizzically. "Why have you got so much faith in me?"

"Because you still love her, that's why. No matter how upset you are, you could never hurt her that way."

"You're right," Jeff admitted, reddening slightly. "Abby's the only woman I've ever loved. I'd take her back in a flash. Answer me this, Dodger, what's the secret?"

"To what?" Dodge asked.

"You and Martine have been together all these years, you've got a terrific thing going on—how do you do it?"

Mitch watched closely as Dodge considered this, the older man's face betraying not one bit of what he'd just revealed to Mitch. "Jeff, there are so many things that factor into it," he answered slowly. "Shared values, common interests and goals. Affection, respect, tolerance. But if I had to narrow it down to one word, it would be the same one that's the secret to a happy friendship."

"What is it?" Jeff pressed him.

Dodge shot a hard stare right at Will Durslag before he replied, "The word is trust."

CHAPTER 2

"DODGE IS HAVING AN affair," Martine Crockett informed Des in a soft, strained voice as the two of them crouched next to the over-stuffed, foul-smelling Dumpster behind McGee's Diner on Old Shore Road, waiting for the kittens to show.

Des drew her breath in. Martine had never confided anything even remotely intimate to her before. Now this, a bombshell out of nowhere. "Who's the woman?"

"I don't know," Martine answered miserably. "I don't want to know."

It was just before dawn, which was happy meal fun time in the world of strays. Esme, Martine's famous daughter, was crouched in wait on the other side of the Dumpster with Des's roommate, Bella Tillis. It was Esme who'd spotted the two hungry kittens nosing around the trash bin late last night when she and Tito had pulled into McGee's for a late meal of fried oysters after a night spent drinking tequila shooters on the beach. Somebody had dumped the kittens there, most likely. Summer people did that. Esme had decided that she *had* to adopt them, and since Martine was the unofficial queen of Dorset's rescuers, the four of them were out there now with their dog cages, trying to lure the poor, starved things in with jars of Gerber's strained turkey. A length of string was tied to each cage door. Once a kitten was inside, they could yank the cage door shut behind it.

The predawn often found Des, Bella, and Martine staked out near a Dumpster somewhere, strings in hand, discussing life, love, and men—three subjects they freely admitted they knew nothing about. They made for an oddly mismatched trio. One tall, cool, late-forties WASP from old Philadelphia money. One round, feisty, seventy-six-year-old Jewish grandmother from Brooklyn. And Des Mitry, a highly gifted artist who was twenty-nine, black, and Dorset's resident Connecticut State Police trooper. Throwing a bona-fide Hollywood movie star into the mix just added more flavor. Not that the girl looked like much at this hour. It was obvious to Des from her puffy eyes, disheveled hair, and soiled clothing that Esme Crockett hadn't been to bed yet.

Unexpectedly, Martine had suggested that her famous daughter and Bella team up together. Obviously, it was so she could drop her bombshell on Des. But why had she?

Des studied her there in the early morning light. Martine was a strikingly pretty blue-eyed blond with good, high cheekbones. The age lines in her tanned face were like the gentle creases in fine leather. She wore her shiny, silver-streaked hair cropped appealingly at her chin, a hair band holding it in place. She wore a pink Izod shirt, khaki shorts, and a pair of spotless white Keds. Martine was almost as tall as Des, who was a legit six feet tall in her stocking feet, and she was very active. Played golf several times a week at the country club, swam for an hour a day at the beach club. It showed. Her figure was excellent—shoulders broad, hips narrow, her long legs toned and shapely.

At first, Des had had some trouble warming up to her. Martine was still very much the belle of the debutante's ball, a privileged white aristocrat who'd never wanted for anything. All she'd had to do was smile and it all came right to her, just like mumsy and daddy had promised. It was all just so *easy* for someone like Martine Crockett. Des had her problems with such women. She, well, hated them. Couldn't help it. But now that she was resident trooper of Dorset, which boasted even more millionaires per square mile than Easthampton, she was coming in contact with a whole lot of them. And she really did need to give them the benefit of the doubt. Besides, she genuinely liked Martine, who was unaffected and caring and sweet. She rescued feral strays, volunteered at the Shoreline Soup Kitchen, and the Dorset Day Care Center. Plus she was bright, perceptive, and good to talk to when you were camped out behind a stanky Dumpster waiting for a feral animal to show.

And now her husband was cheating on her, thereby confirming Bella's old axiom: Most rescuers are ladies with good hearts and bad husbands.

This had certainly been Des's own story. "How do you know he's having an affair?" she asked, crouched there in her tank top and gym shorts.

"I can tell. You can always tell, can't you?"

"Yes, I suppose you can."

Not that Des had been able to herself. Not when it came to Brandon. They were living in Woodbridge at the time, a leafy suburb of New Haven. He was in the U.S. Attorney's office. And she, the Deacon's daughter, was flying high on the Major Crime Squad out of Meriden. After Brandon left her, Des crashed. Bella, the no-bull Yale faculty widow next door, recruited her as a rescuer. And saved her. Woodbridge was now in both of their rearview mirrors. When Des started her new life here in Dorset Bella unloaded her own big barn of a house and came with her. It was working out fine. Between the job, the art academy, and the doughboy, Des wasn't home much. Plus Bella was a fastidious housekeeper, great cook, funny, independent, and thoughtful. True, theirs was not what other people might consider a typical living arrangement, but quite honestly Des couldn't think of a single thing about her life these days that was typical.

"How long has this been going on, Martine?"

"A few weeks," she replied, wringing her hands. She had strong hands with long, graceful fingers. She painted her nails pink. "I'm sorry to be burdening you with this. I just, I feel you're someone who I can talk to. I don't have anyone else."

Des pushed her heavy horn-rimmed glasses back up her nose, frowning. Martine Crockett had a million friends, women who she'd known a lot longer than she'd known Des. Why not confide in one of them? One possibility jumped right out.

Because it *was* one of them.

"You won't tell anyone about it, will you?" she asked Des urgently. Now she seemed sorry she'd brought it up.

"Of course not. But what will *you* do?"

Martine raised her chin, and said, "Oh, I've moved on."

"I see," said Des, although she flat out didn't. Moved on meant what—that she'd gotten past it emotionally, taken a lover of her own, loaded up a van with her most precious possessions? God, these Dorset people could be so cryptic sometimes. No one just *said* what they meant.

Esme moseyed over toward them now, looking sleepy and bored. She was a blond like Martine with flawless porcelain skin and the same good, high cheekbones. Her hair was a wild, frizzy mane of curls that cascaded halfway down her back. To Des, Esme still looked very much like a child. Her heart-shaped face bore soft, slightly malleable remnants of baby fat. Her big blue eyes held wide-eyed innocence. And her hands were a girl's hands, chubby and unblemished by time or work. Esme Crockett was famous for her mouth. It was a pouty, highly erotic mouth with a short, upturned top lip that made her look as if she were in a constant state of sexual rapture. She was also famous for her figure. She was a good deal shorter than Martine, perhaps five feet six, but so ripe and voluptuous that she looked positively illicit in the outfit she had on—a deep V-necked halter top cropped at the belly to show off her gold navel ring, super-low denim cutoffs slashed way high up on her thighs and cheap rubber flip-flops. "Where *are* they, Mommy?" she demanded petulantly. "How long do we have to wait for them?"

"Hours, sometimes," Martine answered.

"Sometimes they don't even show at all," Des said.

Esme flopped down carelessly next to Des on the pavement, reeking of tequila and sweaty girl. She was highly unkempt, in contrast to her spotless, stay-pressed mother. Her hair was unclean, armpits unshaven, ankles soiled. Des noticed that she also had splotchy bruises around her upper arms, as if someone had grabbed her and squeezed her hard. Also a number of scratches on her neck and shoulders.

"Girl, what happened?" Des asked her, as Bella joined them. "Did you get in a fight?"

Esme immediately reddened. "It's not what you think."

"Me, I'm thinking Tito beats the crap out of you," said Bella, who did not know how to mince words.

"No, never. We just get *physical* sometimes when we're, you know . . ."

"Getting physical?" asked Des.

She nodded, glanced awkwardly at her mother, who bristled noticeably.

"I never did understand that," Bella said flatly. "If Morris ever put a welt on me when we were in the throes of connubial passion he would have found his bags on the front porch in the morning, packed and ready to go."

"He'd never *hurt* me," Esme insisted, a defensive edge creeping into her voice. In the flesh, she didn't seem nearly as bright or mature as the characters she played on screen. "I bruise easy, that's all. Honest."

"I believe you," said Des, who believed no such thing. Not with Tito Molina's reputation for violent eruptions.

"I wish they'd get here." Esme sighed, scratching irritably at a mosquito bite on her thigh. "This waiting thing sucks."

"Patience is everything in life," Bella said. "Allow me give you an example. When I was your age I desperately wanted to look like Elizabeth Taylor. Which, God knows, I did not. But guess what?" Bella raised her bunched fist of a face to the sky, preening. "*Now* I do, see?"

Esme gaped at her blankly. "Not really."

"Time, tattela," Bella explained. "It's the great equalizer."

"Do you still date men, Bella?"

"When the occasion arises. Lord knows, the men don't. But you have to be very, very careful when you get to be my age."

"Careful how?"

"One of Morris's dearest friends, Velvel, started wooing me last year. Very cultivated man. A renowned mathematician, seventy-four years old. Before I'd so much as let him give me a peck on the cheek I had to, you know, check him out," Bella said waggling her eyebrows at Esme.

"Wait, check him out how?"

"I made a date to go dancing with him, okay? Waited for a nice slow dance, got out him out there on the floor . . ."

"And? . . ."

"I gave him a good hard whack on the leg. *That's* when I heard it."

"Heard what, Bella?" Now Martine was curious, too.

"The slosh," Bella replied. "You hear a slosh it means the man's wearing a catheter bag. You don't want nuttin' to do with him."

Esme smiled at her, a smile that lit up her entire face. "Bella, you are the coolest."

"That's me, all right, the queen of cool." Bella stood there staring down the front of Esme's halter top at her considerable cleavage. "So did you have your boobs done or what?" she asked her bluntly.

"No way. These are all mine. Want to feel them?"

"Not necessary."

"That whole deal was just Crissie doing what she does," Esme explained.

"Which is what exactly?" Martine demanded.

"She plants the denial before there's ever a story."

"So as to create the story?" asked Des.

Esme nodded. "That way she keeps the tabloids fed and off of our backs."

"That woman is so crass," Martine said. "Honestly, I can't tell if she's part of the solution or part of the problem."

"None of it's real, Mommy. It's just some tabloid trash about tits."

"Those are *your* tits they're talking about. And I don't care for it. Or Crissie."

"Yeah, I kind of sensed that," Esme shot back. They had a definite mother-daughter thing going on. "But don't blame me. Tito's agent hired her. He had to. That's how the business is—if we don't give them *something* then they just make up stuff about how our marriage is in ruins or whatever. It's not like we're real people to them. We're just characters in some twisted interactive soap opera. They shout things at Tito, you know. To bait him."

"What things?" asked Des.

"They tell him I'm a slut. That I'm having sex with Ben Affleck or Derek Jeter or Justin Timberlake, anyone. They're hoping he'll lose it so they can sell a picture of him attacking them. They try to climb over the wall of our Malibu house. They follow us when we leave. It's horrible. If the public knew what really went on, they'd freak. But since it's the press they somehow think it's all noble and decent."

"Those people aren't the press." Bella sniffed.

"No, they totally are," Esme insisted.

Des couldn't disagree. She'd seen the tabloids in action when she'd worked murder investigations. "Do you two keep a bodyguard around?"

"Tito won't live that way. He wants to keep it real, or at least try. He figures, how can you hold on to your street edge when you live like royalty?"

"You can't," Des concurred.

"Besides, Chrissie's staying in the guesthouse while we're here, so she keeps them at bay. And the road we're on is private. The beach association has a gate, and they can't get past that. Or at least they aren't supposed to."

"If they do, let me know," Des said.

"I would, Des, except Tito's deathly afraid of the police. He has *so* many childhood scars." Esme let out a soft laugh. "But, hey, who doesn't, right?"

Martine stiffened at this last comment, Des noticed.

"Everyone thinks they know us, but they don't. Especially Tito. Nobody knows Tito."

"So tell us something we don't know about him," Bella said.

"Seriously?" Esme tossed her head, running her hands through her mane of golden hair. "He's the most deprived boy I've ever met, okay? Growing up, he went without so many things that the rest of us take for granted. Like pets—he's never, ever had one. I mean, God, he'd never even had a Christmas tree until he met me. You should have seen the joy in his eyes when we decorated our very own tree last Christmas." Recalling it, tears began to spill out of her own eyes right down her flawless cheeks. "All the things I took for granted growing up. A nice home, friends, parents who I believed I could trust . . ."

Des felt that there was something deliberately pointy about the words Esme used to describe her parents. Crouched there beside her on the pavement, Martine definitely seemed ill at ease.

"Tito never knew any of those things. That's why he's so *out there* as an actor. It's like he's experiencing everything for the first time."

Des thought she heard some small movements now in the forsythia bushes out behind the Dumpster. "We better get on that other trap," she whispered, tiptoeing around to the other cage and grabbing on to the string attached to its door.

Esme joined her. "Here, let me," she whispered, holding her hand out to Des.

That was when Des noticed the thin white lines on the inside of her wrist. Both wrists, in fact. On-screen, the makeup artists were able to cover them over. But up close and in person Des saw them instantly for what they were. Esme Crockett had tried to slit her wrists at some point in her past. Des found herself wondering what could possibly have driven someone so lovely, gifted, and privileged to want to end her life?

"Shhh, hear them . . . ?" she whispered, clutching the string anxiously.

Des did hear the tiny mewings. And now she could see the two of them coming out of the brush together. They were mixed gray, no more than four or five weeks old.

"Aren't they the sweetest?"

Des didn't like the unsteady way they were moving.

"Hi, babies," Esme cooed as they edged hungrily toward the baited cage, moving closer and closer. "Come get your breakfast. . . . Come on, babies. . . ."

Until they were inside the cage and Esme had yanked the door shut behind them.

"In the house!" Des called out, latching it shut.

Bella and Martine immediately joined them.

"I can't wait for Tito to see them!" Esme cried excitedly, clapping her hands together with girlish delight. "We're going to name them Spike and Mike."

Martine stood there looking down at them in grim silence. So did Bella.

"What, don't they look like a Spike and a Mike?" Esme asked.

What they looked like, all three rescuers knew only too well, was a pair of very, very sick little kitties. Their eyes were rheumy, their noses caked with pus, coats scabby and oozing with sores. Feline influenza, most likely. It was very common in the summer. If left untreated, it often led to pneumonia.

"They look awfully sick to me, honey," Martine said gently. "I think we'd better take them to the vet."

"What do *you* think, Des?" Esme asked.

"I don't meant to be your dream killer, but I think you should prepare yourself for the worst."

Esme let out a gasp of horror. "You mean he might put them to sleep?"

"They're very sick, tattela."

"It was real nice of you to alert us," Des added. "You've done them a solid, because they're *so* miserable."

"Mommy, *noooo*!" Esme threw herself into Martine's arms, weeping.

"We'll get you another pair," Martine promised, hugging her tightly.

"I don't *want* another pair! I want Spike and Mike! They're ours! We found them!" Now Esme released her mother, swiping at her eyes with the back of her hand. "Sorry, I don't mean to be such a baby. This is just so sad. And it's not their fault."

"Me, I'd like to take a baseball bat to whoever dumped them here," Bella growled.

"We do everything we can, honey," Martine said. "We get them neutered. We find homes for as many as we can. But the truth is that there are just too many kittens and not enough people to love them."

"Now, if you'd like to adopt a couple of good, healthy ones," Des offered brightly, "we can certainly help you out."

Esme tilted her head at Des curiously. "You mean you have some at your place?"

"We, uh, happen to have a few." Twenty-eight at last count. "Come on over, girl. Check'em out."

"No, no," Esme said abruptly. "I mean, thanks, but I don't think so."

Martine Crockett took her daughter by the hand now and led her back to Martine's 1967 silver Volkswagon Beetle convertible. They got in and drove off. Des and Bella loaded the cage with the sick kittens into the back of Bella's Jeep Wrangler with its personalized CATS22 license plate.

"What do you think?" Des asked her.

"I think Dr. Bill will put them down as soon as he lays eyes on them."

"No, I mean about *her*."

"Who, the great Esme Crockett?" Bella let out a hoot of derision. "I think she has the worst BO I ever smelled in my entire life."

Why did Martine tell her about Dodge's affair?

Des couldn't imagine. Being human, she also couldn't help wondering who the other woman was. She didn't say anything about it to Bella on the way home—she'd promised Martine she'd keep quiet, and she did. But it was certainly on her mind as they dropped off Spike and Mike with Dr. Bill, knowing full well they'd never see those two helpless kittens again. It was still on her mind when they pulled into her driveway in gloomy silence. She and Bella always felt lousy when a rescue mission turned out sour.

Bella marched straight inside to scrub the kitchen floor and listen to one of her Danny Kaye records, which was what she did when she was blue. Des hung out in the garage for a while with the Pointer Sisters, Mary J. Blige, Bootsy Collins, Master P, Jay-Z and the others that they *had* rescued. She cooed at each of them, stroking the ones who'd let her. Some, like Method Man, just hissed. No problem. He'd come around. Des was patient. She made sure they all had food and water, then went upstairs.

Des had bought and renovated a snug little cottage tucked into a hillside high above Uncas Lake. Mostly, she'd bought it for the sunlight. The living room, which she'd turned into her studio, had floor-to-ceiling windows overlooking the shimmering lake. Her kitchen and dining area were very airy and open, with French doors leading out onto the back deck, which had a teak dining table and chairs, and a dynamite view. The deck practically doubled her living space during warm months. There were three bedrooms, all of them small. The spare room was where Des worked out with twenty-pound dumbbells five mornings a week. Her weight room door was closed currently and there was a steady chorus of meows going on in there. Their five in-house cats were unable to resist the allure of a wet kitchen floor—whenever Bella was in scrub mode she herded them in there.

Des kept a portrait that she'd drawn of Mitch hanging over her bed. She'd drawn it when she was still trying to figure out how she felt about him. He looked very lost and sad in the portrait. He didn't look nearly so sad now. It was the only sample of her art that was visible anywhere in the house. She did not display her haunting portraits of murder victims that were her life's work and her way of coping with the horrors of her job. These she kept tucked away in a portfolio.

She did not like to look at them after she'd finished them.

Right now, Des snatched a graphite stick and Strathmore eighteen-by-twenty-four-inch sketch pad from her easel and started across the house with them as Mr. Danny Kaye was busy singing "Madam, I Love Your Crepes Suzette." Or make that shrieking. Des did not understand that man's appeal. Apparently, you had to be Jewish, old, and from Brooklyn in order to dig him. Also, possibly, deaf.

"I put your breakfast out on the deck," Bella called to her from the kitchen floor, where she was on her hands and knees, scrubbing away like an old-time washerwoman.

"You didn't have to make me breakfast, Bella."

"I did so," Bella shot back, scrubbing, scrubbing. There was a sponge mop, but she wouldn't go near it. "Otherwise you'll tromp all over my wet floor with your big feet."

"They are not big. They're *long*." Twelve and a half double A, to be exact. "Besides, Mitch likes them—especially my toes."

Bella made a face. "*Genug shen!*" Which was Yiddish for *No mas*. "I don't want to hear these things about you two."

"Don't blame me, girl. You're the one said I should snag me a Jewish gentleman."

"And did I steer you wrong?"

"Nope. Just don't tell him that—I don't want his ego swelling." Des tilted her head at Bella curiously. "Real, if I stick around long enough will I *ever* dig Danny Kaye?"

Bella puffed out her cheeks in disgust. "No one appreciates true talent anymore."

"Oh, is that what you call it?" she said sweetly.

"If you want to put on your Jill Scott, go ahead. It's your house."

"It's *our* house. And I'm just woofing on you." Des started out of the kitchen, then stopped. "We can't save them all, Bella."

"I know that," Bella said tightly.

Des went out onto the deck, closing the French doors behind her, and sat down at the table in front of her Grape Nuts, skim milk, and blueberries from Mitch's garden. It was a drowsy, humid morning. A young couple was paddling a canoe out on the lake, their giddy laughter carrying off the water as if they were right there next to Des. Otherwise, it was quiet enough that she could hear the cicadas whirring.

As she ate, she flipped through her drawing pad, looking at her latest work. Her figure drawing professor at the Dorset Academy of Fine Arts, a brilliant and maddening guru named Peter Weiss, had urged Des to take a complete break from her crime scene portraits this summer and draw nothing but trees, an exercise that he claimed would prove highly beneficial to her. He wouldn't explain why this was so, merely said, "You'll find out what I mean." Leaving Des to solve the mystery on her own. She'd tried to do what he said. Spent the past six weeks working on trees and trees only.

And, so far, the results had been a total disaster.

Page after page of her drawing pad was filled with one crude arboreal rendering after another. Her lush, midsummer oaks and maples looked like stick figures topped with meatballs. Her evergreens resembled television aerials. It all looked like something an eight-year-old kid would do. She'd tried graphite stick, vine charcoal, conte crayon, pen, pencil. The results were all the same: *dreck*.

Bella had been the soul of tact when Des showed them to her. "I like everything you do," she said.

Mitch, who was always brutally honest, had said, "Jellystone National Park—they look exactly like the background drawings from the old *Yogi the Bear* cartoons. Remember Yogi and Boo Boo?"

To which Des replied, "Back slowly out of the room while you are still able to."

Knowing full well that he was right. For some reason she kept drawing her way *around* the trees as opposed to getting inside of them. She wasn't *grasping* them. She'd tried to learn her way out of her personal abyss. Pored over book upon book by arborists and nature photographers. Studied the Connecticut shoreline's grand masters such as Childe Hassam, George Bruestle, and Henry Ward Ranger, landscape painters whose works she admired tremendously. But it was no use. Not any of it. She could not translate what her eyes saw into lines and contours and shapes. Her trees were two-dimensional, lifeless, and crude, her drawing hand stubbornly blind.

She slammed her sketch pad shut, boiling with confusion and frustration. Because there was no instruction manual for this, no road map that could direct her to her inner soul. There was only her. The wisdom was within her.

The enemy was within her.

All she could do about it now was punish herself physically. She stormed back down to her weight room. Out went the cats, in came the crazed artist. First, she stretched for twenty good minutes on her mat, freeing her mind, feeling the blood flow through her as she worked the kinks out of her lithe, loose-limbed body. Then she did one hundred push-ups and two hundred sit-ups. Then she hit the irons—two full circuits on her pressing bench with the twenty-pounders, two sets of twenty-four reps each time around. Pushing herself. Working it, working it, working it. Pump, breathe . . . Pump, breathe . . . Muscles straining, veins bulging, the sweat pouring off of her. Pump, breathe . . . Pump, breathe . . . Pump, breathe . . .

Why did Martine tell her about Dodge?

Des could not imagine. These blue-blooded locals genuinely perplexed her. They did not believe that the shortest way between two points was a straight line. They did not believe in lines—only negative space. And she did not know what to do about this. Mitch raved about Dodge Crockett day and night. Should she break it to him his new walking buddy was a snake? Or should she keep it to herself?

She made it through her last set of reps on adrenaline and fumes, and collapsed on the bench in a heap, gasping. She gulped down a bottle of water, then showered off.

Des spent very little time in front of the bathroom mirror these days. She wore no war paint. She needed none. She had almond-shaped pale green eyes, smooth glowing skin and a wraparound smile that could melt titanium from a thousand yards. She kept her hair so short and nubby that it was practically dry by the time she'd put on her summer-weight uniform and polished black brogans. She strapped on her crime-girl belt, complete with top-of-the-line SIG-Sauer semiautomatic handgun, and called out good-bye to Bella. Then she jumped into her cruiser and headed out.

Des lived in was what was considered a mixed neighborhood by Dorset standards, which meant it enjoyed a highly diverse white population. There were tidy starter houses owned by young professional couples. There were rambling bungalows bursting with multiple generations of blue-collar swamp Yankees. There were moldering summer cottages rented by old-timers from New Britain who played bocce out on their lawns. Right now her mail carrier, Frank, was out walking his golden retriever, and a pair of young mothers were on their way to the lake with a brood of kids, complete with pails, shovels, and water wings. They all waved to Des as she drove past. She raised a hand in response.

Summer was her busy season. Dorset's seaside renters nearly doubled the town's year-round population of less than seven thousand, plus the inns, motels, and campgrounds were filled to capacity. More people meant more traffic and more trouble. So did the warm weather. During the cold months, people did their drinking and their fighting behind closed doors. Now it all spilled out onto the front lawn. Dogs barked, tempers flared, neighbors started throwing punches at one another. It could get a little ugly.

And then, dear God, there were the tourists.

First, she headed for the historic district. The lawn in front of the old library on Dorset Street was being set up with chairs for a noon summer concert by Dorset's town band, which was quite accomplished if you happened to be into oompah music. Des rated their sound one solid notch below Danny Kaye on her own personal hit parade. The concert was part of a full day of quaint small-town activities. Crafts stalls were being erected next door on the lawn in front of Center School, where local artisans would be offering their handcrafted candles and soaps, their driftwood sculptures and wind chimes made of seashells and bits of broken glass. Des pulled in at town hall to see if there was anything of interest in her mail slot—there wasn't—and to work on Mary Ann, First Selectman Paffin's new secretary, a lonely widow who desperately needed to adopt two healthy, neutered kittens and just didn't know it yet. Then she resumed her patrol of the historic district, with its lovely two hundred-year-old homes, steepled white churches and graceful old oaks and sycamores. Trees again. Trees, trees, and more trees . . .

I should just give up and move to the damned desert.

The art academy was located in the historic district, in the old Gill House. So were the better galleries and antique dealers, the cemetery, firehouse, John's barbershop with its old Wildroot sign and barber pole.

It was only when she got to Big Brook Road and made a left that she returned to the twenty-first century. Here was Dorset's shopping center, which had an A & P, pharmacy, bank, hardware store, and so on. Across the two-lane road from it were the storefront businesses like the insurance and travel agencies, realtors and doctors. It was all exceedingly underwhelming. There was no ostentatious display of signage allowed in Dorset. No Golden Arches, no big box stores, no multiplexes. Most businesses were locally owned.

As a rule, the business district was quite laid back, too. Not much traffic, plenty of parking. It was possible to get around even during the summer. But not this summer. Not with Tito and Esme in town. News vans were crowded into parking spaces wherever they could find them. Des could spot crews from at least a dozen Connecticut and New York television stations, not to mention CNN, Fox News, *Entertainment Tonight*, and *Inside Edition*. News choppers hovered overhead. And the sidewalks were positively bursting with sun-burned tourists cruising back and forth in the bright sun, back and forth, hoping to catch just one glimpse of *them*.

Madness. It was just plain madness.

As she nosed her way around, making her presence felt, Des came upon a genuine traffic jam at Clancy's ice cream parlor. Cars were at a total standstill. Drivers were even honking their horns, which was unheard-of in Dorset. She flicked on her lights and veered over the yellow line so she could get around to it. When she reached Clancy's she discovered a whale-sized white Cadillac Escalade double-parked out front with its doors locked. Its owner had simply left it there and walked away, blocking the entire lane of traffic. No one else in town could get by.

Des hopped out, straightening her big Smokey hat, and took a closer look. The big SUV had New Jersey plates. No special handi-capped tag, no media or law enforcement markings. Just a selfish, thoughtless owner. Shaking her head, she got busy filling out a ticket. She was just finishing it when a middle-age guy with an expensive comb-over came sauntering toward her licking a double-scoop chocolate ice cream cone that he really, truly did not need. His gut was already straining hard against his tank top. It didn't help that he was wearing shorts. His skinny, pale legs just made his stomach look even bigger. Summer clothing was very unforgiving.

But not as unforgiving as the resident trooper of Dorset, Connecticut.

"Hey, I just went inside for a second," he protested when he caught sight of her. "One second."

"Sir, that was a very expensive second."

"Now you just hold on," he ordered her, as more drivers honked their horns. "You're *not* giving me a ticket over this."

"Oh, I most certainly am. You've created an unsafe situation, and you've inconvenienced a lot of people. Next time, park in the lot."

"The lot was full."

"Next time, wait," she said, as pedestrians began to gather around them, gawking.

"But everyone does it."

"Not in my town they don't."

"I don't fucking believe this!"

"Please watch your language, sir."

"You've got a real attitude, haven't you, doll?"

"Sir, I am not a doll. I am Master Sergeant Desiree Mitry of the Connecticut State Police, and you are illegally parked." She tore off the ticket and held it out to him.

He refused to take it. Just stood there in surly defiance, his ice cream melting under the hot sun and running down his wrist. Too often, Des had discovered, people on vacation were people at their worst. In their view, the world pushed them around seven days a week, fifty weeks out of the year. When they got their two weeks off, they felt entitled to shove back.

"Take the citation, sir," Des ordered him in a calm, steady voice. "Take it and relocate your vehicle at once. If you don't, I will place you under arrest."

"What is it, Tommy?" His slender frosted-blond wife was approaching them now, two appallingly fat little kids in tow, both eating ice cream cones. "What's wrong?"

"Aw, nothing," he growled, snatching the ticket from Des disgustedly. "You give some entry-level person a little taste of power and right away they bust your balls."

Des knew all about this. "Entry-level person" was a code phrase for *N-e-g-r-o*. But she had learned long ago not to mix it up with jerks. It wasn't as if they got any smarter if she did. She simply flashed her mega-wattage smile, and said, "You folks have yourselves a real nice vacation." And stood there, hands on her hips, while they piled back in their SUV and took off.

Once the traffic flow returned to normal she got back in her own ride and continued on down Big Brook Road, making her rounds, her mind still working it, working it, working it . . .

Why did Martine tell her about Dodge?

CHAPTER 3

WHY DID DODGE TELL him about Martine?

Mitch couldn't imagine. And it weighed on his mind all morning. It was there while he logged some quality loud time on his beloved sky blue Fender Stratocaster, doggedly chasing after Hendrix's signature opening to "Voodoo Chile," deafening twin reverb amps, wawa pedal and all. It was there while he helped Bitsy Peck move an apple tree to a sunnier spot in her yard, in exchange for unlimited access to her corn patch. It was there while Mitch steered his bulbous, plum-colored 1956 Studebaker pickup across the causeway toward town: Why had the older man chosen to confide in him this way? It wasn't as if the two of them were that close. Not like, say, Dodge was to Will, who was practically like a son to him. So why had he? Only one possible explanation made any sense to Mitch:

Because it was Will who was sleeping with Martine.

True, Martine was fifteen years older than Will. True, Will was supposedly happily married to Donna. But there was no denying that Martine Crockett was still a major babe. And Will was an exceedingly buff younger man. Plus Will had grown up around Martine, meaning that he'd doubtless harbored moist, Technicolor fantasies about her since he was thirteen. What healthy young boy wouldn't have? Certainly, this would explain why Dodge had flashed such a hard stare at Will on the beach this morning.

Because it was Will who was sleeping with Martine.

Mitch was supposed to meet Des for a low-fat lunch at The Works, but as he reached Old Shore Road he noticed that his gas tank was almost half empty. Probably ought to fill up at the Citgo minimart on his way, he reflected. A very nice, hardworking young couple from Turkey, Nuri and Nema Acar, had recently taken over the operation, and Mitch liked to throw his business their way. So did a lot of the local workmen, whose pickups were nosed up to the squat, rectangular building like a herd of cattle.

Mitch pulled up at the pump and hopped out. The Citgo was that rarest of modern-day phenomena, a full-service station. But only tourists and summer people sat there in their cars and waited for Nuri to pump their gas for them, clad in his immaculate short-sleeved dress shirt and slacks. True locals got out and pumped it themselves. When Mitch was done filling up he went inside to pay his money and respects to Nema.

Just like the half dozen other guys who were gathered there at her counter, their tongues hanging out.

Lew the Plumber was there. Drew Archer, the town's best cabinetmaker, was there. So was Dennis Allen, who serviced the village's septic tanks. Mitch knew those three well enough to say hello to. The others he knew by sight. They were Nema's regulars, just like Mitch. Could be found there at the Citgo almost every morning between the hours of ten-thirty and eleven. Although not a one of them referred to the place as the Citgo.

They called it the House of Turkish Delights.

Because the Acars offered way, way more than the usual minimart menu of candy, soda, and Lotto tickets. They offered Nema's own homemade native pastries and deliciously strong, sweet Turkish coffee. Her baklava was the best Mitch had ever tasted. She also made boreks, which were triangles of layered, wafer-thin pastry filled with chopped nuts and cinnamon. And lalangas, which were fried pastry dipped in syrup and brushed with powdered sugar. The lalangas were especially popular with the workmen who'd grown up on fried dough, a regional delicacy.

The House of Turkish Delights was Dorset's best-kept secret. The local workmen, who considered The Works a yuppified tourist trap, had staked it out as *their* place. And so they told no one about it. Mitch sure as hell didn't. He didn't dare tell Will that he was buying pastry from his competitor, and he couldn't breathe so much as a word to Des—every time he inhaled the air in there he was breaking his diet.

The Acars were the first native-born Turks ever to live in Dorset. They were in their early thirties. Nema was tiny and slender, with large, lustrous dark eyes that reminded Mitch of the '50s film actress Ina Balin. Always, she wore a Muslim headscarf. Nuri was courtly and unfailingly polite. Almost but not quite unctuous. The two of them were from Istanbul, where Nuri had graduated from Bosporus University with a degree in mathematics. Nema told Mitch they had emigrated to America because their parents didn't approve of the marriage. Mitch couldn't imagine why they didn't, since any two people who could work side by side fourteen hours a day and never stop smiling clearly belonged together.

"And how are you today, Mr. Berger, sir?" Nema said to him as Mitch pointed directly to the lalanga that had his name on it.

"I'd feel a lot better if you'd call me Mitch."

"Very well, but you are a naughty, naughty boy, Mr. Mitch."

"God, don't tell me a certain resident trooper stopped by."

"No, no. I was reading your review in this morning's newspaper, of *The Dark Star*, and you almost made me spit up my orange juice." Nema let out a devilish little cackle. "Most amusing and yet insightful."

He thanked her and hopped back into his truck, waving to Nuri, who was filling the tank of a minivan that had New York plates. Then Mitch resumed his trip into town, devouring his gustatory no-no in hungry, fat-boy bites.

It was not easy to find a parking place near The Works. Not with all of the news crew vans and tourists taking up every available curb-side space. Mitch had to leave his truck in the A & P parking lot and hoof it two blocks. The traffic on Big Brook Road was unbelievably hectic. Some nut in an immense white Cadillac Escalade almost ran him down when he tried to cross the street. Honestly, he would not mind when Labor Day arrived and everyone left. Because Dorset didn't feel like Dorset right now. It felt like a resort town crowded with hyperactive strangers. And this upset Mitch's new sense of order in his life. New York was his place for rushing around on noisy streets that were teeming with people. Dorset was his place for quiet reflection. Briefly, he wondered if he was feeling bothered this way because he was becoming rigid and middle-aged.

He decided this could not be possible.

Dorset's sprawling 130-year-old piano works had provided jobs for generations of highly skilled local workers until it shut its doors in the 1970s. Often, there had been talk of leveling the abandoned riverfront factory. Instead, Will and Donna Durslag had rescued it. Not a small undertaking. They'd had to sandblast its red brick, reroof it, repoint the mortar, restore the windows—and that was just the shell. Inside, the 148,000-square-foot factory had no plumbing or wiring, no heat, no nothing. But the architect and contractor who'd tackled the job were tremendously talented, and the transformation was remarkable. The old brick eyesore was now a lively European-style food hall with stalls selling fresh, locally grown produce and eggs, cheeses, olives, fresh-baked breads and desserts, pizza, gelato, fresh fruit smoothies. There was a coffee bar that stayed open until ten at night. There were nuts and grains sold in bulk, coffee beans, teas, spices. There was a butcher, a fishmonger, a deli counter offering salads and sandwiches and take-home meals like veal piccata and meat loaf.

An informal eating area anchored the center of the hall with tables and chairs where people could meet for a sandwich or read the newspaper over a cup of coffee. An arcade housed shops like Jeff's Book Schnook and a wine store. Several of the retail spaces still hadn't been leased yet. There were condominium apartments that faced right out onto a newly constructed riverfront boardwalk. These were mostly occupied.

Mitch did not see Des there yet so he stopped in to sign books for Jeff, as promised. A glass wall separated his shop from the food hall. The first time Mitch had walked in the door of the Book Schnook he knew instantly that it was every publishing person's dream book-shop. It felt more like a private library than it did a place of business.

The space was two stories high with towering dark-wood bookcases. Rolling library ladders allowed customers to reach the higher volumes. A spiral staircase led up to a wraparound loft where there were even more books. Jeff had filled his place with cozy armchairs and brass reading lamps. There was a huge fireplace in the old red brick exterior wall, and tons of little nooks and crannies where customers could browse for hours in front of the windows as sailboats scudded past on the Connecticut River. Often, some very tasty music was playing. Right now, Ella Fitzgerald was singing Cole Porter.

Jeff's shelving system was beyond quirky. Nothing, but nothing, was alphabetical. His own favorite authors were arranged near the front on a wall of shelves he called Store Picks. It was a fluid and eclectic array, subject to his latest whim. This week, his picks included the contemporary novelist Richard Ford, British-born travel writer Jonathan Raban, the late food essayist M.F.K. Fisher, the bleak '50s hardboiled crime writer Jim Thompson, Dorothy Parker, Emily Dickinson, Philip K. Dick, Wallace Stegner and H.L. Mencken.

Popular sellers that Jeff didn't like but had to offer were stashed way up on the second-floor shelves. If it was Mary Higgins Clark that a customer wanted, or a copy of *The Corrections* by Jonathan Franzen, Jeff made them go climb for it. It was his store and his system. And it was just about the choicest bookstore Mitch had ever been in. Jeff had everything a bookseller could ask for.

Everything except for customers. The Book Schnook was deserted. And so silent after the din of the food hall outside that Mitch felt as if he'd just entered a shul.

The little guy in his crooked black-framed glasses was dusting stock in hushed solitude when Mitch got there, sucking his cheeks in and out in a decidedly carplike manner. Jeff's shopkeeper outfit wasn't much different from his hiking outfit. He still wore shorts and sandals with dark socks. Only his shirt was different—Jeff had on an oversized Book Schnook T-shirt adorned with a portrait of Dan Quayle and the store's motto: A Mind Is a Terrible Thing to Lose.

"Hey, Mitch, good to see you!" he exclaimed, dashing back to his storeroom. He returned a moment later toting two cartons of Mitch's paperback reference volumes. They began unloading them onto a library table. "You're doing me a real favor, man. Believe me, I need all of the help I can get."

"Jeff, I'm an author," Mitch chided him gently. "You're the one who's helping me."

He got started signing the books, passing each one along so Jeff could slap an Autographed by Author sticker on its cover. As they worked their way through the stack a boy of twelve or so came in the door, looking very intimidated.

"What can I do for you, buddy?" Jeff called to him encouragingly.

"I-I was just wondering if the new *Codfather* book came in yet," he stammered, his voice soaring several octaves.

"I don't sell that garbage in my store," Jeff snarled in response. "Try Borders. Try Amazon. *Anywhere* but here, got it?"

Which sent the little kid scurrying out the door in bug-eyed terror.

"I can see you're really working on your people skills," Mitch observed.

"*Ab-so-tootly*," Jeff responded with great sincerity. "The old me wouldn't have mentioned those other outlets at all." On Mitch's doubtful look he added, "Mitch, we have to measure our progress in inches. I learned that from my dear sweet mother, right along with another heartwarming chestnut: 'You'll never amount to anything.' That's why Abby dumped me, you know. She thinks I *want* to fail because deep down inside I think I deserve to. Didn't want to be around my vibe anymore. Said it was contagious. What do *you* think?"

"I think that you have a beautiful shop and you should be very proud."

"You really think so?" he asked Mitch imploringly.

Needy. That was the word to describe Jeff Wachtell.

"I really do," Mitch assured him.

Pleased, Jeff began moving Mitch's signed books to a prominent spot by the front door. Mitch browsed a bit. Among Jeff's Store Picks he spotted a paperback copy of *Horseman, Pass By,* the slender first novel by Larry McMurtry that Martin Ritt had made into the movie *Hud*. Mitch had lost his copy and had been meaning to reread it, so he brought one up to the counter and paid Jeff for it.

As Jeff rang it up he started sucking his cheeks in and out again, peering at Mitch uncertainly. "Mind if I ask you something else? I just scored Abby's tour itinerary from her Web site, and she's making her way straight through Connecticut this week on her way to Boston. She's already stopping at C. C. Willoughby and Company in Sussex, right? And her publicist, Chrissie Huberman, is here in town with Esme and Tito, right? Would it be out of line for me to ask her if she'd maybe schedule Abby to stop *here*? Abby sure would bring in the customers."

"Jeff, you don't carry any of your wife's books, remember?"

"I could have fifty copies of *The Codfather of Sole* here by noon tomorrow," he said in a determined voice. "All I have to do is pick up the phone."

Mitch raised his eyebrows at him. "This is a tectonic shift for you."

"Dead on," he acknowledged, adjusting his glasses. "But I need to make certain allowances if I'm going to survive in this business. What do you think?"

"I think this is a very healthy development."

"No, I mean about me approaching Crissie."

"Why don't you just talk to Abby?"

Jeff shook his head vigorously. "We only speak through our lawyers—at a cost of three hundred and fifty bucks an hour. Saying 'Hi, how are you?' runs me twenty-nine ninety-five."

"I guess it couldn't hurt. The worst thing Chrissie can do is say no, right?"

"Right," Jeff agreed, a bit less than convinced. "Thanks, man."

Mitch headed back out to the food hall with his book. It was lunchtime and the place was teeming with hungry Dorseteers, the din of their voices rising up toward the skylights. A lot of them were lined up at the deli counter. Mitch took his place at the end of the line, watching Donna merrily take phone orders, chat up customers, and move the line along with a smooth assist from Rich Graybill, the young chef they'd brought in to help manage the place. Will was busy horsing a huge basket of baguettes over from the bakery. All three of them were moving at an astonishing speed. It takes superhuman energy to work in the food trade, Will once told Mitch. Mitch believed it.

As he got closer to the counter, Mitch carefully studied the enticing platters and bowls on display in the refrigerated case, his stomach growling.

Now Donna was serving the young woman in line ahead of him. "What can I get you, Marilyn? God, I love your hair. Who did it? I've got to go see her. Mine looks just like a Brillo pad. . . . Shut up, it does so."

Mitch liked Donna a lot. She was peppery and funny, and she held nothing back. Always, her pink face was lit with a warm, genuine smile. She liked being who she was. Donna was a bit on the short side, nearly a foot shorter than Will, and more than a bit on the chubby side. And her hair did look like a Brillo pad, frizzy and black with streaks of premature gray. She wore a blue denim apron with The Works stitched across it, as did everyone who served food there.

"Hey there, stretch, what can I get for you today?" she asked, squinting at Mitch through her wire-rimmed glasses with feigned astonishment. "Time out, Berger, is that *you*? My God, you're nothing but skin, bone, and wrinkled khaki." Donna had a pronounced Boston accent, the flat, Southie kind. "How much weight have you lost this summer, fifteen pounds?"

"Ten pounds . . . well, nine."

"That's a lot, Mitch," Will said, unloading his basket of baguettes.

"Not enough to satisfy a certain resident trooper."

"Oh, what does that scrawny gazelle know about poundage?" Donna shot back. "Me, I like a full-bodied man. A man whose ass is bigger than mine. That's all any woman wants."

"So that's it," Will joked. "I always wondered."

"Okay, I'm getting mixed signals here," Mitch told her. "You and Des have to get on the same page."

"Not a chance. She's the one who sees you naked. I just sell you food. Not that I wouldn't like to trade places."

"Donna, are you making a play for me in front of your husband?"

"It's okay, Mitch, I'm used to it," Will said, smiling at her.

Mitch studied their playful banter closely, wondering if Will *was* cheating on her with Martine. He had no idea. None.

Donna said, "If you're *not* going to whisk me away to Bermuda on your yacht then you'll have to place an order. This is a business, Berger. I can't just stand here all afternoon talking dirty."

Mitch went for the grilled shrimp Caesar salad, an onion mini-baguette and a fresh-squeezed orange juice. He placed it all on a tray and ambled over toward an empty table, pleased to see that people at three different tables were intently reading his review of *Dark Star* in that morning's paper. Mitch enjoyed watching people read his work. He was not alone in this—it was just about every journalist's guiltiest pleasure. He sat and opened his book, keeping an eye on the big glass doors to the street.

Des came striding through them a few minutes later and made her way lithely across the bustling food hall, a supremely relaxed smile on her face as her eyes alertly took in everyone and everything in the place. She was becoming an exceptionally good resident trooper, Mitch felt. She was confident, helpful, and straight with everyone. People in town genuinely respected her. Plus there was a refreshing absence of head games with Des. She didn't try to bully or intimidate anyone. She didn't need to. Whatever came along, she knew she could handle it.

Mitch loved the way her face lit up when she caught sight of him seated there. Loved the special smile that she reserved for him and him alone. As she started toward him he wondered what would happen to him if she were not in his life right now. He would go right down the drain, that's what.

But she must never know this—she thinks I'm the one who has it all together.

They did not kiss when she got to his table. Des had an ironclad rule about Public Displays of Affection when she was in uniform.

But there was no avoiding the way they glowed in each other's presence. Just as there was no missing the curious glances that they got from neighboring tables. Because they were a different kind of couple, no question. And when you're different people wonder about you. The glances didn't bother either of them one bit. They knew how happy they were together.

"Hey, bod man," she said, her pale green eyes shining at him from behind her horn-rims.

"Back at you, Master Sergeant."

"I'm going to fetch me some lunch."

"Lucky me," Mitch said brightly.

She cocked her head at him curiously. "How so?"

"Now I get to watch you walk away," he replied, rubbing his hands together eagerly. Among her many attributes, Des Mitry possessed one of the world's top ten cabooses.

"Dawg, would you be talking trash at me?"

"I'm sure trying."

"You'd better behave yourself before I perform a strip search."

"Could I please get that in writing?"

She let out a big whoop and headed over toward the deli counter, her big leather belt creaking, her stride long, athletic, and totally lacking in self-consciousness. She wasn't showing off her form. Didn't need to. Des knew perfectly well what she had. She kidded around with Donna for a minute, then returned with a Greek salad and an iced tea, and sat across from Mitch, her brow furrowing intently. She had something unsettling on her mind. He knew her well enough to know this.

Mitch raised his orange juice in a toast. "Here's looking at you, kid."

"Wait, wait, I *know* this one! We watched it together. Humphrey Bogart, right?"

"In? . . ."

"Um, was it *The Maltese Falcon*?"

"Almost, it was *Casablanca*. But you were *so* close that we're going to give you one of our very fine consolation prizes."

"Which is? . . ."

"Me."

"And if I'd won—what would I have gotten then?"

"Me."

"Sounds like I can't lose," she said, attacking her salad hungrily. "Looks like I've got me some catching up to do, though. I see you've already had your dessert. I'm guessing something from the doughnut food group."

"Wait, what are you talking about?"

"Powdered sugar on your collar, boyfriend."

He glanced down at the collar of his short-sleeved khaki shirt. There were indeed tiny flecks of white there. "I can't put anything over on you, can I?"

"Don't even try. I'm a trained detective. Besides, I know you. Whenever you're upset about something you break your diet."

"I'm not like you, you know," Mitch said defensively. "I can't survive on such a drastically reduced food intake. Pretty soon you'll have me subsisting on a handful of vitamin pills, just like the Jetsons."

"Well, at least you've moved off of Yogi and Boo Boo," she said tartly.

"I sure do wish you'd let me take that one back."

"Not even. You told me the truth. That's what I need to hear if I'm going to get any better. Hell, that's why I keep you around."

"So that's it."

Des gazed at him steadily from across the table. "What's going on, baby?"

"You first."

"Me first what?"

"Something's bothering you, too, isn't it?"

"No way. You broke your diet—you go first."

"Okay, I can accept that. But we have to keep this between us, okay?" Mitch leaned over the table toward her, lowering his voice. "Dodge Crockett dropped a neutron bomb on me this morning— Martine is having an affair."

"My, my," Des responded mildly. "Isn't *this* interesting."

Mitch frowned at her. "You're not reacting the way I thought you would at all. You seem . . . relieved."

"Only because I am," Des confessed. "Real, Martine told me this morning that *Dodge* was having an affair."

"No way!"

"Oh, most definitely way."

"Well, who with?"

"She didn't say. Why, did he? . . ."

"No, not a word," Mitch said, electing to keep his hunch about Will to himself. At least for now.

"Well, this is certainly tangled up in weird," she said, taking a gulp of her iced tea. "I wonder why they've dumped it on us."

"Why pick the same morning?" Mitch wondered. "And why pick *us*?"

She considered it for a moment, her eyes narrowing shrewdly. "I hate to say this, but part of me feels like we're being moved around."

"Moved around how?"

"She told me about Dodge's affair so she could get out in front of any rumors about her own. This way, if word leaks out that she's seeing someone, people will say 'The poor dear had no choice—Dodge has been cheating on her for months.'"

"You think he told me about her for the very same reason?"

"It's a theory, Mitch."

"But that would mean they're expecting us to blab this all over town."

"Not very flattering, is it?"

"Not in the least," Mitch said indignantly. "Dodge told it to me in confidence. I'd never run out and tell everyone in Dorset that Martine is . . . Wait, what am I saying? This isn't Dorset, it's Peyton god-damned Place." He paused, poking at the remains of his lunch with his plastic fork. "Do you think they'll stay together?"

Des shrugged her shoulders. "This may be totally normal behavior for them. Some couples get off on the jealousy. It lights their fire. Hell, for all we know this whole business could be nothing more than air guitar."

"As in they're not really playing?"

"What I'm saying."

"Is that what you think is going on?"

"Boyfriend, I wouldn't even try to guess."

"Neither would I," said Mitch, who had learned one sure thing about Dorset since he'd moved here: no one, absolutely no one, was who he or she appeared to be. Everyone was fronting. That didn't necessarily mean you didn't like or admire people like the Crocketts, it just meant you didn't know them. They didn't let you. "The Crocketts seemed like the perfect couple, too."

"There is no such thing," Des said with sudden vehemence. "And there's no such thing as the face of a dying marriage either." She was drawing on her own painful breakup with Brandon, Mitch knew full well. "If they choose to, a couple like the Crocketts can hide what's really going on from *everyone*."

"So what are we supposed to do now?"

"Besides keep our mouths shut? Not a thing. Not unless they ask us for help." She finished her salad and shoved her plate away. "I did me some hanging with Esme this morning."

"What's she like?"

"Sweet, childlike—at times it seems like nobody's home."

"That's why they call them actors. They're not like you and me. They're instruments. When they aren't performing they're no different than the cello that you see lying on its side in the orchestra room, waiting to be picked up and played."

"If that's the case then why does everybody worship them?"

"They don't. They worship the fantasy that's up on the screen. The performers just have a bit of the stardust sprinkled on them, that's all. It's all about the fantasy. People vastly prefer it to reality, which is depressing and painful and filled with really bad smells. Reality they already know plenty about." Mitch gazed at her searchingly. "Des? . . ."

"What is it, baby?"

"Let's not play games like that with each other."

"Games I can deal with. You sleeping with another woman, that's something different." She drained her iced tea. "Damn, I'm thirsty today."

"Want me to get you a refill?"

"What are you trying to do, spoil me?"

"That's the general idea."

"Yum, I could get used to this idea."

He grabbed her Styrofoam cup and climbed to his feet. "Excuse me, weren't you going to say something?"

"Such as? . . ."

"Such as how lucky you are—you get to watch me walk away."

Des let out her whoop. "Word, you are the only man I've ever been with who can make me laugh."

"Is this is a positive thing?"

"Boyfriend, this is a huge thing."

"Well, okay. Remember now, no wolf whistles." He yanked up his shorts, threw back his shoulders and went galumphing back to the counter for a refill.

"Well, well," Donna said to him teasingly. "The resident trooper certainly has you well trained."

"Nonsense. We like to do favors for each other."

"I think that's very nice," spoke up Will, who was working a baked ham through the meat slicer. "Don't listen to my wife, Mitch. I certainly don't."

"I'm just jealous," she said. "The last time Will fetched something for me was . . . actually, Will has *never* fetched anything for me."

Mitch was watching her refill the iced tea when he suddenly heard *it*—the reverent hush that comes over a room when someone famous walks in. It was as if a spell had been cast over the entire food hall. The boisterous beachgoers and tourists all fell eerily silent, their mouths hanging half-open, eyes bulging with fascination. All movement ceased.

Mitch swiveled around, his own eyes scanning the hall. It was Tito and Esme, of course. They were walking directly toward the deli counter, hand in hand, with Chrissie Huberman running interference. The celebrity publicist wore an oversized man's dress shirt, white linen pants, and a furious expression—because the three of them were *not* alone.

"A little *space*, guys!" Chrissie blustered at the herd of photographers and tabloid TV cameramen who were dogging their every step, crab-walking, tripping over each other, shouting questions, shouting demands as Tito and Esme did their best to pretend they weren't there. Chrissie threw elbows and hips to keep them at bay. She was no one to mess with. She was a strapping, big-boned blond with a snow-shovel jaw and lots of sharp edges. Also the hottest client list in New York. Everything about Chrissie Huberman was hot, including her own image. She was married to a rock promoter who ran an East Village dance club. "Damn it, give us some room to breathe, will you?" she screamed, as the golden couple strode along toward the deli counter, just like two perfectly normal young people out for a perfectly normal lunch.

Hansel and Gretel, Dodge had called them.

Esme had cascading blond ringlets and impossibly innocent blue eyes. Her features were so delicate that Mitch had once called her the only woman on the planet who could make Michelle Pfeiffer look like Ernest Borgnine. She wore a gauzy shift and, seemingly, nothing underneath it. Her breasts jiggled with every step, the outline of her nipples clearly apparent through the flimsy material.

Tito Molina was not a big man, no more than five feet ten and a wiry 165 pounds. And yet his physical presence commanded just as much attention as that of his fantastically erotic young wife. Tito had the edginess of a pent-up bobcat as he made his way across the food hall, that same sexually charged intensity that Steve McQueen once had. The man smoldered. He was unshaven, his long, shiny blue black hair uncombed, and was carelessly dressed in a torn yellow T-shirt, baggy surfer trunks, and sandals. No different from half the young guys in town. And yet he looked like no other guy. No one else had his incandescent blue eyes or flawless complexion that was the color of fine suede. No one else had his perfectly chiseled nose, high, hard cheekbones, and finely carved lips. No one else was Tito Molina.

"Here you go, Berger. . . . ." Donna was holding Des's iced tea out to him. Mitch was still staring at the golden couple. "Earth to Mr. Berger, Mr. Mitch Berger . . ."

"Sorry, Donna," he apologized, taking the cup from her as Tito and Esme arrived at the counter with Chrissie and their tabloid retinue.

Mitch was starting his way back toward his table when he suddenly felt a hand on his arm. It was Tito's hand.

"Did I just hear what I thought I heard?" Tito's voice was tinged with a faint barrio inflection. "Are you that film critic guy?"

"That's me," Mitch said to him, smiling. "That film critic guy."

"Okay, this is good," Tito said, nodding his head up, down, up, down. He was so wired that sparks were coming off of him. "I wanted to let you know what I thought of your review in today's paper."

"Sure, all right," Mitch said, keeping his voice low. He did not want to get into a very public shouting match with Tito Molina. Neither of them would come away the winner. "Go ahead and tell me what's on your—"

Mitch never got another word out—Tito coldcocked him flush on the jaw. The punch connected so fast Mitch didn't see it coming. Just flew straight over backward, the back of his head slamming hard against the floor.

"Tito, *no!*" Mitch heard Esme scream as he lay there, blinking, dazed. "Tito, stop it!"

Now Tito was astride Mitch with both hands wrapped around his throat, trying to squeeze the very life out of him as the tabloid cameramen crowded around them, catching every last bit of it. "How do you like *my* review, hunh?!" the young star screamed at him, pelting Mitch with his spittle. "You *like* it?!"

Mitch could not respond. Could not, in fact, breathe.

Not one of the cameramen tried to pull the actor off of him. They were too busy egging them on.

"You gonna let him get away with that, Mitch!?"

"Throw down, Mitch! Go for it!"

The folks who'd been shopping and eating were getting in on it, too, clustering around them as if this were a street theater performance. Tourists filmed the fracas with their camcorders as Tito continued to choke him, Mitch lying there on the floor like a rag doll, his limbs flailing helplessly. No one seemed to care that he was actually about to die.

It was Will Durslag who vaulted over the counter and yanked the lunatic off him, grabbing Tito roughly by the scruff of the neck. "Let him go, man! Let him go, right now!"

"Get your hands off of me!" Tito spat, struggling in the bigger man's grasp.

"Tito, stop!" Esme sobbed, tears rolling down her cheeks. "Please! . . ."

Now Des had muscled her way through the crowd to Mitch, crouching over him with a stricken expression on her face. "Are you okay? Need an ambulance?"

"No, no, I'm fine," Mitch croaked. "Never better." He sat up slowly, gaacking much the same way Clemmie did when she was trying to bring up a six-inch fur ball. His Adam's apple felt as if someone had just driven a dull spike into it. And his jaw felt numb. He fingered it gingerly, opening and closing his mouth. Everything still seemed to work. "How come I'm . . . all wet?"

"You're sitting in my iced tea."

Will was still going at it with Tito. "I want you out of my market, man!"

"Go to hell!" Tito snarled back at him.

"No, *you* go to hell! You are in *my* place and *I* make the rules here!"

"All right, gentlemen, let's chill out," Des barked, stepping in between the two of them. "Mr. Molina, you need to get a hold of yourself at once, are you comprehending me?"

Tito didn't respond. Esme and Chrissie immediately surrounded him, Chrissie murmuring soothing words at him while Esme hugged him and kissed him.

"Please step back, everyone," Des told the crowd. "Please step back now. And I want these damned cameras out of my face!" she roared angrily.

Miraculously, the paparazzi beat a hasty retreat. Des had explained this phenomenon to Mitch once: no one, not even the lowest tabloid whore, wants to be around a sister when she's armed and pissed.

Esme and Chrissie seemed to be calming Tito down now. He stood there nodding his head obediently as he listened to them, his shoulders slumped, eyes fastened on the floor.

"How are you feeling, Mr. Molina?" Des asked him.

"I'm cool," he said quietly, running a hand through his long, shiny hair. "Everything's cool. No big."

Now Chrissie hurried over to Mitch and said, "God, Mr. Berger, I am *so* sorry about this. If there's *anything* I can do to make it right, just name it."

Mitch sat there in the cold puddle of tea, fingering his jaw. "I'm fine."

The commotion had brought Jeff Wachtell out of his store. "Mitch, I saw the whole thing if you need a witness."

"I'm *fine*," Mitch repeated.

"Can you walk?" Des asked him.

"I can try," he said, struggling unsteadily to his feet.

"Okay, good, my ride's outside," Des said. "We'll sort this out at the Westbrook Barracks together."

"Whatever you say," Tito said with weary resignation. "You're the man."

"Wait, what's to sort out?" Mitch asked.

Des raised an eyebrow at him, clearly wondering if he was punch-drunk. "The paperwork, Mitch. You have to swear out a formal complaint before we can file criminal assault charges."

"No way," Mitch said hastily. "That's absolutely not happening."

Tito gazed at Mitch, stunned.

He wasn't the only one. Des moved over closer to him, hands on her hips, and said, "What do you *mean*? That man just had his hands wrapped around your throat."

"He was only trying to make a point."

"Yes, that's he's a homicidal lunatic. Guess what? He succeeded."

"Des, we had a simple professional disagreement. He sucker punched me and I slipped on an ice cube. It was really no big deal."

"Mitch, he tried to kill you! You can't let him off the hook just because he's famous."

"I'm not."

She shook her head at him. "Okay, then I don't understand."

"This is already going to be bad enough, media-wise. Do you have any what idea what'll happen to me if it actually heads to court? I'll become a tabloid freak. I'll never be taken seriously as a critic again. My reputation will be ruined. My *life* will be ruined. This is my worst nightmare, Des. Just forget about it, *please*."

"I can't," she said stubbornly. "I'm not satisfied."

"Fine, then tell me how to satisfy you," he shot back.

"Yes, please, Des," Esme said pleadingly as the tabloid cameramen quietly, inevitably, rolled back in like the tide, the shoppers crowding in behind them.

Des stood there in judicious silence for a moment, chin resting on her fist. "Okay, I want you two men to smack meat."

"You want us to *what*?" Tito asked incredulously.

"Shake hands, or I'm running you both in."

"You're kidding, right?" Mitch said to her.

"I said it and I meant it. I don't tolerate fighting in my town. This is Dorset, not Dodge City."

"True enough," Mitch said. "But we're not in the Cub Scouts anymore, Des. We're a pair of grown men and—"

"Smack meat!" Des snapped. "Or we're going for a ride."

Mitch shrugged his shoulders and stuck a hand out. Tito Molina shook it, his own hand smaller and softer than Mitch was expecting. The media horde duly recorded it for posterity.

"What do you have to say, Mitch?" one cameraman asked him.

"Not a thing," Mitch answered curtly. "I spoke my piece, Tito spoke his."

"Sure you don't want to take a poke at him?"

"What do *you* say, Tito?" another paparazzi called out.

"Get your own damned life," Tito snarled, instantly tensing all over again. "Stop living off of mine, hunh?"

"All right, let's go!" Des said, herding them away.

The scene was over. The cameramen headed for the doors, anxious to run with what they had. The shoppers dispersed.

"Hey, Chrissie!" Jeff called out to the publicist, who was fending off the autograph seekers in Esme's face. "Can I have a quick word with you?"

Chrissie shot an impatient glance his way, then a slower double take. "Wait, I know you. . . ."

"I'm Jeff Wachtell, better known as Mr. Abby Kaminsky."

Chrissie smirked at him faintly. "Oh, sure, and I should be standing here talking to you because . . . ?"

"I was just wondering if you could convince Abby to swing by for a signing at the Book Schnook," Jeff said, sucking his cheeks in and out. "She'll be coming right past Dorset on her way to and from Boston, and it sure would help me out a lot. What do you say, will you ask her?"

Chrissie raised her jutting jaw at him. "This is like a joke, right?"

"No, I'm perfectly serious."

"Jeffrey, let me see if I can draw you a picture. My client wishes to see you stripped naked, hung by your thumbs—actually, not your thumbs but a much, much tinier part of your anatomy—and slowly pecked to death by hungry birds."

"Does that mean no?"

"It means," Chrissie replied, "that she thinks you are the lowest, most contemptible creature on the face of the earth. If I so much as mention to her that I bumped into you today she'll need a cold compress and a Valium. You ruined her life. She detests you. Am I getting through to you now?" And with that she turned on her heel and ushered Esme toward the door.

"Maybe this is a bad time," Jeff hollered after her in vain. "Could we talk about it later?"

Tito made a point of hanging back, sidling his way over toward

Mitch with the predatory stealth of Jack Palance in *Shane*. Des was about to intercede but Mitch held up his hand, stopping her. He did not want her fighting his battles for him.

"Just one more thing, critic guy," Tito said to him, his voice low and murderous, blue eyes boring in on Mitch's. "I don't want to see you in here again. If I do, I'll mess you up for real. And I don't care if your bitch is around to protect you or not, *understand*?"

It had been a long time since Mitch had been in this position. But as he stood there in The Works, nose to nose with Tito Molina, Mitch was right back in Stuyvesant Town all over again, a porky twelve-year-old going jaw to jaw with Bruce Cooperman, the playground bully who wouldn't let him pass through the gate to the basketball court. Mitch had known what he had to do then and he knew what he had to do now. He stared right back at him and said, "This town is where I live, and you don't tell me where I can or cannot go. If you want to fight, we'll fight. But we won't do it in front of the cameras. We'll do it somewhere quiet. You'll probably win, since you're such a tough guy, but I do outweigh you and I promise you that I'll put every pound I possess into messing up your precious face. By the time we're through people won't know you from Hermione Gingold, *understand*?"

Tito glowered at him in lethal silence for a long moment—until he broke into sudden, side-splitting laughter. Uncontrollable hysterics. "God, that was so cool," he finally managed to say, gasping. "Thanks for that moment, man. I'll have to use it in a scene someday."

"It's all yours," Mitch said, wondering just how much of Tito's erratic behavior was for real and how much was simply designed to keep people off-balance and afraid. He couldn't tell. Could Tito?

"Tito?!" Esme called out to him from across the food hall. She and Chrissie were waiting at the door. "Come on, let's go!"

Tito waved in acknowledgement and started toward her.

"One more thing," Mitch said, stopping the actor in his tracks.

"What is it *now*, man?" Just like that he'd switched over to irritation.

"This kind of stuff is really beneath you."

"You know dick about me, man."

"I know you're better than this. Much better."

Tito considered Mitch's remark for a long moment, tugging thoughtfully at his lower lip. Then he abruptly spat on the floor at Mitch's feet and stormed off.

"Then again," Mitch said to himself softly, "maybe you're not."

Chapter 4

The Citgo minimart was three miles down Old Shore Road from the village, past McGee's Diner, past Jilly's Boatyard, just before the turnoff for Peck's Point. There were some summer bungalow colonies clustered another couple of miles down the road, so the Citgo usually did a thriving business this time of year. Right now, Des found only a couple of pickups parked outside as she pulled up in her cruiser and got out. Right now, she found trouble.

Their big plate glass window had been smashed to bits.

Most of those bits were scattered inside all over the floor, Des discovered as she strode through the open door, crunching them under her feet. Some pieces remained framed in place, their sharp jagged edges exposed. A young workman was using a rubber mallet to tap them onto a tarp he'd laid on the pavement outside.

The owners of the station, the Acars, were visibly upset. Behind the counter, Mrs. Acar, a tiny woman in a headscarf, was trembling, her dark eyes wide with fright. Her husband was busy sweeping up and acting extremely brisk and take-charge. Also really unhappy to see Des. He wouldn't so much as look at her.

It wasn't either one of them who'd placed the call to her. It was the young workman, a customer.

"I got me some plywood I can let you have, Nuri," he said. "Until you can get a new piece of glass, I mean."

"That would be very kind of you, Kevin," Mr. Acar responded, glancing up at him. Which meant he could no longer pretend that Des wasn't standing there in the doorway "Good afternoon, Trooper. How may I help you?"

"You can tell me what happened here."

"This happened," Mrs. Acar responded, placing a smooth, round, granite stone on the counter. It was about the size of a man's fist. In her tiny hand, it looked huge. Someone had painted 9/11 on it in red paint. "It struck very near to my head," she said, pointing to a dent in the Sheetrock wall behind her. "It was fortunate we had no customers in line at the time or they might have been hit, with dire consequences."

"As you can see, no one *was* hurt," Mr. Acar spoke up, forcing a tight smile onto his face. "The window is easily replaced. So there is no trouble."

"Did either of you see who threw it?"

"We saw nothing," he replied crisply. "It was one of our quiet moments. I was in the back room replenishing some supplies for the men's lavatory. And Nema was—"

"Where were you, Mrs. Acar?" Des asked, not liking the way he was trying to stampede her. The man was a bit too anxious for her to pack up and go.

"Restocking my case," Nema replied, indicating the glass case next to the cash register, which was filled with exotic homemade pastries.

"You didn't see it happen?"

"I heard the crash of broken glass. And I ducked. I saw . . . nothing," she said, glancing meekly at her husband. "Then I heard a car pull away very rapidly, a screech of tires. That is all."

"Did you get a make or license number of the car?"

"No, this was not possible. It was gone before I could get a look."

"Which way was the car heading when it left—back toward town?"

"The other way, I believe. I am not positive."

Des went to the door and glanced outside. On this stretch of Old Shore there were no businesses on the other side of the road, just an overgrown tangle of vines, creepers, and wild berries. About a hundred yards past the Citgo, heading away from town, there was a sharp left turn onto Burnham Road, a narrow, residential lane that snaked its way through some old farms and ended up back in the village. Whoever did this most likely turned there and was gone in a

69

flash. Probably two kids in a pickup—one drives, the other crouches in back and throws the stone. Swamp Yankees, if she had to guess. Indigenous lost boys with a hate thing for immigrants. Especially immigrants who were operating a successful new business.

"Have you folks had any trouble like this before?" Des asked Mr. Acar.

"No trouble at all, Trooper," he answered. "Everyone has been very welcoming. And, while your presence is greatly appreciated, I wish you'd not pursue this matter any further. It will only draw more attention toward it, which we do not consider desirable. We shall happily bear the cost of replacing the glass. As you can see, this gentleman is already helping."

Des shoved her horn-rims up her nose, and said, "Look, I understand where you're coming from, Mr. Acar—"

"Please, call me Nuri," he purred, smiling at her ingratiatingly. More than ingratiatingly. The man was starting to ogle her long form right in front of his wife.

"Nuri, a crime has been committed here," she said, her stomach muscles tightening involuntarily. The smarm wasn't just undressing her with his eyes, he was licking her. "I have to file a report—that's my job. Furthermore, the message on that stone is an obvious reference to the attack on the World Trade Center. We've got a task force operating out of the state's attorney's office that specializes in hate crimes such as this."

"But who would hate us?" he asked her imploringly. "We are Turkish people, peaceful people. Turkey is America's good friend."

"You and I know that, but the morons who did this may not be too up on their international coalitions. Besides which," she added, glancing at Nema's headscarf, "you *are* Muslims, and that makes you different. Some people don't care for different. I happen to know a little bit about what that's like. I also know that when this kind of thing happens, it doesn't just hurt you, it hurts the entire community. Look, let me show you something, okay?"

She went back out to her cruiser and fished around in her briefcase for the four-by-seven laminated Hate Crime Response Card that the

Connecticut State Police had developed in conjunction with the Anti-Defamation League. When she returned with it the Acars were talking heatedly to one other. They broke it off at once. Des had a definite feeling that Nema was more anxious to cooperate than her husband was. Clearly, he didn't want to involve the law at all. How come? Was something else going on here—say, somebody running a protection racket on him?

"Please, listen to this," she said, reading to them from the laminated card. "It defines a hate crime as 'a criminal act against a person or property in which the perpetrator chooses the victim because of the victim's real or perceived race, religion, national origin, ethnicity, sexual orientation, disability, or gender.'" Des glanced up at the Acars, who were staring at her now in tight-lipped silence. "That's why the task force needs to be brought in. They know the different hate groups and how they operate. They'll know if someone's been pulling this elsewhere around the state. It might be part of a pattern."

"Foolish boys," Mr. Acar sniffed at her dismissively. "Just a prank by foolish boys."

"You're probably right," Des said, although she did have some nagging doubts. Why during daylight? Early afternoon was not the local bad boys' usual hour for committing random acts of stupidity—late night was. "But this way we'll know for sure, okay?"

"As you wish," Nuri Acar said with weary resignation.

A customer in a BMW pulled up at a gas pump out front. Mr. Acar darted outside to help, grateful for the chance to get away from her.

Des was just as happy to see him go. One of the things in life that she was truly bad at was being civil to people who she thought were creeps. *Get along.* That was the Deacon's motto, and he had ridden it all the way to the tippity toppity—deputy superintendent of the Connecticut State Police, highest-ranking black man in the state's history. But Des was not her father, and that was why she wasn't working homicides anymore. At age twenty-eight, Des had been Connecticut's great nonwhite hope—the only black woman in the state to make lieutenant on the Major Crime Squad. She had produced, too. Outperformed every single man in the Central District.

Except she didn't *get along* with the so-called Waterbury mafia—the inner circle of Italian-American males who pretty much ran things in the state police. They liked to have their big, fat egos stroked, especially by the pretty girls. Des hadn't played along, hadn't respected them. And they could tell. And when the chance came to knife her, they had.

"May I offer you a coffee?" Nema asked, smiling at her uncertainly. "A baklava, perhaps?"

"I'm all set, thanks," Des said, as Kevin began hammering the plywood into place over the broken window.

"I regret the circumstances, but I am so pleased to meet you at long last. Your friend is my friend, after all."

"My friend?"

"Mr. Mitch Berger," Nema said. "He is a fine, fine man. And one of my very best pastry customers."

"I'll just bet he is," Des said, her eyes scanning the case of sweets. Some were covered with powdered sugar, just like the powdered sugar he'd had on his collar at lunch. So this was where he came to blow huge holes in his diet. It did occur to Des, standing there at the counter, that Mitch was at heart a fat little boy and always would be. Still, if this was the worst kind of lie he was capable of then she was lucky and she damned well knew it.

"Such a modest gentleman," Nema added. "No airs, despite his prestigious position with the newspaper. And quite the gourmet. Very discerning."

"That he is." Des did not mention his penchant for eating pot-loads of his god-awful American chop suey, or that she had once found a box of Great Starts microwave sausage-and-egg breakfast burritos in his freezer. She did not want to shatter any illusions, or slow Nema down. The lady was working her way up to telling her something.

"Nuri does not mean to be difficult," she finally said, clearing her throat uneasily. "We wish only to blend in. Surely you can understand that."

"Absolutely," Des said, because she could understand. She just couldn't blend in. "Your husband said he was in back when it happened. You were here behind the counter?"

"Yes, that is right."

"Sure there's nothing else you want to tell me, one friend to another?"

Nema glanced nervously out the glass doors at her husband. "No, nothing."

Clearly, the lady was holding back. She was also frightened. Of what? Who? "Well, if you remember anything . . ." Des handed Nema her card and urged her to give her a call, knowing she never would. Then she bagged and tagged the rock, which would go to the Westbrook Barracks along with her report. The task force would take it from there.

Still, it wouldn't hurt to do a bit of canvassing.

Mr. Acar was washing the BMW's windshield. She tipped her big hat to him politely. He acknowledged her gesture with an equally polite wave. She got into her cruiser and eased it down Old Shore to that quick left onto Burnham, where she parked on the shoulder and got out. She knelt and inspected the pavement carefully for fresh skid marks. Saw none.

Three old farmhouses were clustered there on Burnham not far from Old Shore Road. No one was home at the first house. At the second house she managed to wake up a young man who'd worked the overnight shift at Millstone, the nuclear power plant in Waterford. He hadn't heard anyone speeding by his house in the past hour and was very grumpy about saying so.

Des approached the third house with some reluctance. This one belonged to Miss Barker, an elderly spinster who had called Des twice in past weeks with dire emergencies. A prowler who turned out to be a meter reader from Connecticut Light and Power, and a suspicious-looking hoodlum dumping toxic waste in the marsh who was, in fact, a marine biologist with the Department of Environmental Protection. Still, Miss Barker wasn't a bad person, just lonely and scared. And she missed nothing that went on out on her street.

It took the old girl a while to get to the door. She didn't move very

73

well, which was why Des hadn't tried pressing a kitten on her—she was too likely to trip over it and fall. She was a slender, frail thing with Q-Tip hair, partial to pastel-colored pantsuits. Today she was pretty in pink. The scent of Miss Barker's heavy, fruity perfume wafted out of the doorway with her. She wore so much of it that Des got lightheaded if she went inside the house.

"Sure, it's those darned kids," she responded promptly after Des had explained the purpose of her visit. "They all come tearing around that corner too fast. Especially at night. I hear their tires screeching when I'm lying here in my bed. I'm afraid of what'll happen, dear, I don't mind saying. One of those fool boys is going to smash right into the side of my bedroom some night. The explosion will kill me dead in my bed. Incinerate me sure as I'm standing—"

"This would have happened within the past hour, Miss Barker," Des said, trying to rein her in.

"We ought to have a speed bump out there to slow those boys down, but do you think they listen to me at town hall? I've only been paying property taxes here since 1946, never missed a single payment."

"Miss Barker, did you hear any screeching tires within the past hour?"

"Why, yes, right in the middle of *All My Children*, which I don't know why I still watch. Loyalty, I guess. Not a very popular virtue anymore, is it?"

"Did you see what type of vehicle it was?"

"I absolutely did not *see* anyone," Miss Barker said with a sudden flash of indignation. "So, naturally, I would not have the slightest idea what type of vehicle it was. How could I?"

Des peered at her in surprise. This was a lady who always butted in, never out. Why the dumb act? First Nema Acar, now her. What was this? "Well, did it sound more like a car or a truck?"

"More like a car," she replied after a moment's hesitation. "The pickups have those huge tires now with the big treads that make so much noise. Why do they *need* such huge tires? My daddy drove a truck his whole life, never a single accident, and his tires were just normal, proper tires." Miss Barker paused, her pale pink tongue flicking across her thin, dry lips. "But I really couldn't say *anything* for sure."

Des didn't press her any further. Just thanked Miss Barker for her time and started back toward her cruiser, puzzled and frustrated. So much so that she could feel the beginnings of a deep blue funkadelic haze coming over her.

My job is pointless and stupid. My entire existence is pointless and stupid. I am wasting my life.

She knew the real reason why she was feeling this way. Sure she did. But knowing why didn't make her feel one bit better.

She got back in her ride and cranked up the air conditioner and sat there glowering through her windshield at the huge old sycamore that grew in Miss Barker's front yard. It was so splendid and lovely that it actually seemed to be mocking her with its presence. Either that or she was going totally nutso. She lunged for her cell phone and called her short-relief man. Whenever she needed a save, she reached out for him. As his phone rang, Des sat there wondering what would happen to her if Mitch Berger were not in her life right now. She would go right down the drain, that's what.

But he must never know this—he thinks I'm the one who has it all together.

His phone machine answered. She waited, waited, waited for the beep and said, "Hi, it's me."

And he picked up. "I'm here," he said hurriedly. "I've just been getting a gazillion calls from the media about Tito."

"They're making a big deal out of it?"

"Big doesn't begin to describe it. *Brokaw's* people called me for a quote."

"How's your jaw?"

"Actually, it feels very similar to that molar implant I had done last year. The only difference is that was administered by a board-certified oral surgeon."

"Well, if it makes you feel any better I just met some huge fans of yours."

75

"Oh, yeah, who?"

"The Acars, Nuri and Nema." Total silence from his end. "She said you're just about her best customer."

"Well, sure," Mitch said slowly. "I fill up my truck there all the time."

"You are so busted, boyfriend."

"Busted," he confessed guiltily. "I throw myself on your mercy, Des. You must be so disappointed in me."

"No, baby, I'm not," she said, easing up off of the gas pedal. Because he could be so much worse. He could be Brandon. "You're my boy. All I want is you, no matter what size you are—large, extra-large, jumbo, economy. . . ."

"Okay, you made your point, Master Sergeant. I'll tell you one thing—I'm going to get Nema for this."

"Cut her a little slack. She's had herself a bad day." Des told him what had happened to their window.

"Oh my God, that's awful. Truly detestable. You wouldn't think . . ."

"You wouldn't think what?"

"Nothing. I was just about to say 'You wouldn't think something like this could happen here,' but I stopped myself because any time something bad happens in a small town the bystanders always say 'This is more the kind of thing you'd expect to happen in New York City.' And, as a New Yorker, I always get hopping mad. Things like this go on everywhere, because there are total assholes everywhere. Will you catch who did it?"

"That's up to Hate Crimes, but if I had to guess I'd say yeah."

"They're a smart crew?"

"They are, plus the people who go in for these types of crimes tend to be genuinely stupid. Real, I think Nema knew more about it than she was letting on."

"Why would she hold out on you?"

"Because her husband told her to."

"You don't like him, do you? You think he's oleaginous."

"Damn, is it that obvious?"

"Only to me, girlfriend." From the first day they met Mitch been able to read her mind. Des had never understood how. "I'm glad you called—I was just going to call you and tell you to press your white flannels."

"You just said what?"

"We've been invited to the highly exclusive Dorset Beach Club for dinner tonight, lovey," he said, putting on his best Locust Valley Lockjaw. Which was not good at all. It traveled by way of Canarsie, where his parents were from. "Esme told Dodge what happened between Tito and me. Dodge thought if he got all of us together for a cookout and a swim it would help chill things out."

"And Tito's down with this?"

"Esme said she'd get him there. Dodge is inviting the rest of the Mesmers so as to defuse any possible tension."

"The Mesmers?"

"That's the name of our walking club."

"I didn't know that."

"They don't know it either. I'm bringing corn. Will and Donna are bringing everything else. You like them, right?"

She did like Donna. Will was polite but a bit reserved. Some of the locals were like that. Hell, most of the locals were like that.

"Jeff will be there, too."

Jeff Wachtell she could live without. Des thought he was a whiner, plus he walked like a duck. "I thought you didn't like to socialize with movie people."

"That's absolutely true. But under the circumstances I think this is something I need to do. Tito and Esme are going to be around for a while. I don't want to get into a fight with this guy every time I try to go to the store."

Which was why Des had wanted to march the actor straight to Westbrook in handcuffs. But she held her tongue. They'd been over this already.

"So are you game? I was kidding about the white flannels—it's casual."

"Thanks, baby, but I don't think I'm up for that tonight."

"You're still mad that I didn't press charges against him, is that it?"

"No, no. It's not about you. I need to draw tonight, that's all."

"It'll happen, Des," he said encouragingly. "You just have to be patient."

"Damn it, doughboy, don't you *ever* get tired of being so supportive?"

He didn't respond. Just gave her back a big dose of stung silence.

Now she sat there cursing her bad self. When she was frustrated she could go bitch cakes and then some. All the more reason she should be alone tonight. "That's exactly what Professor Weiss told me," she acknowledged. "He said I'd get it, and that the process would make me stronger. But it's just not happening."

"So why don't you talk to him some more about it?" Mitch said, his voice a good deal cooler than it was before she bit his head clean off.

"I can't."

"Why not? Who is he, the Dalai Lama?"

"I have to figure it out myself, that's all. I just wish I knew *how*. I keep, I don't know, thinking this bolt of inspiration will strike me or something."

"Tex in the stamp stalls, sure."

"Tex in the what?"

"In *Charade*, when James Coburn is walking through the stamp stalls in the Paris park and suddenly, kerchunk, the whole plot falls right into place."

"Damn it, Mitch, this is not some fool movie!"

"I do know that," he shot back. "And I know something else— that I've already had my bellyful of childish, self-absorbed, pain-in-the-asses today, thank you very much."

Des drew her breath in, stunned. He'd never spoken to her this way before. Not ever. "You're right, baby," she said. "My miss. I'm sorry. Really, really sorry."

But she was too late.

Mitch Berger, the kindest, sweetest love of her life, had already hung up on her.

Chapter 5

MITCH WAS NOT HAPPY that Des wouldn't come with him to the beach club.

In fact, he was so not happy that he decided he'd better get off the phone awfully damned now. His jaw ached. His mood was vile. And he didn't want to say anything that he might really regret. He found it hard to believe she was so self-centered she couldn't see that he was in the midst of a monstrous professional crisis and that he needed her by his side—not going on and on about her damned trees.

His situation could not have been more of a nightmare. The twenty-four-hour cable news channels were already broadcasting video highlights of The Fight by the time he got home to Big Sister Island. The digital photos of Tito with his hands wrapped tightly around Mitch's throat were out all over the Internet. There was Tito astride him like a wild beast, teeth bared, ready for the kill. There was Mitch pinned helplessly underneath him, looking like some form of slow, terrified water mammal.

It was America Online's top news story of the day. The headline on the service provider's main screen read "Tito Lowers Boom on Highbrow Critic."

The arts editor of Mitch's paper, Lacy Mickerson, had e-mailed him twice and left an urgent message for him on his phone machine. Dozens of his fellow critics from around the country had sent e-mails as well, many humorous. He would respond to them at some point, but right now he was too busy fending off calls from one media outlet after another. Everyone wanted a comment, a quote, something, anything. The very same tabloid TV vans that had been following Tito and Esme all around Dorset were now pulled up on Peck's Point at the gate to the Big Sister causeway, desperate to get out there and film *him*. Mitch was having none of it. He did not want to comment. He did not want to appear on camera.

He was not an entertainer. He was a critic.

Or at least he used to be.

He sat at his desk, an ice pack pressed against his jaw, and called Lacy back.

"Honestly, Mitch, I thought your review was *gentle* compared with a lot of the others I've seen," she said after he'd given her his version of what happened. Among her many attributes Lacy was fiercely protective of her critics. "Hell, this film has been positively trashed by everyone. People are walking out in droves. Why did he pick on you?"

"Because I was there," Mitch grunted, adjusting his ice pack. It didn't help with the pain, but it gave him something to do. "He's a genuinely talented actor. I feel sorry for him, actually."

"Well, I don't. I've seen these so-called bad boys come and go over the years." Lacy was in her late fifties and claimed to have bedded Irwin Shaw and Mickey Mantle in her youth, not to mention Nelson Rockefeller. "They *all* have talent. It's what they do with it that counts."

"What do I do, Lacy? What's my next move?"

"You shut it down," she said firmly.

The two of them cobbled together a brief statement that would be posted immediately on the newspaper's Web site—just as soon as Lacy ran it past someone with a larger office and, possibly, a law degree. It would also appear on the lead arts page in tomorrow's paper. The statement would serve as Mitch's one and only response to the attack:

This newspaper's chief film critic, Mitchell Berger, and the actor Tito Molina engaged in a spirited creative disagreement yesterday afternoon in a popular eating establishment in Dorset, Connecticut. Mr. Berger feels the matter is fully resolved. He believes that Mr. Molina is a gifted artist with a wonderful career ahead of

*him and he looks forward to his future film work with as much
excitement as ever.*

After he and Lacy were done Mitch swallowed three Advils and
spent the rest of the afternoon ducking phone calls. His phone
machine got quite a workout that day.

He did pick up when Dodge called. And was pleased that Dodge
wanted to broker a peace deal at the beach club. It seemed like a genuine solution. Dodge was smart and tactful. He'd make the perfect
intermediary.

As for Des, well, Mitch hoped she'd figure out what she needed to
figure out—and soon—because when she was stuck in the deep
muck she had a way of dragging him down there with her, whether
he felt like going or not. And that could be awfully damned hard to
handle sometimes.

Not that love was ever supposed to be an easy thing.

When it came time to leave he dressed in a white oxford button-
down shirt, khaki shorts, and Topsiders. He had a welt on his jaw
and red finger marks around his throat, otherwise he looked fit,
casual, and terrific. It was a warm, hazy evening with very little
breeze. The sun hung low over the Sound, casting everything in a
soft, rosy glow. He threw a pair of swim trunks and a towel into the
front seat of his truck, then moseyed over to Bitsy Peck's garden with
a galvanized steel bucket to pilfer a dozen ears of corn.

It was Will who'd taught Mitch the best way to cook corn—plunge
the fresh-picked ears directly into a bucket of water, soak them for at
least a half hour, then throw them on the grill to steam in their husks.

Bitsy was busy digging up her pea patch with a fork, dressed in
cutoff overalls and a big, floppy straw hat. She was a round, bubbly
little blue blood in her fifties with a snub nose and freckles, and just a
remarkably avid and tireless gardener. Hundreds of species of flowers, vegetables, and herbs grew in her vast, multileveled garden.
Actually, Bitsy's garden looked more like a commercial nursery than
it did somebody's yard. When Mitch first arrived on Big Sister she

had gleefully stepped into the role of his garden guru. The lady was a fountain of advice and seedlings and composted cow manure. Mitch liked her a lot.

Although lately she hadn't been nearly as upbeat as usual. Not since her twenty-three-year-old daughter, Becca, a ballet dancer, had come home to mom and the massive three-story shingled Victorian summer cottage where she'd grown up. Becca had gotten herself addicted to heroin out in San Francisco, and had just finished a stint at the Silver Hill Rehab Clinic in New Canaan. Mostly, the two ladies kept to themselves. Hardly left the island at all, and seldom had guests. Bitsy went grocery shopping every couple of days. Otherwise, Mitch would find her toiling diligently in her garden refuge from dawn until dusk.

Becca was out there working with her right now, weeding a flower bed in a halter top and shorts, her own efforts rather distracted and halfhearted. Mitch had seen old photographs around the house of Becca in her full ballerina getup. She had been a slender and graceful young swan of a girl. Truly lovely. But that was before the needle did its damage. Now she was a gaunt, frail shell of a woman with haunted eyes that were sunk deep in their sockets and rimmed with dark circles. Her long brown hair was twisted into tight braids that looked like two lifeless hunks of rope.

Mitch smiled and said hello to her. Becca mouthed "Hello" in polite response, although scarcely a whisper came out. She was painfully quiet. This, too, was the needle, according to Bitsy, who said Becca had been the most outgoing, popular girl in her high school class. Looking at her now, Mitch found it hard to believe.

"So sorry about all of those press vans at the gate today, Bitsy," he said, toting his bucket over toward her corn patch.

"They didn't bother us one bit," Bitsy assured him.

"Well, they sure bothered me."

Bitsy swiped at the perspiration on her upper lip, leaving a smear of mud behind. "My, my, aren't you all fresh scrubbed and smell-goody," she observed with motherly pride as he began stripping choice ears of corn off their stalks and plunging them into his bucket. "And here we are like a pair of sweaty farm animals, aren't we, Becca?"

"Yes, Mother," Becca responded faintly.

"What's the occasion, Mitch?" Bitsy asked, her good cheer a bit forced.

"I've been invited to the beach club. I'm kind of anxious to check the place out, actually. No one's ever invited me before."

"And who did, dare I ask?"

"Dodge Crockett."

Becca immediately dropped her trowel, which clattered off a low stone retaining wall onto the ground. She stared down at it briefly, but didn't pick it up. Just walked away instead—straight into the house, her stride still uncommonly graceful.

Bitsy watched her go, biting down fretfully on her lower lip. "She doesn't like to talk about Dodge."

"I noticed. How come?"

"I'm worried about that girl, Mitch. She spends too much time alone. It's not good for her. She needs stimulation. I wish Esme would come see her."

Mitch glanced at her curiously. "They know each other?"

"Oh my, yes. They were best friends when they were girls. The great Esme Crockett practically grew up out here. Slept over almost every night during the summer. There were slumber parties and pillow fights, and poor little Jeremy was *so* in love with her." Becca's younger brother, a senior at Duke, was away serving a summer internship in Washington. "He'd follow her around like a gawky little puppy. The house was full of kids and laughter then," Bitsy recalled fondly. "Not like now." She went back to her forking, throwing every fiber of her body into turning over the soil. "I didn't realize you and Dodge had become buddies."

"We walk together every morning. I like him a lot."

"People do think very highly of Dodge," she allowed, nodding. "There was even talk about the party running him for lieutenant governor some years back. I suppose it's just as well they didn't."

"Why do you say that?"

"Yes, he's a bright, enthusiastic fellow, all right. More than willing to do his part around town. So is Martine, who is so generous with her time, always ready to throw herself body and soul behind a good cause. And such a decorative creature, too." Now Bitsy trailed off, glancing up at Mitch uncertainly. "Just promise me one thing. Promise me you won't be too taken in by them. Will you do that for me, Mitch?"

"Okay, sure," Mitch said, frowning at her. "But why?"

"Because they're cannibals," she said quietly. "They eat people."

The Dorset Beach Club was located at the end of a narrow and perilously bumpy little dirt road that snaked its way back through a half mile of marsh and wild brambles off of Old Shore Road. It was a private dirt road. No sign on Old Shore marked its presence. In fact, the roadside brush was so overgrown at the beach club turnoff that if you weren't looking for it you would never know it was there.

Which, this being Dorset, was the whole idea.

In fact, Mitch wasn't even sure he was bouncing his way down the right dirt road until he reached a grassy clearing filled with beat-up old Ford Country Squire station wagons, Mercedes diesels, and Subarus. Then he knew this had to be the beach club—in Dorset, the richer they were the junkier their ride. Only the working poor drove shiny new cars.

At the water's edge sat a modest, weathered gray shingled cottage-style clubhouse that looked as if it had been built in the 1930s. Mitch got out, corn bucket in hand, and made his way around to the beachside on a raised wooden walkway, passing through a portal directly into a different time and place. Here, on a wide wooden dining porch beneath a striped blue awning, Mitch found properly attired club members being served their proper lobster dinners by hushed, respectful waiters in white jackets. Proper attire for men was apparently defined as a madras sports jacket and Nantucket red pants. Proper attire for women was anything Katharine Hepburn might have worn to a summer concert under the stars in, say, 1957. A rather

84

tinny sound system was playing soothing, vaguely Polynesian-sounding music. Not a single one of these members was under the age of seventy. Actually, not many appeared to be under the age of eighty. They seemed lifelike enough, although none of them actually spoke and all of them moved in slow motion, as if this were a dream. Standing there on the walkway with his bucket, Mitch had the astonishingly powerful feeling that this *was* a dream, that none of it was real, just his own Jewish schoolboy fantasy of what a private club like this might have been like in bygone days.

Mitch had experienced these paranormal phenomena several times before since he'd moved to this place. He'd taken to calling them Dorset Interludes.

Dodge had instructed him to continue past the dining porch to the long wooden veranda that faced the sand. Here there were showers and changing stalls, a cold drink stand and other amenities for beachgoers. Umbrella tables and built-in barbecue grills were provided for members who wanted to cook out and eat right there on the beach. It was all pretty unassuming considering just how exclusive the beach club was. Three letters of recommendation and a certified check for $10,000 were required—and that was the easy part. The hard part was that the membership roll capped out at a strict maximum of two hundred families, meaning that in order to get in you had to know people and then those people had to die. Not that it looked as if it would necessarily be a long wait, given the median age of the members who were politely gumming their lobster and corn back there on the dining porch.

Of course, the main attraction of the club was the beach itself—and a very nice, wide stretch of clean white beach it was, the sand so immaculate it looked as if it were raked hourly. No trash, no doggy poop, and above all, no beer-bellied pipe fitters from New Britain with their loudmouthed wives and squalling kids. Only the right sort of people were to be found on this beach. People who *belonged* here. Mitch didn't and he never would and he knew this. But he plodded his way toward the barbecue grills anyway, footsteps thudding heavily on the wooden walkway. He was not here to fit in. He was here to bury the hatchet with Tito Molina.

The Crocketts had commandeered two umbrella tables at the far end of the veranda, where they were sharing a pitcher of iced margaritas with Will and Donna and Jeff. Tito and Esme hadn't arrived yet. A big spread of cheeses and crackers was laid out on the table. No one seemed to be touching any of it. They were too busy drinking and talking, their eyes bright, voices animated.

"Hey, it's macho man," called out Donna, who was the first to spot him.

"Mitch, you look like you just went three rounds with Roy Jones Jr.," observed Will.

"How does the jaw feel?" asked Jeff, who sat huddled under the umbrella with a beach towel over his exposed knees. Being a redhead, he burned easily.

"It's really not so bad as long as I don't smile, talk, or eat."

"Where's our resident trooper?" asked Dodge as he refilled everyone's glasses. The pitcher was already half empty—they'd gotten a serious head start.

"I'm afraid she couldn't make it."

"That's an awful shame," clucked Martine, who was stretched out languorously on a lounge chair in the sun, looking tanned, terrific, and not a day over thirty-five in her snug-fitting black one-piece swimsuit. Martine's hips were slim, her legs long, shapely, and smooth. She glanced fondly up at Dodge as he brought her a refill, stroking his arm with tender affection. Then she turned her inviting blue-eyed gaze on Mitch, drawing him effortlessly toward her. "But I'm so glad *you* could join us."

"Wouldn't miss it," said Mitch, his mind straying back to that word Bitsy Peck had just used to describe the Crocketts—*cannibals*. "Beautiful evening, isn't it?"

"Beautiful," she murmured, gazing at the soft glowing sky over the Sound.

"It will be raining by midnight," Dodge predicted. "My left knee aches—old lacrosse injury."

"Darling, I always thought it was your right knee," Martine said teasingly.

"It's *always* been the left," he kidded back.

"Oh, goody, Berger brought corn," observed Donna, her eyes gleaming at Mitch. She already seemed a bit tipsy. "Some men bring flowers and champagne, others bring hog feed. Speaking as one of the hogs, I say thank you."

"Speaking as another one of the hogs, I say you're welcome." Mitch delivered the bucket to Will, who was building a fire in one of the grills out of seasoned hardwood chunks and mesquite. Dressed in a tank top, nylon shorts and leather flip-flops, Will could easily be mistaken for the club's lifeguard. To Mitch he also seemed a bit less lighthearted than the others. Distracted, maybe. Was it being around Martine when both her husband and his wife were around? Mitch wondered.

"Seriously, Mitch, how is your jaw?" he asked with genuine concern.

"Seriously, it hurts like hell. I really don't like getting hit."

"But you're okay to eat?"

"Oh, I'll manage," said Mitch, his stomach growling as he checked out their dinner—racks and racks of baby back ribs, potato salad, red cabbage slaw, fruit salad, brownies.

"For what it's worth, I've known Esme since she was in pigtails," Will said. "She's always had good instincts about people. If she likes somebody, there's some good in there."

"I believe it."

"Care to try a margarita, Mitch?" asked Dodge.

"I'll settle for a beer, thanks." Mitch fetched a Dos Equis out of the cooler, popped it open, and settled into a deck chair with it. "This is nice here," he said, taking a long, thirsty gulp.

"You'll have to be our guest more often," Martine said lazily, crossing her ankles. "We vastly prefer it down at this end. You'll find all of us club rebels down here. That dining room crowd is *so* stuffy." A cell phone rang in the canvas tote bag next to her. She reached for it. "I'll bet that's Esme. She's *always* late. . . . Hi, sweetie," Martine said into the phone, nodding her blond head at them. "We're all here waiting for you. . . . It's lovely out, although Daddy is absolutely convinced it's going to rain. His right knee's acting up."

"Left knee," Dodge interjected, grinning at her.

"Sweetie, when are you two—?" Now Martine's face fell, her brow furrowing. "What do *mean*, you're not . . . No, I absolutely *don't* understand. This is very important. You *know* it is. Tito needs to— Esme? Esme, are you still there? . . ." Martine flicked off the phone, sighing, and tossed it back into her bag. "She couldn't get him to come. They quarreled about it and he drove off in a huff. Everything with them is such a battle, Dodge. I wish we could do something."

"They have to work it out for themselves," Dodge said. "It's their marriage."

Now Mitch heard sharp footsteps coming their way.

"Oh, great, here comes Little Mary Sunshine," muttered Jeff.

Chrissie Huberman was marching toward them, the wooden veranda shuddering under each of her onrushing strides. The publicist's face was set in a determined scowl, her fists clenched. She did treat Dodge and Martine to a great big toothy smile when she arrived at their table. "Hi, Mr. and Mrs. Crockett!" she exclaimed, all sugar and spice for the parents of a prized client. But then Chrissie abruptly whirled, stuck her finger in Mitch's face and snarled, "Don't you *ever* try to pull something like this again! I *forbid* it, you hear me!"

Mitch took a sip of his beer and said, "I hear you, Chrissie. But I have no idea what you're talking about."

"Like hell you don't," she raged. "You're trying to feed off of Tito behind my back. No way! You want face time with my client then you come through me! I protect those kids. I bleed for those kids. And there will be no secret sessions with Tito Molina as long as I'm—"

"Before you go any further," Mitch interrupted, "it's my duty to inform you that you're way off base."

Chrissie tilted her head at him mockingly. "Tell me this wasn't a secret meeting."

"It really wasn't, Chrissie," Dodge spoke up. "It was simply an informal get-together between family and friends."

"Of which *you* are neither," Martine said to her pointedly.

"Honestly, all I want is for this situation with Tito to go away," Mitch said.

Chrissie let out a derisive laugh. "Yeah, right. I know all about you, Mitch Berger—how you're the Mother Teresa of film critics. Won't do the junkets, won't accept gifts. Well, guess what? I don't believe any of it. What Tito did to you today is *every* critic's wet dream. You're no different than the rest. You *all* want a taste," she jeered at him, grabbing her own crotch for lewd, crude emphasis. "You want it so bad you can't stand it."

Mitch gazed at her in stunned silence. They all did. Heads were even starting to turn all of the way back at the dining porch. It was safe to say no one had ever seen such a public display of behavior by a female at the fabled Dorset Beach Club. Certainly not by one over the age of three.

"Young lady, I would like you to go," Martine said to her between gritted teeth. "This club is for members and their guests only. You will kindly take your potty mouth and leave right now."

"Are you trying to tell me this seedy dump is *private?*"

"Get out of here, Chrissie," ordered Will, moving over toward her. "Get out or I'll throw you out."

"Fine, whatever. Just remember what I told you," she warned Mitch.

"Not a problem. I don't think I'll be forgetting this for quite some time."

Satisfied, Chrissie stormed off, her footsteps clunking on the veranda. Heads turned to stare as she went charging past the dining porch.

"Well, it's been quite some day for histrionics," Mitch said wearily. "Sorry about that, folks."

"No need for you to be sorry," Jeff assured him. "Not your fault."

"Not in the least," echoed Dodge.

"That woman thinks everyone else in the world is exactly like her," Will said, gazing after her. "Greedy, two-faced, and conniving. And when you try to explain to her that you're not, she calls you a goddamned liar right to your face. She couldn't get away with that if she was a guy. She'd get punched."

"You should have given me the signal, honey," Donna said, putting up her dukes fiercely. "I would have had no problem decking her."

"She has a hard job," Dodge said. "That's not to defend or excuse her."

"What she has is a personality problem," Martine argued. "I wish Esme would get rid of her."

"She didn't hire her," Dodge said. "Tito's agent did."

"Fine, then I wish Tito would get rid of her."

"Hey, let's not let her ruin our party," Dodge said, forcing a smile onto his face. "Why don't you folks take a swim while we start the chow?"

"I think I will," said Mitch. Although in his case "float" would be the operative word. A true child of the pavement, Mitch hadn't known how to swim at all when he moved to Dorset. But thanks to diligence and hard work, he'd taught himself how to float on his back—the main thing was to relax and trust in his own considerable natural buoyancy. As he started his way toward the changing stalls with his swim trunks he discovered Jeff was tailing him, stride for stride. "Going to take a dip, Jeff?"

"Not exactly . . . I wanted to ask you something personal," Jeff said, sucking his cheeks in and out. "Would you go talk to her for me?"

"Talk to who, Jeff?"

"Abby—when she's at C. C. Willoughby on Thursday. She's just got to come sign books for me, Mitch. I *need* this, or I swear I'll go under. Chrissie totally blew me off, and Abby hung up on me as soon as she heard my voice."

"What makes you think she'll speak to me?"

"She'll at least hear you out. She doesn't *hate* you. Will you do it, Mitch?"

Mitch really didn't want to get involved in Jeff's marital problems. But the little guy seemed so desperate and alone that he didn't know how to say no. "Can I think it over?"

"Does that mean yes?"

"It means I'll think it over."

"Sure, sure," Jeff said with great relief. "Mitch, you're a real pal. I don't know what I'd do without you. Honest."

Mitch continued on behind the open-air showers now to the weathered knotty pine changing stalls, which were grouped on either side of a center aisle, maybe fifty of them in all. Each stall was about three-by-five feet, with a door that was cropped a foot short at top and bottom for ventilation. Mitch's stall was bare except for a wooden bench and a few pegs to hang clothes on.

He emerged a moment later in his baggy surf shorts, and padded back out to the veranda. Martine was already swimming laps in a roped-in area out by the float. There was no one else out in the water. Will and Dodge were busy laying the ears of corn around the edge of the fire, which was getting good and hot. Jeff was seated back under the umbrella in the shade.

Now Donna joined Mitch, wearing a generously cut one-piece suit and a self-conscious look on her round face. Donna was no long-stemmed bikini babe—she was stubby and short-waisted, and she knew it. "Berger, is that you?" she joked, groping blindly at the air before her. She had removed her wire-rimmed glasses for the swim.

"It is."

"How do you like my new hot girl suit?" she asked, modeling it with a dainty curtsy. She was definitely feeling her margaritas.

"I like it fine. You ready to go in?"

"Absolutely, but you have to go in ahead of me. I don't want you staring at my big butt."

"But this way you get to stare at mine."

"That's right, honey." she giggled, swatting his arm with her hand.

The tide was out, the bottom sandy and soft. It fell off gradually as they slogged their way out, the water calm but surprisingly chilly.

It was still only about chest deep as they neared the float, where Martine continued to swim laps back and forth, the hazy sunlight glistening on her smooth, tanned flesh.

"What's up with that Rocky Dies Yellow tattoo?" Donna asked, peering at his biceps. "Are you some kind of a Stallone boy toy?"

"No, Cagney."

"Oh, sure, that's from the end of *Angels with Dirty Faces*. I love that movie."

"I didn't know you were into old movies." Mitch's eyes continued to follow Martine, her stroke so effortless and graceful that she barely made a ripple in the water.

"Mitch, there are more layers to me that you can possibly imagine. I'm like a really good lasagne Bolognese—but I'm also old-fashioned."

"How so?"

"I believe that when you go swimming with one girl you shouldn't be staring at another."

"I wasn't staring."

"Were."

Mitch lowered his voice. "What do you think of her?"

"That's a funny thing to ask," Donna responded slowly. "I *should* hate her guts."

Mitch widened his eyes at her. "Really?"

"Oh, totally. There's never been a day in her life when she wasn't pretty, popular, rich, could have any boy she wanted. And look at her now, she's pushing fifty and she's still built like I was when I was *never*. Which is, like, so not fair." Donna paused, letting out a sigh. "But the truth is that she's a real doll, and she's been nothing but nice to me since I moved here. Why are you asking?"

"Just curious."

"And does Trooper Mitry know you're just . . . curious?"

"Not that kind of curious."

"Yeah, right."

Donna headed farther out now, so that the water was up over her head and she had to paddle a little. Back on the veranda, Dodge was busy working the grill. Will was busy staring out at the two of them—so intently that Mitch couldn't help wondering if he was jealous. Jeff was still seated by himself at the umbrella table, shoulders slumped.

"What's up with our Mr. Wachtell tonight?" Donna wondered, squinting back at the shore. "He seems somewhat bummed."

"He's got money worries."

"Hey, who doesn't?"

"Come on, The Works is an incredible success story."

"Incredible," she agreed. "Just as long as you don't look too close."

"What's that supposed to mean?"

"Mitch, let me put it to you this way—what am I doing right now?"

"You're, well, you're at the beach club. You're in the water. You're . . ."

"*Work* with me here, Mitch," she said impatiently.

"Okay, I've got it—you're treading water."

"And what happens if I stop paddling?"

"You sink to the bottom and drown," he replied, nodding. "But how can that be? Your place is mobbed morning, noon and night."

"Overhead," Donna answered simply. "We owe the butcher, the baker, and the candlestick maker. Our payroll is huge. Our debt load is huge. Everything we hold near and dear is tied up in The Works, including the note on our house. Long term, Dodge is convinced we've got a winning idea. He thinks we can even franchise it all around New England—anywhere there's an abandoned mill. But short term, we are just total kitchen slaves. This is the first time I've had fun in I don't know how long."

Martine started back in toward shore now, waving at them as she swam past, her smile dazzling and white.

"I wasn't kidding this afternoon, Mitch," Donna said, coloring slightly.

"About what?"

"Sailing off to Bermuda with you." Her eyes were locked on to his now.

Mitch swallowed. "What about you and Will?"

"Don't look too close at that either."

"You're having problems?"

"I don't know what we're having," she confessed. "Things just haven't been the same since we went into business together. But, hey, enough with the Oprah-babble. I'm trying to seduce you, handsome. Do you want to sail away with me or not?"

"This is the margaritas talking," Mitch said lightly.

"No, it's all me. I'm dead serious."

"I don't have a sailboat, Donna. I don't even know how to sail."

"Do you know how to swim?"

"Why do you—?"

She dunked him hard, pushing him underwater with both hands. He surfaced, sputtering, and paid her back. And the fight was on, the two of them frolicking and shrieking like a pair of twelve-year-olds. When they'd laughed themselves out Mitch noticed that Will was waving at them to come in. Dinner was ready.

As they waded in Dodge got busy lighting a dozen or so citronella candles to ward off the mosquitoes. Donna wrapped a towel around herself and made straight for the grill to see how everything was doing.

Mitch rinsed off under one of the open-air shower heads and padded back to his changing stall, where he stripped off his wet trunks and toweled himself dry, feeling tingly and invigorated. As he dressed he heard someone's footsteps clomp past him on the decking toward a neighboring stall. He heard a stall door slap shut. Then he heard something else.

He heard a man whisper, "Not *here*—someone will catch us!"

And a woman whisper, "I don't give a damn! *He* does what *he* wants. Why can't I?"

Mitch froze, drawing his breath in.

"You're insane!" the man whispered, groaning softly. "We can't just . . ."

"I *want* you," she gasped. "Hurry! Give it to me *now*."

Mitch could not recognize them by their furtive whispers. But there was no mistaking what he heard next—the quick, heavy breathing, the slapping of bare flesh against bare flesh, the steady, rhythmic creaking of the wooden floorboards. The two of them were having it off in there together like a pair of sex-starved high school kids.

And then there was silence.

Mitch immediately tiptoed to the back of his stall and climbed up onto the built-in bench. From this vantage point he'd be able to see over his cropped stall door when they headed back out to the veranda. He was being a snoop and he knew it. But there was no way he was not going to find out who these lovers were.

A few moments later he heard their stall door swing open on rusty hinges. And footsteps, leather sandals clacking against the decking. Martine Crockett walked past, calmly straightening herself. She'd changed into a polo shirt and shorts, and she was striding a bit unsteadily, but she looked as cool, collected, and fresh as she always did.

Mitch waited, breathless with anticipation. After a moment a man emerged, looking flushed and shamefaced.

It wasn't Will Durslag.

It was Jeff. Martine's lover was Jeff Wachtell.

Ab-so-tootly.

The party was still going strong at ten o'clock when Mitch decided to say good night.

A dense fog had settled in, signaling that the rain wasn't far off. His jaw ached and his head was spinning. All he wanted to do was go home, take three Advils, and crawl right under his bed. He could not look at either Jeff or Martine throughout dinner. And yet he was also unable to stop picturing the two of them together, groping each other's naked, tumid flesh in that changing stall. Nor could he turn off the quiz show that was broadcasting nonstop inside of his mind.

Question: Could this GET any weirder?

Answer: Please, God, no.

Mitch felt so whipped by the time he'd steered his way across the fog-shrouded causeway for home that he didn't even bother to turn on the living room lights. Just made straight for the kitchen, where he replenished the cats' kibble bowl, fished an ice pack out of the freezer, and swallowed his Advils, hearing the mournful call of the foghorn on the Old Saybrook Lighthouse across the river. He was halfway up the steep, narrow stairs to his sleeping loft when something undeniable and truly frightening suddenly occurred to him.

He was not alone in his house.

Noises. He distinctly heard noises. The clinking of a glass. A cough.

His heart racing, Mitch flicked on a light and discovered Tito Molina sitting there in his one good chair, drinking up his scotch. Clemmie dozed contentedly in the actor's lap.

"Geez, Tito, scare people much?" he demanded.

"I like sitting in the dark," Tito answered, his blue eyes blazing at Mitch defiantly.

Mitch stood there in guarded silence, wondering what the combustible young star wanted. And whether he should be afraid for his life. Should he try to call Des? Should he arm himself? What with, the fireplace poker? He ended up just standing there, his eyes falling on Clemmie. "She hasn't sat in my lap all summer."

"Animals take to me. I'm one of them." Tito took a gulp of Mitch's scotch, the glass trembling so violently in his hand that it clinked off of his teeth. The man was wrapped beyond tight.

Clemmie awoke with a yawn, jumped out of Tito's lap, and wandered off toward the kitchen. Mitch watched her go, jealous in spite of himself.

"That guitar of yours is a piss," Tito said, his eyes falling on Mitch's Stratocaster. "Play me something."

"Kind of tired right now, Tito. What is it you want?"

"To talk."

"Okay, sure." Mitch sat on the edge of his loveseat, keeping the coffee table between them. He'd made that himself by bolting a discarded wooden storm window onto a leaky old rowboat. He was very proud of his coffee table. "But how did you get here?" he asked, snugging the ice pack against his jaw.

"What, you think because I'm Chicano I don't know how to use a damned phone book?"

"Of course not. I didn't see a car parked at the gate, that's all."

"I swam out. My ride's back at the town beach."

Tito's hair was indeed wet, Mitch now noticed, as were the yellow nylon shorts that he was wearing. The orange-and-blue T-shirt he was wearing was dry. It was one of Mitch's T-shirts. In fact, it was Mitch's treasured and exceedingly threadbare New York Mets 1986 World Series T-shirt. He'd owned that shirt since he was in high school. And Tito had gone and helped himself right to it.

"That wasn't very smart of you," Mitch told him. "People have drowned trying to swim out here—the river currents can be treacherous. That's how the island got its name. Back before they built the causeway they used a little ferry boat, and it capsized and a Peck daughter washed out to sea." Mitch stared at the young actor, wondering what it would be like to be *so* handsome. Everyone in the world wanted to look like Tito Molina—and yet his unparalleled good looks hadn't brought him anything even remotely close to happiness. "It would have been better if you'd buzzed me. I'd have raised the gate for you."

"How could you do that, man? You weren't here."

"I was at the beach club. I thought you'd be there, too. I thought we'd have a chance to talk then."

Tito didn't respond. Just poured himself some more of Mitch's scotch, his hand wavering unsteadily.

Mitch abruptly rose and marched into the kitchen for his emergency stash—the family-sized squeeze bottle of Hershey's chocolate syrup that he kept hidden under the sink behind the laundry detergent and furniture polish, away from Des's disapproving eyes.

"What are you doing in there?" Tito called to him.

Mitch returned with the syrup and sat. "Just getting comfortable," he replied, squirting a generous shot of it onto his tongue.

"You have really disgusting personal habits, man," Tito observed, curling his lip.

"Hey, you pick your remedy, I'll pick mine."

"Fair enough," the actor conceded. "I hear you're hooked up with the trooper lady."

"So what?"

"So nothing. I'm envious, that's all."

"You're married to the sexiest woman in America and you envy me?"

"Totally. Yours is the real deal. The way that she took charge of our situation today. Charged right in, no fear . . ." Tito gazed out the window, his knee jiggling nervously. "That was so cool."

"Esme said you'd be at the beach club tonight."

"She shouldn't have. I told her I wouldn't go." He drank some more scotch, his finely sculpted features tightening. "She's my Miss America, know what I'm saying? All she needs is the damned crown and that . . . what's that thing they wear across their boobies, says where they come from?"

"A sash?"

Tito nodded. "Right. But she doesn't listen to me when I tell her things. I'd never go near a place like that. It's filled with dead men walking. I start hanging at their damned beach club with them then I'm not *me* anymore, know what I'm saying?"

"Yes, I think I do."

"Okay, what did you mean by that?" Tito demanded suddenly.

Mitch shook his head at him, perplexed. The man was an absolute master at keeping people off-balance. "By what?"

"This afternoon, you said I was better than this. What did you mean?"

"It doesn't exactly require a translation."

Tito gazed at him searchingly. "I'm just a poor dumb beaner, jack. I need one, okay?"

Tito Molina sure needed *something*. He seemed to be consumed by inner disquiet. Mitch just didn't know what it was he needed, or why he seemed to feel he needed it from him.

Mitch settled back on the loveseat with his syrup bottle, listening to the foghorn. "I was there on opening night when you were in *Salesman*. I saw it happen, Tito. I saw you blow Malkovich right off of that stage. You're the real deal. You have the talent and looks and pure unadulterated star quality to do whatever you want. They can't stop you. And that's rare. One, maybe two actors in a generation have what you've got. Newman had it. Redford had it. Right now, there's you and there's only you. For me, it's as if you're holding a fortune right in the palm of your hand and instead of investing it wisely you're pissing it away on crap like *Dark Star*, and I wish like hell you wouldn't."

Tito threw down another hit of scotch, shuddering. "Sometimes it's like a trade-off. You've got to do that stuff so they'll let you do what you really want."

"I understand that," Mitch said. "But what is it that you really want to do?"

"Man, I don't know," he replied, staring gloomily down into his glass.

"I don't believe that. You know exactly what you want to do."

Tito peered up at him suspiciously. "Okay, so maybe I do. What I want . . . I want to make a movie about my father. It would be, like, a way to understand where I come from, know what I'm saying? See, he was just this really angry, screwed-up juicehead and he died—"

"In a bar fight, I know."

"I'd play him myself, see. And Esme would play my crazy mother. I've written the script. Most of it, anyway. And I want to direct it myself, too, which means I'd have to raise the money myself, which my agent totally hates. But that's okay, because I don't think I'll be straight with myself until I do this. I *need* to do this." He glanced at Mitch uncertainly. "You're a smart guy. You know about things. Word up, what do you think?"

Mitch stared back at him for a moment. Now he knew why Tito Molina was here, what he wanted. Tito was an actor. He wanted Mitch to direct him. "I think you should do it."

"Really?"

"Absolutely, because you're passionate about it. You should always work on whatever you're most passionate about. Otherwise you're just another meat sack, wasting your time, wasting your life . . ." Mitch applied more syrup to his tongue. "Unless you can't afford to do it, that is."

"Hell yes, I can afford it. They gave me twenty mil for *Dark Star*. That's my going rate now. I'm in the club, man. But, see, my agent wants me and Esme to do this romantic comedy together, *Puppy Love*."

"I'll probably be sorry I asked you this, but what's it about?"

"I play a young veterinarian from the wrong side of the tracks," Tito replied woodenly. "She's a high-class breeder of champion basset hounds. We meet. We fall in love. We fall out of love. We—"

"Say no more. Please." It sounded like a feel-good sapfest, the kind where exhibitors ought to post a sign at the box office reading Diabetics Enter at Own Risk. "Do you like the script?"

"No, I hate it. It's just this bunch of cute, fake moments, strung together like beads. Totally Hollywood, if you know what I mean."

"Oh, I know exactly what you mean."

"But it's a go project. The studio's behind it."

"And Esme?"

"She'll do it if I will. But I don't know, man. I feel like . . ." Tito ran a hand over his face, distraught. "I feel like I don't have any real say in what happens. Like I'm not an actual person, just a character in a movie that somebody else is creating. None of it's real. I'm not real. Esme's not real. Esme and me, Chrissie and me . . ."

"What about Chrissie and you?" Mitch asked, frowning.

"Nothing, man. Forget that. Would you read the pages I've written?" he asked Mitch nervously.

"I'd be honored," replied Mitch, who found himself discovering the same thing about Tito that Dodge had. Mitch liked the guy. He didn't expect to, but he did. There was genuine boyish innocence to him that came through in spite of that twitchy anger. "Mind you, this means I won't be able to review it when it comes out. Hey, wait, is this all just an insidious ploy to disqualify me?"

"No way," Tito insisted. "I'm not that clever, man. I swear it."

"In that case, I'll be happy to read your pages. Drop them by any time."

Tito sat there staring out the window for a long moment. "I don't know, it's all just so . . ." He trailed off. Briefly, he seemed very far away. Then he shook himself and drained his scotch. "I'm in the middle of something bad. Something I got myself into. And I can't get out of it."

Mitch watched the actor curiously. Was he still talking about *Puppy Love* or had he moved on to something else? Mitch couldn't tell. "You can get out of anything if you really want to. You're in charge of your own life, Tito. You have the power."

"What power, man? I don't even know who I am."

"Do you want to know?"

"Yes, absolutely."

"Trust me, that puts you way ahead of most people."

Now Tito jumped to his feet, so suddenly that Mitch found himself flinching. It was an involuntary thing, and if the actor noticed it he didn't let on. "Gotta go. Big thanks, man."

"For what, Tito?"

"The T-shirt," he replied, flashing a smile at him.

"I wouldn't mind getting that back, if you think of it."

"You can have it right now," Tito said easily. "I'm all dried off."

"No, go ahead and wear it home. It's damp out. You might catch cold. Besides, it looks so much better on you."

Tito went to the door and opened it, pausing there in the doorway. "Sorry about this afternoon."

"It's forgotten, as far I'm concerned. Can I give you a lift back to your car?"

"Naw, I'm cool. I'll take that bridge thing back. The walk will do me good. Later, man."

Mitch flicked on the porch light and watched Tito Molina melt soundlessly into the fog just like Sinatra did after he delivered the Arabian pony to the young lord in *The List of Adrian Messenger*, one of Mitch's favorite thrillers in spite of George C. Scott's awful English accent. Quirt was curled up on a tarp under the bay window, his eyes shining at Mitch. Mitch said good night to him, then flicked off the light and went back inside, breathing deeply in and out.

He hadn't realized it, but he had been holding his breath practically the entire time since he'd walked in on Tito.

He crawled right into bed, Clemmie snuggling up against his chest for the first time in weeks. Mitch didn't know if this was her trying to atone for being disloyal to him or whether she just felt cold. And he didn't much care. He was just grateful to have her there. Exhausted, he lay there stroking her tummy and listening to her purr. And now the rain started to patter softly against the skylights over his bed. Mitch lay there with Clemmie, listening to it come down and growing sleepier by the second. Soon, they had both drifted off.

His bedside phone jarred him awake. He didn't know how long he'd been asleep. It didn't seem like very long. He fumbled for it, jostling Clemmie, who sprang from the bed and scampered downstairs. "H-Hello . . . Whassa? . . ."

"I'm sorry if I woke you. I just wanted you to know something."

"Okay . . . Uh, sure." Mitch sat up, recognizing the voice on the other end despite the steady, persistent roar in the background. "Where are you?"

"I'm on Sugar Mountain, with the barkers and the colored balloons."

"Wait, give me a second, I know what that's . . . Neil Young, right?"

"You are."

"What's that whooshing noise? Are you hanging out in a men's room somewhere?"

"Not exactly."

"What time is it anyway?"

"It's too late. The damage is done. The hangman says it's time to let her fly."

"*What* hangman? What the hell are you talking about?"

"Good-bye, Mitch."

"Wait, don't—!"

No use. The line had already gone dead.

Mitch lay there trying to figure out what on earth had just happened. Briefly, he wondered if he'd simply dreamed the whole conversation. He decided there was no sense to be made of it now. He was just too damned tired. So he rolled over and fell immediately back to sleep.

Until another phone call awakened him. This time it was Des. It was dawn now and a steady, driving rain was pounding the skylight over Mitch's head.

"Baby, I'm sorry to wake you—"

"No, no. I'm glad you called," he assured her, yawning. "I didn't feel good about how we left things yesterday. I shouldn't have hung up on you."

"Mitch . . ."

"I was just having a bad day. I understand that you have to obsess. If you don't, you won't get anywhere."

"Mitch . . ."

"So was that our first real fight? Because if it was I don't think it was that bad, do you?"

"Baby, please listen to me. . . ."

Something in her voice stopped him now. "Why, what is it?"

"I'm on my way up to the Devil's Hopyard. The ranger's found a body at the base of the falls. A jumper, apparently."

The hangman says it's time to let her fly.

Mitch's heart began to pound. "God, I should have known. The *falls*, damn it. That's what I was hearing. . . ."

"When?" she demanded. "What do you know about this?"

"It's him, isn't it?" he said, his voice filling with dread. "It's Tito."

She didn't need to answer him. Her silence said it all.

Mitch closed his eyes and let out a groan of sheer agony.

His own worst nightmare had just taken a giant leap into pure horror.

CHAPTER 6

THE ROAD UP TO the Devil's Hopyard State Park was intensely twisty and narrow. Des's cruiser very nearly scraped the mountain laurel and hemlocks that grew on either side of it as she steered her way toward the falls, the wet pavement steaming in front of her as the sunlight broke through the early morning haze. Already, she had her air conditioning cranked up high. The Hopyard was situated in Dorset's remote northeast corner. Very few people lived up here. She spotted a farmhouse every once in a while. Mostly she saw only granite ledge and trees, trees, trees.

The road dead-ended at the entrance to the falls, where a uniformed park ranger was waiting for Des next to a green pickup. Due to funding cuts, many of the state parks made do with summer interns, most of them college students. Kathleen Moloney, the trimly built blond who met Des, was exceedingly young and fresh faced.

Des nosed up alongside of the pickup and got out, her horn-rimmed glasses immediately fogging up in the warm, humid air. Des had to wipe them dry with the clean white handkerchief that she kept in her back pocket.

One other vehicle, a scraped-up black Jeep Wrangler, was parked there in the ditch next to the gate.

"It's just awful," Kathleen said to her over the steady roar of the falls, her voice cracking. "I've *never* seen anything like this. I was making my routine morning swing through the park, you know? I didn't even know what I was looking at when I first saw him. I swear, I just thought it was a bundle of old clothes."

"I'm sorry you had to see it," Des said to her sympathetically. Finding a jumper was definitely pukeworthy.

Des paused to take a closer look at the Jeep. The scrapes were fresh—loose flecks of black paint came right off on her fingers. A mud-splattered cell phone lay on the wet ground a few feet away on the driver's side. Before she did anything else Des bagged it and stashed it in her trunk. Then she opened the Jeep's passenger door and poked around inside. She spotted no suicide note. She did find a car rental agreement stuffed in the glove compartment, made out to Tito Molina. She returned it to the glove compartment and closed the Jeep back up.

"Let's go have us a look, Kathleen, okay? And if you start to feel the least bit funky, just sing out. We don't have any heroes in this unit."

The young ranger smiled at her gratefully and ushered her inside the gate on foot, where there was a parking lot adjoined by picnic grounds. At this spot, they were up above the waterfall. "It's happened before," she told Des as they walked. "A pair of lovers jumped off together back in the '80s. And there was a teenaged boy high on drugs a couple of years ago. I was warned. But I still . . . I wasn't ready for this."

"Trust me, no one is," Des said as they arrived at a guardrail that was posted with a sign: *Let the Water Do the Falling. Stay Behind This Point.*

"I think I know where he jumped from. We can take a look before we go down, if you'd like. Just watch your step."

Des followed her over the guardrail and out onto a bare outcropping of rock, stepping carefully. The granite surface was slick and mossy, and the soles of her brogans were not ideal for rock climbing. An empty pint bottle of peppermint schnapps lay there. She eyeballed it to see if he'd left a suicide note rolled up inside of it. He hadn't. Beyond that, she kept her distance, not wanting to compromise the scene. From where she stood she saw a few spent matches. No muddy shoeprints on the granite. Not that she expected any. The night's rain would have washed them away.

"You can see him from here." said Kathleen, crouching near the edge of the outcropping.

Des inched over beside her and peered over the side of the sheer granite face. Mostly, what she saw was the swirling white foam of the river as it came crashing down onto the smooth, shiny gray a hundred feet below. But then her eyes did make out a small patch of color—a figure in an orange T-shirt and blue jeans that lay there down on those rocks.

"Okay, Kathleen, I've seen enough."

They retraced their footsteps back to the guardrail and made their way down a narrow footpath to the base of the falls. It was a steep and demanding descent. The path was not only mucky from the rain but was crisscrossed with exposed tree roots. Des wished she had on hiking boots like the ranger did.

Tito Molina had landed faceup on the boulders that were next to river, his eyes wide open. His arms and legs seemed grotesquely shrunken inside of the T-shirt and jeans he had on. He looked like a small boy dressed in a man's clothing. His famous, chiseled face had crumpled in upon itself, like a high-rise building after the demolition man has imploded it. Blood and brain matter had oozed out onto the rocks from under his shattered head. The back of his skull seemed to have borne the brunt of the impact, which Des found a bit surprising. So did the direction he was facing—his feet were pointing *toward* the outcropping that he'd leapt from. She stood there looking at him for a long moment, feeling that old, familiar uptick of her pulse. She hadn't felt it for a while. Not handing out traffic tickets to obnoxious tourists.

Briefly, her eyes lingered on the T-shirt Tito was wearing. It was a New York Mets 1986 World Series T-shirt, a shirt that she swore she'd seen Mitch wear. In fact, it was one of his prized possessions. Why on earth would Tito Molina be wearing it?

Now she tilted her head back and gazed up, up toward the top of the cliff, which loomed straight overhead. Rooted there in a fissure in the granite face, perhaps ten feet beneath the rock outcropping where they'd found the schnapps bottle, Des could make out a small, hardy cedar tree clinging for life. Tito's fall had snapped off one of its limbs. The raw wood stood out like exposed bone against the darkness of the stone. She stared at the tree, transfixed, certain that it was trying to whisper something crucial to the suffering artist deep inside of her. But whatever it was she couldn't comprehend it. Didn't speak the right language. Didn't even know any of the words. Didn't know. Didn't know . . .

"I didn't move him or anything," Kathleen said, raising her voice. The roar of the falls was even louder down here. "I couldn't bring myself to get near him."

"You did right, Kathleen."

"I have a tarp in my truck. Should we cover him?"

"We don't want to go anywhere near him," said Des. "That's the medical examiner's deal. What we do need to do is secure this scene. Are the other entrances to the park open yet?"

"No, I always open this gate first."

"Well, that's a help," she said, knowing full well that once word of this got out the paparazzi would be coming over, around, and through any gate they could find. "I need for you to stand guard over the body while I radio in. No one, but no one, comes near it, okay?"

"I guess so," she answered, visibly uncomfortable.

"You don't have to look at him, Kathleen. Just stay here with your back toward him. Anyone gets close, you chase 'em off. I'll be back with the cavalry just as soon as I can. Can you do that for me?"

The young ranger nodded at her gamely.

"You the man, Kathleen."

Des hiked back up to her ride and radioed the Troop F Barracks in Westbrook for as many cruisers as they could spare, then the medical examiner's office for a team of investigators. Based on her own observations, Des also made the decision to reach out to her old unit, the Central District headquarters of the Major Crime Squad in Meriden.

Then it was also up to her to notify the next of kin. As the morning sun broke bright and hot over the trees, she phoned Martine, figuring the news might go down easier if Esme heard it from her mother.

"Martine, we have a situation up here at the Hopyard," she said, keeping her voice calm. "It's Tito. We found him at the base of the falls."

"He's . . . dead?" Martine's voice was a frightened whisper.

"He is. Can you inform Esme?"

"Absolutely. We'll be up there right away."

"I'm not so sure that's a good idea."

"She'll need to see him, Des. She'll insist. I won't be able to stop her."

"I understand. That being the case you might want to bring Chrissie along for the ride."

"Why would we do that?" Martine asked, her voice turning chilly.

"It's going to be a total zoo."

"Yes, you're absolutely right. I wasn't even thinking. I'm just so . . ." Martine sighed mournfully. "Why would Tito *do* such a thing? He was so talented and loved. That poor, beautiful boy."

"Martine, you'd better prepare Esme for something else. . . ."

"What is it, Des?"

"Tito's not beautiful anymore."

The first trooper to arrive on the scene established a perimeter by shutting down the narrow Hopyard Road all the way back at Route 82. More cruisers started arriving soon after that. Des directed them to the other park entrances, and sent a trooper down the path on foot to take over for Kathleen. A medical examiner's van pulled up next and a pair of brisk, efficient investigators in blue jumpsuits hopped out. Des directed them to the body. Then the crime scene technicians started arriving in their cube vans, followed closely by a slicktop with two Major Crime Squad investigators in it.

The investigator behind the wheel was a woman of color. A short, muscle-bound man was riding shotgun. Des knew this man only too well—Rico "Soave" Tedone had been her sergeant back when she was a lieutenant on Major Crimes. Soave was one of the Brass City boys, kid brother of a capo in the state police's so-called Waterbury mafia. When they'd knifed her, it was Soave who'd wielded the blade. At the time, she had hated him for it. Not that he was a bad person, just immature, a work in progress, a *man*. Now that Soave was a lieutenant and Des was Dorset's resident trooper, their relationship had thawed considerably, so much so that when he'd finally gotten around to marrying his high school sweetheart, Tawny, Des had been invited and actually gone to the wedding.

"Yo, Des!" he called to her warmly as he climbed out of the slick-top, flexing his body-builder's muscles inside of his shiny black suit. He always wore black. Thought it made him look classy. In truth, it made him look like a chauffeur.

"How are you, Rico?"

"Never better," he said, grinning at her.

Marriage did seem to agree with him. He looked cheerful and relaxed. Possibly even a bit jowly. And he'd finally shaved off his dead caterpillar of a mustache, Des was happy to note, although he had not lost his nervous habit of smoothing it with his thumb and forefinger. Except now all he was smoothing was bare skin.

"What have you got for us, Des?"

"Got you one dead movie actor."

"He jumped?"

"Very good question, wow man. Happily, I don't have to answer that. You do."

Soave's partner started toward them now, dressed in a sleeveless lime green knit top, tan slacks, and chunky boots that gave her a couple of inches on Soave. She was a good five feet nine and built like a rottweiler with jugs. Huge jugs.

"Now, here's a meeting I've been looking forward to," Soave said eagerly. "Des Mitry, give it up for my new partner, Yolie Snipes."

Des had heard about Yolie Snipes on the grapevine. The boys called her Boom Boom because of what she had going on inside of her shirt. She was half-Cuban, half-black, and all player—young, tough and street smart.

"God, this is just such a thrill for me," Yolie exulted as she pumped Des's hand. She wore her nails short and painted them purple. Her grip was like iron. "Where I come from you are a legend and it is such an honor to even be on the same investigation as you." She talked extremely fast and her voice seemed to come all the way up from her diaphragm. "Word, girl, I have been wanting to meet you *forever.*"

"Glad to know you, Yolie," Des said, a bit blown away by her motor. Yolie Snipes was a girl in a hurry. She had a latina's creamy mocha skin and gleaming brown eyes, but her big lips and wide-bottomed bootay spelled sister all the way. So did the braids. She had a thin one-inch scar across her left cheek that looked as if it had been done by a razor, maybe a box cutter. She wore silver studs in her ears, no makeup or lipstick. She was bigged up—had a weight-lifter's rippling arms. She wore the portrait of a woman's face tattooed on her left biceps with the initials *AC* written underneath it.

"Walk this back for us, Des," Soave said. "You have some concerns about the body?"

"I do, although we all know that this was a man with his share of personal problems. And it certainly plays suicide. Looks as if he drove his Jeep up here late last night, got himself drunk, and threw his bad self off a cliff."

"Damned crazy fool," Soave said disapprovingly. "Here's a young guy pulling down millions, is married to a world-class hottie. Why go and do that?"

"It wasn't making him happy, Rico."

"Did you find a note?"

"No, I didn't. But I did bag his cell." She popped her trunk and handed it over. "He placed a call on it from right here at around one-thirty." They could learn the exact time from his cell phone record. "The words he used sounded an awful lot like good-bye."

Soave glanced at her curiously. "You know who he called?"

"I do. It was Mitch."

"Who, Berger?" Soave had always been bewildered by Mitch's presence in her life. "Are you telling me he and Tito Molina were tight?"

"Not exactly. Tito went after him yesterday."

"Sure, sure, I saw it on the news last night," Yolie spoke up. "Tito whooped this movie critic's ass on account of he gave him a bad review."

"You're not saying that's why he killed himself, are you?" Soave asked. "Because Berger hurt his little feelings?"

"No, I don't believe so," Des replied, wondering if Mitch was thinking this.

"Well, what did he say to Berger?"

"You can get the exact words from him. He's waiting to hear from you."

"Okay, good," Soave said. "What else have we got?"

"Tito's ride." Des pointed out the Jeep's freshly scraped paint job.

"Could be this happened earlier in the day," Yolie suggested, kneeling for a better look. "If they phoned in an accident report then the car rental people will have a record of it. Then again, he might have sideswiped somebody on his way up here last night. I'll see if anyone reported it, maybe canvass those farmhouses down the road. Could be somebody heard him hit a tree or something."

This was a sharp one, Des observed. Her mind broke down all of the angles in a flash. "There's an empty bottle of peppermint schnapps up at the top of the cliff. Also some spent matches. I didn't see anything else."

"Yolie, why don't you go have a look?" Soave said. "I'll check out the body with Des."

"I'm on it." Yolie immediately went charging off.

"It's real slippery up there," Des called after her. "Watch your step."

"I always do," Yolie Snipes responded, smiling at her over her shoulder.

"She's an eager one, isn't she?" Des said as she watched her make her way across the parking lot, big bottom shake-shake-shaking. Des could only imagine what was happening to the girl's front end.

"Twenty-four-seven," Soave agreed, smoothing his former mustache. "You slap her down, she bounces right back up. That's Boom Boom. She makes me feel middle-aged, you want to know the truth."

"Rico, you *are* middle aged," Des informed him as they started their way down the footpath to the base of the falls.

"Between us, the wife can't stand her. Thinks she's a scheming slut bomb. Not true. This is a good kid. Tawny's just jealous, you ask me."

"Does Tawny have any reason to be?"

"Hell no," Soave said indignantly. "I'm a happily married man. Me and Tawny just put in an offer on our first house. Besides, Boom Boom's hooked up with my cousin Richie."

"The one who works Narcotics?"

"The two of them are real tight. You know what they're calling her up at the Headmaster's House?" Soave glanced at her slyly. "The next Des Mitry. How do you like that?"

She didn't. It made her feel like she'd retired to Boca Raton or died.

"I'm telling you, Boom Boom's the complete package," he said, stepping his way carefully over the bare roots in the path. "Plus I never have to worry about her drowning."

Des shot a cold look at him in response.

He immediately reddened. "Sorry, Des, you know how I backslide when I've been away from you."

"I do know that, Rico. But I still keep hoping for a miracle."

Tito was in the middle of his final photo shoot as they scampered down onto the rocks. The assistant ME was photographing the star from every possible angle before they transported his body to Farmington for the autopsy, which was automatic whenever there was an accidental or unexplained death.

"What a stupid waste," Soave said, shaking his head at the dead actor disgustedly. "Okay, what are you selling, Des?"

"I'm not *selling* anything, Rico. I just wanted to point out something about the way he landed."

"What about it?

"The back of his head took the brunt of the impact. That's not consistent with a swan dive. He should have landed facedown, not up."

Soave considered this for a moment, his wheels starting to turn. "So he somersaulted in the air, end over end."

"If that were the case then his head would be where his feet are. He's turned completely the wrong way around, Rico."

"You're right, he is." Soave furrowed his brow thoughtfully. "Maybe the water shifted him around after he landed."

"The man's dry, and there's no blood anywhere else. He's lying right where he hit."

"So he spiraled in the air. That would explain it. The wind can do that."

"There was no wind last night."

"What are you saying, Des?"

"That the position of his body is consistent with someone who was standing with his back to the edge of the cliff and then pitched over backwards. *Or* got pushed."

He peered at her, his eyes narrowing. "Still can't get used to the slow lane, can you? You want back in the game."

"I am totally fine right where I am, Rico. I just thought I'd share my professional concerns with you before you call it. But if you want to blow me off that's totally fine by me."

"Come on, don't get all huffy."

"I do *not* get huffy. I get riled. I get pissed. I get—"

"Whoa, I agree with you, okay?" Soave said, holding his hands up in a gesture of surrender. "It don't read right. That makes it a suspicious death. And that's how we're going to play it." He ordered the crime scene technicians to proceed with maximum care, and to relay that up top to Yolie. Then they started their way back up the path toward the gate. It was becoming very hot out. Soave was perspiring heavily. "Good catch, Des," he said, swiping at his face with a handkerchief. "Thanks for the heads-up."

"You're very welcome," she said crisply.

"You're in a lousy mood this morning, know that?"

"I don't mean to be, Rico. These are my people. I know them."

"There's going to be a major media feeding frenzy, am I right?" he asked, his voice filling with dread.

"There is," she said, thinking that this was a new sign of maturity on his part. Earlier in his career, he'd been supremely hyped at the prospect of getting his face on television. But now that he'd gone before the bright lights a couple of times, he knew just how hot they could get. And had the burn marks to prove it.

"I'm giving them no labels on this one," he said, steeling himself out loud. "I don't say suicide. And I for damned sure don't say murder. Neither of those words comes out of this man's hole. Not once. All I say is it's an unexplained death and that we're still gathering information."

"They'll try to get you to confirm that it's an 'apparent' suicide," Des said. "You say—"

"I say that nothing is 'apparent' at this time."

"Even though they'll go right ahead and call it that anyway."

"Damned straight."

By the time they got back up to the gate the TV news vans were already stacked ten-deep on the shoulder of the road. Cameramen and reporters had swarmed the entrance to the park, shouting questions and demanding answers. The uniformed troopers could barely hold them back.

"How did they get past that roadblock?" Soave wondered.

"They're like mice, Rico. All they need is a quarter-inch crack of daylight and they're in."

Now they heard a car horn blaring. It was Martine's VW Beetle convertible. She was trying desperately to get through the horde, but couldn't. Esme finally leaped out of the car a hundred yards short of the gate and ran barefoot the rest of the way. Chrissie Huberman jumped out in hot pursuit. The press people let out a shout. Their cameras rolled.

"I want to see him!" Esme sobbed as she reached Des, the tears streaming down her porcelain cheeks. "I *have* to!"

"I really wouldn't do that, honey," Des said, as Soave stood there gaping at the beautiful young actress.

"Tito, why did you *do* this?!" she cried out, her stage-trained voice carrying over the roar of the waterfall. "Tito, where are you? *TITO?!* . . ." Esme fell to her knees, sobbing hysterically.

Chrissie knelt beside her, tears streaming down her own face, Des noticed.

And that wasn't all Des noticed. Something new about Esme's look caught her eye: The actress was sporting a great big fat swollen lip this morning.

Somebody had recently punched Esme Crockett in the mouth.

"Girl, I heard *so* much about you when I was coming up," Yolie Snipes gushed from the seat next to her as Des piloted her cruiser back down the narrow Hopyard Road. "First sister to investigate homicides in state history, cover of *Connecticut* magazine when you were twenty-three—I can't believe I'm riding in the same car with you."

"You're being too kind," said Des, who was never comfortable with flattery. "Where'd you grow up, Yolie?"

"The Hollow," she grunted. Frog Hollow was Hartford's most burned-out ghetto. It was nowhere. "My mom died of an overdose a year after I was born."

"And your dad?"

"Never even knew who he was. Everyone I came up with was inmate-bound, me included, but my aunt Celia made sure I got out."

"AC?" asked Des, referring to the portrait on her arm.

Yolie's face lit up. "That's right. She kept me together, body and soul, until I got me my four-year ride to Rutgers."

"You played ball, am I right?"

"It's all that," she acknowledged. "My total dream was to play the point for Coach Geno at Storrs. He scouted me, too, but there was no way I was going to beat out Suzy Bird for playing time. Not in this life. So I moved on down the road to Piscataway, played for Coach Vivian. And we scratched and we clawed and we won us a few. Got my degree in criminal justice. Came back home, took the test, and here I am."

They passed through the roadblock at Route 82, waving to the trooper who was stationed there, and Des started toward the shore now, cruising among the lush green gentlemen's farms with their fieldstone walls and two hundred-year-old houses set way back under canopies of maple trees.

"I never worked a town like this before," Yolie confessed, gazing anxiously out her window at the moneyed countryside.

"You'll do fine. The people here are no different than people anywhere else. They just have longer driveways and better manners."

"Can I ask you for some advice, sister to sister? It's about Soave. . . ."

"What about him?"

"He's a decent man, but my read on him is he won't be moving up. What I mean is, he's got the juice but not the smarts. Am I right about that?"

"He's a good officer," Des said tactfully. "Don't underestimate him."

"I'm not. I'm just, at this point in my career I'm looking to hook up with people who I can learn from. And I'm thinking I've gotten just about all I can out of Soave. I don't mean to sound cold. Just being honest, know what I'm saying?"

"Sure, I do," said Des, thinking that Soave would probably be reporting to Yolie Snipes in a couple of years.

"I might put in for a transfer to Narcotics," she went on. "Or maybe the gangs task force. The street's where I can do the most damage. I *know* the street. That sound like a smart move to you?"

"It does. Just bear in mind that he'll be really insulted. He's thin-skinned."

"Who, Soave? Shut up!"

"And he does have the juice, like you said. Trust me, you do not want that little man for an enemy. Those Waterbury boys are strictly about family and we are *so* not related."

"You saying he'd trash me?"

"I'm saying be careful," Des replied as she cruised into Dorset's business district. Big Brook Road was quiet. The vacationers were still in bed. She turned onto Old Shore at the traffic light and headed for Big Sister.

"This Mitch Berger we're talking to—he's your boy, right?"

"That's right."

"How is that?"

Des glanced at Yolie curiously. "How is what?"

Yolie raised an eyebrow at her. "The pink of things."

"So far so good."

"Myself, I've never road tested a nonbrother."

"I thought you and Soave's cousin Richie . . ."

"No, we're just friends. He'd like to get with me, but I'm not playing that game right now. I'm just so damned tired of getting hurt. Word, are they any nicer?"

Des shrugged. "They're still men."

"Soave had him a major chubby for you, you know."

"He *told* you that?"

"Didn't have to. I can see it in his eyes whenever he talks about you. And he talks about you a lot."

"Well, it never went anywhere, if that's what you were wondering. Strictly his chocolate fantasy—you know how that goes."

Yolie nodded her braided head. "I am, like, uh-hunh. They all want to find out what it's like to get with Sheena, Queen of the Jungle. What do they think, that we hang from the chandelier by our ankles?"

"What, you mean you don't?"

Yolie let out a hoot. "Girl, you've got you a bad self. We're going to be okay."

"Yolie, I never had any doubts."

Des turned off Old Shore at the Peck's Point Nature Preserve. The preserve was open from sunup till sundown. There were footpaths, bike paths, a green meadow that tumbled its way down to the tidal marshes, where the osprey nested. The moisture from the night's rain shimmered on the tall meadow grass in the morning sunlight.

Yolie gazed out the window with her mouth open, overwhelmed by the serene beauty of the place.

Des had grown so accustomed to it that she forgot sometimes just how spectacular it was. She eased her way slowly along the dirt road, passing a couple of joggers who were out with their dogs. The road ended at the barricaded causeway out to Big Sister Island. Des had a key to raise the barricade. Slowly, she eased across the rickety wooden causeway, seeing Big Sister through Yolie's eyes as Yolie took in the lighthouse, the historic mansions, the acres of woods and private beach.

"Shut up, girl! No wonder you dig him—man's got his own private island."

"It's not all his."

"Who *is* this man?"

"He's just someone who happens to know everything there is to know about every single movie that's ever been made in the history of the planet."

"Sounds like a geek."

"That he is—but he's my geek."

Des pulled up in the gravel driveway outside his cottage. Mitch was on his knees in his vegetable patch, weeding with furious intent. Quirt sat right by his side, keenly interested in every clump of fresh soil Mitch was turning over. The lean orange tabby came running to greet Des when he heard her get out. Rubbed up against her ankle, talking up a storm. She bent over and scratched his chin as Mitch got up off his knees, swiping at his sweaty brow, and ambled toward them.

He looked sad and confused and hurt. In fact, he looked exactly the way he had the very first time Des laid eyes on him, the day he'd found that man's body buried in this very vegetable garden. The only thing different about him now was his red, swollen jaw.

"Hey, Master Sergeant," he said to her, his jaw clenched tightly shut. It must have stiffened on him in the night.

"Hey, baby," she said gently, putting her hand on his rather damp shoulder. What she wanted to do was hold him tight, make it all go away. "Say hello to Sergeant Yolie Snipes—she's Rico's new partner."

"We came to ask you some questions about Tito Molina, Mr. Berger," Yolie said to him solicitously. "Are you okay with that?"

Mitch was fine with it. "Let's go inside and get a cold drink. Sorry I sound so funny, Sergeant. I feel just like Al Pacino in the first *Godfather* after he got punched by Sterling Hayden. Remember that scene in Brando's study when Michael tells Sonny *he's* going to be the trigger man in the Italian restaurant? The camera moves in on him slooowly as he sits there, commanding the attention of all of the men in the room, and that's when it dawns on you that *he's* the new godfather. Man, that was great moviemaking."

He shlumped inside the house ahead of them, Yolie pausing to whisper, "Girl, does he talk about movies *all* the time?"

"Only when he's awake."

"You didn't tell me he was so cute. He squeak when you squeeze him?"

Des smiled at her. "That's not all he does."

That morning's New York newspapers were stacked on Mitch's desk, the *Daily News* and *Post* featuring identical page-one photographs of Tito astride Mitch with his hands around his throat. Already it was old news.

"Have you been getting a lot of calls from reporters?" Des asked him.

"I wouldn't know. I unplugged the phone after I spoke to you."

He washed his hands and face in the deep, scarred kitchen sink, then poured each of them a tall glass of iced tea with sprigs of mint from his garden. He handed them around, then flopped down in his one good chair as Des and Yolie took the loveseat. "Whew, it's sticky as hell out there this morning," he said, breathing heavily. "I apologize if I smell like a plow horse, but I'm learning that physical work helps me when I'm down."

"I head straight for the weight room myself," Yolie spoke up, her head swiveling as she took in the view of the Sound from three different directions. She was, Des observed, very uneasy here in Mitch's cottage. Also very anxious to make a good impression on the Deacon's daughter. So anxious she was slouching a tiny bit as she sat there beside Des, just enough so that her immense breasts were less of a temptation for Mitch to stare at. Des knew why—Yolie did not want Des thinking that she'd been waving them in her boyfriend's face. This was an aware, careful girl. A girl who missed nothing.

"Mitch, we need to talk about that phone call you got from Tito," Des said, shifting them into business gear.

"Yeah, okay," he agreed, sipping his iced tea carefully. Some of it dribbled down his chin anyway. "I hadn't been asleep very long. In fact, it seemed as if he'd just left."

"Whoa, he was *here* last night? You didn't tell me that part."

"Yeah, he was sitting right here when I got home from the beach club."

"How did he get out here?"

"He swam out, which should have told me something right away."

"Why is that, Mr. Berger?" Yolie asked, gulping down some iced tea.

"Call me Mitch, would you? You're scaring me with that mister stuff."

She flashed a quick smile at him. "Done, Mitch."

"The tide was coming in," he explained. "It's dangerous. Anyone who tries that can't be thinking straight."

"You couldn't have known what he'd do," Des told him. "Besides, it's too soon to say what did happen. We don't know yet."

"I should have known," he repeated stubbornly.

"Did you give him your Mets T-shirt to wear?"

"He sort of borrowed it. I'm never going to see that shirt again, am I?"

"You wouldn't want it back, believe me."

"Please tell us what happened when he was here," said Yolie, politely taking over the inquiry, pad and pen in hand.

"Nothing," Mitch replied, shrugging. "We talked."

"It was a friendly talk? You were vibing?"

"We totally were," Mitch said, his voice filling with regret. "He told me he wanted to make a movie about his father's life. He said he'd already written most of it. He asked me if I'd mind reading it. I said I'd be happy to."

"What time did he leave here?"

"Eleven or so."

"Was he high?"

"You mean on drugs? I don't think so. He did drink a lot of my scotch, but he was plenty coherent. I offered to give him a ride back to his car. He said he was okay to walk."

"Where was his car?"

"He left it back at the town beach parking lot."

"How long does it take to walk there from here?"

"I've never timed it, Sergeant. A good half hour, maybe forty-five minutes."

Yolie jotted this down in her notepad. "That would put him in the parking lot by around midnight?"

"Yeah, I guess."

"Did he mention Esme to you?" Des interjected.

"He said she was his princess. He said she should be wearing a tiara and sash."

"She showed up just now at the falls wearing a fat lip," Des told him. "Did he say anything about them fighting? That he'd struck her, anything like that?"

"No, not at all. The only negative thing he had to say about Esme was that she sometimes didn't listen to him. But he wanted her to play his mother in the movie he was writing. He wouldn't have mentioned that if they were having serious problems, would he?" Mitch paused, sipping his iced tea distractedly. "Tito also wanted some advice from me."

"What about?" Yolie asked.

"Sergeant, I've been asking myself that very same question ever since Des called," Mitch confessed, running a hand through his curly black hair. "We were talking about his career, okay? There was this movie called *Puppy Love* that his agent wanted him to do, and Tito really didn't want to do it. And then he told me he felt trapped. Being a total idiot who doesn't know how to keep his big mouth shut, I told him that if he was caught up in something he didn't want to be in that he had the power to get out of it."

"Sounds fair to me," Yolie said.

Mitch shook his head at her miserably. "What if he wasn't talking about his career anymore when he said that? What if he was talking about *life?* Think about it, he's sitting here, this unstable, deeply disturbed actor. . . . What if he was trying to tell me that he wanted to end it all? Don't you realize what I did? I gave him the green light. Look at what happened—as soon as left here he drove straight up to the falls and jumped right off a cliff." Mitch slumped in his chair despondently. "God, I may as well have pushed him."

"Don't go there, Mitch," Des ordered him.

"Can you tell us about this phone call you got from him?" Yolie said.

"I was in bed asleep," Mitch said hollowly. "He sounded . . . He was just really down. He said that it was too late. Then he started talking about the hangman. 'The damage is done. The hangman says it's time to let her fly.' That's from a Neil Young song."

"Neil Young." Yolie repeated. "He's that weird old hippie guy, right?"

Mitch stared at her coldly. "He's not weird and he's not old."

"Do yourself a solid, girl," Des advised her. "Stay away from pop culture entirely."

"Mitch, what did you take that to mean?" Yolie pressed on.

"At the time, nothing. But now . . . now I take it to mean that he was about to commit suicide, don't you?" Mitch got up out of his chair and went over toward the windows, standing with his back to them for a long moment. When he turned to face them, his eyes had filled with tears. "I'm the last person on earth who spoke to him," he declared, his voice rising with emotion. "If only I'd said something else, *anything* else. Maybe the right words would have changed his mind. Maybe he'd still be alive."

"I repeat," Des said to him sharply. "Don't go there!"

"Des, I'm already there! And I don't know how to deal with it. How do I live with myself from now on? How do I look at myself in mirror every day? I *killed* him, don't you get it? I killed Tito Molina!"

CHAPTER 7

As soon as Des and that chesty new sergeant of Soave's cleared out Mitch threw his Power Book and some blank notepads into his day pack. Put down a three-day supply of kibble and water for Clemmie and Quirt. Closed up the house, jumped in his truck and fled.

He did not tell Des he was leaving. He only knew he had to get gone.

He made a quick stop at the House of Turkish Delights for baklava and good, strong coffee. One look at Nema Acar's face when he walked in and Mitch could tell she'd heard the news about Tito's death plunge on the radio.

One look at Mitch's face and she could tell he didn't want to talk about it.

"You got your window replaced," he observed, his voice sounding a bit husky.

"We did, yes," Nema said brightly. "And we were visited by the Hate Crimes officers. They said our misfortune does not correspond with anything presently in their database. Mitch, they don't know if they will find these people."

"They *won't* find them," Nuri said insistently as he came out from the back room with a bucket and mop. "I have told you this many times. And did you listen to me? No, you did not."

Nema's mouth tightened, but she said nothing in response.

"I made very clear to them my feelings," he went on, speaking to Mitch now. "They offered to station a cruiser here for one, perhaps two, weeks, as protection. I told them no, thank you. I do not wish to frighten away my customers, do I? This is a business matter, and therefore I shall raise it with the Dorset Merchants Association."

Mitch was definitely experiencing the tension between the Acars that Des had mentioned. And he most definitely did not want to get caught in the middle.

He pocketed his change and got out of there as fast as he could, devouring his baklava as he drove to the Old Saybrook Amtrak station. Here he caught what the locals called the Toonerville Trolley, the poky little Shoreliner train that connected up the beach towns with New Haven, where the Metro-North commuter train into Grand Central could be picked up. It was a two-and-a-half-hour trip altogether.

The morning rush hour had passed so he had a seat to himself. His Power Book could run for up to six hours on its battery. He immediately fired it up, drained his coffee, and got to work.

First, he made notes. Tried to remember every single word Tito Molina had said to him as he sat there in Mitch's chair, drinking his scotch. Every mannerism, every inflection. Tried to summon up the phone call that woke him in the night. Then he moved on to his other recollections, such as how exhilarated he'd felt that night he'd seen Tito on stage in *Death of a Salesman*. He wrote about the high point of Tito's movie career, *Rebel Without a Cause*. He wrote about Tito's unfulfilled dream to film his father's life story. When he changed trains at New Haven Mitch kept right on writing. He had to keep on writing—until he could get to the city and find some real relief for what ailed him. Mitch wrote and he wrote, stitching all of his recollections and impressions together now into a cohesive essay. So totally absorbed in his work was he that he was surprised when he discovered they were already arriving at the station at 125th Street. The trip had flown right by.

When his train pulled into the belly of Grand Central he caught the Times Square Shuttle, rode the Number 1 subway train down to Fourteenth Street, and hoofed it the rest of the way home, slowing his pace to a crawl in the fetid noon heat of New York City in July. The street tar was as soft and gooey as fresh-baked brownies underfoot as he crossed Hudson Street; the heat positively radiating off of the cars idling at the intersection. He paused at the little market on

Hudson Street to buy a fresh pint of chocolate milk, then headed for his place.

Mitch maintained a parlor floor-through in a nineteenth-century brownstone on Gansevoort between Greenwich and Washington Streets in the West Village's old meatpacking district. Once, the apartment had belonged to Maisie and him. It was their place. Right now, the place was dim and stuffy and smelled like either very old cheese or very dirty socks. He cranked up the window air-conditioners front and back, flicked on his coffeemaker, and put on Taj Mahal's "Phantom Blues" good and loud. He sorted through his bills and catalogues distractedly for a few minutes while the coffee brewed and the apartment cooled. Then he poured himself a mug of strong coffee, laced it with two fingers of rich chocolate milk, and plunged back into his essay.

When he had finished polishing it he phoned Lacy.

"Young Mr. Berger," his editor said brightly. "I wondered when I'd hear from you."

"I'm responsible for his death, Lacy."

"What are you talking about? The first set of wire stories are labeling it 'an apparent suicide.'"

"I could have prevented it. I gave him some advice. Bad advice. And now he's dead. He was the best damned actor of his generation and he's dead. He deserves a critical tribute in tomorrow's paper, Lacy. His career was so much more than tabloid tiffs and that stupid *Dark Star.* His real story needs to be told. *I* need to tell it. What do you think, am I being too self-indulgent?"

"What I think, darling boy, is that you're the only arts critic I've ever worked with who actually wonders whether someone would be interested in what he has to say. Don't you realize that there are one million avid readers who can't *wait* to read your final take on Tito? They will gobble up every single word. Go for it, Mitch, do you hear me? Give me something."

"On its way," he announced, e-mailing her the file.

Then Mitch went off in search of his relief.

He found it exactly where he had found it ever since he was a small boy. Most of the favorite childhood haunts were long gone now—the New Yorker, the Regency, the Little Carnegie, the Bleeker Street Cinema. Skyrocketing rents and the advent of video rentals had driven them out of business. Fans could watch the old movies in their own homes now. And that was well and good. But for Mitch, the movie up on the screen was only one aspect of his viewing experience. He loved being inside of the theater itself. The world made sense to Mitch when he was in a movie theater after the lights went down. It wasn't merely his refuge from the painful disorder of the outside world. It was his natural habitat.

In the darkness of a movie theater, Mitch Berger came alive.

A precious few sanctuaries still remained scattered here and there across the five boroughs, if you knew where to go. And on this steamy July afternoon Mitch knew exactly where to go—to a matinee double bill of *The Deadly Mantis* and *Them!* at the Film Forum on Houston Street.

He was practically alone there in the blessed darkness. No one sat within ten rows of him as he sank into a seat, loaded down with sandwiches, pickles, potato salad, cookies, candy, and soda. He unwrapped a sandwich and got busy chomping on it, sore jaw or not, as Craig Stevens got busy examining those very curious tread marks in the snow outside the demolished arctic lookout station. And so, as *The Deadly Mantis* played out on the screen, Mitch found his solace.

Until suddenly someone tall and slim slid into the seat next to him and whispered, "Is that corned beef I smell?"

"No, it's pastrami," he whispered back, stunned. "What are *you* doing here?"

"Looking for you, doughboy," Des replied. "What did you think?"

"But how did you know where to find me?"

"I know you, that's how. Besides, this isn't my first stop. I've already been to the American Museum of the Moving Image out in Astoria—"

"Naw, I wasn't in a Bergman mood. Want a half sandwich?"

"Uh-uh. Then I stopped at the Thalia, where they were running a Laurence Olivier retrospective."

"Yech, he was a poseur. How about a piece of pickle?"

"Damn, there sure are a lot of white men in this city who look like you and go to films by themselves in the middle of the day. And here I'd thought you were unique. What *are* we watching? Look out, that's one gigantic bug!"

"It's a praying mantis," Mitch whispered excitedly, as the two of them sat there with their heads together. "This is actually a classic cautionary tale about the effects of nuclear radiation on nature. They're saying that we shouldn't mess around with powers we don't understand, because really bad things can happen. We have to be humble. Can't think that we know everything."

She glanced at him curiously. "Are we still talking about this movie?"

"Well, yeah," he replied, frowning. "Hey, want a Mallomar?"

She leaned over now and kissed him with an urgency that surprised Mitch. "You scared me, baby."

"I'm sorry, Des. I didn't mean to. I just had to get away."

"I know that," she whispered, squeezing his hand. "My ride's double-parked out front. I need for you to come back out into the world, okay? I have some important things to tell you."

"Are we going to come back in and watch the rest of the movie?"

"No, we're not."

He gathered up his food and followed her up the aisle and out into the hot sun, blinking at the bright light and colors. Horns honked. Tires screeched. People shouted. People rushed. The world was never a more vivid place than it was in that first moment after emerging from a movie theater into daylight.

The interior of her cruiser was already hot and stuffy. Des turned on the engine and cranked up the air conditioning to high. Now that he was able to get a good look at her Mitch realized that the love of his life looked exceedingly frazzled and upset.

It was me. She was worried about me.

"We won't get toxicology results for several days, so we have no idea how stoned Tito was or wasn't," she informed him, sitting there with her hands on the wheel, shoulders squared inside her uniform. "But the medical examiner's autopsy has turned up some indications that are not entirely consistent with suicide as the cause of death."

"*What* indications, Des?" Already, he could feel his heart beginning to race.

She turned her steady, green-eyed gaze on him, and said, "They found moss and lichen under Tito's fingernails, which were severely torn. And the tips of his sandals were scuffed. A crime scene tekkie went back with a long-range lens to check out the side of the cliff, and the moss that's growing six feet or so from the top has definitely been disturbed. All of which indicates that the man was hanging there, scrabbling and kicking, before he went over."

Mitch gulped. "He was murdered, is that it? Somebody pushed him."

"Slow down, cowboy," Des cautioned him. "Nothing is obvious yet. If you want to spin it that he jumped, there's still a perfectly plausible explanation."

"Which is? . . ."

"That the man changed his mind at the very last second. Tried to save him himself, failed, and over he went. Which would also explain the position of his body when he landed."

"Oh."

"Except for one other interesting piece of information our canvassing turned up," Des continued. "A lady who lives in one of those farmhouses on the Devil's Hopyard Road says she heard a car sideswipe the guardrail near her house sometime around one in the morning. It's a harsh, god-awful noise. She knows it well. She claims the car was heading in the direction of the falls. This would correspond with the fresh scrapes we found on Tito's Jeep, okay? Now here comes the interesting part—she couldn't get back to sleep. Was still up at about two-thirty, heating up some milk in her kitchen, when she heard another car speed by. Only this car was heading back down to Dorset from the falls. It's a dead-end road, Mitch. That means somebody else was up there when Tito died."

"His killer," Mitch declared.

"Or a material witness, at the very least. Not that we've found any physical evidence to support it. The rain washed all of the shoe prints away. The only fingerprints on the schnapps bottle were Tito's. The only tire tracks in the ditch belonged to his Jeep. Of course, somebody could have just left their car in the middle of the damned road at that time of night." Des paused now, her face tightening. "There's one other ingredient we have to stir into the mix . . . Esme Crockett's fat lip."

"You think Tito hit her, don't you?"

"Somebody sure did."

"How did she explain it?"

"She hasn't. She's in seclusion. Too distraught to talk, according to her big-time New York doctor. Her big-time New York lawyer says he'll make her available for questioning tomorrow. In the meantime, I need for you to come back to Dorset with me."

"What for, I've already told them everything that I . . ." Mitch trailed off, swallowing. "Wait, they don't think *I* killed him, do they?"

"Rico doesn't know what to think. At this point, he just wants to learn whatever he can."

"Is that new sergeant of his any good?"

"Boom Boom? She's got her some game."

"Why do they call her Boom Boom?"

"You trying to tell me you didn't notice?"

"Seriously, Des, am I a suspect?"

"You're a material witness. The last person who had contact with him."

"Other than his killer, you mean."

"Assuming that's how it plays out," she countered. "Real life, the autopsy report supports either suicide or homicide. Let's say it's suicide. . . . He left no note, which doesn't fit the pattern. But he did call someone—you. He didn't plan it out very carefully, putting his business affairs in order and so forth. Again, that doesn't fit the pattern. But, hey, he was an actor, not a notary public. Okay, now let's turn it around, say somebody killed him. . . . Where's the stanky?"

Mitch frowned at her. "The stanky?"

"I'm thinking of a murder I worked a couple of years back. A housewife up in Newington. It played suicide right on down the line—except we had us a husband who'd removed five thousand from a joint account the day before his wife died. He had a girl-friend. He had three different post office boxes in his own name. He just plain stank of it, understand?"

"Yes, I do."

"You said Tito told you he was into something that he wanted to get out of, right?"

"You are."

"Could he have been talking about something *romantic*?"

Mitch considered this. "He sure could have. Of course, Des! He was meeting someone up there for a tryst. He wanted to break it off, and she didn't, and so she killed him. Wait a minute—he made some vague reference to Chrissie Huberman last night. I jotted it down when I was making notes this morning. I remember him saying, 'None of it's real. I'm not real. Esme's not real. Esme and me, Chrissie and me . . .' And I said, 'What about Chrissie and you?' And he quickly changed the subject. I assumed he was talking about Chrissie's influence on his career. But maybe the two of them were involved. That would certainly explain why Martine hates her so much. Although why on earth he'd get mixed up with Chrissie when he's got Esme Crockett—"

"Don't try to understand other people's love lives. You'll get nowhere."

"Well, if this does turn into a murder investigation I just hope the tabloids don't come after *me*. We did have that brawl at The Works and I could be construed as a—" Mitch broke off, gazing miserably across the seat at her. "They can do that, can't they? They can actually turn me into the prime suspect."

"Baby, they've got a license to do anything they damned please."

"But Tito called me from the falls," Mitch pointed out. "His cell phone record will show exactly what time that was. How could I have killed him if I was talking to him on my phone moments before he died?"

"Okay, there are a couple of holes in that," Des answered. "The time of death is never that precise. Twenty, thirty minutes either way is well within the margin of error. You could have had that phone conversation, then driven up there and pushed him."

Mitch sat there massaging his tender jaw, not liking this. "What's the second hole? You said there were two."

"There's no proof it was *you* who he spoke to. Someone else could have answered your phone while you were on your way up to the falls to kill him. Anyone who was in your house at the time."

"You're right. God, I *am* a suspect, aren't I?"

"Boyfriend, if I didn't love you I'd be taking a cold hard look at you. You have motive, opportunity, and no alibi. Unless, that is, do you have an alibi?"

"What kind?"

"Was someone else with you at the time of his death?" she asked tonelessly.

"How can you ask me something like that? You know I was alone."

"I know only what you tell me."

"Okay, I'm *telling* you I was alone."

"Okay, fine," she said shortly.

Mitch gazed out the window at the sidewalk. Two smartly dressed young professional women walked by together. Both were talking on cell phones, though presumably not to each other. "Des, do I need to hire a lawyer?"

"You're a material witness, not a suspect. But I do have to bring you back, understand?"

"I understand."

"Good, then let's ride. We split now, we can still beat the rush hour traffic." Des put the cruiser in gear and eased it along Houston Street, heading west toward Varick. "Will this get me to the West Side Highway?"

"Can't we go back in the morning?"

"Why would we want to do that?"

"Because we never spend any time here together. I want to eat spinach fettuccine with you at the Port Alba Café."

"Yum, sounds totally off the hook," she responded as they came to a dead stop at Varick. The intersection was gridlocked—trucks, vans, horns. "But now isn't the right time."

"It's never the right time," Mitch grumbled, because there was something else going on here. She considered his apartment Maisie's turf. She would not stay over. She would not keep any clothes there. "I left my computer and stuff at my place."

"So we'll stop on the way," she said easily.

"Des, we should stay over tonight. This is something you need to do."

"We are never going to move," she said distractedly as the signal went from red to green to red, the gridlock failing to budge. "Okay, why do I *need* to do this?"

"Because you're lost, that's why."

She drew back, scowling at him. "Is this about those damned trees?"

"You can't find your way, and it's making you crazy. Making you a big nonfat pain to be around, too, I have to point out. Because I can't lie to you."

"Maybe sometimes you should," she said menacingly.

"If I did then you wouldn't believe me when I said no one else was at my place last night, would you?"

"Well, no."

"And you *are* sure, aren't you?"

"Well, yes."

"Then believe me when I tell you this—you need New York."

Des let out an impatient sigh, drumming the steering wheel with her long, slender fingers. "Mitch, I live in the country. That's where the damned trees are, remember? This is the city, nothing but pavement and broken glass and, God, I hate this traffic."

"That's why you don't appreciate it. You have to put away your car keys. New York is for walking and looking and listening. You're bombarded by more of everything when you're here—more beauty, more ugliness, more excitement, more jeopardy. That makes you more alive. And *that* sharpens your senses. Des, this will work for you. I'm sure of it. Have I ever steered you wrong?"

"Totally. You promised me that *Written on the Wind* was a good movie."

"It's a camp classic. The apex of Douglas Sirk's career. You just have no appreciation for kitsch, that's all."

"I consider this an asset, not a liability."

"Besides, Dorothy Malone won an Oscar for Best Supporting Actress."

"Which one was she?"

"The blond nymphomanic. Interestingly enough, she went on to play Constance Mackenzie in the TV version of *Peyton Place*."

"Wow, what goes around comes around. Your brain is like a continuous loop, you know that?"

They finally cleared the intersection and she went barreling west toward Hudson, honking at a bike messenger who strayed into her path.

"There's something else I should warn you about," he added. "Sex is better in the city."

"If it gets any better I'll have to be sedated," she said, flashing a quick smile at him. "I can tell you're starting to cheer up—you're getting your mojo back."

"I have mojo?" Mitch asked, brightening.

"Oh, most definitely." At Hudson she took a hard right and floored it, heading uptown toward his apartment. "Look, when this Tito business gets cleared up, and I get me a day off, maybe we'll give it a try. *If* we can go dancing, that is."

"Dancing?" he repeated, frowning at her. "In public?"

"I'm saying it."

"No, no. I don't do that."

"What do you mean, you don't do that?"

"Have you ever seen me engaged in the physical act of dancing?"

"Now that you mention it, no."

"It's not a pretty sight, Des. I have a spongy bottom, poor flexibility, no actual moves to speak of. Trust me, you don't ever want to see me dance."

"Got to dance, doughboy."

"What, this is a package deal?" he demanded, wondering just exactly how this whole situation had gone so horribly wrong so fast.

"Package deal."

"You don't play fair."

"I don't have to, I'm a girl. And you're my boy. And I want to see you out on that dance floor, shaking what your mama gave you."

"Fine, if that's what it takes to get you here, I'll do it. Because nothing, but nothing, is more important to me than your art. Not even my own personal dignity." Mitch paused, squaring his jaw at her grimly. "I just hope that you realize the sheer, unmitigated horror of what you're letting yourself in for."

CHAPTER 8

ETHEL MERMAN VERY NEARLY bounced Des right out of her bed.

This was all about Bella and her digitally damned remastered cast album of *Annie Get Your Gun*. As far as Des was concerned, waking up to Ethel Merman singing "I Got the Sun in the Morning" was like coming to at the epicenter of an earthquake that registered 5.1 on the Richter scale.

Groaning, Des put on her horn-rims and staggered downstairs barefoot in a tank top and gym shorts. She felt groggy and stiff all over after spending most of yesterday driving to and from New York. Her eyes were bleary and puffy.

The coffee was brewing in the kitchen, where Ethel was even louder. That damned woman's vibrato could shatter a plate glass window as far away as Delaware. Bella, who had to be clinically deaf, was parked at the dining table, eating her All-Bran and leafing through that morning's New York papers.

Their in-house cats all came scampering, hoping to convince Des that Bella had failed to give them a morning treat. Des knelt to pet them before she called out, "Morning, Bella!"

"Good morning, Desiree," Bella yelled back to her.

"Um, haven't you got your Ethel cranked kind of high for a woman whose roommate packs a loaded semiautomatic weapon?"

"My bad." Bella immediately went charging into the living room to turn it down. "That's what my grandson, Abie, always says. 'My bad, Grandma. My bad.' The boy starts Harvard next month and he talks like a three-year-old. Would you rather listen to someone else?"

"I think I'd like to ease into today with a little silence, if you don't mind."

"Not at all." Bella shut off the stereo and sat back down. "Very nice piece about Tito Molina by your handsome Mr. Berger in today's paper," she said, stabbing at it with her stubby finger. "It has a lot of heart."

"Mitch felt real bad about what happened, plus he was a genuine fan of the man's work." Des poured herself some coffee and took a sip, scanning it over Bella's shoulder. "What do they have on the investigation?"

"That Lieutenant Tedone isn't ruling out homicide. Neither is the medical examiner." Bella licked her thumb and flipped her way back to the front page. "Here it is. . . . 'The medical examiner is characterizing the circumstances of Mr. Molina's death as questionable.' Is that true?"

"Reasonably," Des responded, yawning. "What do the tabloids have?"

Bella's face dropped. "You don't want to know."

Des immediately spread the *Daily News* and *Post* out on the table for a good look. Both featured page-one photos of a hysterical Esme Crockett arriving at the gate to Chapman Falls with her fat, bloodied lip. The *News* was awash with speculation about the lip. Sex was the culprit. They even quoted an unnamed source close to the golden couple as saying, "They liked it rough." Des wondered just exactly who this source was. The *Post,* meanwhile, was already trying to link Mitch to Tito's death: "Although Mitchell Berger is not considered a suspect at this time, an unnamed source added, 'Obviously, the authorities want to learn everything they can from him.'" Which definitely made it sound as if they thought he was hiding something. Who *was* this unnamed source?

And how can I get my hands around his or her throat?

"Nu, what happens now?" Bella asked eagerly.

"Another day in paradise," Des replied, burying the tabloids under Mitch's paper so she wouldn't have to look at them. The cats roughed up her area rugs in much the same way after one of them had puked on the floor. "Thought I'd start out with another tour of Jellystone with Yogi and Boo-Boo."

"Okay, I'm nodding but I don't actually understand what you're saying."

"Then I'll put on my uni and saddle up. Got me some parking tickets to write."

"Desiree, what do *you* think happened to Tito?"

It was a hazy, humid morning, the sky the color of dishwater. Des went over to her windows overlooking the lake and slowly stretched out her hammies, feeling the tightness in her legs as she bent down to touch her toes. "What I think," she said, "is that it's not my job to think about those things anymore."

"But you must have an opinion. You can't just turn it on and off like a faucet."

"Can, too."

The doorbell rang now. Des padded to the door and opened it.

It was the Crockett girls.

Esme with her wild, uncombed mane of blond hair and her raw, bruised lower lip. The actress wore a pair of military fatigue pants, a tube top, and a somewhat dazed expression on her lovely young face.

Martine held her firmly by one arm, a brave, determined smile creasing her own face. "Go ahead and tell her, sweetie. Tell Des what you've decided."

"The kittens," Esme announced to Des in a trembly voice. "I want to see the kittens. Can I?"

"You totally can," Des assured her. "I never turn away a prospect. We were just having some coffee. Can I pour you ladies some?"

"We're all set, thanks," Martine said, the thin soles of her chic patent leather sandals clacking smartly on the polished wood floors as she strode in. "Good morning, Bella!"

She and Bella launched into cheery chitchat as Esme fell to her knees and started playing with Missy Elliot, Christie Love, and the rest of the in-house crew.

"Hi, there," she cooed, stretching out on the floor with them. "Hi, girls."

"Some of them are boys," Des pointed out. "That big orange stud standing directly on your hooters is Kid Rock."

"Figures." Esme giggled, stroking him gently.

Martine looked around at the house admiringly. "You've done wonders with this place, Des. It's absolutely darling."

"I like the light," said Des, who had never before in her life known someone who used the word "darling" to describe, well, anything.

"Your boyfriend's article was real nice," Esme said to Des. "But he was wrong about Tito's script, you know."

"How so?"

"There are no pages. They don't exist. Never have. The project was all just a fantasy. A lovely, lovely fantasy."

"Des, may I be frank?" Martine cut in briskly. "Esme felt, we both felt, that it would be a good idea to make her available to you right away this morning. She wants to help the authorities any way she can. And there are some . . . things she'd like to get off of her chest."

"Would this have anything to do with your lip, Esme?"

"It would," Martine answered for her.

Esme was back into playing with the cats.

"I appreciate you coming forward." Des said, starting toward the kitchen phone. "I'll reach out to Lieutenant Tedone and we'll get the ball rolling."

"No ball," Esme said abruptly. "No lieutenant."

Des stopped in her tracks. "You just said what?"

"I want to talk to *you,* Des. I like you."

Des smiled at her. "I like you, too, Esme, but I'm not involved in this investigation. I'm just the resident trooper."

"Mommy, I don't like this now," Esme said, slowly shaking her head from side to side.

"Just take it easy, sweetie. We'll figure something out." To Des, Martine said, "You could be present at the questioning, couldn't you?"

"Could you?" Esme asked her pleadingly.

"I can *request* to be present, if you'd like," Des responded carefully. "But that's strictly the lieutenant's call. Before we go any further, does your lawyer know you're here?"

"She's fired him," Martine answered.

"I *hate* lawyers," Esme lashed out suddenly. "They get paid to lie."

"You don't have to tell Des that," Bella pointed out. "She was married to one."

"What about Chrissie?" Des wondered. "Where is she this morning?"

"Chrissie worked for Tito, not Esme," Martine said frostily. "She's been sent packing as well."

"She's left town?"

"We should be so lucky. She refuses to go, Tito's death being such a huge story and all. But she no longer represents Esme's interests and she's no longer living with her."

"Mommy's moved in with me," Esme said.

"I thought she could use the company. It means poor Dodge has to hold down the fort alone at our place, but he can manage for a few days."

"Des, can't I just talk to *you*?" Esme pleaded once again.

"Yes, can't we do that?" echoed Martine, who seemed real anxious to avoid the standard Major Crime Squad channels herself.

Des wondered why. Was she just being protective of her daughter or was there more going on here? Mitch had told Des all about Martine and Jeff—not that Des had for one second been able to get her mind around it. Had Martine also been sleeping with her own son-in-law? Was *she* the other woman who Tito was meeting up at the falls? Was such a thing possible?

This was Dorset. Of course it was.

"I have to shower and throw on some clothes," Des said. "Bella will take you down to the garage and introduce you to the kittens."

"The kittens!" Esme clapped her hands together like a little child. "I want to see the kittens!"

"Take your time. Get to know them. Then we'll figure something out, okay?"

Bella led the Crockett girls downstairs. As soon as they were out of the room Des phoned Soave and told him to get his ass over there. Then she jumped in the shower.

She was buttoning her uniform when the doorbell rang. She raced to the door and answered it. Bella and the girls were still down in the basement.

"Thanks large for the heads-up, Des," Soave said as he came through the door with his chest puffed out, bulked-up muscles flexing inside his shiny black suit.

"No problem, Rico. I'm just glad you were nearby." They'd set up a temporary command station over at town hall.

Yolie came in a bit more slowly, her brown eyes flicking around at the contents of Des's house with intense curiosity. Today she was wearing a loose-fitting dark blue top made of a synthetic silk that didn't cling so conspicuously to her front end. A conscious choice, Des figured.

"Girl, you *live* here?" Yolie marveled, her voice hushed. "This is sweet! And look at that deck. You can sunbathe *buck* out there if you want to. Mind if I ask, what's the rent on a place like this?"

"I own it."

"Shut up!"

"Rico, is it okay with you if I sit in? Esme might feel more comfortable."

"Cool with me," he said, smoothing his former mustache. "Is there a lawyer?"

"She canned him."

"Even more cool."

"You folks want some coffee?"

"That'd be great, Des," Soave said.

The two of them went out on the deck while Des poured it. The Crockett girls came back upstairs now, minus Bella.

"Bella said to tell you she's taking her 'shtarker' walk," Martine informed her. "Whatever that means."

"Once around the lake," Des translated. "It's three-point-six miles, the last mile uphill."

"So many sweet kittens," Esme said dreamily. "I just love the Pointer Sisters, especially the one with the white paws."

"That's Bonnie. They're a sister act—you want one you have to take all three."

"Can I, Mommy?"

Martine was gazing out at the deck. "That's the officer who was at the falls yesterday," she observed. "And that woman with the braids was there, too."

"What do *they* want?" Esme demanded.

"To talk," Des said gently. "It's going to be fine. I'll be with you."

At the sound of their voices Soave and Yolie came back inside. Soave approached Esme slowly and with tremendous care, as if she were made of fine crystal and were liable to shatter if he squeezed her too hard. "I am incredibly grateful that you could give us some time this morning, Miss Crockett. Anything you can tell us about your late husband will be a tremendous help."

"Where's Tito?" Esme demanded.

"Tito?" Soave was instantly thrown. "The body's . . . He's in Farmington, with the medical examiner."

"When can I bring him home?"

"Soon. A few days."

"Please answer me this, Lieutenant," Martine said. "Is my daughter a suspect?"

"At this point no one is a suspect. We're still trying to determine what happened."

"You're saying you don't know?"

"That's exactly what I'm saying."

"Well, what makes you think Esme knows anything?" she demanded.

"Martine, this is strictly an informational interview," Des said.

"That's right," Soave agreed. "Informational."

"Well, okay, then," said Martine, apparently satisfied.

They sat around Des's dining table. Major Crimes didn't usually tape record informational interviews, although a signed, written statement might be asked for later. For now, Yolie produced a notepad and pen, and parked her rippling bare arms before her on the table as if she were getting ready to arm wrestle somebody.

From across the table, Esme watched her every move warily. The actress sat next to her mother, gripping her hand tightly.

Des had her own eyes on Soave, who took a sip of his coffee and then sat back with his hands clasped behind his head, which told her that Yolie was his inquisitor. Des sat back in her own chair, curious to see Boom Boom's moves.

"How are you feeling today, Esme?" Yolie asked, raising her chin at her assertively. She was nervous around these women. Des could tell.

"Okay, I guess."

"I understand you've been under a doctor's care since Tito's death. Are you presently under the influence of any medication?"

Esme shot a sidelong glance at her mother, then raised her own chin at Yolie. "Why?"

"Just answer the question, please," Yolie said brusquely.

"No, this is the real me," Esme responded, smiling faintly. "You know, I just love your scar."

"You love my *what*?" Yolie said, fingering her cheek self-consciously.

"It makes you look so gangsta."

Now it was Yolie who was thrown. "Um, let's try to stay on subject, okay? Esme, when did you get that lip injury?"

Esme lowered her eyes, coloring slightly. "The other night."

"The night Tito died?"

"Yes."

"Want to tell us how it happened?"

"Well, Tito had been out all evening. He was pissed at me, because I wanted him to go to the beach club with me and he wouldn't."

"Where did he spend his evening?"

"I don't know," Esme replied, twirling her blond hair around her finger.

"You have no idea where your husband was all evening?"

"That's what I just said."

Yolie narrowed her eyes at her across the table. "Was that typical?"

"I guess."

"Well, where did *you* go?" she asked, growing a bit frustrated by Esme's vagueness.

"Nowhere. I stayed home. They were running an *I Dream of Jeannie* marathon on TV Land. Do you like that show? It's the one with the astronaut. I am so into it."

"Were you with her, Mrs. Crockett?" Yolie asked Martine.

Martine shook her head in response.

"Was there anyone else in the house? A maid? Cook?"

"We don't like to live like that," Esme said, making it sound as if Tito were still around, still choosing how to live. "We have some daytime help is all."

"A local widow does the shopping and cleaning," Martine explained. "The realtor set it up."

"Gotcha," said Yolie, jotting down the information in her notepad. "So no one else was around?"

"Well, there was Chrissie," Esme offered.

"Your publicist?"

"*Former* publicist," Martine said.

"She was out in the guesthouse," Esme revealed. "It's over the garage. It has a separate entrance and everything."

"Could she hear what went on in the main house?"

"I really don't know. You'd have to ask her."

"Okay, we will. How would you describe your husband's mood that evening?"

"He was pissed at me. I just told you."

"I'm speaking more generally now. Was he morose or depressed?"

Esme stared at her in astonishment. "He was Tito."

Yolie stared right back at her. "Meaning what?"

"Meaning he told me all the time that James Dean had the right idea—live fast, die young, and leave a good-looking corpse. He *always* talked about doing himself in."

"Did you think he meant it—or was he just styling?"

"Tito was never about styling," Esme shot back defensively.

"What time did he come home that night?"

"Around midnight, I think."

"What happened then?"

"He went straight to our bedroom and put on a pair of jeans instead of the swimming trunks he was wearing. Then he started rummaging around in his closet."

"He was searching for something?"

"Maybe. I guess so."

"Any idea what?"

"No, I have no idea."

"Esme, did he keep a gun in the house?"

"No way. Tito hated guns."

"Okay, what happened next?"

"He said he was going right back out again."

"And what did you say to him in response?"

"That he should stay home with me. I got kind of pissed, and that's when . . ." Esme trailed off, her bruised lower lip quivering.

"That's when he hit you?" Yolie pressed her.

"Yes."

"Did he strike you with his fist or his open hand?"

"With his fist."

"He punched you, in other words."

Esme nodded, Martine stiffening noticeably.

"Did he knock you down?"

"Yes."

"Did you suffer any other injuries as a result?"

"Not really."

"Were you angry?"

"I guess."

"You *guess* you were angry that your husband punched you in the damned mouth? Come on, girl, stop fronting me."

"*Yes*, I was angry."

"And what did you do about it?"

"Nothing! He stormed out the door and I never saw him again— not alive, anyway."

"You've got some bruises and scratches on your arms," Yolie observed. "What's up with those?"

"They're from before," Esme responded, glancing down at them. "He and I . . . we fought a few days ago."

"So he had a habit of knocking you around, is that it?"

"I-I wouldn't call it a habit."

"What *would* you call it?"

"We *fought*, okay? That's what two people do when they love each other. They fight. They care. That's what it means to be in love." Tears began to spill out of Esme's big blue eyes. "I guess you wouldn't know anything about love, or you wouldn't ask me anything so lame and insensitive and stupid!"

Des got up and fetched her a tissue. "If I might just ask one quick question . . ." she interjected, hoping to cool things off.

"Go ahead, Des," Soave said, nodding his head approvingly.

Yolie just stared across the table at her with her mouth open, clearly taken aback by the interruption.

Des sat back down, flashing a warm smile at Esme. "The other day, you told me that those bruises happened during rough sex," she reminded her in a slow, soft voice.

Esme dabbed at her eyes, sniffling. "I know I did."

"So you were lying to me?"

"I was. I'm sorry, Des."

"And that story about your lip in this morning's *Daily News*?"

"Also a lie. I don't even know how it got there, but it's a lie."

"Why did you lie to me about it, Esme? Was it to protect Tito?"

"Yes," she admitted. "I didn't want you thinking just what *she's* thinking." Meaning Yolie. "That he was a bad person. He wasn't bad. He was just messed up."

"Were you ever afraid of him?"

"No."

"Did he ever threaten to harm you?"

"Never."

"Okay, good. I just wanted to clear that up," Des said. "We all know how hard this is for you, Esme, and we appreciate it. You're doing great."

"Really great, sweetie," Martine agreed, squeezing Esme's hand.

"Sorry for the interruption," Des said to Yolie. "She's all yours."

"You two were having marital problems?" Yolie asked, her tone a bit less prosecutorial now.

"Yes, we were," Esme said bleakly.

"Straight up, was Tito seeing someone else?"

Esme's mouth tightened. "Yes, he was."

"For how long?"

"I don't know. I think it started after we came here."

"I see," Yolie said, clicking her pen between her teeth thoughtfully. "Do you know who the woman is, Esme?"

"No, but . . ." Esme trailed off, twirling her hair around her finger again.

"But what?"

"Tito was never faithful to me. Not ever. That's just the way he was."

"And did this bother you?"

Esme shrugged, saying nothing in response.

"What happened after he punched you in the mouth?"

"I told you that already," she replied coldly. "He left."

"This was about twelve-thirty?"

"Something like that, yeah."

"Did he take anything with him?"

"A bottle of peppermint schnapps."

"And what did you do after he left?"

Esme glanced over at her mother, reddening, then looked back at Yolie and shrugged once again, saying nothing.

Soave tilted his head at the actress curiously.

So did Yolie, who leaned forward a bit, her breasts jutting out over the table. "Esme, we believe that Tito died sometime between one-thirty and two. Were you at home at the time of his death?"

"Not really," she answered in a quavering voice.

Now Martine was looking at her curiously, too.

"Esme, where were you?" Yolie persisted.

"Out," she whispered.

"Out where?"

Esme sat there in pouty silence for a long moment before she turned to Des and said, "Do I have to answer that?"

"I would if I were you," Des advised. "They're going to find out eventually. Better all the way around if they hear it from you."

"Well, okay," Esme said reluctantly. "I was with a man."

Martine glared at her with withering disapproval. "You've been seeing someone yourself?"

"Yes, Mommy," she admitted guiltily. "After Tito split, I went to his place."

"And you stayed there with him how long?" Yolie asked.

"Until maybe four in the morning."

"What did you do then?"

"I went home."

"What did you think when you got home and Tito wasn't there?"

"I didn't think anything. I took a shower and went to bed."

"You weren't worried about where he was?"

"No."

"Who is this man, Esme?"

Again the actress turned to Des. "Do I have to say?"

"It's kind of necessary, Esme. Tito's death is still unexplained, and this man is in a position to vouch for you."

"Well, if you say so . . ." Now Esme's face broke into a naughty little smile. "It's Jeffrey Wachtell."

The composed beauty of Martine's face instantly turned harsh and ugly. "Why, you little *whore*!" she cried out, smacking her daughter hard in the face.

Des grabbed Martine roughly by the wrists and yanked her to her feet. "Okay, we're not having any of that in my house!"

"Yo, what the hell *is* this?" Soave wondered, baffled.

Esme scarcely reacted at all. Just sat there, unfazed, as her split lip started to ooze fresh blood. Clearly, this was someone who was used to getting hit. Des had encountered her share of female punching bags before, but they were never rich, pretty, and white. In this regard, Esme was a first for her.

"Why did you come back?!" Martine screamed at her daughter, struggling in Des's grasp. She was a handful, amazingly strong. "You could have gone anywhere in the world—why did you have to come *here*?!"

"Yolie, want to get her an ice cube and a towel?" Des said as she muscled Martine toward the French doors.

"Got it," Yolie said, springing into action.

"You did it on purpose, didn't you?! You *wanted* to hurt me!"

"What if I did?" Esme shot back, sneering at her.

"You are *sick*!"

"Well, you ought to know!"

"Okay, let's take it outside," ordered Des, hustling Martine out onto the deck.

Soave followed them out there. "So, what, they're *both* boinking this guy Jeff?" he asked, stroking his former mustache.

"So it would seem," Des replied, as Martine began to pace back and forth across the deck, hugging herself, utterly distraught.

"Who is this guy, the stud of the century?"

"Rico, I truly don't know how to respond to that."

He went back inside now, shaking his head. Des stayed with Martine. It felt warm and muggy out there after the coolness of the house.

"How could she do this to me, Des?" Martine sobbed as she continued to pace. "My own daughter—how could she?"

"When you told me about Dodge you didn't tell me that you were seeing someone else, too."

Martine stopped in her tracks. "You sound disappointed."

Des said nothing to that, just gazed at her.

"Our marriage is not exactly healthy these days," Martine confessed. "Dodge goes his way and I go my mine. Jeffrey is ... not exactly Brad Pitt, I'll grant you. But he's funny and he's sweet and he's the most attentive lover I've ever been with. He bathes me. He reads Emily Dickinson to me by candlelight. He licks whipped cream from between my—"

"Really don't need to hear this part," Des growled.

"Do you have any idea what that's like after twenty-six years of Dodge?" Martine demanded. "Twenty-six years of wham-bam-good-night-ma'am? Jeffrey makes me feel like *me* again. And that sick little bastard has been having it off with my own damned daughter this whole time. I will hurt him for this. I will make a bow tie of his balls and—"

"Martine, I wouldn't say things like that in front of me."

"You're absolutely right," she said hurriedly. "I didn't mean to make threatening remarks. I'm just so *hurt*. I know exactly why she did it, too. To get back at me."

"For what?"

Martine's face darkened, but she didn't answer. Just went over to the railing and faced the lake, her back to Des, posture rigid.

Des studied her there for a long moment. "Martine, were you and Dodge home in bed together when Tito died?"

"I do believe I can see Bella from here," she said, shading her eyes with her hand. "That fierce little bowling ball of a person striding along the footpath at the edge of the water. See her?"

"If Esme was with Jeff when it happened . . ."

"It means that I wasn't," Martine acknowledged. "I was home."

"Was Dodge home with you?"

"It's very pleasant out here, isn't it?" Martine said evasively. "Still, I would have thought there'd be a bit more breeze coming off of the water."

Yolie came out there now to tell them she was done with Esme. Martine asked if she could take her daughter home. Yolie said she could, but only after the lady solemnly promised to behave herself.

Yolie remained with Des after Martine had gone inside. "Girl, is *this* your idea of better manners? Because I can get this for free back in the projects morning, noon, or night."

"I was as surprised as you were."

"Word, did I just choke in there?" she asked, glancing at Des uncertainly.

"No, not at all. It's all okay."

"But you took the ball out of my hands. How come?"

Des kept quiet. It wasn't her place to criticize Sgt. Yolie Snipes.

But Yolie wasn't having that. "Please tell me," she pleaded. "I'm not on my home court here. And I get, like, *no* help from Soave when it comes to how to behave."

"Well, okay," Des said. "You were moving in for the kill, which is fine. But you didn't see that she was on the verge of wigging, which isn't fine. That's a delicate young performer in there. She just lost her husband. If you'd kept at her one minute longer, she would have shut down on you completely."

"Kinder and gentler is not my style."

"I'm not saying it should be. Do what works for you. Keep the funk alive. Just keep an eye on your subject's temperature gauge, too. Know when to back off."

"Yeah, I can be a raw dog sometimes," Yolie admitted, nodding her head. "Especially when I'm uptight. I mean, she's so famous and all. Only, why did she say that to me about my cheek?"

"She's an actress. Everything in her world is make-believe. Pay no attention. You're doing fine."

"Real?"

"Real."

"Big thanks," Yolie said gratefully. "Ready to go?"

"Go where?" asked Des, frowning.

"Interviews. Soave wants you along, since you know the people."

"Okay, sure." Des started back inside, then stopped. "Oh, hey, you didn't give up anything to the tabloids yesterday about Mitch, did you?"

"Who, me?" Yolie let out a huge laugh. "Not even. Soave won't let me anywhere near the press. 'One voice, one message,' he always says. Between us, I think Tawny's on the receiving end of a big happy whenever that little man sees himself on television. Why are you asking?"

"Just curious," Des said, smiling at her. "Come on, girl. Let's do Dorset."

CHAPTER 9

IT WAS SUCH A sultry, sticky morning that there wasn't even a breath of breeze out on Big Sister. Mitch could barely make out the Old Saybrook Lighthouse through the haze as he stood at his windows, drinking his morning coffee and listening to the shrill whine of the cicadas in the trees. The Plum Island workboat was chugging its way out, the Sound as calm as a bathtub. But no summer yachtsmen were setting out for a day's sail. There was no point in leaving the boatyard when the weather was like this.

He hadn't slept well. For one thing, Clemmie was way unhappy about him traipsing off to New York that way. She made her displeasure known by bounding across his bed like a playful faun every half hour all night long. In Clemmie World, this was known as payback.

Not that Mitch would have been able to sleep anyway. Not after he'd made the mistake of checking the Web sites of the New York tabloids to see what they'd be featuring about Tito's death in their morning editions.

Garbage, that's what.

Snide quotes from unnamed sources implicating him in Tito Molina's death. Dirty hints that he knew more than he'd let on, possibly even had something to do with it. . . . *Obviously, the authorities want to learn everything they can from him.* . . . Why on earth did someone, anyone, think he was holding out? Mitch didn't have the slightest idea. But he did find it deeply, deeply disturbing. Despite his own best efforts, he was being turned into a featured player in this ongoing media sideshow. . . . *And costarring chubby, good-natured Mitch Berger as the thinking man's Kato Kaelin* . . . And now he had no control over what was happening to him. Zero. None.

And so he'd tossed and he'd turned all night long as the ceiling fan stirred the warm, steamy air around his sleeping loft and Clemmie periodically leaped across his stomach, yowling. And he was up well before dawn, getting shaved and dressed. Naturally, as soon as he started stirring Clemmie curled up in his chair and went fast to sleep, one paw over her eyes to block out the rising sun.

Mitch didn't log on to his computer. He didn't want to read any more stories connecting him to Tito's death. He didn't even want to look at his own story about Tito in this morning's paper.

What he wanted was to get his life back.

He was looking forward to his daily hike with the Mesmers. He could use a good honest dose of Dodge Crockett's upbeat reassurance, Will Durslag's croissants and quiet strength, even Jeff Wachtell and his kvetching.

But there was no Dodge waiting there in the haze when he trudged his way across the causeway with his birdwatcher's glasses— just big Will and little Jeff.

"Hey, man, we missed you yesterday," Jeff called to him cheerfully.

"I had to wait around for the police."

"Do they seriously consider you a suspect?"

"I seriously don't know. But I didn't push Tito off any cliff."

"We all know that," Will assured him, standing there with his knapsack filled with fresh-baked goodies. "Real nice article you wrote about him, Mitch."

"Thanks, Will," Mitch said, peering down the misty path in search of Dodge. "Don't tell me our captain's actually late."

"Maybe Dodger ought to buy himself a wristwatch," Jeff cracked.

"Sure, let's chip in and get him one," Mitch joined in, still trying to fathom the concept of the little guy and Martine naked together. He couldn't imagine what went through Jeff's mind every morning as he walked along next to Dodge, stride for stride, knowing that he was shtupping the man's tall, blond beauty of a wife behind his back. How did he feel—gleeful, superior, guilty, all of these things?

"Dodge is *never* late," Will said, frowning. "I don't know where he is."

"He must be tied up with Esme this morning," Mitch said. "Don't you think?"

"No, I don't," Will said. "When I talked to him on the phone last night he said Martine was going to stay with her for a few days, and that he'd see us out here in the morning."

"So something came up," Jeff said. "Come on, men, let's march. I've got a full morning of unpacking ahead of me."

Will didn't budge. "If something came up he would have called me," he said stubbornly. Will always carried a cell phone on their walks in case Donna needed to reach him. He pulled it out of his back pocket and punched in Dodge's number and waited as it rang, an intent expression on his face. "Machine," he grunted, shaking his head. He left no message. "This is really not like Dodge, I'm telling you."

Mitch studied Will curiously. "Do you have a feeling something's wrong?"

"I really don't know," Will said with obvious concern. "But he *was* all by himself last night."

"Does he have a health problem that we don't know about?" Jeff asked. "A heart condition or something?"

"Hell no," Will responded. "He's in great shape."

"Then what's the big deal?"

"I just think we should go take a look, that's all. Make sure he's okay."

"If that's what you want," Mitch said. "You know him best."

"Well, I think you guys are wasting your time," Jeff argued. "This is the only break I get all day. Me, I'm going to walk our walk." And with that he marched off down the path, toes pointed outward in an exceedingly ducklike fashion.

They took Mitch's truck, Mitch helping himself to a warm croissant as he eased his way down Peck's Point's rutted dirt path to Old Shore Road. Will bounced along next to him, big and broad shouldered, his lean face etched with worry as he gazed out the windshield at the road. Mitch found himself wondering why. What did Will know that he wasn't sharing?

"I think I've figured out your secret," Mitch said, munching.

"My secret? . . ." Will seemed startled.

"Your great-tasting croissants. I know how you do it."

Now Will's face broke into a lopsided grin. "Okay, Mitch, take your best shot."

"Butter," he declared.

"What about butter?"

"My theory is that when something tastes really, really good it generally has something to do with extra butter. A whole lot of extra butter. Would you say I'm right or wrong?"

"Mitch, you are not wrong," Will conceded, laughing.

"You see?" Mitch exclaimed triumphantly. "I knew it."

The Crocketts lived on ten acres of lush green meadow and marshland overlooking the Connecticut River on Turkey Neck Road, an exclusive little lane that twisted its way along a narrow peninsula off of Old Shore Road. The land had been in Dodge's family for many generations. Mile Creek ran along the edge of the property, which was enclosed by fieldstone walls that dated back to the 1820s, when the land was first cleared for farming.

As Mitch pulled in at their driveway, Will asked him to stop so he could hop out and see if Dodge had retrieved that morning's *Wall Street Journal* from their mailbox. Dodge had. Then Will climbed back in the Studey, gazing down the long gravel drive at their rambling, natural-shingled house. Long ago, it had started out as a modest summer bungalow. Then it had been winterized. Then modernized. Then added on to—a music room for Dodge's piano, an office, a gourmet kitchen with French doors that opened onto a blue-stone terrace overlooking the tidal marshes.

"My dad used to plow this driveway when it snowed," Will said, slamming his door shut behind him. "I'd come with him sometimes. It was always early in the morning, freezing cold. God, I loved those mornings. He had an old truck like this one, and the heater never worked."

"This one doesn't work either," Mitch said to him encouragingly.

He enjoyed hearing Will's Rockwellesque remembrances of his youth.

"One year, when I was twelve, two feet of pure white powder fell overnight," Will recalled fondly as they rumbled up the drive toward the house. "It was a bright blue morning, and when we got here there was this snowman, must have been twelve feet high, standing right in front of the house. Dodge had built it for Esme in the night. She was tiny then, three or four. It had a carrot for a nose, coals for eyes, a scarf, hat, the whole nine yards. Most amazing thing I'd ever seen. Even my dad couldn't get over it. H-He died just a few months after that, cancer of the pancreas. Went real fast. The amazing thing is I've been down this driveway a million times since then, but every single time I pull in here I flash right to that morning, that snowman, riding next to my dad in that cold truck." Will hesitated, glancing shyly over at Mitch. "Do you ever do that—live inside of your memory that way?"

"God, yes. There are certain street corners in the West Village, every time I see them I think of Maisie and start to mist up. There are restaurants I haven't gone back to since she died. Fire Island is off-limits. The Mohonk Mountain House up in New Paltz is flat-out haunted, so is Tuscany, where we spent our honeymoon. Hell, I almost had to give up our apartment."

"But you didn't, right?"

"No, I did something much smarter than that—I came to this place. That's how I met Des. And you and Dodge."

"Dodge is a rock. If it hadn't been for him, I'd never have made it after my dad died. Martine, too. I owe both of them so much."

Will obviously cared deeply about the Crocketts, Mitch reflected. So why had Dodge glowered at him that way on the beach? And if they'd been so good and kind to Will, why had Bitsy Peck called the two of them cannibals?

The garage door was open, Dodge's diesel wagon parked inside. Mitch pulled up by the front porch and killed the engine. It was very quiet, so quiet he could hear the flapping of gull wings overhead.

"Want to ring the bell?" he asked Will as they got out.

"Let's check around back. They usually leave the kitchen door unlocked."

A wrought-iron dining table and chairs were set up out on the terrace to take maximum advantage of its view of the tranquil tidal marshes. A juice glass and coffee cup, both emptied of their contents, sat there on the table. So did the *Wall Street Journal*, a set of car keys, a pair of sunglasses, Dodge's birdwatching binoculars, Dodge's sun hat . . . everything but Dodge.

"This is really weird," Will said fretfully, trying the French door to the kitchen. It was locked. "I don't like this at all."

They put their noses to the glass, shielding their eyes against the sun's glare with their hands.

Will let out a gasp. "Oh no . . ."

Dodge was sprawled out on the tile floor behind the kitchen's center island. Mitch could make out only the lower part of his body—his hiking shoes and shins. But he could definitely hear faint whimpers of pain coming from in there.

"Better call nine-one-one, Will."

Will had other ideas—he threw his big shoulder against the glass door with all of his might and shattered the whole damned frame. As the lock gave way he stormed inside, Mitch on his heels. But what they barged in on was not Dodge writhing in pain on the floor.

Because Dodge was not alone.

He was going at it with someone there on the kitchen floor, his hiking shorts bunched down at his knees. The naked woman was slender and pale and appeared to be quite young, although frankly Mitch couldn't tell much about her because she had a canvas gunny sack over her head, the drawstring pulled tight across her throat. The whimpers that they'd heard were hers. She was pinned there beneath Dodge on her hands and knees, her wrists lashed together around a leg of the massive maple chopping block next to the stove.

As Mitch and Will burst inside Dodge tumbled back against the counter in surprise, reaching for a dish towel to cover himself. He lay there, his chest heaving, sweat pouring from him as Mitch and Will stood there with their mouths open, too flabbergasted to speak.

"W-We phoned," Will finally stammered dumbly. "When you didn't answer we got concerned."

"No reason to be," Dodge assured him with remarkable calm. "Another opportunity presented itself this morning, that's all. What with me bunking alone and all."

From the floor next to the chopping block, the woman bucked and strained against her wrist restraints, moaning incoherently inside of that gunny sack over her head. Mitch stood there, shuddering with revulsion. He felt as if he'd just walked in on a porn film that had been custom-tailored for ranking members of the Gestapo.

"There's nothing unusual going on here, men," Dodge pointed out, in response to Mitch's look of sheer horror. "Just two adults having consensual sex."

What Mitch wanted to do was run right out the door. Go straight home and wash out his brain with soap and water. But he didn't. Instead, he crossed the kitchen floor and knelt next to the woman, who was so slender her ribs and vertebrae were plainly visible.

She recoiled in animal fright when he touched her.

"Sshh, it's okay," he whispered, gently removing the bag from over her head.

Her eyes were wild with panic and she was gagging for air—some kind of black material had been stuffed into her mouth. Her panties, Mitch discovered as he reached in and pulled them out. She immediately began gulping down huge lungfuls of air, her breathing rapid and ragged. Mitch dug his pocketknife out of his shorts and cut through the leather cord that bound her hands together. Her thin cotton summer dress lay in a heap next to her on the floor. Mitch helped her on with it.

Then he held his hand out to her, and said, "Come on, Becca, I'll take you home."

CHAPTER 10

"I DIDN'T HEAR TITO smack her around," Chrissie Huberman insisted. "I didn't hear *anything*—and you can't make me say I did."

"We're not trying to, Miss Huberman," Yolie said back at her, somewhat helplessly. "We're trying to figure out what happened that night."

"Well, don't look at me, okay? And if *I'm* the best you can come up with as a suspect then you are just totally brain challenged."

"You're not a suspect," Soave said, trying to cool the publicist's jets. As if he or anyone else could. "We're investigating an unexplained death."

"Can you boys and girls even *deal* with a case this hot?" she wanted to know. "You should consider bringing in an outside consultant. I can pick up the phone and get you a retired NYPD chief of detectives here by three o'clock. He'll be up to speed by the five o'clock news. You want me to make the call?"

"What we want," Des said slowly, "is for you to relax and answer the questions that are put to you."

"Fine, whatever," Chrissie blustered, puffing out her cheeks.

They were grouped around a conference table in the spare conference room of Dorset's musty-smelling town hall. The Major Crime Squad computers were up and running in there, and a couple of uniformed troopers were busy working the phones. Outside, there was total insanity—news vans with satellite transmitters lined up every which way on Dorset Street, reporters and cameramen waiting in a noisy, impatient cluster out on the curb for their twelve o'clock feeding.

Chrissie sat erect at the end of the table, dressed in a yellow silk blouse, white linen slacks, and suede loafers. Her hands were placed palm down on the table, fingers spread wide. She had big hands and wrists. She was a big woman, tall, rangy and very sure of herself. She was not pretty, but everything about her manner suggested that if you didn't think she was then you'd been seriously misinformed.

"At present, we're still trying to fill in the blanks," explained Soave.

"What if I told you I'd like to have my lawyer present?" she demanded, glaring at the three of them.

"That's totally your right."

"Not necessary," she said dismissively. "I have a law degree myself."

"I thought you were a publicist," he said, frowning.

"That doesn't mean I can't be well educated, does it?" Chrissie raised her longish nose in the air, sniffing. "You know, this building smells an awful lot like my grandmother's house in Great Neck. What am I . . . Wait, that's *moth balls* I'm smelling, right? And something else . . ."

"Ben-Gay," Des informed her quietly.

"*Definitely* Ben-Gay," she exclaimed. "God, I would have been up all night wondering about that. Thank you, Trooper."

"You're very welcome."

Yolie said, "We understand from Esme that you're planning to stay around Dorset, even though she's terminated your services."

"If by that you mean I was fired, I wasn't," Chrissie said smoothly. "Esme can't fire me. I didn't work for her—I worked for Tito. And now is when he needs me the most. His whole legacy as a screen star is on the line. The lasting image that audiences around the world will have of Tito Molina is being cast right at this very minute. I will not quit on him. Too much is at stake."

"Pretty big story for you, too, I imagine," Yolie suggested.

"What are you trying to do, girlfriend, fit me for a hooker hat?" Chrissie snarled at her angrily.

Yolie drew back, a bit overwhelmed by this savvy, hard-shell New

York image broker. Clearly, this would go down as a learning day in Boom Boom's personal diary. "I'm just wondering why you're still around."

"I'm *around* because I cared about that kid," Chrissie said. "Both of them, actually, whether Esme believes it or not. She's a helpless little lamb. If I don't stay in town she'll be slaughtered by those predators out there. Who else does she have watching her back? Her aging preppy bitch of a mother? Besides, I have another client passing through this area today, so it made no sense for me to go back to New York. I'm bunking at the Frederick House Inn for a few days."

"How did you manage that?" Des asked her curiously.

"How did I manage what?"

"It's the peak of the summer beach season. Plus every tabloid reporter in America is in town. How did you get a room there on such short notice?"

"No biggie," Chrissie said offhandedly. "A writer for the *Daily News* swapped me her room for an exclusive."

"What exclusive would that be?" Des asked.

Chrissie looked down her nose at her. "You don't really care about shop talk, do you?"

"Just answer the question, please," Des persisted, as Yolie watched them go back and forth, content to be riding the bench for now.

Chrissie shrugged her shoulders. "Okay, sure. I fed her that rough sex spin to explain Esme's split lip. Kinky sex between two beautiful stars the public will eat up. Wife beating they will not—bad for Tito's image."

"Not to mention Esme's lip," Des said. "So *you* were the informed source close to the golden couple. Girl, you have you some skills. I'm impressed."

"I work hard for my clients," Chrissie said simply.

"Most definitely. But now you've got to show us the love, too."

"What are you talking about?" Chrissie wanted to know.

"I'm talking about you sitting here telling us that you couldn't hear what went on that night between Tito and Esme. That's just not going to get it done, is it, Lieutenant?"

Soave shook his head gravely. "Not even maybe."

"But it's the truth!" Chrissie protested.

"Tell us what you heard, Chrissie," Des said, raising her voice at her. "Give us some news we can use."

"Look, it's a big, big piece of property. There are acres of lawn in between the guesthouse and the main house. They're nowhere even near each other."

"Where were you earlier that evening?" Soave asked.

"I went out to dinner with a couple of reporter friends. Got home at about ten-thirty, climbed into bed, and worked the phone."

"Who were you talking to at that time of night?"

"My other clients, for starters. They're my babies. I have to tuck them into bed. And I called Gunnar, my husband. We talk every night when I'm away. Then I, let's see, I talked to Tito's agent on the coast, then a guy I know at *Daily Variety*. What can I tell you? I live on the phone. I was too wired to sleep, so I took a Valium."

"How often do you need to do that?" Yolie asked her.

"Are we here to talk about my personal shortcomings?" Chrissie shot back.

"Please answer the question, Miss Huberman," Soave said.

"Fairly regularly, okay? I get kind of wound up. Maybe you noticed."

"And you heard no yelling going on between Tito and Esme?" Yolie pressed her doggedly.

"For the thousandth time—no."

"What about cars?" Des asked. "Did you hear any cars come and go?"

Chrissie thought about this for a second. "I did, now that you mention it. The driveway there is gravel, and it makes a definite crunching noise. Somebody pulled in about eleven-thirty, maybe twelve. Then went out again a few minutes later. Another car took off not long after that."

So Chrissie was corroborating Esme's story, Des reflected, that Tito had come and gone in a huff and that she, Esme, had then gone running to Jeff Wachtell. "We're placing the time of Tito's death at between one-thirty and two," Des said, shoving her horn-rimmed glasses up her nose. "You were in bed?"

"Asleep," Chrissie replied, nodding. "I dropped off at around one."

"Alone, yes?"

"Alone, yes," she answered frostily. "Next thing I knew Esme was in my bedroom screaming about how the police had just found Tito, and I had to hit the ground running in six different directions at once. It's been like that ever since."

"She doesn't seem all that crazy about you," Des said. "Esme, I mean."

"She doesn't have to be."

Des stepped into the batter's box now and swung from her heels. "Would that have anything to do with the fact that you were sleeping with Tito?"

Chrissie wouldn't take the bait. "Why, what did she tell you about us?" she asked, not the least bit flustered.

"Not one single thing."

"Then how do you . . . Oh, I get it. Tito must have told someone. He wasn't real discreet, to put it mildly." Chrissie fell silent for a moment, staring down at her hands on the table. "Esme probably did know, yeah. And my personal rule of thumb is whatever she knows, Mommy knows."

"How long had you two been involved?" Des asked.

" 'Involved' isn't the word for it. Tito didn't get involved. The boy was strictly a midnight rambler. Showed up bombed on my doorstep late one night."

"And you let him in?"

"Are you kidding me? He was the sexiest man in America. Who was I not to? And in answer to your next question—Gunnar and me, we're not about being possessive. So this was not a major deal, okay?" She paused, lowering her voice confidentially. "Neither was Tito, for that matter. In the sack, I mean. Besides, we only slept together a grand total of four times. Three, technically. The last time he couldn't even rise to the occasion."

"Too bombed?"

"Too *something*. Don't ask me what. The boy didn't exactly confide."

"Was he upset about it?"

"Well, he wasn't thrilled, if that's what you mean."

"This is a very interesting angle, Des," Soave spoke up. "I am liking this large."

"I heard that," Yolie agreed, nodding her braided head.

Chrissie's eyes immediately widened. "Whoa, do not even go there," she said, her voice rising with urgency. "Tito did *not* toss himself off of that waterfall because of me. This is ancient history I'm talking about. Five, six months ago. It happened when I was staying with them out in L.A. And he never, ever knocked on my door again after that. We've been strictly business ever since. And in case you're thinking I'm some kind of a Sally Home Wrecker, forget that, too. Their marriage was already a joke."

"You saying he got around?" Yolie asked her.

Chrissie let out a sharp bray of a laugh. "Don't put it all on him. Esme more than kept up her end. And that girl's taste in men isn't the greatest, believe me. She's a slut for big dumb clods. That's the real reason why Tito wouldn't have bodyguards around. She was always giving 'em some in the pool house."

"This made Tito jealous?" Des asked, leaning forward.

"Totally," Chrissie affirmed. "Understand this about Tito Molina. He was a genuine rebel—angry, soulful, gifted, all of that. But when it came to women he was strictly old school. He wanted to chase puss whenever he felt like it, and he wanted Esme waiting patiently at home for him. And if she talked back to him, *wham*, right in the kisser. Trust me, she wasn't going to take that from him much longer. A few more months at most. The marriage was toast. That's why Tito's agent was so anxious for them to make *Puppy Love*. It was going to be their last big payday together. I am talking north of thirty million between the two of them. But it was absolutely vital that they start filming it right away."

"Vital for who?" Des asked.

"For everyone," Chrissie replied, bristling. "We are talking about two mega-stars. When they work, hundreds and hundreds of other people work. And I'm not talking about the glamour people. I'm talking about the assistant wardrobe girl and the guy who drives the catering truck. These people depend on that work to feed their families. And I'm talking about the fans. The millions of young people who wait in line for hours in the rain just for a chance to see those two up on screen together." Chrissie broke off, her eyes glittering at Des defiantly from across the table. "You think we were *using* them, don't you? You think we were manipulating poor little Tito and Esme for our own selfish personal gain. Well, you're wrong. I happen to know actors better than you do, and do you know what they fear the most in life? *Being ignored.* If those two had made *Puppy Love* together, it would have been sheer tabloid heaven—just like Taylor and Burton in *Cleopatra*. And, believe me, they both would have loved every single crazy minute of it." Chrissie sighed, her voice heavy with regret. "But now it's never going to happen."

"Tell us what Tito was up to since they arrived in Dorset," Yolie said.

"Okay, sure," Chrissie said easily. "What would you like to know?"

"Were you aware that he was seeing someone?"

"I assumed he was. He slipped out a lot late at night."

"Who was she?"

"You're assuming it was one particular she. It's more likely that there were several women."

"Can you give us a name? One name?"

Chrissie shook her head. "I don't do that. I don't gossip about a client."

"Shut up," Yolie exclaimed. "What do you call what you were just doing?"

"Dishing like nobody's business, you ask me," Soave said, nodding.

"I was not. I was talking about Tito and me. I mentioned no other names. Go ahead, look it up in your notes." Now Chrissie focused her gaze on Des. "How come you haven't asked me who *Esme* was seeing?"

Des didn't respond.

"It's because you already know his name, am I right?"

Again, Des didn't respond.

"I see, so you get to ask questions and I don't." Chrissie heaved her chest, exasperated. "Then let me put it to you this way—are you at least taking a good, hard look at Mitch Berger as your killer?"

"Why do you say *killer*?" Soave fired back. "We're investigating an unexplained death, remember? Or do you know something we don't know?"

"I know that he's very well connected." Chrissie stared right at Des as she said this, purposely trying to push her buttons. "I know that he and Tito really threw down at The Works."

"Tito threw down," Des corrected her. "Mitch hit the deck."

"All the more reason for him to come after Tito that night," Chrissie went on. "The man was publicly humiliated. Guys hate that. It drives them nuts. Seriously, shouldn't you be talking to him?"

"We *have* talked to him," Yolie blurted out.

"Really, what did he say?" Chrissie asked eagerly, smelling a choice morsel she could feed to the hungry horde outside.

"We're talking to everybody," Soave said brusquely, shooting a warning look at his young partner. Boom Boom still had a lot to learn about the Chrissie Hubermans of the world.

"And I sure do hope I don't pick up the paper tomorrow and read that we're focusing our attention on him," Des added in a low, steely voice. " 'According to a high-level source close to the investigation.' "

"You have to admit it makes a good story," Chrissie said.

"Good for who, girl?"

"You do your job, I do mine."

"I'm down with that, only maybe you ought to pull into Jiffy Lube and get your value system checked."

"What's *that* supposed to mean?"

"That you are not going to pump up the volume by trashing

Mitch Berger," Des told her. "If you try that I will come after you and I will put you in the hospital."

"You're a law officer," Chrissie objected. "You can't threaten me that way."

"This isn't the badge talking. This is me. Do we understand each other?"

"Sure, whatever. I mean, God, it's so obvious that you people have nothing."

"We're talking to everybody," Soave repeated coldly. "We're especially interested in Tito's lovers."

"Well, don't look at me," she said. "A meaningless fling—that's all we had, I swear. Why would I lie to you about it? I have no reason to."

"You have every reason to," Des countered. "Not only were you and Tito involved but you have no one to vouch for your whereabouts at the time of his death."

Chrissie sat there in heavy silence for a moment. "You're right, I don't. So I can't help you *or* myself. Live and learn. The one night when it would have paid for me to drag a warm body home, I have to hop into bed with my cold hard cell phone. There's a valuable lesson to be learned here."

"What lesson is that, Miss Huberman?" Soave asked.

"If you don't watch out, being a good girl can get you in a whole lot of trouble," she replied. "Now can I get the hell out of here? I have a client who needs me."

CHAPTER 11

"WHY WOULD BECCA LET Dodge treat her that way?" Mitch asked Bitsy Peck as the two of them sat there in rocking chairs on her shaded porch, gazing out at the dead calm Sound. "What was she even doing there?"

"Mitch, that man has always had a peculiar power over her," Bitsy replied, sipping her iced tea. "It's something I had to face up to a long time ago. When it comes to Becca, Dodge is leaning on an open door. She's weak and she's pliable and she so wants to please him. He was her first, you see."

"Her first lover?"

"Love had nothing to do with it," Bitsy said bitterly.

Becca hadn't said a word the whole way home in Mitch's truck. Just sat there in between Mitch and Will, staring out the windshield as if she were in a trance. And she smelled bad—rank and coppery, like a handful of moist, dirty pennies. Will was very quiet himself. He seemed terribly upset by the scene they'd walked in on.

As for Mitch, he could not get over that this shell-shocked, twenty-three-year-old recovering heroin addict was Dodge's idea of a lover. True, Becca was a consenting adult, as Dodge had taken pains to point out. But strictly in a legal sense. In a human sense, she was a lost little girl. What was she to Dodge—someone who he cared about? Or merely a limp rag he could tie up and plug to his heart's content? Mitch had no idea. How could he?

He obviously didn't know Dodge Crockett at all.

When he pulled up next to Will's van at the entrance to Peck's Point, Mitch told Becca he'd be right back, then hopped out with him, and said, "Will, did you have an idea that this was going on?" Keeping his voice low.

"I don't know what you mean." Will unlocked his van and got in.

"You seemed so worried about Dodge not showing up. Did you know about him and Becca?"

Will didn't respond. Just started up his engine and sat there behind the wheel, a remote and silent keeper of secrets.

Mitch found himself wondering what those secrets were. What else did Will know about the man? How much was he holding on to?

"Don't judge him, Mitch," Will said, putting his van in gear. "The man's not perfect, but here's some news for you—none of us are."

Then he'd driven off and Mitch had taken Becca across the cause-way to Big Sister, where a silver VW Beetle was parked outside of the Pecks' sprawling summer cottage.

Esme was seated there cross-legged on the veranda in a string bikini, calmly shucking peas with Bitsy, her signature mane of tou-sled blond hair tied back in a ponytail. Mitch couldn't get over how much the beautiful actress resembled a ten-year-old child as she sat there intently popping open the pea pods, her pink tongue flicking distractedly at her raw, swollen lip. She had a girl's tiny, delicate ears and snub nose, a girl's blond peach fuzz on her tummy. But she was not a girl. She was a lithe, voluptuous woman who had cheekbones the camera loved, an Academy Award to call her own, and a very famous, very dead husband.

As he stood there looking at her, Mitch noticed that Esme Crock-ett also had thin, faint white scars on the inside of each of her wrists.

"Hey, girlfriend!" the actress called to Becca, smiling at her warmly. Until, that is, she spotted the thousand-yard stare coming from her old school chum. Then Esme said no more—just put down the bowl of shucked peas, hopped nimbly to her bare feet, and led Becca inside the house by the hand.

"She wasn't . . . isn't on drugs, is she, Mitch?" Bitsy had asked him first thing, her eyes wide with fright.

"I don't believe so, no."

"Well, that's a relief. I only worry about that girl every minute of every day. I don't suppose you feel like telling me what happened to her, do you?"

Mitch hadn't felt like telling her one bit. "What brings Esme by?"

"The poor dear's having such a hard time, what with the police and the media and the grief. She needed a bit of a breather," Bitsy said, fanning herself with her floppy straw hat. "We've been sitting here shucking peas and making girl talk, just like we used to."

Esme came padding back out onto the porch, alone. "Becca's taking a hot shower," she said, reaching for a man's white dress shirt to throw on. "I'd better get going. Mommy will freak out if I'm gone for long."

"I'm sorry about Tito, Esme," Mitch said.

"I know you are," she said coolly. "Everyone is."

"What I mean is, I liked him."

Esme glanced at him searchingly, as if she were noticing him for the first time. "Thank you." Then she went over to Bitsy and kissed her on the forehead. "I love you, Bits."

"I love you, too, sweetheart," Bitsy said affectionately. "Come back any time. You're always welcome."

Then the actress had headed off and Bitsy had asked Mitch, once again, what had happened to Becca. And so Mitch told her, Bitsy's round cheeks mottling with anger as he detailed where and how they had found her.

"Dodge has always had a thing for teenaged girls," Bitsy revealed to him now as they rocked back and forth, the floorboards creaking under them. "Some men can't be trusted with other men's wives. Dodge Crockett can't be trusted with their daughters. That's why they couldn't run him for lieutenant governor—he's left too many tender young virgins in his wake."

"Like Becca?"

"Like Becca. And now he wants her again, apparently. And if that man nudges her off of her road to recovery, I swear I will load up one of father's old hunting rifles and shoot him down like the wild dog that he is. I don't care if I go to jail for the rest of my life."

"Don't talk crazy, Bitsy."

"Mitch, I'm telling you the God's honest truth."

A long black cigarette boat filled with sunburned summer people went tearing by the island, leaving an incredible roar of noise in its roiling wake.

"God, I wish they'd outlaw those horrible things," she observed irritably. "What kind of morons ride around in them anyway?"

"Morons who like to make a lot of noise."

"Why on earth would they want to do that?"

"So that people like you will notice them. Otherwise, you wouldn't." Mitch glanced at her curiously. "Exactly how old was Becca when she and Dodge first got together?"

"She was of legal age, eighteen. It wasn't statutory rape, just unsavory. And drugs were involved. She was high on pot half the time, and eager to try anything new. He took advantage of her poor judgment to grab himself a piece of fresh young girl. I'd like to point out that Becca wasn't in any serious trouble before that, Mitch. She was just a headstrong girl who liked to kick up her heels. It wasn't until after she got mixed up with Dodge that she got into heroin."

"I wondered why you called him a cannibal before. Now I know why."

"Mitch, you don't know the half of it," Bitsy said darkly.

Mitch rocked back and forth in guarded silence, wondering what else there was. Part of him hoped she'd spill it, part of him hoped she wouldn't. Because there were some things about people that you were better off not knowing, he had come to realize.

Bitsy took a long, slow drink of her iced tea before she said, "It was that golden summer when the girls turned fifteen. They were inseparable, those two. Esme was such a sweet girl, Mitch. A sunny, happy girl who loved to swim and windsurf. And so pretty that there were always lots of boys around. Nice boys, good boys. All of them so healthy and bright, full of enthusiasm. Mind you, she and Becca both had huge crushes on Will Durslag, who was lifeguard at the town beach in those days. All of the girls did. He was a great big handsome boy—an *older* boy. They were like pesky kid sisters to him." Bitsy let out a long, pained sigh. "God, that seems like such a long, long time ago. . . ."

"What happened that summer, Bitsy?"

She rocked back and forth, her brow furrowing. "I'm not even sure I should tell you this. But I feel like you're family, and I've always trusted you to do the right thing. You have to promise me you'll never, ever tell a soul about this. Except for Des. I know you confide in her. But no one else, okay?"

"Okay . . ."

"Esme was Dodge's first, Mitch," Bitsy said quietly.

Mitch swallowed. "Freeze-frame, are you saying? . . ."

"I'm saying he started sexually abusing his own fifteen-year-old daughter that summer. The change in Esme's personality was noticeable and truly alarming. She became gloomy and distant. She looked unwell. She . . . even tried to take her own life."

Those scars on her wrists. Mitch discovered he was scratching at his own wrists now, as if something were crawling around under his skin. He stopped himself, squirming in his seat.

"I honestly don't think Esme would have survived if she hadn't found her way into acting," Bitsy went on. "Acting was her escape. It got her away from this place. Away from *him*."

"Did she ever press charges against him?"

"No, never. All she wanted to do was go far, far away. And she did. She hasn't been back here since she finished high school. Not until this summer."

"What about Martine?"

"What about her?"

"How could she stay married to him? How could she stand by him?"

"By refusing to believe it. She insisted that Esme was making it all up. That she was merely trying to *hurt* her father."

"So she was a full-time resident of the state of denial?"

"Denial is not uncommon under such circumstances, Mitch. The alternative is simply far too horrible to contemplate. Esme's silence was also quite typical. She was afraid to tell anyone. The only reason I know about it is that the night before she left for New York she finally told Becca everything. And Becca told me."

Just another day in paradise, Mitch reflected as he rocked back and forth on Bitsy's porch. One more slice of family life in this Yankee eden called Dorset. "Why did Esme come back now? Why did she bring Tito here?"

"I honestly don't know, Mitch."

"Maybe the wounds have finally healed."

"Wounds like those never heal."

"I'm thinking that one other person may know about this. . . ."

"Such as who, Mitch?"

"Will Durslag."

"You're not wrong," Bitsy concurred, shoving her lower lip in and out thoughtfully. "Will's role in life has long been to clean up the sobbing, broken messes that Dodge leaves behind. He delivers the parting gifts, mends the broken hearts. There was an au pair girl on Turkey Neck Road some years back, a lovely Scottish girl. And when she got pregnant it was Will who claimed responsibility and paid her way back home. Even though everyone *knew* she was Dodge's little beach blanket plaything. Will has always stuck by him. He so looks up to Dodge."

"My God, how can he?"

"Because he was so young when he lost his own father. Dodge is all he has as a role model."

"Some role model."

"Besides, it's not as if he hasn't profited from their little arrangement. Dodge put him through the Culinary Institute of America, after all. And Dodge has bankrolled The Works."

"Between us, Donna told me they're barely getting by."

"Between us, I'm not surprised to hear that," Bitsy said, raising an eyebrow at him. "Dodge is seriously cash strapped these days."

"How do you know this?"

"I know it because there isn't a plumber or an electrician in Dorset who will work for them anymore. The word is out—the Crocketts don't pay their bills. Martine has bounced so many checks at the beauty parlor that Rita won't let her set foot in the door unless she has cash on her."

"But how could this happen?"

"The NASDAQ, that's how. Dodge risked everything he had on tech stocks. When the dot-com bubble burst, so did his entire portfolio. The man's not a wise investor."

"But he seems so, I don't know, on top of things."

"Well, he's not, believe me. He's run through two considerable family fortunes in the past twenty years, his and Martine's. That house of theirs is mortgaged to the rafters. All he has left is The Works. If *it* doesn't succeed, he and Martine may actually be out on the street."

"Amazing," said Mitch, who was beginning to wonder if there was any one single facet to Dodge's life that wasn't a complete sham. Now he heard footsteps on the floorboards of the veranda and turned to see Becca standing there barefoot in a sleeveless white cotton nightgown, damp and fragrant from her shower. Her wet hair was combed out straight and shiny. She looked very young and innocent. "I think I may lie down in my room for a while, Mother," she said softly.

"Of course, darling," Bitsy said, mustering a reassuring smile.

"Thanks for the save, Mitch," Becca said with a shy smile of her own.

"No problem. That's what neighbors are for."

"He told me he still cared about me. That he thought about me a lot and missed me."

"So you've been seeing him?" Bitsy asked her pointedly.

Becca lowered her eyes. "Maybe a little," she admitted, scuffing at the floorboards with her big toe. She had a dancer's feet, knobby and calloused. "We went for a walk on the town beach together the other night."

"Was this the night before last?" Mitch asked her curiously.

"Well, yeah. It was raining. We walked and talked for hours in the rain. It was nice. He was very sweet."

"What time did you meet him there, Becca?"

"Why do you want to know that?"

"Because it might be important."

"Midnight. I met him at midnight. You were in bed asleep, Mother."

"This morning, too, I imagine." Bitsy was not pleased that Becca had been slipping out on her this way.

"I'm an adult, Mother."

"You absolutely are."

Clearly, they had boundary issues, which were of no concern to Mitch. What did interest him was that Becca Peck was apparently walking on the beach with Dodge at the time of Tito's death. This being the case, where was Martine? Who could vouch for her?

"I-I thought it would be different this time," Becca said haltingly. "I thought *he* would be different. I was wrong, Mitch. And by the time I realized it, it was too late to stop."

"You don't have to explain yourself to me, Becca."

"No, I need to. I just can't imagine what you must have thought when you walked in on us. What you ... must be thinking of me right this very minute."

"I'm thinking that you got played. It can happen to anyone. Believe me, you're not alone. Not by a long shot."

"I'd like to repay you somehow."

"You don't have to do that either."

"Can I make you lunch one day? I'm a decent cook, if you don't mind vegetarian."

"It's true, she is," Bitsy chimed in encouragingly. "She's taught me all sorts of inventive ways to use my zucchinis."

"Sounds great."

Becca padded back inside now, leaving them alone there on the veranda. They rocked back and forth in silence for a long moment.

"What are the chances she'll stay clean?"

"Not good," Bitsy answered flatly. "You have to like the person who you see in the mirror every day, and Becca doesn't. She needs to feel good about herself again. Find something she can care about. For years, it was dance. But she's stopped dancing and she hasn't come up with anything to take its place. That's what she needs in her life right now—*not* a degrading affair with a man who preys upon her own sense of worthlessness. She tells herself Dodge treats her that way because she *deserves* to be treated that way. It isn't so, Mitch. She's sweet and she's lovely and she's never been a harm to anyone in this world but herself." Bitsy trailed off, fanning herself with her hat. "Something you'll learn when you have children of your own—and I sincerely hope you will, because you'll make a wonderful father—is that you can't protect them from their own mistakes. All you can do is love them."

"Why do you think I'd make a good father?"

"I believe the word I used was 'wonderful.'"

"Well, why do you?"

"Because you care about other people. A lot of couples who have children don't. Too darned many."

"Tell me about Martine."

"What do you want to know about her?"

"Well, she must at least be aware that Dodge chases after young girls."

"Of course she is."

"How can she tolerate it?"

"Mitch, the most important thing to remember about Martine Crockett is that she's a crushed flower."

Mitch glanced at her curiously. "A crushed what?"

"That's an old Miss Porter's expression. I guess no one uses it anymore. It means that she's, well, she was a great beauty who married unwisely. And has paid dearly for it ever since with a life of regret, resentment, and muted desperation. It means . . ." Bitsy hesitated briefly, her chest rising and falling, round cheeks reddening. "It means that she's Dorset's town tramp. Has been for a good twenty years. And I can never forgive her for that, Mitch. Not because I give a good goddamned whose husband she's sleeping with—and, believe me, I can think of a dozen without even breaking a sweat—but because she was that poor girl's mother and she let it happen. Instead of protecting Esme from that awful beast, she was out chasing after her own selfish pleasures. And when she was presented with the horrible truth, when Esme *told* her what Dodge was doing to her, she simply chose not to believe it. And look what happened to her beautiful little girl, Mitch. Look what happened to *my* girl. My b-beautiful, sweet—" Bitsy broke off with a sudden choked sob and went barreling into the house with her hands over her face, her straw hat falling from her head and fluttering to the veranda floor.

She didn't want Mitch to see her cry. Crying was something that was done behind closed doors. Bitsy was very old-fashioned.

Mitch picked up her hat and hung it from a hook outside the door, then trudged home by way of the lighthouse on the island's narrow, rocky strip of beach, his hands in his pockets and a hollow, sick feeling in the pit of his stomach. Quirt was taking a nap in the shade under the butterfly bush by the front door. Clemmie was nowhere to be seen.

There were several more phone messages from news outlets wanting to talk to him about Tito's death. These he ignored. There were also three messages from Dodge. *"Mitch we need to talk. . . . Mitch, I really don't want to leave things this way. . . . Mitch, please call me. Mitch. . . ."*

These Mitch carefully erased. He did not call Dodge Crockett back.

C. C. Willoughby and Co. was situated smack-dab in the center of the quaint little main drag of quaint little Sussex, a highly desirable shoreline commuter town sandwiched in between Greenwich and Cos Cob. At latest count, a hefty 38 percent of the homes in Sussex were valued at more than $1 million apiece. Pristine white colonial mansions, immaculate green lawns and shiny new silver Lexus SUVs abounded. No handyman specials, no weeds, no clunkers. It occurred to Mitch, as he tootled his way slowly through town in his old Studey, that he had entered a world apart, a world where virtually no one was not rich, blond, slender, and stylish. At least Dorset had a few middle-class working stiffs who were misshapen, dark, and shlumpy.

Well, at least it had *him*.

Most of the shops were located in vintage brick row buildings. The parking out front was on the diagonal, just like in that Connecticut village in *Bringing Up Baby*, the one where Cary Grant and

Katharine Hepburn stopped to buy meat for Baby. There was a movie theater that played foreign films for mature audiences, a barbershop, dry cleaner, a coffee shop called The Beanery. There were chic boutiques selling things like really expensive baby clothing and kitchenware.

And there was C. C. Willoughby and Co., which had started out in the space where the village hardware store had once been and had proven to be such a success that it had spread not only upstairs but to the buildings on either side of it. C. C. Willoughby was the rarest phenomenon in the book business—an independent bookstore that made money. Book lovers didn't just come to C. C. Willoughby to shop, they came to spend the whole day. And they came from all over the state of Connecticut. This made it a must-stop for best-selling authors on tour. Most of the big names, from Tom Brokaw to Toni Morrison to Abby Kaminsky, author of the Codfather Trilogy, held signings there on their way from New York to Boston.

Mitch couldn't even get near the place on this particular July afternoon. People were lined up by the hundreds to get in the door and meet Abby. Many of these people in line were children wearing pointy Carleton Carp fish-head costumes. As he drove by them in search of a parking space, it dawned on Mitch that they looked disturbingly like a legion of very short Ku Klux Klansmen in town for a rally.

He wondered if anyone else had every noticed this before.

He ended up parking in a municipal lot three blocks away and strolling back. He entered through the bustling café, which was connected to the gift shop, where high-end stationery, soaps, and scented candles were sold. The herbal scents filled the entire bookstore. Mitch had always thought a bookstore should smell like, well, books. Not like lavender. Still, he admired C. C. Willoughby. He admired anyone who could turn a profit selling books. Most of the vast downstairs was reserved for current hardcover fiction and nonfiction. Abby was signing copies of her new novel upstairs, where the children's books were. The line of kids and their parents waiting to meet her snaked all the way down the stairs and out the front door.

Mitch squeezed past them and tried to get to her by way of an adjoining room. But the doorway was intentionally blocked. All he could manage was a peek of her seated there at a table, greeting her fans one by one and signing copies of *The Codfather of Sole*. Abby was a chubby little blond in a cream-colored linen suit. Flanking her were Chrissie Huberman and Abby's escort, a six-foot-four inch slab of granite who favored the goatee and shaved head look. Mitch supposed it was intended to make him look menacing, and as far as he was concerned it worked.

There was no way Mitch could approach her now. None.

So he waited outside on a bench across the street, nursing an iced cappuccino from the café while he tried to keep his mind off of the horrifying image of Dodge and his own teenaged daughter in bed together. He could not do it. The image would not fade away.

A half hour later, Abby finally emerged out front with Chrissie. The two women chatted for a minute as Abby signed books for a few more grateful young readers. Meanwhile, her escort made his way over to a black town car parked two doors down, unlocked it, and waited there for her, holding a rear door open. Mitch was on his feet now, inching his way steadily closer. Abby and Chrissie exchanged a hug, then Chrissie went back inside and Abby started toward the car. As soon as she'd climbed in the escort slammed her door shut and got in behind the wheel.

This was when Mitch yanked open her door, jumped in beside her and said, "Abby, we need to talk."

"Hey, what do you think you're doing!" she objected angrily.

"I'm sorry, but this was the only—"

"Back off, Mr. Stalker Nut!"

"I'm not a stalker, I'm—"

"Yo, who is this guy, Abby?" her escort demanded, twisting around in the front seat and seizing Mitch by the collar of his rumpled button-down.

"Wait, I *know* him. . . ." Abby shook a manicured finger at Mitch now. "I've seen your picture in the paper. You're—"

"Mitch Berger," he gasped.

"Right," she exclaimed. "And you're all mixed up in this Tito Molina mess with Chrissie. . . . Let him go, Frankie." Frankie complied. "I know who this man is, although I don't have the slightest idea what he wants. What *do* you want, Mitch?"

"It's about Jeff," Mitch said, straightening his collar. "I'm a friend of his."

Abby's face fell. "Oh, I see."

Abby Kaminsky was a little bitty thing, barely five feet tall. And there were two things Mitch knew about her right away. One was that she was someone who had been told that she was adorable for as long as she could remember. The other was that she was someone who had always fought her weight. For some reason, Abby reminded Mitch of Muriel Bloom, the teacher who he'd been madly in love with when he was in the fifth grade. Something about her heart-shaped face, milky complexion, and startled blue eyes. Abby wore her frosted blond hair in a smartly styled bob. Her makeup, lipstick, and nail polish all came together in a way that indicated a professional had supervised her entire look—right down to the linen suit she wore, which accentuated her generous curves rather than fighting with them.

On the seat next to her were a box of Cocoa Pebbles kids' cereal and a water bottle. She reached for the water bottle, her eyes studying Mitch carefully. "Look, I have to be in Boston. I don't have time for this—whatever *this* is."

"It'll only take a few minutes," Mitch promised. "Have you eaten lunch? I happen to know they make a superior BLT at The Beanery."

"God, cookie, you know the way right to my heart."

The Beanery was narrow and dark. The floors were of well-worn wood, as were the high-backed booths, which had several generations of initials carved into them. Since it was after two o'clock, no one else was in there eating lunch. They took the booth next to the front window. Frankie stayed outside, leaning against the town car with his big arms crossed, glowering at Mitch.

"Don't mind him, Mitch," Abby said, hanging her linen jacket on a coat hook by the door. She wore a sleeveless white silk camisole underneath. Her bare arms were round but well toned, as if she'd been going to the gym regularly. "He's just very protective. And we had a brief, a-a *thing*, so he gets all hormonal."

"You're not with him any longer?" Mitch asked, recalling how enraged Jeff had been over their affair.

"I don't stay with anyone for very long. Listen, I have to go wash my patties. I've just spent the past hour shaking hands with my you-know-whos. Do you have *any* idea where those fingers of theirs have been? In their mouths, in their noses, in their . . . God, it's too horrible to even think about." She paused, looking Mitch up and down. "I'm going to take you on faith. Order me a BLT and a chocolate shake."

He ordered the same for both of them from the elderly waitress as Frankie continued to glare at him through the window.

"That was so terrible about Tito," Abby said when she returned to their booth, sliding in across from him. "It must feel weird knowing you were the last person on earth to speak to him before he jumped."

"Actually, that may not be what happened. He may have been murdered."

"*You* didn't kill him, did you?" she demanded breathlessly, her big blue eyes widening. "Please tell me it wasn't you, Mitch. You've just jumped into my town car. You're notorious. You're desperate. You've got the wounded teddy bear thing going on. Already I have a mad crush on you."

"It wasn't me," Mitch said.

"Oh, thank God."

The waitress returned now with their shakes, fussing over Abby, who she obviously recognized.

Mitch tasted his. It was frosty and good. "But until they do know how Tito died, I won't get over this. I need to know if I could have saved him."

"Mitch, I wouldn't blame myself, I were you. Tito Molina didn't know up from down. That was one hurtin' puppy."

Mitch gazed at her curiously. "You sound as if you knew him."

"I did." She took a gulp of her shake, the tip of her pink tongue flicking at the residue on her upper lip. "We had a brief, a-a *thing*."

"Really, when was this?"

"Before I left on my tour. Would you believe I've been on the road for over six weeks? I've hit twenty-three cities in forty-nine days, not that I'm counting or anything. My face is breaking out for the first time since the Reagan years. I have no life and no one to talk to except for Frankie, who is not exactly Mr. David Halberstam, in case you didn't notice. These past few nights have been the first nights I've slept in my own actual bed since, like, Memorial Day. When I woke up my first morning home, I didn't recognize my own room. I couldn't even remember what city I was in. That's when you know you've been on tour too long. And already I'm back on the road again, two nights in Boston and . . ." She trailed off, suddenly realizing that she hadn't answered Mitch's question. "Chrissie brought me by Tito's hotel for breakfast one morning. He was in New York to meet with some British playwright, and the studio was hoping he'd agree to be the voice of Carleton for the film version of *The Codfather*. He ended up passing, but he wanted to hear my thoughts about the character before he committed."

Mitch nodded. The first Carleton movie was a state-of-the-art animated production that had been two years in the making. It was going to be its studio's big Christmas release. Freddie Prinze Jr. was providing the voice of Carleton.

"I thought he was very sweet," Abby went on. "And after Crissie took off, I found myself upstairs in his hotel room, naked. Scout's honor, I boinked Tito Molina—little Abigail Kaminsky from Margate, New Jersey, thunder thighs and all. Honestly, I was so nervous I felt just like I do when I'm at the gynecologist's office. My little hands and feet were all clammy, and I couldn't stop shaking. But he was very gentle and considerate."

The waitress arrived with their sandwiches now. "Miss Kaminsky, my granddaughter *ab-so-tootly* loves your books," she said as she set down their plates. "Could I get your autograph?"

"You *ab-so-tootly* can!" Abby responded sweetly, scribbling her name on a napkin and handing it to her. "Tell her I said hi!"

"Oh, I will." The waitress scurried off, thrilled.

They dove hungrily into their sandwiches, two chubby people who prized their eats.

"You sure do know your sandwiches, Mitch," Abby proclaimed after several bites, licking mayonnaise from her manicured fingers. "This is the best BLT I've ever had. What's the secret?"

"The tomatoes are right off of the vine, I think. Makes all the difference." Mitch sipped his shake distractedly, his mind racing. Could Abby somehow be a player in this? "How long were you and Tito an item?"

"We weren't," she said flatly. "It wasn't that kind of a deal at all. It was strictly a one-shot matinee. The proverbial quickie. Besides, like I told you, I don't stay involved with anyone for long."

"Not even Jeff?"

Abby reddened instantly. "Jeffrey Wachtell broke my poor heart into a million pieces. I gained twenty pounds after we split up. I couldn't write a single word. I couldn't leave the house. All I could do was eat and cry. I cried and I cried. I still cry myself to sleep every night. Look at me, Mitch—I'm rich, I'm famous, I'm buffed to within an inch of my life. Believe me, this is as fantastically cute as I'm ever going to look. And I can't remember the last time I went out on an actual date." She shot a brief, disdainful glance out the window at Frankie, who appeared to have fallen asleep on his feet, rather like a barnyard animal. "What's wrong with me anyway? Am I that disgusting?"

Mitch went back to work on his sandwich. "You're just worn down from your tour, that's all. You'll meet someone real soon."

Abby smiled at him coyly. "You really think so?"

"I do. And I'll tell you something else—Jeff's out of his mind."

She reached across the table and put her hand over his. "Come with me to Boston, Mitch. Have dinner with me tonight. Stay over with me."

"I can't, Abby," he said, staring down at her soft little hand.

"Why not?"

"Well, for starters, I've known you for less than an hour."

"Sometimes it happens that way," she said, squeezing his hand tightly.

"Plus it would not be a good idea for me to leave the state right now."

"I can vouch for you. I'm famous. I'm credible."

"*Plus* I'm involved with someone."

"Damn, I knew it. The good ones are always taken." Abby released his hand and took a long gulp of her shake, peering at Mitch over her fountain glass. "So how do you know Jeffrey?"

"We walk together on the beach every morning."

"How is he?" she asked, her nostrils flaring. "Not that I care."

"Still in love with you, or so he says."

Abby let out a shrill, mocking laugh. "Yeah, right," she said scornfully. "Listen to me, Mitch, the single most important thing to remember in regards to Jeffrey and women is that every single word out of his mouth is a lie. And the little putz gets away with it, too. You know why? Because he happens to be among the world's greatest swordsmen. You wouldn't know it look at him, but it's true. Jeffrey has absolutely spoiled me for other men. That's my curse. I swear, when I was there in that hotel bed with Tito Molina all I kept thinking was 'God, if only he were Jeffrey Wachtell.' That's crazy, isn't it?"

"Not if you still love the little guy."

"I *hate* the little guy! The little guy is despicable. The little guy is . . ." She fell silent, dabbing at her mouth with her napkin. "I understand he has a mother-daughter tag team thing going on now—he's boinking Esme Crockett *and* her old lady at the same time. Chrissie told me all about it. You look surprised, Mitch. Don't be. That man is the craftiest little pussy hound imaginable. Even beautiful women instinctively get all motherly and protective toward him. They can't help themselves. Half of the time *they* seduce *him*—despite knowing he's absolutely no good for them. Believe me, I'm the expert. I paid the price in the worst possible way." Abby sat back in the booth, hugging herself with her bare arms. "I'm the one who walked in on him boinking my own baby sister, Phyllis, in our own bed in our own apartment. Mitch, you have no idea how violated I felt. How dirty."

"I'm sorry, Abby."

"So am I," she said, shivering. She had goose bumps up and down her bare arms now. "That's why I won't give him a nickel of my earnings. He's not the injured party, *I* am."

Mitch got up and fetched her linen jacket for her.

She snuggled back into it gratefully, studying him with her startled blue eyes. "I don't know what Jeffrey's told you about our settlement battle. . . ."

"That he's asking for twenty-five percent of the proceeds from the first book. He claims he was involved early on in the creative process, and therefore should participate in it."

"Not in a million years." Abby sniffed. "Never."

"I don't blame you at all. Still, you have to admit that, well, Jeff *is* Carleton, isn't he?"

"Carleton is fiction," Abby shot back, bristling. "Carleton is *my* creation. Jeffrey had nothing to do with him. Not one thing!"

"Are you *ab-so-tootly* sure of that?"

"And he does *not* own the copyright to that *stupid* expression! No one does. I was free to use it. And I'll keep on using it for as long as I damned please. Carleton is *not* Jeffrey Wachtell. How could he be? Carleton isn't a liar. Carleton doesn't whine about every single thing twenty-four hours a day, seven days a week. Ask yourself this: Can you imagine Carleton hosing his wife's sister?"

"No, of course not. Carleton's not old enough. He's still a little boy. Or fish. Or . . ."

"Carleton is *good* is what he is," she asserted. "Carleton is honest and brave and true. And I will bankrupt Jeffrey Wachtell with lawyer fees before I ever give him one shiny nickel of my proceeds." Abby took a deep breath and let it out slowly, silently mouthing a ten-count. Jeff was way under her skin, no two ways about that. "How is his bookstore doing, anyway? Chrissie told me it's a real dump."

"Not true. It's a lovely little store. Although he is struggling to get by."

"Good."

"In fact, that's the reason why I'm here—he was wondering if you would stop in and do a signing. You'll be passing right by Dorset on the interstate, and he could really use the boost."

"Not a chance," she replied sharply. "After Boston I'm in Bar Harbor, then Martha's Vineyard, then home. I am not stopping at some neighborhood bookshop in some out-of-the-way village no one's ever heard of. It's not worth my while, Mitch. How many books could he move—fifty? I just sold ten times that this afternoon."

"Still, you could do it if you really wanted to."

"It's true, I could," she admitted. "But you've put your finger right on it, Mitch. I really, really, don't want to."

"It sure would help him out, Abby."

Abby cradled her chin in her palm, gazing at him in wonderment. "Cookie, have you been totally ignoring every single word I've been saying to you?"

"Absolutely not."

"Then answer me this—why on earth would I help Jeffrey out?"

"Because you still love him. And he still loves you. You two should be looking out for each other, not trying to draw blood."

"You're sweet, Mitch, but you're living in a make-believe world. In real life, people who hate each other really do hate each other."

"You want real life? A tabloid has offered Jeff a quarter of a million dollars for dirt on you."

"Dirt?" Abby immediately paled. "What dirt? What has that weasel been telling you about me?"

"That you hate kids so much you made him get a vasectomy."

"That was his idea, not mine," she said heatedly. "He's the one who's terrified of parenthood. I want to be a mother more than anything in the world. Don't you think I'd make a good mother?"

"I honestly don't know."

"Well, I do, because I know what's in my heart. Besides, the procedure he had is totally reversible. God, I don't *believe* he's trying to peddle such crap! Wait, what am I saying? Of course I do. This is *Jeffrey* we're talking about."

"My sense is that he really doesn't want to dish, Abby. In fact, I don't believe he will. But he's in a tight spot financially."

Abby recoiled, shaking her finger at him. "Wait one lousy minute. Now I know why you're here—you're trying to strong-arm me! Sure, that's it. You came here to tell me that if I don't show up at his crummy store he'll go to the tabloids. You're his stinking messenger boy, aren't you? Tell me I'm wrong, Mitch. Go ahead!"

"Okay, you're wrong. The thought never even occurred to me."

"Maybe it didn't," she conceded. "But I can guarantee you that it occurred to him."

"Abby, that's really not how I read the situation."

"Then you'd better go get your eyes checked, cookie. I know Jeffrey. I know how his mind works. And he's telling me, through you, that if I don't do this for him he'll sell me out."

"But he swore he wouldn't," Mitch pointed out. "He told me you were the only woman he's ever loved, and that he'd take you back in a second."

"And you *believed* him?" Abby demanded incredulously.

Mitch drained his milkshake and slumped there in the booth, suddenly feeling profoundly deflated and used up. "Abby, I honestly don't know who to believe anymore."

"If I were you," Mitch advised, feeling the gentle lift and dip of the swell beneath him, "I'd do some checking up on Abby Kaminsky's whereabouts the past couple of days. Or, more specifically, nights."

"Jeff's ex-wife?" asked Des, who was floating on her back next to him, wet skin gleaming in the moonlight. "Why is that?"

"Because she slept with Tito Molina."

"No way. Her, too?"

"Scout's honor."

"You think she might be involved in this?"

"She's certainly in the mix. Quite the humid little pepper pot, too."

The two of them were enjoying a late-night skinny dip off Big

Sister's private beach. The water was bracing and the night air had turned gloriously crisp and clear. Overhead, the moon was full, the stars bright.

Mitch had spent much of the evening seated there on his favorite beach log, gloomily sampling the bottle of peppermint schnapps he'd bought out of morbid curiosity. It tasted awful, in his opinion. Strangely familiar as well, although he could not imagine why. Des had pulled up outside his carriage house at around ten o'clock and joined him on the beach a few minutes later, clutching two cold Bass ales and two towels.

He had never been happier to see her in his life.

As they floated there naked in the moonlight, the lights of the town a glow in the distance, Mitch reminded himself just how lucky he was to be here on this night with this woman. It was the one positive thing he had taken from losing Maisie the way he had—not a day went by when he took the good things for granted.

"How did you happen to meet up with said humid little pepper pot?"

"Jealous?"

"I'll ask the questions, mister."

"Jeff asked me to look her up. He wants her to sign books at his store."

"Since when do you do Jeff's bidding for him?"

"Since everything stopped making sense. I need for this to make sense."

"It may not, Mitch. A lot of times things just get more and more confusing."

"That's not what I need to hear tonight, Des. Tonight I need to hear that life is nothing but one big long Frank Capra movie. And I actually detest Frank Capra—with the possible exception of *Dirigible* with Jack Holt and Fay Wray."

"My miss," she said, flashing a smile at him. "And thanks for the heads-up. I'll pass it along to Rico."

"Abby's been sleeping with her escort, too—a big goon named Frankie. I don't know his last name, but he might be worth looking into. Meanwhile, get this, Jeff's actually been two-timing Martine with her very own—"

"With Esme. Yes, I know."

"Esme told you?"

"She had to. Jeff's her alibi. And, believe me, the news came as a real unpleasant surprise to Martine. I had to pull her off of the girl."

"What did Jeff say about it?"

"He backs Esme up all the way. At the time of Tito's death, she was getting busy with him at his condo. Yolie and I confirmed it with him this afternoon."

"Hmm, that means each of them is the other's alibi. . . ."

"Where do you think you're going with that?"

"Nowhere," Mitch said, as they floated along. "Except, well, what if Esme and Jeff killed Tito together?"

"Why would they?"

"Revenge. He hated Tito for getting it on with Abby. Esme hated him because he beat on her and cheated on her. Do we know for a fact that Tito's killer acted alone?"

"Mitch, we don't know anything for a fact," she said wearily, glancing over at him. "You cast an awesome glow in the moonlight, you know that?"

"You've obviously never gone skinny-dipping with a white boy when the moon was full."

"No, I'm serious, Mitch. Check out your stomach—you look like you've swallowed something radioactive."

"Only because my stomach happens to be sticking up out of the water," Mitch growled at her. "But thanks for pointing it out to me, slats."

"What I'm here for, doughboy," she said sweetly. "Got anything else for me?"

He fed her the highlights of his morning. How he and Will had walked in on Dodge and Becca having rough sex together. How Becca had told him she and Dodge were taking a midnight stroll on the beach together when Tito died, meaning that he had someone to vouch for his whereabouts—and Martine very likely didn't.

"Why would Martine want to kill her own son-in-law?" she wondered.

"Maybe she was romantically involved with Tito, too. Maybe he broke her poor, cheatin' heart. It makes about as much sense as Martine and Esme both having extramarital affairs with Jeff Wachtell. I mean, once you get your mind around that unwholesome factoid nothing seems out of the realm of possibility, does it?"

"Now that you mention it, no."

"Did Esme know about Jeff and her mom?"

"Totally, judging by the little smirk on her face when she gave out with the news. It was her own special way of inflicting pain on mommy dearest. For what specific reason I don't know."

"I do, Des," Mitch said quietly. And now he told her about how Dodge started molesting Esme when she was fifteen. How Martine had refused to believe her. How Esme had attempted suicide. How Dodge had long been a plague on Dorset's young girls and Will had been his enabler, in exchange for future considerations.

Des listened in stony silence before she said, "Well, that does explain the way Esme reacted this morning when Martine smacked her."

"How did she? . . ."

"Like she'd been getting smacked around her whole life."

"What, you think Dodge beat her up?"

"Believe me, a bright, beautiful fifteen-year-old girl doesn't spread her legs for daddy without a fight. I'm with you, Mitch—she hates her mom for not protecting her. But I don't buy that Martine didn't know what was going on. She knew. That's why she was so anxious to go to the police this morning. Because the longer this drags out, the deeper we'll dig. And she's terrified we'll unearth it. How did you hear about it, anyway?"

"From Bitsy. Becca told her. I don't think anyone else knows, except for Will."

"And possibly Tito. Esme may have told him."

Mitch glanced over at her, wondering where her mind was going. "Bitsy said I could tell *you* this. Does Soave have to know about it?"

"Maybe I can withhold it from him," Des answered slowly. "If it's not vital to the investigation, that is."

He smiled at her. "You're one of us now, you know that?"

"One of who?"

"A Dorseteer."

"Let's not get carried away, doughboy. I said maybe."

"Sure, sure. Are you getting cold?" he asked, paddling gently to stay afloat.

"A little, but I'm okay. You?"

"I'm fine. This is why I maintain the extra layer of subcutaneous fat."

"So that's it."

"*Ab-so-tootly.*"

"Mitch, I want you to promise me you'll never say that word again."

"Promise," he said, grinning at her. "Bitsy did tell me one other thing about the Crocketts—they're so strapped for cash that Martine can't write a check anywhere in town. Apparently, just to round out the whole bogus illusion, Dodge sucks as a businessman." He gazed back ashore at Bitsy's rambling house. There were several lights on upstairs, a porch light downstairs. "She's real worried about Becca being mixed up with him again. Becca's fragile and vulnerable, and there's no way that having some guy stuff your panties in your mouth can be good for your . . . Oh, hell, never mind."

"No, it's okay, baby. What are trying to tell me?"

"I just don't want to be friends with Dodge anymore, that's all."

"I don't blame you. But what about the Mesmers?"

"I won't be walking with them again."

"I'm sorry, Mitch."

"So am I. That was something I really looked forward to doing every morning. But I can't now. Not without my skin crawling. Would you believe Will actually *defended* the guy to me this morning? 'Don't judge him,' is what he said. He and Donna are having some problems of their own, by the way. Donna told me."

"Since when does Donna Durslag talk to you about her marriage?"

"Since she had one too many margaritas at the beach club."

"Sounds like maybe she made her a little play for you, too."

"Jealous?"

"I already told you. I'll ask the questions, mister."

"Des, I don't belong around these people," Mitch confessed. "I gave it my best shot. I tried to be a normal, socialized member of the species. But if this is what passes for normal—"

"Believe me, Mitch, this *is* normal. It's what I deal with every single day of my life."

"Then I'm proud to be a maladjusted geek who sits in the dark by myself all day, staring at flickering images on a wall." He reached for her hand in the water and found it and squeezed it. "When do people stop surprising you?"

"They don't. But the surprise doesn't always have to be an unpleasant one. In fact, when you least expect it, you might bump right into somebody who just makes you feel good all over."

"Are you trying to cheer me up?"

"Actually, that was me flirting with you shamelessly. Not very good at it, am I?"

"That all depends—do you put out?"

"Only for a certain glowing gentleman."

Mitch maneuvered his way over closer to her and planted a salty kiss on her wet, cold mouth. "Am I that gentleman?"

"Could be," she said, her almond-shaped green eyes glittering at him in the moonlight.

"Then as far as I'm concerned, you flirt great. Care to start back in?"

"Hell, I'll even race you back to the house."

"You're on. Provided you promise me one thing."

"Name it."

"Let's steer clear of the kitchen floor tonight, okay?"

"Not a problem, boyfriend."

They dashed back in the crisp night air, teeth chattering, and jumped right into a hot shower together, howling and snorting like a couple of rambunctious little kids. After they'd toweled each other dry they made their way up into Mitch's sleeping loft, where they forgot about everything and everyone and there was only the two of them and it was wonderful.

They were blissfully asleep at 4:00 A.M. under a blanket and a Clemmie when Des got paged. She started rummaging hurriedly for her clothes as the Westbrook Barracks dispatcher gave her the details over her cell phone.

"Wha' is it?" Mitch groaned at her after she'd hung up.

She was already lacing up her shoes. Des could get dressed unbelievably fast. It was her four years at West Point. "Night manager of the Yankee Doodle Motor Court just found . . . There's a woman dead in the tub with part of her head smashed in."

Something in her tone of voice set off alarm bells. Mitch swallowed, fully awake now. "Who is it, Des?"

"Baby, it's Donna Durslag."

CHAPTER 12

IF DORSET POSSESSED WHAT could be truly called a seedy side it was found up Boston Post Road just before the town line for Cardiff, Dorset's sleepy, landlocked neighbor to the north, which benefited not at all from summer tourism and which elderly locals still called North Dorset, even though it had been a separate town since 1937. Here, just past Gorman's Orchards, could be found a tattered strip of businesses operating out of wood-framed buildings that had once been residences. If someone needed to have their sofa reupholstered or their unwanted facial hair removed, they came here. Pearl's World of Wigs, Norm's Guns, and Shoreline Karate Academy were here. The Rustic Inn, a beer joint popular with the Uncas Lake swamp Yankees, was here.

And so was the Yankee Doodle Motor Court, which was a living relic from the bygone days of drive-in movie theaters and poodle skirts. To the casual passerby, it was a wonder that the decaying little bungalow motel hadn't been torn down twenty years ago. It had no swimming pool, was not near the beach or the interstate. There was no apparent reason for anyone on earth to stay there—not unless they were terribly lost or desperate.

But Des knew better.

The Yankee Doodle enjoyed a prized niche in Dorset society—it was the place where married people came to mess around. Des had learned early in her career that every town, no matter its size or degree of affluence, had just such a place for illicit trysts. Mostly, what the Yankee Doodle offered couples was privacy. The bungalows were spaced a discreet distance apart, and the parking spaces were around in back so that people driving by on Boston Post Road couldn't see who was parked there. The management was reputed to be very discreet.

She got there in the purplish light of predawn. Danny Rochin, the sallow, unshaven night manager, came right out of the office to greet her wearing a too-large Hawaiian shirt, slacks, and bedroom slippers. He was a stringy, sixtyish swamp Yankee with a jet black Grecian Formula hair job that looked totally unnatural under the courtyard floodlights, especially in contrast with his bushy white eyebrows. They always neglected the eyebrows. Big mistake.

"Is anyone still staying here from last night?" Des asked him as she climbed out of her cruiser.

"No, ma'am, we're all empty," he replied, eyes bright with excitement. He was missing a few teeth, and his narrow shoulders were hunched against the morning's unusual chill. It had dipped down into the forties, which was a shock to the system in July.

"Let's go have us a look, Danny."

There was blood. The spread on the double bed was spattered with it. So was the wall behind the bed. So were the shades on the night table lamps. Donna's wire-rimmed glasses, which lay neatly folded on one of the night tables, were spattered, too. The bed did not appear to have been used. The covers were still crisply folded, and the pillows had no depressions in them.

The Yankee Doodle was the sort of a place where things like lamps and televisions were bolted down, just in case some low-class guest might be tempted to walk off with them. But Donna's killer had still managed to find something to club her with—a night table drawer. It lay on the rug next to the bed, smashed, splintered and bloodied. Her shoulder bag was on the dresser next to the TV, as was her gauzy summer peasant dress, carefully folded. Also a seethrough black nightie, very slinky, very hopeful, very sad.

The bungalow was tiny. There was barely enough space to squeeze around the bed to the bathroom, where Donna was on the floor. From where she stood, Des could just make out her bare feet.

"Did you touch anything, Danny?" Des asked him as he remained outside, pulling nervously on a cigarette.

"Not a thing, I swear. Her purse is just as I found it. I'm not here to steal no twenty bucks from some poor woman's billfold."

"I know that, Danny," she said, flashing a reassuring smile at him. "I'm just trying to assess the crime scene." Now she went farther in for a better look.

Donna was naked on her knees before the bathtub with her big butt sticking up in the air for the whole wide world to see. Not that she was obese but she wasn't a nineteen-year-old runway model either. And the bathroom floor is not the most dignified place to die. Go ask Elvis. There was a foot of blood-tinged water in the tub. By the look of things, her killer had knocked her unconscious with the drawer, dragged her in there and held her head underwater until she was gone. Her center of gravity had tumbled her a bit backward after she'd died, lifting her face up out of the water. There were broken blood vessels around the eyes, and her lips were blue. The bloody wounds to the back of her wet head were readily apparent to Des from the bathroom doorway. There was some blood on the floor, but not much. No bloody shoeprints. The floor had been wiped. Des could not see any bloody towels in there. No towels at all, in fact. He'd taken them with him. Whoever he was, he was careful.

Standing there gazing at Donna Durslag, Des experienced that same mix of despair, horror, and fascination that she always felt when she saw what people were capable of doing to each other. She would need crime scene photos. She would need to get this down on paper. Possibly life-sized, so she could bring forth the full impact of Donna's figure as it knelt there in death. She would draw this. *Had* to draw this. It was how she kept it together.

And to hell with Professor Weiss and his damned trees.

"How often do you run the vacuum in here, Danny?" she asked, starting back around the bed toward him.

"Once a week . . . maybe," he replied.

Meaning there would be tons of hairs in the rug from past guests. Most likely, the tekkies wouldn't even bother with it. But they would for sure check the surface of the bed for hair or fiber transfers, and the blood spatters for a blood sample that was not the victim's. Also the smashed night table drawer for prints, although he'd doubtless wiped that clean same as he'd wiped down the bathroom. Des was certain that they'd find nothing. It smelled like a clean kill all the way.

"Where's her car, Danny?"

"Around in back."

It was faded gray Peugeot station wagon. Locked. Both the passenger seat and backseat were strewn with empty take-out coffee cups and food wrappers. There was one other vehicle parked back there, a red Nissan pickup truck that belonged to Danny.

He led Des back to his office now, where there was a reception counter made out of fake wood, a Coke machine, television, a couple of green plastic chairs. The worn linoleum on the floor was the color of canned salmon. A door marked Private led back to the inner office.

"What time did she check in?"

"Just after ten o'clock," Danny replied, taking his place behind the counter. The man seemed much more at ease now that he was back there, straighter and taller.

"Was she alone?"

"Yes, ma'am."

"Did she sign the register?"

"You bet. We run a clean operation here. No hookers, no minors, no monkey business."

Des glanced at the register—Donna had signed her own name, clear as can be. "Did she pay you in cash?"

"Credit card," he said, his bony hands shaking slightly as he produced the credit card slip for her. She suspected he was in need of a drink. He settled for another cigarette.

"The lady had a husband," Des said, surprised that Donna had made no apparent effort to cover her tracks. "Is this typical?"

"Yes and no," Danny answered, thumbing his stubbly chin shrewdly. "Some of 'em are real careful about keeping their after-hours activities off the household books, others aren't. Depends on who takes care of the bills every month, is how I always figured it."

"Had you ever seen her before?"

"No, ma'am. She was a first-timer. On my shift, anyway, and I been here on overnight for thirteen years."

"How did she seem to you? Had she been drinking? Was she high?"

"She was nervous. A lot of 'em are. Men and women both."

"And what does that generally tell you?"

"That they're doing something they never thought they'd be doing."

Des turned and glanced through the front window at Donna's bungalow across the courtyard. "Did you see him arrive?"

"No, ma'am, I didn't. Got no idea who he was."

"Maybe you saw his car pull in. Think hard, please. This is important."

"I wish I could help you, ma'am, but we're real busy that time of night. Eleven, twelve o'clock is my rush hour. Lots of folks coming and going. Going, mostly. Some drop the key off in here with me. The rest just leave it in the door—the ones who don't want to be seen together by *anybody*, if you know what I mean. Shoot, I must get one suspicious husband in here a week, offering me cash money for the lowdown on his missus."

"And do you give it to him?"

"Hell no," Danny replied indignantly. "Our guests have a right to their privacy. That's why they come here."

Des had happened upon this peculiar phenomenon before—people with tremendous professional pride where you least expected to find them. And why not? Danny Rochin certainly had more class than, say, Dodge Crockett. "That lady got herself pretty beat up in there. You didn't hear them going at it?"

"Well, maybe . . ." Danny cast a longing glance over his shoulder at the office door.

"You want to go take care of what you need to take care of?"

He slipped gratefully into the back room, shutting the door softly behind him. Des could hear a desk drawer slide open and shut. A moment later Danny returned, smelling of whiskey. "I did hear a woman . . . shriek, I guess you could say. And it did come from the direction of that bungalow, number six."

"What time was this, Danny?"

"About one-thirty," he replied. "Look, it may have been nothing. Some couples, they make certain noises when they're . . ." He trailed off uncomfortably, his eyes avoiding hers.

"I'm right with you, honey. Just keep on going."

"So I didn't think much of it—not until I started cleaning out the bungalows this morning and I found her in there. I'm real sorry if I did wrong, ma'am." He seemed genuinely upset. "But I can't go knocking on doors every time somebody lets out a shriek, can I?"

"Don't be so hard on yourself, Danny. There's no way you could have known what was going on in there."

"Do you really mean that?"

"I really do."

"I never had nothing like this happen before on my watch. Worst thing was an attempted rape charge three, four years ago. And that just turned out to be a lover's quarrel."

Outside, Soave and Yolie pulled up alongside of Des's cruiser and got out. Each of them clutching a Bess Eaton take-out coffee container. Each of them wearing an angry glower. Soave's lips were tightly compressed. Boom Boom's chin was stuck out. They'd been spatting. Or they were just getting on each other's nerves. It happened. Partners had to spend a lot of time together. And that's not easy—especially when the case they're working suddenly goes way bad.

Soave seemed relieved to see Des standing there in the office doorway. "Another early start to the day, hunh?" he said, forcing a weary smile onto his face. His eyes were bloodshot, his bulky shoulders slumped with fatigue.

"This could get to be a habit, Rico."

"God, let's hope not."

Yolie couldn't get away from the man fast enough. "I'll check the register, put together a list of guests for us to canvass," she told him hurriedly as she started inside, wearing a bulky yellow cotton sweater that made her entire upper body look huge. "Maybe one of them saw somebody, recognized somebody. . . ." She halted in the doorway, smiling brightly at Des. " 'Morning, girlfriend."

"Back at you, Yolie. You'll find the victim's car behind the bungalow."

"I'm on it."

Des led Soave toward the crime scene, their footsteps crunching on the gravel. As they made their way across the courtyard two more cruisers pulled up, followed by a team of tekkies in a cube van. The uniformed troopers secured the perimeter. The tekkies got busy unloading their gear.

"I swear, that damned Boom Boom is going to drive me crazy," Soave complained. "Right away, she wants to brace our movie star this morning. She's convinced that Esme Crockett's behind all of this. Her and Jeff Wachtell both, since each is the other's alibi."

"That's interesting," Des said. "Mitch went there, too."

Soave glanced at her coldly. "So, what, Berger's backstopping my investigation now?"

Des let that one slide on by. "What did you tell her, Rico?"

"I told her we don't have enough yet. This is *Esme Crockett* we're talking about, not some gang-banger. She can hire the best team of criminal defense lawyers in the world. We have to get all our ducks in a row before we go anywhere *near* her."

Des had to smile at this. When they were a team it was always Soave who was Mr. Great Big Hurry, Des who was Ms. Go Slow.

"So guess what she says back to me."

"Rico, I can't imagine."

"She says I'm not secure enough in my manhood to accept her input. That I feel, quote, sexually threatened by her performance on the job, unquote. *And* that she finds it hard to respect me. Can you believe that?"

"She possesses what my good friend Bella Tillis calls moxie. Got to like that in a girl."

"*You've* got to like it—I don't. She's busting my balls, Des."

"She's hungry, Rico. Better that than a slacker, don't you think?"

He shook his head at her. "Somehow, I *knew* you'd take her side."

"Chump, I'm not taking anyone's side," Des shot back angrily. "And I have an excellent idea—solve your own damned personnel problems, okay?"

"Real sorry, Des," he apologized, reddening. "I didn't mean that. I'm just, I got like two hours of sleep last night and this case is now totally out of hand. I appreciate your input. Really, I do."

They arrived at the bungalow. Soave went inside to take a look at Donna's body on the bathroom floor, his face tightening. "Did you know her?"

"I did. This was a nice lady, Rico. A professional chef. She ran The Works with her husband, Will."

"If she was such a nice lady what was she doing here?"

"Playing in the dirt."

"Who with?"

"I wish I knew. As questions go, that's the big kahuna."

The crime scene technicians wanted to squeeze in there and start taking pictures.

Soave made way for them, moving back outside. "No, Des," he countered. "The big kahuna is how does this fit into the Tito Molina death?"

"You think the two are connected?"

"Don't you? Two violent deaths three days apart in a town this size—they can't be unrelated, can they?"

"I agree, Rico. Although there was no effort to make this one look like a suicide."

"That could have been dictated by circumstances," he suggested, taking a noisy slurp of his coffee.

"Again, I agree. But why did Donna pay for the room with her damned credit card? What kind of way is that to sneak around?"

"Des, I can't get my mind around what's going on here, can you?"

"Not even."

"Tito Molina and Donna Durslag are both dead and there *has* to be a reason why," he mused aloud, smoothing his former mustache. "You know what I keep coming back to? I had me a very wise loot once who had this saying: 'It's never complicated. It's about money or it's about sex. Or it's about money *and* it's about sex. But it's never complicated.'" He paused, grinning at her. "She was a wise person, that loot."

"Still am, wow man. Don't kid yourself."

They stood there in silence for a moment. A car drove by on Boston Post Road, the driver slowing for a look before he sped past.

"Any chance Donna was romantically involved with Tito?"

"I doubt that, Rico. If she was mixed up with Tito then what was she doing here last night? Or, more precisely, *who* was she doing here last night?"

"You have a point there, Des."

"Then again, so do you."

"Which is? . . ."

"That Donna wasn't so nice. She slept around on Will. Mitch did tell me they were having marital problems. Let's say she *was* involved with Tito. Say Tito wanted to break it off, and she didn't, and she killed him in a jealous rage. Maybe someone else, someone close to Tito, figured it out and paid her back last night."

"Like who?" he wondered.

"Then again," she went on, "it's not as if her killer brought a weapon along. He had to use a drawer to beat on her."

"Meaning we could be looking at a spontaneous crime of passion," Soave said, nodding.

Yolie came charging across the courtyard from the office now. She took a look inside the bungalow at Donna, then reemerged, grim-faced.

"Rico, we'd better notify Will," Des said.

"Would you mind delivering the news?"

"Not a problem. I can try to feel him out while I'm there, if you'd like. He might know who her boyfriend is."

"Go for it," he urged her.

Yolie joined them now, hugging herself tightly with her big arms. She was either cold or freaked by the sight of Donna. Both, maybe. "Check it out, are we thinking it was a man who did her?"

Soave shot a blank look at Des, then turned back to Yolie, and said, "Why, where are you going with this?"

"That bed wasn't slept in," Yolie replied. "Her nightie was never worn. They can't say for sure until they swab her, but it sure doesn't *look* like she had sex before she died."

"So he killed her before the two of them got busy." An impatient edge crept into Soave's voice. "So what?"

"So if there's no evidence she had sex with him then there's no evidence it was a *him*," Yolie answered, her own voice getting sharp.

"She's right, Rico," Des agreed. "A reasonably strong woman could have done this."

"Maybe Donna was waiting for her boyfriend to show," Yolie continued, encouraged by Des's backing. "Maybe her boyfriend's jealous woman showed up first and decided to take care of business."

"All possible," Soave conceded. "But how would she know that Donna was shacked up here?"

"Easy," Des said. "She listened in on another phone extension when they made the date. Or intercepted their e-mail. Or maybe she just followed her here."

"*Or* how about if the woman and the boyfriend were in on it together?" Yolie offered eagerly. "What if it's a *couple* we're after—a jealous, desperate woman and her boy toy? Esme and Jeff. First they killed Tito, now Donna."

Soave immediately let loose with an exasperated groan.

Yolie lowered her eyes, pawing at the gravel with her boot. "Well, what do *you* think, Des?"

"Yolie, it's not totally out of left field," Des answered guardedly, not wanting to get caught in between them. "Esme doesn't come across as a major-league schemer, but she *is* an actress and great beauty. For the sake of argument, let's say she could manipulate Jeff into killing Tito for her. It still comes back around to this: What's so damned special about Donna Durslag?"

"Okay, I'm not hearing you," Yolie said, frowning at her.

"Then you need to take a deep breath, count to ten, and listen up," Des explained. "When it came to Tito and other women it was strictly take a number, the line forms on the right. That boy slept with everyone. Esme knew this. In fact, she was plenty busy herself. So say he and Donna *were* sleeping together—why would Esme suddenly care?"

"Maybe Tito wanted to divorce her and marry Donna."

"Get outta here!" Soave erupted. "He's going to dump one of the world's top hotties for that butterball in there? No way!"

"Life is not a P. Diddy video, Rico," snapped Des, who was immediately sorry. Right away, she was caught in their crossfire.

"Now, what's that supposed to mean?" he demanded, flexing his shoulders defensively.

"It means," Yolie shot back, "that love is about more than a tight butt, *dawg.*"

"Hey, I know that, Yolie."

"Sure didn't sound like it, *dawg.*"

"Can we please move on?" Soave said angrily. "Because I'm about solving these murders, not arguing sexual politics with you all morning, okay?"

"Cool by me," Yolie huffed. "I'm not about arguing. That's not what I'm standing here doing."

"Have you got anything local for us?" he asked Des abruptly, clearly desperate to scramble his way back to safer ground.

Des fed them what she'd learned from Mitch about Dodge Crockett walking on the beach with Becca Peck when Tito went over the falls, thereby putting Martine in the same apparent category as Chrissie Huberman: without an alibi. "You might also look into the whereabouts that night of another Chrissie Huberman client, Abby Kaminsky, who happens to be Jeff Wachtell's estranged wife."

Yolie perked right up at the mention of Jeff's name. "What about her?"

"She had a fling with Tito."

"Shut up!" Yolie clapped her hands together excitedly. "I am loving this."

"That's good work, Des," Soave echoed. "Anything else we should know?"

"Not that I can think of," she said tonelessly, twirling her big Smokey the Bear hat in her fingers.

"Okay . . ." Soave narrowed his red-rimmed eyes at her, sensing that she was holding on to something else. They knew each other too damned well. Plus she was not the world's greatest liar.

"Any idea where this Abby is?" Yolie asked.

"Boston, I think. Chrissie will have her exact itinerary. I can check with her if you'd like."

"I want you to do more than that, Des," Soave said. "I want you to go interview her."

"Whoa, Rico, I'm resident trooper, remember? I don't do road trips."

"I know that, but me and Yolie are going to be buried here all day, and I don't have time to run all of this by somebody new. And, look, I'm really up against it, okay? They're going to muscle me out of the way if I don't score in the next twenty-four." So he was feeling the hot breath of the bosses on the back of his neck, Brass City family ties or not. "I need you on this one, Des. You know the players. You've got the game skills. Will you come off of the bench for me?" he pleaded, his voice catching slightly. "I'd be unbelievably grateful. I really, really would. Honestly, I don't know what I'll do if you say no. . . ."

"Damn, Rico, pull on over to the curb and park it, will you?" Des said, flashing a grin at him. "All you had to say was please."

Will Durslag's mother had left him a farmhouse up on Kelton City Road, a bumpy dirt road that forked off Route 156 just past Winston Farms. Des piloted her cruiser along it slowly, realizing that Mitch had been totally right last night.

I am a Dorseteer now.

When put to the test, she had put the interests of the locals ahead of Meriden. She'd seen no vital need for Soave to know that Dodge had sexually abused Esme and so she hadn't shared it. And this was something entirely new for her. She'd heard plenty of shocking news on the job before. But hearing it about people who she knew—this was fresh. So was withholding it from a colleague. Not that any of this should have surprised her. She was well aware now that being resident trooper required a whole lot more moral dexterity than she'd realized going in. Nothing about her new job was black or white. Each day brought a brand-new shade of gray.

The Durslag place was at the very end of Kelton City Road, down a rutted, muddy driveway. It was a rundown circa 1920 two-story farmhouse on three acres of stony ground. The porch sagged. The roof sagged. Everything sagged. There was a jack under one corner of the foundation, and a blue tarp was stretched over a section of the roof that needed replacing. Numerous windowpanes were cracked, the glazing crumbling or missing entirely.

Will and Donna had started paving the driveway at some point, but after they'd done the stretch between the house and the wood-shed they'd stopped. A portable basketball hoop was set up there, and their catering van was parked alongside of it. Will hadn't left yet—for his morning beach walk or work or anywhere else.

Des pulled up behind the van and got out, smelling tangy wood smoke in the chill morning air.

At the sound of her cruiser Will came out the door onto the rotting porch. "Do you know something, Des?" he called out anxiously, running his hands through his lanky hair. Dressed in a sweatshirt and cutoffs, he looked like a college kid home for the summer. "Where is she? I've been up all night worried sick."

"Let's go inside and talk, Will," she said, starting her way up the steps.

"Why, what do you know?"

The front parlor was small, dingy, and damp. There was a Victorian loveseat upholstered in purple silk brocade shot so full of holes that the stuffing was spilling out. There was an armchair with a blanket thrown over it. There were stacks of old magazines and newspapers. There was dust and there were cobwebs. Whatever they were, the Durslags were not tidy housekeepers. Will had a fire going in the old potbellied Franklin stove, which gave off some welcome warmth against the chill in the room.

"I've been calling *everywhere*," he said fretfully. "I even called nine-one-one to see if there'd been an accident on the highway. Where *is* she, damn it?"

Des smelled coffee in the kitchen. "How do you take your coffee, Will?"

"Black, why?"

The kitchen was a whole different scene—bright and sunny and cared for. It was a spacious farmhouse kitchen equipped with a commercial Viking range, Subzero refrigerator, and a massive butcher block island. Well-used copper pots hung from a rack overhead. A paint-splattered dining table was set before sliding glass doors that overlooked the woods. Clearly, this was the room where they spent their time. Des found a cup in the cupboard, filled it from the coffeemaker and came back to the parlor with it, hating what she was about to do to this man.

Will had lifted the lid of the stove and was feeding the fire with stubby logs, his movements edgy and urgent. "I'm sorry it's so cold in here this morning. This house has absolutely no insulation, and this wood's kind of damp. It's been so humid out."

"You'd better sit down, Will."

"How come?" he asked, looking at her warily.

"It's bad news about Donna. I'm sorry to tell you that she's been found murdered."

Will sank slowly down onto the loveseat. "Oh no, this can't be . . . It *can't.*"

"Here, drink this," she said, holding the coffee out to him.

He didn't reach for it. Just sat there, dazed.

"Will? . . ."

Again, he didn't respond. Just sat there goggle-eyed, his breathing quick and shallow. He was a big strapping guy but size meant nothing when it came to shock. At West Point, Des had seen rock-hard specimens of fearless fighting manhood faint dead away over a flu shot.

She darted into the kitchen and rummaged under the sink for some ammonia. Came back, uncapped it and waved it under his nose.

Will barely reacted to the first two whiffs. After the third whiff he recoiled from her, his eyes starting to clear. Then the recognition of the news set back in. "Oh, God," he gulped. "She was my soul mate, my *everything*. What am I going to do?"

"You're going to drink your coffee, and we're going to talk. Come on, take this. The caffeine will help."

Obediently, he reached for it and took a sip, his chest rising and falling. "How did it happen?"

She sat in the armchair facing him and crossed her long legs. "The details aren't pretty."

"I don't care," he said, his eyes searching her face. "Tell me everything. I *need* to know."

"She was found at the Yankee Doodle."

Will's eyes widened in surprise. "The motel?"

"She checked in there last night at about ten o'clock. She was meeting somebody, Will. Whoever he was, he knocked her unconscious and he . . ."

"And he what?" Will demanded.

"Drowned her in the bathtub."

"No, this can't be," Will groaned, rocking back and forth on the sofa. "You've made a mistake. Take another look. It's got to be somebody else, not Donna."

"It's Donna. I saw her with my own two eyes."

He drank some more coffee, clutching the mug tightly in both hands. "Will they have to cut her open? Please tell me they're not going to do that."

"I don't believe that's called for," Des replied. "Have you got someone who can stay with you, Will? You shouldn't be alone at a time like this."

"I have no one," he replied woodenly. "Just Donna—and now she's gone."

"May I use your phone?"

He didn't respond. Barely seemed to hear her.

Des went in the kitchen and called Mitch, who promised he'd be right over. Then she returned to Will and sat back down. "Mitch is going to hang out here for a little while, okay?"

"Who did this to her, Des?" Will demanded suddenly. His shock had given way to raw anger. It often happened this way. "Who murdered my Donna?"

"We don't know yet. You can help us out. If you're up to it, I mean."

"Of course, but how?"

"By answering some questions. I have to warn you, this might be rough."

"You can ask me anything. I don't give a damn. I've spent the whole night going crazy. She didn't come home. She never, ever did that before."

Des took out her notepad and pen. "Do you have any idea where else she was last night?"

"She had her meeting of the Dorset Merchants Association. They get together for dinner twice a month."

Will's mention of the Merchants Association set off a faint flicker of recognition in the back of Des's mind. "Where do they usually meet?"

"At the Clam House. There's a back room for club meetings." The Clam House was a seafood restaurant adjacent to the Dorset Marina, popular with boaters and tourists. "It usually runs from seven until about nine."

"Did she typically go without you?"

"Yeah, the association was her deal. We've always divided up the workload according to our strengths. Donna was good at working the room. She liked it, even. Me, I'm a cooker. I belong in the kitchen with my pots and pans."

"Were you expecting her home after that?"

"Not directly, no. She had to meet somebody about a catering gig on her way back."

"Any idea who that was?"

Will furrowed his brow in thought. "She may have told me their name, but I'm drawing a total blank. Things are always just so hectic. It was a cocktail party. A bon voyage thing. That's all I remember."

"Where did she keep track of her appointments? Could she have input it somewhere?"

Will smiled very faintly. "No, no, she hates . . . she hated computers. But it ought to be written down in her date book. It's black leather."

"This would be in her shoulder bag?"

Will nodded his head, swallowing.

"Okay, good," Des said, knowing full well that it wouldn't be written down. That there was no catering gig. It was simply the little white lie she'd told Will to buy herself enough time to stop off and screw her boyfriend. "What time did you get home last night, Will?"

"I rolled in about nine-thirty. I was expecting her by ten, ten-thirty. We always stayed in touch by cell phone. If she knew she was going to be later than that she would have called. I tried calling her about eleven. When she didn't answer I started to worry. I phoned our late man, Rich Graybill, to see if she'd stopped by The Works. Rich is usually there until about midnight, cleaning up and getting things set up for the morning. But he said he hadn't seen her."

"Tell me more about him. What's his story?"

"Who, Rich? He's a young guy, good guy. Lives with his girl-friend, Kimberly. She's one of our pastry chefs."

"Her last name?"

"Fiore."

"What did you do after that, Will?"

"Paced around a whole lot," he confessed. "Kept calling her cell phone. Kept getting more and more worried. Like I said, I called the state police to see if there had been any accidents. I can't even remember what time I did that. . . ."

"Not important." And even if it were they would have logged his call.

"At one point I actually decided to go look for her at The Works. I thought *maybe* she'd decided to get an early start on tomorrow's baking. Which makes no sense, because if that's where she was she would have called me. But I was just so desperate. I couldn't just sit here, you know?"

"Yes, I do."

"I left her a note on the kitchen counter in case she got home while

I was out." He loped into the kitchen and returned with it, gazing down at it as if it were the last piece of concrete evidence that Donna and their marriage and their life had ever existed. Gently, he placed it on the coffee table for Des to see. He'd scrawled it in pencil on a piece of lined yellow paper: "Don-Don—I'm out looking for you. Where are you? Be home soon. Love, Willie Boy"

"When I got back here, she still wasn't home," he added quietly. "And I've been sitting up ever since."

"Will, there are some things I need to ask that might seem pretty cold and hurtful. But I need to ask them, and you need to answer them. If you can, that is."

"I understand." He sighed, flopping back down on the loveseat. "Fire away."

"Was Donna involved with someone else?"

Will glared at her, his jaw clenching. For a second, he looked like a vengeful Viking warrior. Then he relaxed, his gaze dropping to the worn rag rug at Des's feet. "We had our troubles," he admitted. "All couples do. Especially when they're together twenty-four hours a day. But I swear to you, I wasn't sneaking around on Donna with another woman. That's the God's honest truth."

"I understand." Des was patient with him. The man was blown away. "And what about Donna? Was she seeing someone?"

He looked up at her miserably. "You want to know if she had a boyfriend—the short answer is yes."

"Who is he, Will?"

"No idea. She never told me. In fact, we never so much as discussed him. But I knew. There were these hang-ups on the phone all the time when I'd answer it. There were the errands she'd run during the afternoon—she'd be gone for an extra hour without any explanation, and be real anxious to take a shower as soon as she got home. I'd notice scratches and bruises on her body that she wasn't real specific about explaining. She . . . she acted different, smelled different, *was* different. I don't know what else to say, except that when you've been married to someone for a while you can just tell."

"How long had this been going on?"

He shrugged his broad shoulders. "Three, four months."

"Her not coming home last night," Des said. "Did it occur to you that—?"

"That she was with *him*? Sure it did. Except that she never, ever did that to me before. She never just disappeared for a whole night. I mean, she didn't want me to know about it, okay? Me or anyone else. Dorset's a small town. Everyone knows you. If you're sneaking around in this place, you have to be incredibly careful." Will reached for his half-empty coffee cup. "One other thought did cross my mind," he admitted, sipping from it. "I thought maybe . . . that she'd run off with him. Left me for good. Our bank has one of those automated eight-hundred numbers you can call day or night to find out your current balance. I called it to see if she'd withdrawn anything from our joint checking account."

"Had she?"

"No."

"You say you kept a joint checking account. Who paid the monthly bills?"

"Me, usually."

"So you would typically see her credit card statements?"

"I guess," he replied, frowning. "Why?"

"Will, Donna paid for the bungalow at the Yankee Doodle with her Visa card. Is this something that would have caught your eye when you sat down to pay the bills?"

"Most likely. I mean, yeah. Definitely."

"What would you have thought when you saw it?"

"Well, I know what sort of a reputation the place has, if that's what you're asking me."

"Maybe she was planning to intercept next month's statement and pay it herself. Does that seem reasonable?"

"Des, why does *any* of this matter?"

"Because her behavior last night wasn't typical, that's why. Like you said, she'd been so careful to hide this affair from you, and yet she showed up at the Yankee Doodle at ten o'clock. She *had* to know she'd get home late enough to set off alarm bells with you. Now, why did she do that? And why didn't she pay cash?"

"Maybe she was *out* of cash," he replied helplessly. "Maybe she was feeling horny and reckless. Who knows, she may have been drunk as a skunk."

"Did she have a problem with alcohol?"

"No! I'm just trying to . . ." Will broke off into heavy silence. "I honestly don't know what she was doing there at that hour, okay?"

"Okay, Will," Des said gently.

She heard the rumble of an engine outside now and went to the window. Mitch's old plum-colored pickup truck was bouncing its way up the dirt drive. She went out onto the sagging porch to greet him, her gallant, uncombed love, her pudgy white knight in his frayed oxford button-down and shlumpy khaki shorts.

"How is he?" he asked, giving her a quick bear hug.

"Not so good."

"God, I am hating this," he murmured glumly. Then he took a deep breath and went charging in the front door with a smile forced onto his face, Des on his heel. "Whoa, it's like a meat locker in here, Will," he exclaimed, rubbing his hands together. "Your place is just as bad as mine. Zero insulation, am I right?"

Will scarcely seemed to notice Mitch. Just sat slumped there on the loveseat, lost in his grief.

Mitch clomped over to the stove to warm his hands, glancing at his friend uncertainly. "I'm really sorry about Donna."

The mention of her name seemed to rouse Will. "Thanks, man," he said hoarsely. "How . . . was the beach this morning?"

"I didn't walk," Mitch replied.

"Yeah, me neither." Will ran a hand over his face, his eyes filling with tears. "I don't think I'm going to make it, Mitch. I really don't."

Mitch came over and put his hand on Will's shoulder. "That's exactly how I felt when I lost Maisie. I know it doesn't seem like it right now, Will, but you're going to make it. It'll get a little better every day, I promise you."

"I can't even *see* tomorrow," Will confessed. "All I can see is that I'm all alone. Donna was my *everything* . . . my best friend. My soul mate. My partner."

Mitch drew back from him, startled.

Des couldn't imagine why. Perhaps he had once said those very words himself about Maisie. "I'll be heading out now, Will," she spoke up.

Will nodded absently, saying nothing to her.

She motioned for Mitch to join her out on the porch.

He did, closing the door softly behind him. "Whew, this is not going to be a lot of fun."

"Not even close," she said, putting her big hat back squarely on her head. "Just wanted to let you know I'm heading up to Boston now."

"You going to talk to Abby?"

"Yeah."

"Give her my regards. And, hey, if you go through Cambridge on your way back, stop at East Coast Grill and pick up a large quantity of their eastern North Carolina shredded pork, okay? We can have it for dinner when you get home. Trust me, it's outstanding."

She cocked her head at him curiously. "Man, how can you think about barbecue at a time like this?"

"I'm not like you. Food is all I think about when I'm upset, remember?"

"That's not something I forget, believe me."

"East Coast Grill," he repeated. "It's on Cambridge Street, just off of Prospect. Anyone will be able to give you directions. And, please, whatever you do, don't take that damned Ninety-five the whole way up. Get off at exit seventy-four, take Three-ninety-five through Norwich and then change to the—"

"Mitch, I *know* how to get to Boston from here."

"Promise me you won't take Ninety-five," he said urgently.

"Why is my route so damned important?"

"Because there's a fatality on that highway at least three times a week and I love you and I don't want to lose you."

She utterly melted. Never had a man made her go gooey the way this one did. She leaned over and kissed him softly on the cheek. "Okay, I promise."

"I don't get it, Des," he said, shaking his head in bewilderment. "Why would someone want to kill Donna? What the hell's going on here?"

"Boyfriend," she sighed, "I wish I knew."

As Des steered her cruiser back down Route 156 she gave Yolie a heads-up on her cell phone about Donna's so-called catering gig and her black leather date book. Des also fed her the name of the Durslags' late-shift man, Rich Graybill. Yolie agreed that he was definitely someone worth talking to. She said she'd also hook up with his girlfriend, Kimberly Fiore, to see if Kimberly backed up what time Rich got home.

Before Des got onto the highway for Boston she pulled in at the Acar's minimart and got out to fill up her gas tank.

Nuri came out at once to do it for her, dressed in his customary white shirt and slacks. "Good morning to you, Trooper," he said politely. His eyes were not nearly so polite. Once again, they were working their way over and around every single inch of her body. "Shall I fill it up?"

"Yes, please," she responded, shuddering slightly. She felt positively creeped by this man. She spotted Nema inside through their sparkling new front window and waved to her. Nema waved back, smiling broadly. "Have you had any further problems, Mr. Acar?"

"Not a one, as I anticipated," he replied, starting in on her windshield with a soapy squeegee. "Everyone has been most supportive. Most particularly my fellow members of the Dorset Merchants Association, who have agreed to offer a cash reward of one thousand dollars to anyone who can provide useful information regarding the identity of these vandals."

Des leaned against the side of the cruiser with her arms crossed. "You folks had your monthly meeting last night, am I right?"

"That is correct," he said, clearing the soap from the window with careful, precise movements. "At the Clam House. The surf-and-turf combo is particularly delicious, in my opinion."

"Did you happen to see Donna Durslag there?"

"I sat right next to her," he said easily. No hesitation or tinge of color to his cheeks, no nervous glance over his shoulder at his wife. "Very nice lady, Mrs. Durslag. So full of personality. Jolly is an appropriate word for her, is it not?"

"So she seemed in good spirits to you?"

"She did. Very upbeat and pleasant."

"What did you two talk about?"

"Nothing very specific. Local business concerns. Tourism and so forth."

"Do you remember what she had on?"

Now Nuri Acar glanced at her curiously, aware that her interest in Donna was more than casual. "A white dress, I believe. It was not anything fancy."

"Like a peasant dress?"

"If you wish."

"Did she happen to say anything about where she was going afterward?"

"I don't believe so, no." Nuri dumped the squeegee back in its soapy tub and returned to the gas pump nozzle, gripping it tightly as he finished filling her tank. "Why do you wish to know so much about Mrs. Durslag?"

"What did *you* do after the meeting broke up, Mr. Acar?"

"I came back here to help Nema. We stay open until ten."

"What time did you get here?"

"Perhaps nine-fifteen," he said, as the nozzle clunked to a halt. Her tank was full. "That will be twenty-two dollars even, please."

"You came straight here?" she asked, handing him her credit card.

Nuri took it from her, scowling. "What is the point of this, young lady?"

"Mr. Acar, if you have anything at all to tell me, it'll go down a whole lot better if you do it before rather than after."

"After *what*, may I ask?"

"After I say out loud that Donna Durslag was murdered last night."

Nuri's eyes widened. "My goodness gracious. By who?"

"By her boyfriend," Des replied, raising her chin at him. "Whoever he is."

"I was not involved with that woman," he shot back. "And I resent your insinuation."

"I insinuated nothing. You asked me a question, I answered it."

"How dare you doubt my veracity?" he demanded, highly indignant. Or staging one hell of an imitation, especially for someone who was so overtly smarmy. "I am a respectable businessman. A married man. How dare you?"

"I simply have a job to do, Mr. Acar."

"Then you have a filthy, horrible job. A proper young lady would not hold such a job. She would not." Glowering, he turned on his heel and sped inside to run her credit card. Service without a smile.

Des got back in her cruiser and waited calmly for him to return.

When he did, he refused to make eye contact with her. She was too far beneath him.

"I carry a pooper-scooper, Mr. Acar," she explained as she signed the credit card slip. "I'm the girl who cleans up after the other human beings. You're right—sometimes it's not a very nice job. We're not a very nice animal. In fact we're the cruelest, most thoughtless animal on the planet. I try not to let it get to me, but, wow, some mornings it just turns me all upside down." She tore off her copy and handed his back to him, treating him to her biggest smile. "You have yourself a good one, okay?"

Abby Kaminsky lived plenty large when she was on tour.

The best-selling children's author had herself a condo-sized suite on the ninth floor of the highly choice Four Seasons Hotel on Boylston Street, complete with a drop-dead view of the lush green Public Garden, the Common, and Beacon Hill. It was a bright, crisp New England afternoon, the sky a deep blue, the clouds puffy and white. Off in the distance, the Charles River shimmered in the sunlight.

"It's like I told you on the phone," Abby chattered gaily as she showed Des in. "I am insanely busy today. I can only give you a few minutes. I have two bookstore appearances, a radio call-in show, and then I'm talking fish with the *Zoom* kids." Jeff Wachtell's estranged wife was a bustling, impeccably groomed little thing with a frosted head of architecturally designed, stay-put hair that made her seem a bit taller than she really was, which was barely five feet tall. "A stylist will be here in twenty minutes to make me gorgeous. It's just a really tight, tight day."

"Understood," Des said. "I appreciate you squeezing me in."

There was a fruit basket and a bouquet of flowers in the living room. There was a portable wardrobe rack full of Armani linen suits and silk blouses. There was a life-sized cardboard cutout of Abby clutching her new Carleton Carp book under a balloon caption that read: *Go Fish!*

And there was a goateed no-neck seated on the sofa, drinking a diet soda and staring at a rerun of *Baywatch* on the television.

"This is my escort," Abby said. "Frankie, say hello to Resident Trooper Mitry. She's come here all the way from Dorset, Connecticut."

Frankie gave Des a brief nod, barely bothering to look her way. He was too busy maintaining his cultivated air of bad-assdom.

One whiff and Des could smell yard all over him. "Glad to know you, Frankie," she said pleasantly. "Your last name is? . . ."

He glowered in silence for a long moment before he said, "Ramistella."

"You work out of New York?"

"Bay Ridge."

"What's your address?"

He gave it to her, peering up at Des now with eyes that were heavy lidded and immensely hostile. "Why so many questions?"

"Behave, Frankie," Abby ordered him. "She's just doing her job. You need to leave us alone now, okay? Go take a walk or something. And have the car ready for me downstairs at two sharp."

He got up very deliberately, turned off the TV, and started for the door.

"Oh, hey, cookie?" Abby called after him. "Take my cutout, will you?"

Grimacing with disdain, Frankie carried the cardboard Abby out of the room under his arm, shutting the door softly behind him.

"Can I get you anything from the minibar, Trooper?" Abby asked her. "Water, juice?"

"I'm all set, thanks."

Abby sat on the sofa and kicked off her little pumps, one stocking leg folded under her, a box of Cocoa Pebbles kids' cereal cradled in her lap. She reached inside for a handful and munched on it. "Want some? What am I saying? Of course you don't. Pebbles are my own thing," she explained merrily. "Can't help myself. Now what can I do for you?"

Des took off her hat and sat in an armchair across the coffee table from her. "You can tell me where you've been the past couple of nights."

"Sure, I can do that," Abby said easily, chomping on her cereal. "Only let me ask you something first—why do you want to know this?"

"Because we're trying to ascertain the whereabouts of anyone and everyone who was involved with Tito Molina."

"Oh, sure, I get it," she said, nodding her head of hair. "You found out that I had a little, a-a *thing* with Tito. Did Chrissie tell you? No, wait, it was your boyfriend, wasn't it? It was Mitch."

Des didn't bother to answer her.

"It's okay, Crissie's told me all about Mitch and you. And now that I've met you both I must say you are the last two people in the world I'd guess would *ever* end up in the feathers together. I mean, talk about an odd couple. You're black, he's Jewish. He's a critic, you're a cop. You're skinny, he's . . . not." Abby wagged a manicured finger at Des, her big blue eyes gleaming. "You know, you two would make a terrific pair of fish."

Des let out a laugh. "I'll make sure to pass that one along to him."

"No, no, I'm serious. I've been wanting to get more racial for some time. The inner city kids need role models. And you're so tall and gorgeous and self-assured. Seriously, I am adoring this. May I use you?"

"I can't imagine anything more flattering—just as long as you don't name me something like Hallie Butts."

"Cookie, I am *stealing* that!" Abby squealed with delight. "You are so lucky, you know that? Mitch is one you'll never, ever have to worry about. Trust me, I personally road tested him."

"Road tested him?"

"I came on to him like gangbusters yesterday," she confided, girl to girl. "Did everything but dive under the table and go for his zipper with my teeth. See, when I'm tour I can get a little, you know, horny. But I could not generate so much as a mild whiff of interest out of him. That one is a keeper, believe me."

"Oh, I believe you," Des said, wondering what America's parents would think if they found out that their kids' favorite author was a little bit nutty and a whole lot slutty. "So about your activities these past couple of nights . . ."

"Okay, sure." Abby folded her little hands in her lap and took a deep breath, collecting herself. "I got home to New York from my tour the day Tito died. I was on the six P.M. flight from Los Angeles." She gave Des the name of the airline and what time it had left L.A.

"Was Frankie with you?"

"He sure was. I can't travel alone anymore. Too many kids want to talk to me and touch me. Puh-leeze . . ." Abby shivered, fanning herself with fluttering fingers. "A limo met us at the airport to bring me home. Frankie helped me shlep all of my stuff upstairs—I had to take a ton of clothes."

"Where do you live?"

She gave Des her address on Riverside Drive. It was a doorman building on the corner of West Ninety-first Street.

"What time did you get settled in?"

"Maybe eight."

"Did Frankie stick around?"

"No, he took the limo on home."

"And how did you spend your evening?"

Abby got up suddenly and padded over to the window in her stocking feet, silent as a kitten on the plush carpet. "I realize this is going to sound terrible, but I can't lie to you because I happen to be the soul of honesty—except for when I'm not. You do believe me, don't you?"

"I really couldn't say. So far, you've told me jack."

"You're absolutely right," Abby admitted, letting out a nervous laugh. "The truth is, I was in Dorset. I-I've been in Dorset a lot lately."

Des leaned forward in her chair, watching Abby closely. "Doing what?"

Abby went over to the minibar and pulled out a small bottle of Perrier and opened it. "Sitting parked outside of Jeffrey's condo in my car," she replied, taking a dainty sip.

"What are you, stalking him?"

"God, no. I'm not parked out there with an Uzi or anything. Just a box of Cocoa Pebbles and a pair of b-binoculars." She paused, reddening. "Okay, maybe I'd better explain myself."

"Maybe you'd better."

"I just . . . I wanted to see for myself who he's sleeping with. I need to know. And I am so humiliated to admit this out loud to you that I could just about crawl under that sofa. I mean, how pathetic am I? But it's the truth. I've been sitting in my damned car every night, watching that little weasel entertain one gorgeous woman after another and crying my poor baby blues out."

"Have you been in direct contact with him?" Des asked, shoving her horn-rimmed glasses up her nose.

Abby returned to the sofa and sat back down. "Define direct contact."

"Well, does he know you've been watching him?"

"*God*, he'd better not. I would just die if he found out."

"You haven't spoken to him?"

"Of course not. Why would I?"

"Because you still love him, that's why."

"I do *not* still love him," Abby said angrily.

"Tie that bull outside, as my good friend Bella Tillis likes to say. A girl does not sit in her car all night with a pair of binoculars unless she feels the love."

"Okay, so maybe I feel it a little," Abby admitted reluctantly. "That's really beside the point."

"And the point is? . . ."

"That I'm telling you the truth. Check with my garage on Broadway and Ninety-second. They'll tell you what time I took my car out and when I brought it back. It's a black Mercedes station wagon. I've practically been living in it since I got back. Night after night I sit there—until dawn, when I drive back. What a rotten drive that is, too."

"Have you been making it alone?"

"Of course. Who else would sit there with me all night like some nut?"

"Frankie would."

"I am not involved with Frankie. We *were*, very briefly. But not anymore. I've been alone. Just little me."

Which meant that Abby Kaminsky had no one to vouch for her, Des reflected. No one who could say she hadn't pushed Tito Molina off that cliff. True, she was a tiny thing. But the element of surprise can add a good deal of muscle. And that granite ledge was plenty slick. Only, what about Donna Durslag? Why would Abby want to see *her* dead?

"You do believe me, don't you?" Abby asked, watching her uncertainly.

"I don't disbelieve you," Des responded. "How about you tell me what you saw while you were parked out there?"

"Sure, okay, I can do that. I saw, let's see, I saw Esme Crockett show up there the first night."

"This is the night Tito died?"

"Correct. She got there at around midnight. I could see her and

Jeffrey sucking face through the kitchen window—until he turned the lights out and they did God knows what unspeakable things to each other in the dark. She left at about four in the morning."

Which backed up what Esme and Jeff had said. "And the next night?"

"Her mother showed up at around eleven."

"Did Martine stay the night?"

"She was there less than ten minutes," Abby said gleefully. "Tossed a major hissy fit on the front porch. She even threw a flower pot at Jeffrey."

"She'd found out he was two-timing her with Esme," Des ventured.

"You got that right, cookie. And what a mouth that bitch has on her. She's standing out there screaming at the top of her lungs about how she's going to make a bow tie out of his balls. Unbelievable! Then she took off in a huff."

"And what did you see last night?"

"Last night I was here in Boston," Abby said hastily. "But . . . why are you asking?"

"Because someone else got murdered last night, that's why."

"Really, who?"

"Donna Durslag."

"Oh, sure. She owned The Works with her husband."

"You knew her?"

"By name. Jeffrey rents his space from them."

"So you're saying you *weren't* watching his condo last night, am I right?"

"That's right," Abby said, lowering her eyes.

"Don't disrespect me, girl. If you took your town car out of the hotel parking garage last night, I'll know. If you rented a different car, I'll know. If you so much as walked out that lobby door, I'll know. I have the means. I have the skills. I have the—"

"Okay, okay, no need to get all huffy on me."

"I do *not* get huffy."

"I *was* at Jeffrey's last night," Abby conceded. "I was staked out just like the other two nights—from eleven till about four. I took the town car."

"Why lie to me about it?"

"Because I'm embarrassed," she wailed plaintively. "Wouldn't you be embarrassed? I mean, God, this is *so* humiliating."

"Who visited Jeffrey last night?"

"No one, I swear."

"Did he go out?"

Abby shook her head. "He was there by himself all night."

"Did you think about knocking on his door?"

"Not a chance."

"Why not, was Frankie with you?"

"Look, I'd rather not involve Frankie in this, okay?"

"That's not an answer."

There was a tapping at the suite door now.

Abby let her breath out, clearly relieved by the interruption. "Would you mind getting that, cookie?"

Des got up and went to the door and opened it.

A frail young man with a concave chest and a two-day stubble of beard stood out in the hallway clutching a pair of battered metal carrying cases. "I'm here for Abby," he announced.

"Come in, Gregory!" Abby called to him as she bustled over toward the desk. "I'm afraid I'll have to cut this off now, Trooper. Gregory has to do my mouth."

"That's fine," Des said. "I got what I came for. Where will you be tonight?"

Abby frowned at her. "Right here in Boston, why?"

"Just checking. You're a happening little girl. Liable to turn up anywhere."

"Well, I'll be here. That's the truth. And I always tell the truth."

"Except for when you don't," Des said, smiling at her. "Right, I heard that."

One of the doormen down in the lobby gave Des directions to the

East Coast Grill. Her cruiser was double-parked out front. She got in and called Yolie on her cell phone to tell her what she didn't want to hear—that Abby Kaminsky backed up Esme and Jeff's story.

"Did you believe her?" Yolie asked, sounding thoroughly dejected.

"Yolie, I honestly don't know. She's rich, wiggy, in love. Anything's possible. What have you got?"

"So far, not a damned thing. None of the guests at the Yankee Doodle saw our boy come or go. And, Lordy, were they not happy to be questioned. Kimberly Fiore backs up her boyfriend, Rich Graybill. He got home from his late shift at The Works by midnight. Word, we are *nowhere*," she grumbled at Des.

"Hey, we'll lick this, Yolie. You keep that chin up for me, okay?"

"Girl, I am *all* about that," Yolie vowed before she hung up.

Des started up her cruiser and glanced in her rearview mirror, spotting big Frankie. He was seated at the wheel of the black town car parked behind her in the hotel's loading area, glowering at her with as much menace as he could muster. Definitely a yard face. The man had done time. She was positive.

As she pulled away, Des ran a check on him on her digital radio. She got her answer before she'd made it across the Charles into Cambridge on the Massachusetts Avenue Bridge. Frank Ramistella had wriggled his way out of two assault charges when he was in his late teens, then served three years of New York state time for armed robbery. As far as the law knew, he had been clean for the past six years.

All well and good, Des reflected as he steered her way toward Central Square. The man was still hired muscle. And he was way into Abby. He'd do what that little blond asked him to, even if it meant pushing Tito Molina off a cliff. But that still begged the question about Donna. What possible reason could Abby have for wanting Donna dead?

This question Des could not answer.

And it troubled her big-time. Actually, this whole case did. Because the more she learned the more confused she got. In truth, she wasn't getting any closer to figuring this one out at all.

In truth, her damned fool head was reeling.

CHAPTER 13

"UM, OKAY, TELL ME again why we're sitting here like this?"

"Because I have a feeling, that's why," Mitch explained to her for the umpteenth time.

"You have a feeling," Des repeated from next to him in the darkness. She was still in uniform, her collar opened, sleeves turned back.

"I do. I have a definite, undeniable feeling."

"Oh, it's undeniable, all right."

They were sitting in his pickup a hundred yards up Turkey Neck Road from Dodge and Martine Crockett's driveway, their bellies full of barbecue. Carriage lanterns framed the driveway entrance, bathing it in a dim, golden glow. Across the darkened meadow, lights were on inside the house. It was just past eleven. Warm, sticky air had moved in from the south as the afternoon had given way to evening, bringing low clouds and fog with it. Now it was humid and still and the cicadas were whirring. In the distance, Mitch could hear the foghorn on the Old Saybrook Lighthouse.

"What's more, you need my help," he added. "You've got two murders that don't seem to connect with each other except for the simple fact that they must. And you're totally flummoxed by it— you, Soave, Yolie, all of you."

"Well, you're not wrong there," she growled at him.

"Would you like to know why you're so flummoxed?"

"One way or the other, I have a feeling you're going to tell me."

"Because all three of you think inside the box. I'm not being critical, mind you. I'm just saying that you're encumbered by the rules and procedures of your job, and I'm not. This allows me to function as a freer thinker. You might even think of me, well, as a visionary."

Des reached over in the dark and squeezed his hand. "Baby, I'm not going to have to hit you, am I?"

"What you'll be doing, before this night is over, is thanking me."

"Mitch? . . ."

"Yes, Des?"

"*What* damned feeling?!"

"That we've let our heads get turned by all of this sex. We've got so many Dorseteers hopping in and out of bed with each other that we don't know who loves who, who loathes who, who might want who dead. . . . Are you with me so far?"

"You're talking, I'm listening."

"Okay, good. We've got Abby, Chrissie, and Martine all without alibis for the night Tito died. Two of them had been romantically involved with him. The third was his mother-in-law. Now, we don't know why Donna Durslag had to die. Therefore we have no idea which one of those three had any interest in killing her. But here's something that we *do* know—that Dodge Crockett is a sick, bad, morally depraved guy."

"I won't disagree with you there."

"Let's say that this qualifies him to be our prime murder suspect, okay?"

"That's a bit of a leap, but go ahead and run with it."

"We know that he's home alone tonight. He told me so this morning. So all we have to do now is wait and he'll show his hand."

"What hand?"

"Something is going to happen tonight," Mitch declared with total certainty. "I'm telling you, I can feel it."

"Whoa, time out, cowboy—*this* is your feeling?"

"Well, yeah. Put yourself in his shoes, Des. It's not as if a perverted sociopath like Dodge is going to spend his night watching *Send Me No Flowers* on American Movie Classics. Not that it's a bad movie, mind you. Rock Hudson and Doris Day were an underrated comedy team, and Paul Lynde absolutely goes to town as a funeral home director who loves his work just a bit too—"

"Okay, I *am* going to have to hit you."

"Someone is going to visit Dodge tonight. Or he's going to go see someone."

"And? . . ."

"And that's our chance to find out what he's really up to and who he's up to it with. If he leaves, we follow him. If someone comes by, we tiptoe our way to the house and put our noses to the glass. It's smart, it's simple, and it'll work. What do you say, Master Sergeant, am I right or am I right?"

Des sat there in the darkened silence for a long moment before she said, "You do know that this particular move is straight out of the Hardy Boys, don't you?"

"Maybe it is," he admitted. "But it was a darned effective maneuver when they'd exhausted their other options. Besides, Frank and Joe cracked a number of Fenton's toughest cases."

"You do know that was fiction, don't you—for little boys?"

A possum moseyed its way out of the brush and up the Crocketts' driveway, its long, slinky tail trailing along behind it. Truly one of God's ugliest creatures, Mitch observed. Right up there with the lowly woodchuck. Just one of the many new things he had learned since he moved to Dorset. "You think this is a stupid idea, is that it?"

"Actually, I'm sitting here thinking you make a shocking amount of sense."

"So what's the problem?"

"For starters, I think you have you a personal vendetta thing going on. You admired Dodge and he's turned out to be a total sleaze and now you want him to fry. Your judgment is clouded, Mitch. That's not to say I disagree with you. The man is bad news, and he should pay for what he's done to Esme and Becca and who knows who else. But that doesn't necessarily make him a murderer. Just a sleaze."

Mitch considered this for a moment. "Okay, what else?"

"I also think there's an exceptionally good chance that we're going to sit here until four in the morning and have nothing to show for it except stiff necks."

It *was* awfully quiet. They hadn't seen so much as single passing motorist since they'd been parked there.

"Maybe, but at least we're together." He leaned over and kissed her smooth cheek. "You don't mind that part, do you?"

"No, baby, I don't mind," she said, her own knowing lips finding the sweet spot under his ear, the one that turned him into a quivering mass of man Jell-O.

"Did I remember to thank you for stopping at East Coast Grill?" he murmured, finding her mouth with his.

"Three times . . . This makes four."

"I'm overwhelmed. I've never had a woman bring me pork before."

"If I'd known you were this easy I'd have done it a lot sooner," she said, groaning softly. "But you'd better pass me some of that coffee. I've been up since before dawn."

Mitch poured her some from the thermos he'd brought, thinking about what she'd said. Because she wasn't wrong. Not one bit.

He did want it to be Dodge.

They'd had words that morning at Will's house. Mitch hadn't needed to stay there with Will for long. As soon as Des took off the poor guy headed straight for the phone to call his father figure. Dodge's arrival was Mitch's official cue to leave. Mitch was in no mood to hang around with that man.

Still, their paths crossed out on the front porch as Dodge came bounding up the steps, looking all tanned, virile, and fit, a manila folder tucked under one arm. "Mitch, I'm so glad you're here," he said, face etched with concern. "This is just such an awful business. Why would anyone want to hurt Donna?"

"I really don't know, Dodge."

"How is our boy holding up?"

"Our boy is pretty shook."

"We missed you out there this morning," he said, eyeing Mitch carefully. "The tide was out. It was beautiful."

"I couldn't make it," Mitch said, rather stiffly.

"Sure, sure." Dodge seemed stung by Mitch's chilly response. "Oh, hey, I've got something for you," he said, holding the manila folder out to him. "This is the application for that teen mentoring program over at the Youth Services Bureau. They'd love to have you if you can spare an hour a week."

Mitch reached for it gingerly. He did not actually wish to touch anything that Dodge had touched. In fact, he felt a form of visceral revulsion just standing on the same porch with him.

After an awkward silence Dodge said, "I'm sorry you had to walk in on my . . . private moment with Becca yesterday."

Mitch said nothing. He knew that the older man was waiting for him to put his mind at ease. But Mitch didn't particularly feel like doing that.

"I can tell that you're still upset," Dodge persisted.

"Dodge, I really don't want to talk about this right now. Why don't you go inside? Will needs you."

"It's wasn't what it looked like, Mitch. Becca and I have a real history together. We go way back."

"Kind of like you and Esme?" Mitch snapped, immediately regretting it. He should have kept his mouth shut.

Dodge didn't lose his composure. He simply looked Mitch straight in the eye and said, "I don't know what you've been hearing, or from who, but I love my daughter, and I would never, ever hurt her. Anyone who says otherwise is a liar."

"You never touched her?"

"I'd like to have an opportunity to discuss this further with you, Mitch. Martine will be with Esme tonight. I'll be home all evening. We can have a drink on the terrace and talk it through, okay? Maybe by then you will have cooled off."

"Dodge, one thing keeps puzzling me—why'd you tell me that Martine was having an affair?"

"Because she was," he said. "And because you and I are friends. Or at least I thought we were."

"Okay, right, I get it now," Mitch said, nodding his head. "*I'm* the one who has the problem."

"Mitch, we all do things that we don't understand and we can't control," Dodge offered as explanation. "Things that we feel bad about. That's what makes us human beings. Our only real failure is when we don't make the effort to understand one another. Will you at least try? Will you do that much for me?"

"Sure, I'll do that much, Dodge," he replied grimly, seized by the horrifying certainty that his friend had just confessed to killing Tito Molina and Donna Durslag.

And then Mitch had said good-bye to him and headed home to prowl Big Sister's tidal pools alone with his hands in his pockets. He pruned his tomato plants, mowed his lawn, picked wild blackberries and beach plums. He was fine as long as he kept moving. Until at long last Des returned to him from Boston, one-quart tub of shredded pork in hand.

And now they sat there together in his truck, Des sipping coffee and stabbing holes in his theory. "What about the fact that Dodge has an alibi for when Tito was murdered?"

"His alibi is Becca," Mitch pointed out. "I don't mean to sound cold, because I like Becca, but if Dodge can convince her to get down on all fours with a bag over her head, he can convince her to fib for him."

"I'll give you that one," she responded. "But answer me this—why would Dodge want to kill Tito?"

"Maybe he didn't. Maybe it was the other way around. Let's say Tito found out about Dodge and Esme. Maybe Esme told Tito, okay? And let's say Tito called Dodge out on it. Think about what Tito told me at my house that night. He said he'd gotten himself into something bad, something he couldn't get out of. This certainly fits the bill, doesn't it? *'The hangman says it's time to let her fly,'* Maybe Tito was telling me that Dodge was about to pay for his sins."

"Except that Dodge got the best of him up there," she mused aloud. "Is that what you're saying?"

"Well, why not? There's no actual proof that it was a woman who pushed Tito off of that cliff, is there?"

"Not one bit," Des said. "Only answer me this, boyfriend. Why did Dodge turn right around and kill Donna? What's the connection?"

"Maybe there isn't one. Maybe it was just some rough sex that got out of hand. It happens."

"No sale. You can't tell me that he *accidentally* happened to kill his second person in three days."

"Look, I saw with my own two eyes what this guy is capable of doing to women. Frankly, it's a miracle that more of them haven't died while they were getting freaky with him."

"This wasn't getting freaky, Mitch. Donna was brutally, violently murdered. I am talking about walls spattered with blood."

"Was there a lot of blood?"

"There was enough. Why, what's the significance of—?" Des broke off suddenly, drawing in her breath.

Mitch sat right up, hearing the same sound she had—a car starting. It came from across the Crocketts' meadow. Headlights flicked on now in front of their house and, slowly, the lights turned and made their way down the long gravel drive toward them. Mitch recognized the flatulent burble of the car's diesel engine. It was Dodge's old Mercedes wagon.

It was midnight and Dodge was heading out.

"I don't believe this," Des muttered at him.

"And I don't believe you doubted me," Mitch exclaimed triumphantly. "If I were a less secure person I would actually be hurt."

"Hush!"

The Mercedes was nearing the carriage lamps at the entrance to the drive. From where they sat, it was impossible to tell if Dodge was alone in the car. For that matter, it was impossible to be sure that it was Dodge who was behind the wheel. As the Mercedes paused at the road, Mitch reached for his key in the ignition.

Des stopped him with a warning hand. "Not yet. Let him get rolling first."

Dodge pulled out and headed toward Old Shore Road, leaving plumes of diesel exhaust in his wake. Mitch waited until he'd gone around a bend before he started up the pickup and put it in gear.

"No headlights," Des cautioned him. "Just zone in on his taillights."

Mitch took off after the Mercedes in the blackness. Fortunately, there were occasional streetlamps to mark his way. Otherwise he would have driven into a ditch for sure.

Old Shore Road was deserted at that time of night. The Mercedes was about a half mile ahead of them, chugging in the direction of town, its headlights casting a soft, film noir glow in the foggy mist that reminded Mitch of the opening sequence of *The Killers*, when William Conrad and Charles McGraw are pulling into that sleepy small town in search of the Swede. All that was missing was the ominous Miklos Rozsa score.

Mitch chugged along after it at a steady forty-five.

"Don't get too close," Des said anxiously from next to him, her knees jiggling with excitement. "Give him room."

He grinned at her. "Want to take the wheel, Master Sergeant?"

"Heck no. You're doing great."

"You miss this, don't you?"

"Miss what?"

"The hunt. You are loving this. I can see it in your eyes."

"Doughboy, it is pitch-black in this cab."

"So maybe I'm imagining it."

"So maybe you ought to keep your imagination on the road. Careful, he's slowing down. . . . Watch it!"

Mitch hit the brakes, coming to a dead stop. Up ahead, Dodge was pulling into the Citgo minimart, even though it was closed up for the night. The illuminated sign was dark, the big floodlights out. There was only the night-light that the Acars left on inside when they went home. Nonetheless, Dodge drove around in back, where the rest rooms and trash bins were, and shut off his lights.

"Man, what the hell is he doing?" Des wondered as they idled there.

"Meeting somebody?"

Des jumped out, shutting her door silently behind her. "Catch up with me real slow," she said to him through the open window. "Hit your lights when I signal you, got it?"

"Got it."

She was off and running now, streaking her way toward the minimart, her knees high, her arms pumping. Mitch eased along behind her, seeing her backlit by the night-light inside. Now he could see her cutting across the parking lot toward Dodge's car, raising an arm high over her head. Now he could see her lowering it. . . .

And now Mitch flicked on his headlights.

And there stood Dodge Crockett intently spray-painting 9/11 WTC on the side of the minimart in two-foot-high red letters.

"Hold it *right* there, Mr. Crockett!" Des bellowed at him angrily.

First, Dodge froze. Then he hurled the aerosol paint can at her. Then he tried to run, which was futile—Des was faster than he was. He scarcely got twenty before she overtook him and threw him roughly to the pavement, jamming her knee into the small of his back. She slapped a handcuff on him and dragged him over to the rear service door, which had a heavy steel handle on it, and cuffed him to that. Then she called for a cruiser on her cell phone. She also got the Acars' home number and put in a call to them.

Mitch climbed out of the truck and walked slowly over toward Dodge, his eyes hungrily searching Dodge's face in the headlights for some insight into what was going on in this man's mind—this man who he had looked up to and confided in and thought of as a friend.

Dodge did not hang his head in shame or defeat. He remained unbowed and unapologetic, the same way he had when Mitch and Will had walked in on he and Becca.

"A cruiser will be here in five," Des announced, pocketing her phone.

"How about the Acars?" Mitch asked.

"No answer. I left a message on their machine."

Mitch frowned. It was after midnight—kind of late for them to be out. Then again, maybe they didn't pick up after they went to bed. A lot of people didn't.

"This finally makes some sense," Des said, staring coldly at Dodge "I get it now."

"You get what?" wondered Mitch.

Dodge wasn't saying a word.

"Why Miss Barker got weird on me," she explained. "The old girl clammed right up when I asked her if she'd seen anybody drive by her house after that rock got thrown. Same with Mr. Acar, who was way too anxious to button it all up. Because it wasn't any stupid kids who were messing with him. It was *you*, Mr. Crockett, and you're someone who still matters in this town. Miss Barker knew it was you—she recognized your car. And Mr. Acar knew because you'd warned him, hadn't you? You'd told him what might happen if he didn't back off."

Mitch turned to Dodge and said, "Why have you done this? What did the Acars ever do to you?"

"They've cut our morning take-out trade in half, that's what," Dodge spoke up, his voice calm and matter-of-fact. "They're absolutely killing us with those Turkish pastries of hers. The locals haven't come anywhere near The Works since she started selling them. I begged Nuri to give us a break. I said to him, look, you've got a thriving gasoline business. Kindly leave the food trade to us. He refused. I even offered to buy the damned pastries from him myself and sell them at The Works. Again he refused. He just wouldn't listen to reason. Those Acars are unbelievably stubborn people."

"So, what, you're trying to scare them into leaving town?" Mitch asked.

"I'm *trying* to protect my investment. This is business I'm talking about, Mitch. People play for keeps. Believe me, some fellow who was truly ruthless would have burned this damned place to the ground a month ago and never lost a night's sleep over it. We will have to shut down half of our bakery operation if they don't back off. As far as the banks are concerned that's a red flag. I won't be able to raise any more capital. I won't be able to meet my overhead. The Works will go into receivership, and I'll be cleaned out. I'll lose everything."

"In other words, the Acars are smart businesspeople and you're not."

"Don't judge what you don't understand," he shot back gruffly.

"Actually, I understand you perfectly, Dodge," Mitch said.

"You're the single most arrogant egomaniac I've ever met. You think the rules that apply to other people don't apply to you. That you can do whatever you want to whomever you want, up to and including your own daughter. Well, you're wrong, and it's amazing to me that you've lasted all of these years without finding that out. I guess you're just a sheltered small-town boy. But let me just ask you this—why did you have to push Tito off of that cliff? And how did Donna qualify as competition? It seems to me she was one of your biggest assets."

"Now, you wait one minute." Dodge's eyes widened. For the first time he seemed genuinely rattled. "I've stepped over the line a tad, I'll grant you that."

"You're granting us jack," Des snapped. "We caught you in the act."

"I threw a rock through a window," Dodge acknowledged readily. "I sprayed some graffiti on a wall. But that's all. You can't pin those murders on me. I had nothing to do with them. I am not a killer, I swear."

"All I know," Mitch said, "is that Donna told me not to look too closely at her business or her marriage. And now she's dead and you're out here trying to put a hardworking immigrant couple out of business."

"Where were you last night, Mr. Crockett?" Des asked him.

"I was home all evening."

"Alone?"

"Very alone. I don't seem to be too popular these days."

"I can't imagine why," she said, raising her chin at him. "Were you romantically involved with Donna?"

"Of course not," Dodge replied. "Donna Durslag didn't sleep around. She wasn't the type. Believe me, I know about these things."

Mitch started to say something back but before he could get the words out something went *ker-chunk* inside his head and he just stood there with his mouth open, dumbstruck. Because it hit him now—the thing that had been staring right at him all along. The thing he'd completely ignored.

And now Mitch stood there in the Citgo parking lot with his head spinning. It was spinning when the cruiser that Des had summoned pulled up and an immense young trooper climbed out. It was spinning as Des went over the charges with the trooper. It was spinning as she uncuffed Dodge from the door handle and put him in the backseat. It was still spinning when he and Des stood there watching the cruiser take Dodge away to the Troop F barracks in Westbrook.

"Are you okay, boyfriend?" Des asked, examining him with concern. "You look a little blown away."

"Des, I've figured it out. . . ."

"Figured what out?"

"Who killed Tito and Donna."

"Well, are you going to tell me about it?"

"Of course, only there's absolutely no way to prove it. No conventional way, that is. Des, I'm afraid that this is going to call for some more, well, visionary thinking."

She stood there with her hands on her hips, scowling at him. "Mitch, you have *got* to be kidding me."

"What do you mean by that?" he protested innocently.

"I *mean*, I know that look on your face. You look just like a fat little boy who is about to stick his fat little hand in the cookie jar."

"Okay, first of all I resent the repeated use of the F-word—"

"You want to set some kind of a trap. And you want *me* to watch your back, don't you? Tell me I'm wrong. Go ahead, tell me."

"Well, it worked once before, didn't it?"

"You ended up in the *hospital* before."

"I didn't mind. The wound healed fast, and I got all of the ice cream I could eat. Not to mention tapioca."

"Mitch, it cost me my damned job on Major Crimes."

"And look how much happier you are. Look at how much fun we have together, day in and day out." He strode resolutely back to his truck now and got in, waiting for her join him.

Des followed him reluctantly and climbed in, her eyes shining at him. "Mitch, I'm being serious now, okay? Please, please don't do this—whatever *this* is."

"I have to," he insisted, pulling out onto Old Shore Road and heading for home.

"Why, damn it?"

"Because somebody has been killing people who I care about. You guys can't put a stop to it. I can. And there's absolutely no need for you to worry about me. I can handle myself. I'm perfectly capable of . . ." Mitch frowned, glancing over at her. "What was that noise you just made? I distinctly heard a sound come out of you."

"That was sheer human anguish!" she cried out. "I am involved with a crazy person. You are insane!"

"Am not. I'm just a concerned Dorseteer who's had enough."

"Kindly tell me this, Mr. Had Enough—what am I supposed to do about Rico and Yolie? What do I tell them?"

"Not a thing. If they have so much as a hint of prior knowledge then it's entrapment. That's one of the truly valuable things I've learned from hanging with you, Des."

"Mitch, it's entrapment if *I'm* involved!"

"But you're not. You're simply backing my play in case it all turns sour. They can't fault you for being in the right place at the right time. Perfectly legitimate."

She glowered out the windshield in seething silence. "You're going to do this no matter what I say, aren't you?"

"If you don't want in, just say so. I promise I won't hold it against you."

"You know what I should do? I should cuff you to that steering wheel right now."

"But you won't," he said, grinning at her.

"Why the hell not?"

"Two reasons. One, because I'm your sweet baboo—"

"You *were* my sweet baboo. Our love is like *so* hanging in the balance right now."

"Two, because deep down inside, where your scrupulously high moral standards live, you know I'm right."

She said nothing in response to that. Just rode along next to him, smoldering, as he steered his truck back to Big Sister.

"I can't do it," she finally said, her voice low and pained. "Not again. I won't be there to help you this time. You're on your own. I'm out."

"That's fine. I understand."

"I *mean* it!"

"So do I."

"Mitch, I can't even begin to tell you how much I am hating you right now."

"I'm awfully fond of you, too, Master Sergeant."

The road up to the Devil's Hopyard was narrow and twisting, and the low, dense fog ahead of him in the headlights made the shoulders seem to crowd right in around his truck.

Mitch drove slowly, alone in the cab except for his microcassette recorder and the pint bottle of peppermint schnapps on the seat next to him. His mouth was dry, his palms moist, even though he kept wiping them on his shorts.

When he arrived at the end of the road he pulled onto the shoulder by the gate, just as Tito had when he'd phoned him to say goodbye. The yellow crime scene tape had been removed, but two overflowing barrels of evidence still remained—the trash that the press corps and celebrity gawkers had left behind. Their empty film canisters, food wrappers, coffee cups and soda cans were spilled out all over the pavement.

Stinking garbage. This was Tito Molina's final tribute from his public.

Mitch shut off his engine, grabbed his things and got out, hearing the roar of the falls, feeling the fear surge through his body. He started down the rocky footpath in the fog, making his way by flashlight past the picnic tables toward a wooden guardrail that smelled of creosote. Here he spotted the warning sign that all of the newspaper accounts had referred to, the one that read: *Let the Water Do the Falling. Stay Behind This Point.*

He climbed over it and started his way carefully out onto the slick, gleaming shelf of ledge, the roar growing louder as the water cascaded right by him, crashing onto the rocks down below. It was cooler up here over the falls. But he was still perspiring, his heart pounding as he inched his way slowly out onto the promontory.

Mitch sat now, hugging his knees with his arms, and flicked off his light, alone there in the wet, roaring darkness. And terrified. He would be feeling way more sure of himself if Des were backstopping him, no question. Not that he blamed her for saying no. She had to think of her future. He knew this. But he also knew that she was his safety net. Walking this particular tightrope without her made the trip a whole lot more daunting. He took a sip of the peppermint schnapps, realizing at long last that what it tasted exactly like was Nyquil—although he doubted that a slug of peppermint schnapps would put him to sleep in ten to twelve minutes with drool dribbling down his chin.

In fact, he doubted he'd be asleep for a long, long while.

The waterfall masked all distant noise. Mitch didn't hear the other car arrive. Didn't hear its door slam shut. Didn't hear the footsteps approaching in the darkness—not until they were right there beside him, sure and quick on the slippery granite ledge.

And Mitch heard a raised voice say: "You came alone?"

Mitch reached down and flicked on the microcassette recorder at his feet. It was a powerful little unit. When he'd tested it in his bathroom with the shower and faucet running full blast it could pick up his voice quite clearly from four feet away. "Of course I did," he responded, hearing the quaver of fear in his own raised voice. "I said I'd be alone, didn't I?"

"You said it was urgent, and that I should meet you up here. Why here?"

"Because this is your special place. You feel safe up here. I think I can see why. It's comforting being surrounded by so much darkness and water. You're totally free to be yourself—the self that you hide so well from everyone in the daylight." He took a gulp from the bottle. "Want some peppermint schnapps?"

"I've never liked the stuff. Since when do you?"

"Oh, I don't."

"Then why'd you bring it?"

"As a tribute."

"Does anyone else know we're here, Mitch?"

"Not a soul."

"Why are we?"

"Because we're friends. I want to help you."

"You said on the phone that you know. *What* do you know?"

Mitch reached for his flashlight and flicked it on, its beam illuminating the lean, taut face of Will Durslag. "I know that you loved Tito and you killed him. I know you loved Donna and killed her. But I don't know why, Will. I need to know why."

Will's eyes turned to narrow, frightened slits. He looked like a wild, desperate animal crouched there in the torchlight.

Mitch flicked it off, plunging them back into the darkness. They'd been doing better there. "We talk about lots of things when we walk on the beach together. Can't we talk about this?"

"Sure, Mitch," Will finally said, his voice heavy with sadness. "Let's do that. It'll be good to talk about it. Maybe I won't feel so scared."

"I can't imagine why you're scared. You've got away with it all. There are no witnesses. And the only physical evidence is in your Franklin stove."

"My Franklin stove . . . ?"

"Sure, that's why you made that fire in your parlor this morning. Not because of the chill, but because Donna's blood got all over your clothes. Plus there were the towels you mopped up with. I'm thinking you must not have been wearing rubber-soled shoes when you killed her—rubber stinks out loud when it burns. You must have had on your leather flip-flops. I suppose you could have buried the stuff, but a fire made a lot of sense." Mitch glanced over at him in the darkness. "What are you scared of, Will?"

"Myself. I'm not in control of *me* anymore. My God, I even killed my own wife. That's generally considered to be pretty despicable behavior."

"Generally."

"Tell me, Mitch—how did you know?"

"You told me yourself."

"I did?" Will shot back in surprise. "When?"

"On the beach the other morning, when I asked you about your croissant recipe. You mentioned you'd gotten it from your partner in, I think you said, Nag's Head."

"Yes, that's right."

"When I asked you if you meant *business* partner you said no. But you didn't clarify what you did mean. Just kind of left it hanging there."

"So? . . ."

"So I work with words for a living, Will. Guys our age usually use the word 'girlfriend' when we're discussing a significant romantic partner. Unless, that is, we're going out of our way to be non–gender specific. Unless, that is—"

"Unless we're gay," Will said.

"I didn't think much about it. Not until this morning, when you used the word again in connection with Donna. That's when it dawned on me that you're bisexual. And that *you* were the one getting it on with Tito—who, like you, had relations with both men and women."

"No," Will said emphatically. "You're wrong on both counts."

"Okay, tell me how."

"For starters, we weren't 'getting it on.' That suggests something quick and sweaty in the backseat of a parked car. It wasn't like that, Mitch," he insisted, his voice growing painfully earnest. "It was real love. I was ready to devote my life to him. Give up Donna. Give up everything. We were in love, Tito and me. And Tito *wasn't* bisexual. He was one hundred percent bitch—his word, not mine. Oh, sure, he got married to Esme. And he could perform sexually with women, up to a point. He *was* one hell of an actor, after all. But his heart was never in it. Tito was gay from the time he was a barrio boy, Mitch. He kept telling me: You have no idea what it's like to be a bitch in the barrio. The scorn you face, the contempt. He *hated* being gay. That's why he became an actor—so he could become someone else, *anyone* else. That's why he got high all of the time. And that's why he was always trying out so many different women. He kept hoping that one of them would 'cure' him, as if what he had was a disease. God, he was *so* nineteenth century."

Mitch sat hunched there on the damp granite, recalling that both Abby and Chrissie had pointed out how disappointing the lovemaking with Tito had been. Chrissie even told Des that the screen idol hadn't been able to perform at all the final time they'd slept together.

"Tito was a tortured soul, Mitch. He couldn't be himself. They wouldn't *let* him be himself."

"Who wouldn't, Will?"

"The powers that be, that's who. You of all people should know why."

Mitch nodded his head. "You're right, Will, I do. It's the final frontier. And no one, but no one, has ever been able to cross it."

There was a very short list of bankable Hollywood leading men— the $20-Million-Dollar Men they were known as, by current wage standards. Actors whose name above the title guaranteed a picture instant financing. There were seldom more than a half dozen such actors at any one time. Right now there were the two Toms, Cruise and Hanks, Harrison Ford, Robert De Niro. And, until a few days ago, Tito Molina. These leading men all had very different qualities. But they all had one very important trait in common.

They were not gay. They were never gay.

There *was* no such thing as an openly gay Hollywood leading man. The mass audience simply would not accept him. If anything, gay actors had been driven even deeper into the closet than they had been in the Rock Hudson days, when everyone in the business knew but the public didn't. There was too much tabloid money out there now. Too much ugly fascination in the stars' private lives. Not to mention AIDS awareness. The merest whisper about a lingering respiratory infection or unexplained weight loss could completely short-circuit an actor's rise to stardom. Mitch had seen it happen.

"Will, how was it possible for him to keep his sexual identity a secret?"

"By marrying a great beauty," Will replied. "By sleeping around with a million women. By never being happy one single day of his life."

"You're the first man he slept with since he got famous?"

"No, of course not. He had others. But he hadn't been with a man since he married Esme. Mitch, he was deathly afraid of falling into the clutches of an opportunist. So he was always very careful to choose the right type."

"Which was . . . ?"

"The married type. Men with children and roots in the community. Men who had just as much interest in keeping it quiet as he had. Tito never, ever cruised the bars. Never picked up anyone. Never *told* anyone. Not his agent, not Chrissie—"

"What about Esme? Did *she* know?"

"Never. His marriage to her was the greatest acting performance of Tito's life. Not that he hated her or anything. He genuinely liked Esme as a person. And they belonged together in a weird sort of way. They were both so confused and vulnerable. I mean, God, that poor girl is *so* screwed up after what Dodge did to her."

"How could you let Dodge get away with that, Will? How could you cover for him?"

"I had to."

"Why, because he was like a father to you? That doesn't justify it."

"You don't understand, Mitch. I had no choice." Will fell silent, shifting around next to him on the ledge. "I hit a pretty bad patch after my dad died. Got into some real trouble. I-I stole a car and accidentally ran somebody down in East Dorset. An old lady. I almost killed her, Mitch. Dodge was a state senator then. He went to bat for me. Kept the newspapers out of it. Got the charges dropped. My record is clean, and I have Dodge to thank for that. I *owe* him, okay? And I will always be loyal to him. He's big on loyalty. He's big on trust. Can you understand that?"

"I guess I can," Mitch said, recalling the steely way Dodge had stared at Will on the beach when he'd said the word "trust."

"Esme could never make Tito happy," Will went on. "She never knew why. And it was a source of tremendous pain for her. He felt bad about that, because he was hurting her and he knew it. But there was only one person on the face of the earth who could make him truly happy, Mitch, and that person was me. With everybody else, he was just acting."

"How do you know he wasn't acting when he was with you, too?"

"Because it was *real*, damn it!" Will cried out, enraged. "We *loved* each other!"

"How long were you two together?"

"We met the day he and Esme arrived in town. The Crocketts had us over for dinner and . . . and we just stared at each other across the dining table all evening long. Couldn't take our eyes off of each other. God, Tito had the most beautiful eyes. He made the first move, out on the patio after dessert. I'll never forget those first words he said to me, not for as long as I live. He said, 'I'd better warn you—I'll break your heart.' I said I'd take my chances. And he *did* break my heart—because he loved being a star more than he loved me. It wasn't just the money. It was being *Tito Molina*. He wouldn't give it up for anything, Mitch. I was willing to sacrifice my marriage, my business, everything I'd ever worked for. I was willing to throw it all away for him. But he wasn't willing to do that for me." Will let out a heartbroken sob. "And now he's dead and, God, I miss him so much."

"You should have thought of that before you killed him."

"I *didn't* think, don't you see? I lashed out in a blind rage. I just couldn't stand to lose him. Tito was my true soul mate, Mitch. Someone like that . . . it only happens once in a lifetime."

"It can happen twice, if you're real lucky."

"I loved him, Mitch. And he loved me. Just not enough. He wouldn't leave Esme for me. He wouldn't risk his career for me. That's what he came up here to tell me that night. That he had to b-break it off."

Mitch uncapped the peppermint schnapps and took a swig. "I didn't know what he was mixed up in, Will, but he did tell me he felt trapped. I urged him to get clear of whatever it was. So whatever he said to you that night—it was partly my fault. I should have kept my mouth shut."

"Don't blame yourself, Mitch," Will said to him insistently. "Tito broke it off because he wanted to break it off. And when it came time to do it he was ice cold. Do you want to know what he said to me? He said, 'This doesn't have to end badly, it just has to end.' Like he was talking about a service contract on a kitchen appliance. I wouldn't listen. I couldn't imagine not being with him. I begged him. He refused. We argued. And now I'm all alone."

"Will, how much did Donna know?"

"She knew that I'd been involved with men, if that's what you mean. Not a big deal, as far as she was concerned. Not until lately, that is."

"Since you'd met Tito?"

"I started coming home from work later and later. My physical interest in her fell way off. She kept asking me, 'Who is it?' And I said 'You don't have to worry, it's nothing.' And then one night she caught Tito dropping me off at The Works after we'd been up here together. My own fault. It was late. I thought she'd already gone home for the night. I was wrong. She said, 'What are you doing with *him*?' And I said, 'We're friends.' And she said 'Since when?' Donna was no dummy, Mitch. She knew what was going on. She was hurt. And she was afraid. She started drinking a lot more than usual. And flirting. Trying to make me jealous. I saw her getting all frisky with you at the beach club."

"That was the night you killed him. Did she know about that, too?"

"She put two and two together," Will acknowledged. "She started acting very guarded around me, very uneasy. I didn't think she'd turn me in. She did love me, after all. But I *was* afraid that she'd get involved with someone else. You, maybe. And that one night she'd have herself a little too much to drink and blab my little secret. This is Dorset, Mitch. The most dangerous weapon here isn't a gun, it's a whisper. I couldn't risk it. I couldn't take that chance."

"So you killed her."

"I suggested we try to rekindle our romance at the Yankee Doodle. We'd been joking about the place for ages. She loved the idea. She even bought herself some sleazy black lingerie for our little tryst. We made it all into a game. We arranged to meet there a half hour apart, just like a pair of illicit lovers afraid of being found out. She got there first."

"And she paid for the room with her credit card," Mitch said. "She didn't try to keep it off the household books, or disguise her identity. She didn't have to, because the man who she was meeting was her own husband. Dodge was right about her, you know. He put his finger right on it—Donna wasn't the type to sleep around."

"I couldn't risk it," Will repeated vehemently. "When I spoke to Des this morning I reversed our roles. I told her it was Donna who was slipping out on me. All a lie, of course. There was no boyfriend. And no catering gig after the Merchants Association dinner. I made all of that up. I parked our van behind a beauty parlor just down the road from the Yankee Doodle. I didn't want anyone to spot it in the motel parking lot. That was the one thing I couldn't chance. I brought along a change of clothes as part of our game, and I left nothing behind. Not even the towels I used to wipe the blood off of my hands. I burned it all when I got home. Towels, clothes, my flip-flops—just like you said. And then I got busy acting like the concerned husband. I called our late man, Rich. I called the state police. And I waited there for someone to knock on my door to tell me Donna was dead. Des, as it turned out. I think I was pretty convincing as the grieving widower. I learned a few pointers about acting from Tito. The main thing he told me is you have to *believe* the dialogue. I believed it, all right. I believed every damned word of it."

"How could you do it, Will? How could you murder Donna that way? Tito I can comprehend. It was a momentary spasm of anger. But Donna's death was something that you plotted out really, really carefully. How could you?"

"I *told* you, I'm not in control of myself anymore!" he cried out. "I loved Donna, don't you see? And now I'm all alone and I'm scared and I'm desperate and I—I don't want to go to prison for the rest of my life. *That's* why I had to kill her. If she'd told anyone, I'd be finished."

"You *are* finished, Will. It's all over now. Come on, let's go do the right thing, okay? Let's go call Des. I'll be by your side the whole way, I promise." Mitch fumbled around in the dark for his tape recorder, shut it off and stuck it in the back pocket of his shorts. Then he grabbed the schnapps bottle and climbed to his feet, flicking his flashlight beam on Will. "Tell me something—was it any easier?"

Will remained crouched there on the granite ledge, staring out into the fog-shrouded blackness. He seemed very calm now, very at peace with himself. "Was what easier?"

"Killing Donna. It's supposed to be easier to murder someone if you've already killed once before."

"No, that's a Victorian myth, same as thinking you can be 'cured' of being gay. Just because you've killed once doesn't mean that you've gone over to the dark side, Mitch. I hated what I did, and I'll be haunted by it for as long as I live." Will looked up at him now, blinking in the torchlight. "Quite honestly, I don't think the third time will be any easier either."

It happened so fast.

Will lunged at him with such sudden ferocity that Mitch's flashlight went clattering to the rocks and rolled right over the cliff, plunging them back into darkness as they wrestled with each other there on the slick granite ledge, slipping and sliding. Will trying with all of his might to push Mitch over the edge. Mitch trying with all of his own might to stop him.

"Will, don't do this!" he gasped, struggling to dig his heels in. He did have heft on his side, and a lower center of gravity. But Will had a distinct advantage of his own—he was insane. "You *have* to turn yourself in."

"Never," he gasped back at him.

They fell to the ledge now, rolling around there on the narrow shelf of rock, punching and kicking and clawing for their very lives. And there was only them and the roaring water and the blackness of certain death a hundred feet below.

Will was back up on his feet, kicking blindly at Mitch in the dark, smashing him in his ribs, his shoulder, his neck.

Mitch scrambled away, groping desperately in the dark for a stone, a weapon. His fingers found the schnapps bottle—but Will's powerful hands found his throat. And Will was choking him and choking him. And Mitch was fighting for breath as he raised the bottle high over his head, gasping, gagging, until with the very last bit of power that was left in his body Mitch smashed Will Durslag hard in the face, shattering the bottle and pitching the taller man over backward, right over the cliff.

Which would have been fine by Mitch except for one thing—Will was still holding on to him by his shirt.

And so as he went over Mitch went over, too, his own legs flailing wildly in space as Will hung there in midair, clutching on to him for dear life. Mitch tried in vain to grab on to the moss, to the wet stone, something, anything. Feeling Will's weight pulling him down, down the sheer edge of the cliff, moss coming away in his fingers, bare stone refusing to yield him even the merest finger or toehold as he slid and he slid and he—

Until with a sudden rip Mitch's shirt gave way in Will's hand and Will was gone, screaming, into the blackness of the night, his roar and the roar of the waterfall merging into one.

Freed of Will's weight, Mitch clung there to the sheer side of the cliff for a brief, gravity-defying instant. But now he could feel himself falling again, scrabbling, kicking, trying to put on the brakes. Except there was nothing to hold on to and it was all happening too fast and he was going and he was going—until his hand *just* wrapped itself around a spindly tree branch, halting his fall.

And now he was hanging there by one arm, his body swinging free in the air, and there was only enough time for one final realization.

I am never going to see Desiree Mitry again. I am going to die. I am going to die. I am going to . . .

Chapter 14

Des had to be so damned careful.

As much as she wanted to floor it straight for the falls, she didn't dare. Couldn't take the chance that Will Durslag would spot her cruiser at the gate and wig out. Because there was absolutely no telling what that man was liable to do to him. Assuming that Mitch was right and it *was* Will who'd killed Tito and Donna. Maybe Mitch was totally wrong about his walking buddy. Maybe Will could convince him of this. Maybe he and Will would have a perfectly pleasant conversation, shake hands, and go their separate ways.

Then again, maybe not.

She used an entrance that was way over on the other side of the park, at Witch Meadow. Kathleen Moloney drove over from her cabin to raise the gate for Des. The young ranger had to wonder why Des needed to get into the park at one o'clock in the morning. But she was too sleepy to act genuinely interested, and she did not offer to tag along.

Des made do with her parking lights as she sped through the fog-shrouded park on a narrow service road, asking herself why she was letting herself get dragged into this fool gambit of Mitch's after all. Even though she'd sworn up and down that she wouldn't. Even though his impulsive desire to make things right sometimes seemed as if it came straight out of those old Hollywood movies of his, as opposed to the real world. Even though not one bit of this was smart or sane.

Why, damn it?

Because he was her boy, that's why, and he was what he was. She could not change him. She could only love him, even when he acted crazy. And if *anything* happened to that pudgy pink butthead tonight because she wasn't up there watching his back she would never forgive herself.

She would just die.

She left her cruiser a quarter mile up the service road from the river, hearing the roar of the falls now. She made it the rest of the way on foot, stumbling her way along the footpath in the darkness. She did make sparing use of her flashlight, holding it low to the ground, pointed straight down. But once she'd reached the guardrail she did not dare use it at all. Plunging herself into utter blackness, she climbed over the rail and crept slowly out onto slick bare granite, the river roaring as it raced by her, her eyes and ears straining for some sign of human life. But it was no use. She was blind and she was deaf. It was straight out of a nightmare.

Except this was no nightmare. This was real.

All she needed was a hint of where they were. One hint. A breath of a voice. A trace of movement. But as she crept slowly forward in her crablike crouch, there was nothing. Not one thing . . . Wait, was that the sound of glass breaking? No, her ears were playing tricks on her. It was nothing. She couldn't even be sure they were here at all.

Not until she heard a man's bloodcurdling scream.

It came from very close to her—no more than ten feet away. And now all bets were off and she was up on her feet with her flashlight out, charging toward the edge of the cliff, waving her beam around the granite promontory.

Except there was no one.

They were gone. Both gone.

She was all alone up there—just her and a broken liquor bottle that glistened on the granite. Peppermint schnapps.

Des felt a clutch in her chest. It was pure, animal anguish. She very nearly went over herself. Because she did not want to live. But she held back, standing there frozen, unable to believe, to think, to *breathe*. Until at last she drew in her breath in big ragged gulps and called his name out into the black void below her. *"MITCH!!"* she cried in helpless desperation. *"MITCH!!"*

"D-Des . . ."

She barely heard it over the roar of the falls. It was the weakest of gasps.

"*D-Des* . . ."

From below her. It came from right below her.

She inched her way over to the very edge and shined her light straight downward—directly into the two poached eggs that were Mitch Berger's terrified eyes. The man was swinging there in midair ten feet below her, clinging by his white-knuckled hands to a spindly little cedar that grew out of a crevice between the rocks. It was the very same tree that Tito had snapped when he fell.

"You *came*!" he groaned. "I-I knew you would. . . ."

"I knew that you knew," she called down to him, trying to keep her voice calm. "Where's Will?"

"Dead!"

"That's not going to happen to you, baby. I won't let it, hear me? Just hold on. I got you. Just hold on. . . ."

She had no rope. And no time to run back to her car for one. He'd be dead in a matter of seconds. Swiftly, she whipped off her black leather garrison belt, jettisoned her holstered SIG-Sauer and cell phone, and knotted the tongue around her wrist, yanking it tight. She propped the flashlight up against a stone, pointing downward, and edged her way as far down the sheer granite face as she could without losing solid hold.

Bracing herself, Des dangled the belt buckle out to him. "Reach for it!"

He tried, waving an arm in feverish desperation at the belt buckle as it wavered there in the air above him.

But it was no use—the other end of the belt was still a good two feet shy of him. If only she had a fifty-inch waist. But she didn't. That left her with one last option. It wasn't a good one, but it was the only one she had.

She had to surrender her solid hold. Climb her way down that bare, vertical granite toward him, fingers and toes searching for crevices and holds in the slick stone. "Hang on, baby!" she called to him as she edged down closer, inch by precarious inch. "I'm here!"

"Des, my arms are g-getting . . ."

"I am *not* hearing that!" She dangled the belt out to him once more. Damn, still another foot to go. And not a thing to grab on to. "You *can* hold on. Just one more minute. One minute. Say you'll hang on for me. Come on, say it!"

"I'll . . . I'll hang on. . . ."

She edged lower, clinging to the side of the cliff by her fingers, clawing at the moss with her nails as the river tore on by her, pelting her with cold spray. She could not even think about how she was going to climb back up there with him. One impossibility at a time. "Hang on, I got you," she told him, keeping her voice steady. "You're taking me dancing, remember? I've been waiting for this. Think I'm going to let you weasel out now?" Reaching her belt down to him. *Damn*, still six more inches. Edging lower, surrendering a halfway decent toehold for *no* toehold, seeing him real clearly now in the flashlight's beam, his hair glistening from the spray, his hands trembling around the branch that was the only thing between him and death. The branch that was bending and straining against his weight. "What was the name of that place again?"

"*What* place?"! He was panting wildly, as if he'd been running all out for miles. It was exhaustion and it was panic.

"Where you're taking me dancing."

"T-Tavern . . . The Tavern."

One more good foothold was all she needed. One more. She reached down with her foot, poking blindly, kicking, until finally she made contact with the base of the tree that Mitch clung to. Her shoe was right next to his hand, bracing her there. "They got them a DJ?"

"Just a jukebox . . . Des, I c-can't . . ."

"It's okay, we're all good now," she said, her voice brimming with confidence. "I've got you. Here we go. . . ." Des readied herself, breathing in and out, realizing with a shocking degree of clarity that it was for this singular moment in her life that she had done all of that work. Every weight she had lifted. Every mile she had run and hiked and biked. The four years of iron-willed training at West

Point. All of that was preparation for this moment, this mountain, right here, right now. And she would need all she could bring. Every bit of strength. Every bit of heart. It all.

Because she was about to take on two-hundred pounds of man.

With her left arm, Des dangled the belt out to him. "Grab it, Mitch."

"I *can't!* We'll both go down!"

"No, we won't."

"We *will!*" he cried out, panting. "I'll p-pull you right down with me. Kill us both. Just let me go. . . ."

"I *can't* let you go!" she sobbed, the tears beginning to stream down her face. She could not stop them from coming. She did not even try. "I don't want to be alive unless you are, too. Then I *will* die, don't you get it? Now give me your damned hand, you fat son of a bitch!"

He made an angry lunge for the belt and grabbed hold, the suddenness of his weight very nearly yanking her right off the mountainside. But she held on, wet fingers clinging to wet granite, fingernails breaking, her shoulder feeling as if it were about to pop out of its socket.

But she had him. Now all she had to do was tow him back up onehanded. Nothing to it. Cherry pie. Great big slab of it, à la mode.

Slowly, Des began the agonizing climb back up that sheer cliff to safety, the veins in her neck bulging as she reached up with her right arm, grabbing an uncertain fingerhold, and pulled him up along with her by her left, the muscles in her legs and lower back powering them upward, inch by precious inch. An animal groan of pain coming out of her as she willed them back up. The pain in her shoulder growing so intense that she was positive she could not hold him one second longer, that she *had* to let him go. Or die. She was beginning to feel light-headed now, almost delirious. The mountain was starting to waver and shift on her, like a ship at sea.

"What's our . . . song?" she panted, terrified she was about to pass out.

"Our . . . *what?*"

"Got to have . . . song . . . How's Aretha?"

"Fine . . . by me . . ." he answered, kicking wildly against the side of the cliff. Somehow, he found a toehold in a crevice, freeing some of his weight from both of their shoulders for a precious moment.

Gasping, she clung there, soaking wet, every muscle in her body quivering, knowing she had to keep moving. Forcing herself to keep moving. "Here we go, baby. One more time." Climbing upward again. Gaining a fingerhold, losing it, slipping back down, grabbing on to the wet granite for dear life. And trying it all over again. "Your favorite Aretha . . . ?"

"Has to be . . . 'Respect.'"

"Me, too. Oh, God!" she groaned, as the pain in her shoulder grew even more unbearable. "Tell me about . . . the food."

"Des, we can't. . . ."

"We *can!*" she screamed, inching farther upward toward the dim glow that was her flashlight's beam. "Tell me . . . what we'll eat."

"Spinach . . . fettuccine."

"Love me . . . I love me the pasta. Must be part Italian."

"No, can't be. You're already . . . part Jewish. Bella said so."

One inch, then another. Until at last he could finally swing a leg up over that branch he'd been hanging from. He straddled it, his chest heaving.

She clung there, her face hugging the cold granite as if it were a goose-down pillow. Her shoulder felt dead now. *She* felt dead— ready to surrender to the black void below. She had nothing left. Not one bit of energy. She couldn't make it. *They* couldn't make it.

Mitch worked his foot up under himself, bracing it against the base of the little tree. Then he knotted the belt tightly around his wrist, the better to hold on. "Just a couple more feet and we're there," he said with a sudden rush of bravado. "Two, maybe three. We're going to make it, right?"

Now he was trying to spur her on, even though both of his arms had to be ready to fall off. But he could tell that she was losing it.

"Almost there," she croaked, slowly tilting her head upward, raising her eyes. She could see the flashlight up there. Five feet away. Might as well be five miles. "You . . . still my boy?"

"You know I am. Know something else? Your gas tank isn't empty. You've got two more gallons left."

She tried to smile but was too weak. "I-I do?"

"You come with an emergency reserve tank. I read about it in your owner's manual. Listen to me . . . Des, are you listening to me?"

"Y-Yeah?"

"My turn to do the heavy lifting now. Soon as I get both feet up under me. All you have to do is move us up two more inches. Then I can push you the rest of the way, okay? Can you give me two more inches?"

Groaning, she started to climb again, positive her fingers were about to break right off at the knuckle. And now he had both feet under him on that little tree and he was pushing her upward instead of pulling her down, lifting her up, up, up the side of the cliff just like when she was a little girl and the Deacon would take her for a ride up on his shoulders, laughing and singing. And Des was grabbing for the top now and she was safely up and she was—

Until suddenly there was an awful cracking sound and that little tree gave way.

And Mitch was hanging on to her for dear life again, nothing under him besides blackness and death. But she could brace her knees against solid stone now, and he was making it up, up, and over and they were both collapsed there, alive, covering each other's faces with kisses, grateful for life, grateful for each other, grateful.

They lay there for a long time, soaking wet, too exhausted to stir. The awful pain in Des's left shoulder didn't subside at all. She couldn't move the arm one bit.

"Admit it," she finally said weakly. "Admit that you're glad I made you lose those ten pounds."

"I will never, ever doubt you again," he groaned, sprawled there beside her. "Only, what do I do now?"

"About what?"

255

"I just killed a man."

"Don't go there, Mitch. Will Durslag did that to himself."

"No, that's not what happened," Mitch said with sudden vehemence. "You didn't see it, Des. I smashed him in the head with a bottle. I killed him."

"*Before* he killed you. Which, by the way, he almost did."

"I know, but—"

"No *buts*!" Des said angrily. "Just forget about any *buts* and you listen to me, okay? You will need a story for Rico. And if you don't stake one out and stick to it you'll be looking at the inside of a criminal investigation. Will Durslag murdered two people, and he tried to murder you—it was kill or be killed, understand? Say you understand!"

"What are you so upset about?"

"Because I just saved your fool life and I am *not* going to throw you back. I worked too damned hard."

He was silent for a moment. "Okay, I understand."

"Thank you." She reached over with her good arm and stroked his face. "You got his confession, right?"

"Tape recorder's in my back pocket. Or it was. I don't have enough strength to see if it's still there."

"Roll over."

He rolled over on to his side and she smacked his butt with her fist, striking something squarish and hard. "It's going to be okay. I can work with Rico." Now she fumbled around for her cell phone.

"Hey, Des?"

"What is it, bod man?"

"Have I told you recently how much I love you?"

"It's okay, I don't mind if you tell me again. I've had a pretty hard night."

The sun woke her early. There was no sleeping late on Big Sister. Not in July. Not even with the aid of multiple painkillers.

The morning was warm, but there was a fresh, lovely breeze off the water. Mitch made the coffee and poured them each a cup. She got herself into a tank top and gym shorts and they went strolling barefoot together on the island's narrow beach, sipping their coffee, neither of them moving very fast. They were the walking wounded. Des wore a sling on her left arm and bandages around all five fingers on her drawing hand. Mitch's right cheek was scraped raw, and he had an angry welt on his neck where Will had kicked him. Will had also kicked him in the ribs, cracking two of them.

When they returned to his cottage he picked blueberries for their cereal while Des chilled in a lawn chair drinking iced tea with her long, bare legs stretched out before her and Quirt sprawled out on his back underneath her, his tail swishing happily in the grass. She was on medical leave for at least a week. She had nowhere to go and nothing to do. She could think of worse ways to do nothing, and worse places to do it.

Soave came rumbling over the wooden causeway just past nine, Yolie bringing up the rear in Des's cruiser. They had taken a preliminary statement from Mitch last night at the falls. Soave had not acted the least bit leery. Perhaps a bit blown away.

Yolie had been a lot blown away. "Shut up!" she kept exclaiming as she listened to Mitch's story.

The EMS people had hiked down by flashlight and found Will Durslag dead on the rocks in almost the same exact spot as Tito Molina had been. Will was even lying on his back the same way as Tito. Same head trauma. Same everything. It was eerie just how exactly he had followed the great love of his life into death.

Since it was the middle of the night and Des needed medical attention, Soave had held off on taking a more detailed statement until the morning, when Des assured him it would all start to make sense. Then she had accepted EMS transport to the twenty-four hour Shoreline Clinic in Essex. Mitch followed in his truck.

Everyone was very nice to her at the clinic. A chatty technician x-rayed her shoulder. A kindly nurse plunged her torn, bloodied fingers into a disposable basin of warm soapy water. The orthopedist who was on duty scrutinized her X-ray and pronounced it an anterior subluxation, which was physician-speak for a partially dislocated shoulder. There was some ligament damage, but the bones within the joint were not fractured. He assured her she would not need surgery and would soon be as good as new. After injecting her with a muscle relaxant he manipulated her shoulder back into place, gave her a sling to wear, and told her she might need physical therapy to restore her normal range of motion and strength. He also warned her that when a shoulder has popped out once there's a greater likelihood that it will pop out again under similar circumstances. Not a problem, Des assured him. She had no intention of ever again clinging to the side of a cliff with a grown man hanging from her arm.

It wasn't until she was signing her release forms that Mitch happened to tell the orthopedist that he was experiencing sharp pains whenever he breathed. That was when they x-rayed him and found the cracked ribs. Which they did not tape. They just told him to take it easy.

There was a twenty-four-hour pharmacy in Old Saybrook where they were able to get their prescriptions filled. By the time they got back to Mitch's place her shoulder was starting to ache again. She swallowed a pain pill and climbed into bed with an ice pack, sleeping off and on. Clemmie stayed glued to her hip the whole night, watching over her carefully. Cats were amazing that way. They always knew when you were hurting. Des just hoped Mitch didn't resent this, since he was prone to jealousy in regards to Clemmie, thereby demonstrating that he still didn't totally understand cats.

He himself had stayed downstairs watching a tape of his favorite boyhood comfort film, *The Beast from 20,000 Fathoms*, and putting away an entire box of Entenmann's chocolate chip cookies that he'd had squirreled away somewhere.

Now Des remained on her lawn chair, gazing at the sailboats out on the Sound, while Soave and Yolie went in to talk some more with Mitch and listen to the tape recording of his last conversation with Will Durslag.

Soave strolled back outside first, smoothing his former mustache, and came over and crouched beside her, carefully averting his eyes from her shapely bare legs. "I'll tell the media we've been made aware of the existence of a confession," he said slowly. "Meanwhile, we'll go hard after some physical evidence to backstop it. Could be we'll find remains of burnt clothing in his Franklin stove with traces of Donna's blood DNA on them. Maybe even find one of his hairs on the bedspread at the Yankee Doodle. That'll at least put him at the scene. As far as Tito goes, I don't think we'll ever come up with anything solid." Soave paused now, shaking his head at her. "You were right again."

"I was?" Des shifted her sling, wincing. "How so?"

"It *was* about sex."

"It was about love, Rico. Makes the world go around."

"Your boy says that it was all his own idea to arrange a meet with Durslag—and bring his tape recorder."

"True enough."

"*And* that you were up there without his knowledge and just happened to be in the right place at the right time to save his fat, sorry ass."

"He said that?"

"Everything but the fat, sorry part. What were you doing in the park at that time of night anyway?"

"Nosing around. Some local kids have been holding pot parties up there."

"Uh-huh." Soave narrowed his eyes at her shrewdly. "Me, I'm figuring it's a good thing he didn't tell you his plan in advance—because then it sure might have smelled like the E-word."

"The E-word?" Des gazed at him dumbly. "Oh, you must mean entrapment. *Hell* yeah. Smart of him not to do that."

"You wouldn't think they'd teach him stuff like that at film critic's school."

"Man's a big-league journalist, Rico," she pointed out.

"Yeah, well, your big-league journalist seems a little shook up, you want to know the truth."

"He saw a man die last night. Almost lost his own life in the deal. He's not used to that."

Soave stood back up now, swiping at his shiny black trousers, and let out a sigh. "I have to tell you, Des, my life is a whole lot simpler when you're not in it."

"Yeah, but you miss me so much you can't hardly stand it," she said, smiling up at him. "Can you work with this, Rico?"

"We can work with it," he said, which was his way of finally indicating to her that they were two people who really were there for each other. "And I still say you have the best legs in the whole damned state. Did you notice I didn't stare at them once?"

"I did, Rico. And I was impressed. You're a nascent feminist."

"Okay, I don't know what that means, but I'm looking it up."

"You do that, wow man."

He started back to his car as Yolie emerged from the carriage house with Mitch. "Girl, I left your keys in the ignition," she said, coming over to Des.

"Great, thanks."

"I've, um, decided to stick it out a little while longer with Soave."

"Glad to hear that. You keep your eyes and ears open, you can learn a lot."

"Dig, I'm not sure that what I learned on this one belongs in any how-to manual," Yolie said, crossing her rippling arms in front of her boom booms.

"Why, what did you learn?"

"You're *supposed* to assemble the facts until they point you at the truth, check? But this one's ass backwards. The truth's already a done deal and now we're going looking for the facts."

"In Hollywood they call that retrofitting," Mitch piped up.

"Retro-*what?*" Yolie shot back, cocking her head at him.

"You insert an earlier scene as story foundation for the climax you ended up improvising on the spot."

Yolie peered at him in confusion. "Sure, whatever . . ."

Des said, "Word, it's the stuff they don't teach in the manual that makes you wise." She stuck her bandaged hand out to her. "Stay in touch, Yolie. Put a shout on sometime, hear?"

"I hear," said Yolie, clasping it gently. "It was all good, Des. I'm wishing we can do this again."

"That's something else they don't teach you."

"What is?"

"Be careful what you wish for, girl. Because it just might come true."

CHAPTER 15

NURI ACAR WAS METHODICALLY brushing a thick coat of tan-colored primer over the graffiti Dodge had spray-painted on his wall when Mitch pulled into the minimart for his morning fix. Nuri must have been on his second coat by now, because the red paint was becoming all but invisible to Mitch's eye.

"That doesn't look bad at all, Mr. Acar," he said encouragingly.

"It will be fine." Nuri smiled at him broadly. He seemed more at ease than Mitch had ever seen him. "All we have wished for since we arrived in Dorset is to be good neighbors. I am so glad that this matter is resolved now. I wish I knew how to thank you, Mitch."

"Not necessary."

"No, it absolutely is. Nema and I have decided that from now on we will accept no money from you for coffee or pastry. Gasoline only."

"That's insane. I can't let you do that."

"Mitch, you must allow me to show my appreciation. To deny me is to insult me."

"Well, okay, but the resident trooper won't be happy about this. She's very particular when it comes to my caloric consumption."

"She is one very tough lady, our resident trooper," Nuri observed quietly, his mouth tightening.

"Tougher than you can possibly imagine."

"But she is also what you call a 'straight shooter.' And I respect her for that."

"Good," said Mitch, smiling. "Now I'm the one who's glad."

They shook hands, Mitch wincing slightly as Nuri gave his arm a hearty yank. The ribs felt okay unless Mitch made a sudden movement or, God forbid, sneezed. Then it felt as if someone were jabbing him with a boning knife.

Mostly, he was still just really resentful that Clemmie had chosen to stay up in the loft with Des after they got home from the clinic instead of on the sofa with him. He'd been hurting, too, after all, and wasn't she *his* cat? Didn't he feed her and tidy up her gaaacks? Where was the fairness in this? Where was the loyalty?

Deep down inside, Mitch figured he still didn't totally understand cats.

He tried to slip one past Nema and pay her for his baklava and coffee, but she wouldn't go along.

"Your money is no good here, Mitch," she clucked at him.

"You knew, didn't you, Nema?" Mitch said to her. "You saw Dodge throw that rock through your window."

"I did, yes," she admitted reluctantly.

"Why didn't you say anything?"

"We were afraid," she replied, lowering her large, dark eyes.

"Of what?"

"Mr. Crockett is part of the hierarchy. A man with connections. Who knows, he could get our business license revoked. Possibly even get us deported. So Nuri felt it is best to keep quiet."

"And you went along with him."

"He is my husband," Nema said, as if that answered everything.

For her, it did.

From there Mitch piloted his truck up Old Shore Road to the post office, munching on his baklava. He bypassed Dorset Street entirely so as to avoid the media crush at town hall, where Soave was busy putting out information about Will Durslag's death. Thirty-six hours after the fact, Des's former sergeant was still playing it very close to the vest until the forensics people up in Meriden finished sifting through those ashes in Will's woodstove. Soave had still not made public Will's tortured love affair with Tito Molina. All he was saying was that Will had been found dead at the base of Chapman Falls, that they were in possession of his taped confession, and that an investigation was proceeding.

He had not mentioned one word about Mitch's involvement in Will's death. This was fine by Mitch.

When he arrived at the post office he fetched his mail from his box and was starting back outside with it when Billie, the jovial old girl who worked behind the counter, called out, "Hey, Mitch, I got something for you. Been holding on to it." She reached down under the counter and produced a torn, overstuffed ten-by-thirteen manila envelope. "Somebody dropped this in our mailbox out front the other night," she explained, her eyes gleaming at Mitch with keen interest.

Mitch took one look at the envelope and immediately knew why. It had originally been addressed to Tito Molina—from a talent agency in Beverly Hills. Someone had crossed out Tito's name and box number, and hurriedly scribbled Mitch's name across the top. No box number or address for Mitch, no postage, no nothing. The envelope wasn't even sealed shut.

"You owe me a buck sixty-five, my dear," Billie said apologetically.

Mitch paid her and went back outside and got into his truck, his heart racing as he sat there staring at the envelope. He opened it. Inside he found a fat sheaf of lined yellow legal pages covered with crude, almost childlike handwriting.

On the first page a note had been scrawled in the margin: "Mitch, hope you like it. But *please* be honest—Tito"

It was his unfinished screenplay. He'd called it *The Bright Silver Star*.

Mitch devoured it at once, seated there in the post office parking lot. What he read turned out to be the heartfelt story of a sensitive, special little Chicano boy named Ramon who sees imaginary creatures he calls the Bad People and fears they are about to murder him in his sleep. Ramon has an Anglo mother who lives in her own dream world. His Chicano father, a day laborer, can't understand either one of them. Enraged, he lashes out in a violent drunken outburst, beating Ramon's mother half to death before he packs up and clears out.

Mitch found *The Bright Silver Star* brutal yet surprisingly delicate and poignant. It reminded him quite a bit of *The Glass Menagerie* by Tennessee Williams. In fact, it was written more as a play than a movie. The action, such as it was, consisted of a series of conversations that took place over a single day in a squalid two-room apartment.

There were no exteriors, no camera directions. Tragically, there was also no second act. Tito had managed to write only the first fifty or so pages, leaving the crisis in little Ramon's family life unresolved. Even so, this glimpse into the private hell that was Tito Molina's childhood was so painful that it very nearly brought tears to Mitch's eyes.

He was still sitting there in the cab of his truck, totally decked, when Martine Crockett pulled up next to him in her silver VW Beetle convertible, her golf bag tossed across the backseat. Mitch was pretty hard to miss there in his '56 Studey half ton, but Martine did her best anyway, scrupulously avoiding eye contact with him as she got out and strode inside, her gait long and assertive.

Mitch took a deep breath and followed her in. He found her waiting in line to buy stamps from the vending machine. A couple of her lady friends were asking her how Dodge was doing.

"He's home, he's fine," Martine replied with a brave smile. Her face was composed, her gaze clear. "*We're* fine. It's all just a terrible misunderstanding."

Warm hugs were exchanged, lunch invitations extended. They weren't shunning her. She was one of *theirs* after all, a cherished member of the inner circle, and by repudiating her they'd only be repudiating themselves. If she wasn't afraid to show her face in public, they weren't afraid to stand by her.

Mitch found this rather amazing, but he shouldn't have. This was Dorset, where appearances mattered. Hell, appearances ruled.

And then her friends were gone and Martine was alone. She stiffened at the sight of Mitch standing there.

"How is he, Martine?" Mitch asked.

"Anxious to clear his name," she answered tightly. Martine started to say something more, stopped herself, then plowed ahead. "He was very hurt that you turned against him, Mitch. I guess where you come from people define friendship differently."

"Martine, how much did you know?"

Martine paid for her stamps and tucked them into her purse. "About what?"

"About Dodge and Esme."

"I have no idea what you mean."

"Yes, you do."

"Look, I don't know what she or anyone else may have told you—"

"Yes, you do."

"You've been lied to, Mitch. And you've chosen to believe those mean, ugly lies instead of the simple truth."

"Which is? . . ."

"Esme has always enjoyed a warm, wonderful relationship with her father. And she . . . And they . . ." Martine's lower lip quivered, her flawless blond composure starting to crumble. For one brief second, Mitch thought she might give in to the horrifying reality of what her husband had done to their daughter. But she didn't. When it came to the fine art of keeping up appearances, Martine Crockett was a master. "They have nothing but love for each other—not that I expect someone like you could ever believe something decent or good about a man like Dodge."

And with that she turned on her heel and marched stiffly out of there, leaving Mitch convinced of something he had never really believed about people before. Not until this very moment, standing in the Dorset post office.

When someone can't accept the truth about the person who they love, they don't accept the truth. They accept the illusion instead.

They have to.

The news about Abby Kaminsky's unscheduled appearance at the Book Schnook got out incredibly fast.

Kids wearing carp heads were lined up all the way out the door of the bustling food hall into Big Brook Road for the chance to buy an autographed copy of *The Codfather of Sole*. The Works was still doing a bang-up lunch trade, Mitch couldn't help but notice. Rich Graybill was running the show for now.

Inside the Book Schnook, Abby was seated at a table in front of a giant *Codfather of Sole* poster, signing copies and chattering gaily with her excited young readers. Chrissie Huberman was near at hand, watching over her protectively. It was Chrissie who was responsible for the huge, last-minute turnout. She'd not only blitzed the local radio stations with ads but had hired a private plane to pull a sign along the shoreline beaches all the way from Madison to New London. Thousands upon thousands of beachgoers had seen the message.

Jeff was bustling back and forth between the cash register and the stockroom, his manner lively and animated. "Hey, it's my main man Mitch," he exclaimed brightly. "Did you walk this morning?"

"No, did you?"

"Couldn't. I had to drive up to the warehouse in Springfield for copies of Abby's book. Otherwise they wouldn't have gotten here in time." He deposited an armload on the table next to Chrissie. She immediately began opening them to the title page for Abby, who was signing books and shaking hands with the brisk, focused efficiency of an assembly line worker. Jeff started back to the cash register, where parents and kids were stacked up six deep. "Mitch, I don't know how to thank you for this. You're a true-blue friend."

"You have a slightly different take on me than Martine does."

Jeff gulped. "Shhh, not so loud," he pleaded, shooting a nervous glance over his shoulder at Abby.

Mitch lowered his voice. "What's the official story, are you and Martine finished?"

"There was nothing *to* finish. Reports of our 'affair' have been greatly exaggerated. And I would appreciate it if you'd never, ever mention that woman's name in my presence again."

"Whatever you say, Jeff." Now Mitch moseyed over to Abby to say hello.

"How are you, cookie?" Abby said to him as she signed and shook, signed and shook.

"Surprised to see you here. Pleasantly so."

"No big. I called Chrissie from Boston last night and we decided it was something we actually could squeeze in."

"And why not?" Chrissie deftly arranged an open book in front of Abby as the next eager kid in line stepped up. "It shows what kind of a classy, above-the-fray person you are."

"And you were right, Mitch," Abby added. "It's a lovely little store. Jeffrey even laid in a supply of Cocoa Pebbles for me. Can you believe he remembered?"

"Where's Frankie, out in the car?"

Abby's saucer eyes widened in panic. "Listen, I barely knew that yutz, understand? And, besides, he's history."

"She fired his tight, hairy buns last night," translated Chrissie.

"I've decided to travel a little lighter from now on," Abby acknowledged, her eyes following Jeff as he scampered back into the stockroom for another load of books. "Maybe I should help him with those. He gets back spasms if he shleps too much weight."

"You stay here and sign—I'll shlep." Chrissie dashed off to help him.

"You may be seeing a bit more of me in Dorset from now on, Mitch," Abby confided.

"Working on a new book?"

"A new venture," she replied, graciously handing over a signed book and moving on to the next kid. "You might even say I'm looking out for my own interests by being here today. This whole operation is going into receivership, and my business manager thinks it has a really huge upside if some new investor is willing to take it on."

"And that investor is you?"

"Why not? I love food, I love New England. . . ."

"And they've barely scratched the synergy surface here," Chrissie said, setting down a huge load of books. "My God, I can see Emeril Legasse and Jacques Pepin giving cooking demonstrations out there while Jeff's selling copies of their cookbooks in here. In fact, I can see *you* here, Mitch."

"Me?"

"Sure, dinner and a movie with Mitch Berger, noted New York film critic. What do you think?"

"We'll talk," he replied. To Abby he said, "So you'll be Jeff's landlord?"

"Partner is more like it," she said.

"We're not divorced yet, Mitch," Jeff pointed out as he dumped another load of books in front of her. "Technically, we're still husband and wife."

"Technically, we still are," Abby allowed.

"I *knew* it—you two are going to end up back together again, aren't you?"

"Not a chance," protested Jeff. "Word of honor, Mitch. That could never, ever happen."

"Not in a million years," Abby chimed in, blushing furiously. "Like, *ab-so-tootly* never."

Esme was building a huge sand castle with Becca on the beach near Big Sister's lighthouse. Bitsy was watching them from her covered porch, fanning herself with her floppy straw hat. The day was bright and hot, with very little breeze.

"She's hiding from the press," Bitsy told Mitch as he stood there next to her, observing the two of them out there in their string bikinis, working away. "I don't blame the poor thing. She can stay here as long as she wants to, as far as I'm concerned."

"How long will she?" Mitch wondered.

"You'll have to ask her that."

He went down the wooden steps to the beach and plowed through the hot dry sand toward them. They were on their hands and knees before their rising castle, both of them filled with laughter and high spirits. From fifty feet away, they looked like a pair of impudent, playful fourteen-year-old schoolgirls full of lollipop dreams. From closer up they were the very picture of innocence lost—two battle-hardened veterans who between them had logged enough years on the dark side for ten lifetimes. Becca was nothing but skin and bone, with dark circles under her sunken eyes. Esme had that fat, scabby lip to go with the expression of dazed confusion that wracked her delicate, lovely face. Her eyes were those of a woman who was now completely lost and fearful.

"This is quite some castle," Mitch observed, because it was. A good five feet high, with turrets, towers, and a fine, deep moat.

"Are you going to help us?" demanded Becca, wetting her hands in a water pail. "Or are you just going to stand there like a big boss man?"

Mitch promptly flopped down on his knees and started scooping out more sand for the moat. "How long are you planning to stick around, Esme?"

"Until they release Tito's body," she answered quietly as she continued molding the castle walls with her hands. "I want to take him back to Bakersfield and bury him with his parents."

"That's a really nice idea," Mitch said. "Listen, there's something important I need to talk to you about. The night Tito died, do you remember when he came home and was rummaging around in his closet before he went back out?"

Esme didn't respond for a moment. Just kept fashioning the castle wall with her shapely hands. "I remember," she finally said in a voice that came from somewhere on the other side of the ocean.

"It was his script he was getting. He must have mailed it to me on his way up to Chapman Falls that night. I just got it today. It really does exist, Esme."

"How is it?" Becca asked eagerly. She seemed vastly more excited about Mitch's discovery than Esme, who'd scarcely reacted at all.

"I have to tell you, I was pretty knocked out by it. Honestly, it's terrific. He called it *The Bright Silver Star*."

Esme sat back on her haunches now, swiping at the hair in her face. "I never once saw him working on it. He must have done it when I was asleep." She let out a heavy sigh, her breasts straining inside the tiny bikini top. "Tito did get up a lot in the middle of the night. The poor thing had such awful nightmares."

"I have it back at my house," Mitch said, climbing to his feet. "I'll go get it for you right now."

"No, don't," Esme said abruptly. "I mean, please don't. Tito wanted you to have it."

"It's your property, Esme."

"He gave it to you."

"But this is something of great value. You can get a lot of money for it."

"I don't want it. I don't even want to read it. It will just make me sad. I'm tired of being sad, Mitch. Can't you understand that?"

"Sure I can. Only, what am I supposed to do with it?"

"Something good," she said simply. "Something decent. You're a smart man. You'll know what to do."

"Getting a little dry here," Becca announced, taking their empty water pails down to the water's edge to fill them.

"Can we talk about something personal?" Mitch asked Esme.

"If you'd like."

"Did you know that Tito was gay?"

The actress peered at him curiously. "You must think I'm a total bimbo, asking me that."

"No, not at all. It's just . . . Will told me that you didn't know."

"Will was wrong."

"He said that's what Tito told him."

"Then Tito lied to him," she said, her voice growing heated now. "I *always* knew he was gay. It was obvious. Gay is gay."

"And yet you stayed together," Mitch said. "Why?"

"I loved him. Is that so hard to understand?"

"Not to me," said Becca, returning now with the water pails. "I think you guys were really great together. And I always will."

"Besides," Esme added, her face darkening, "after what I went through with Daddy dearest, Tito and me just seemed kind of . . ."

"Kind of what, Esme?"

"Normal."

"How much did Tito know about that?"

"Not a thing."

"Why, were you afraid of what he might do to Dodge?"

"No, not really."

"Then what was it?"

"That was the past," Esme explained. "I don't like to go there— there's never anything back there that's any good. So I never, ever look back. Only forward."

"Is that why you never went after your dad?"

"You mean like call the law on him or something?"

"No need to do that," Becca spoke up, her own sunken eyes getting a steely look. "His current punishment is much worse."

Esme nodded her head in grim assent.

"What punishment is that?"

"Daddy has to live with himself," said Esme.

"Each and every day," Becca added.

Mitch let this one go. He didn't tell them that Dodge seemed to have no regrets, no remorse, no functioning conscience at all. Esme and Becca both needed to believe that he did, and Mitch wasn't about to take it from them. They had so little else to cling to. "Esme, why did you come back here this summer?"

"I thought Dorset would be good for us," she replied, shrugging her soft shoulders. "I was wrong."

A pair of kids on jet skis went hurtling past them now, shrieking with high-decibel delight. Mitch sat back on his ample haunches, watching them. "Look, maybe we ought to talk about Tito's script again in a few days," he suggested.

"No, Mitch," Esme said. "I don't ever want to talk about that again. Just promise me one thing, okay?"

"Of course. Anything."

"His fans deserve to know who Tito really was. Tell them. It can't hurt him now."

"What about you? It can hurt you."

"No, it can't," Esme said softly as she continued working on their castle, her wet hands fashioning its walls higher, higher, and still higher. "Nothing can hurt me anymore. Not a thing."

Chapter 16

"Hey, Tina — long time no see."

"Mitch, it has been *too* long!" Tina's round, pink face lit up with motherly delight as she planted wet kisses on both of Mitch's cheeks. She was a chubby, bustling little strawberry blond in her fifties. "Now tell me," she commanded him, gazing up, up at Des. "Who is this lovely creature?"

"Say hello to Desiree Mitry."

"Welcome to my restaurant, Desiree."

Des smiled at her. "Thank you, I've heard a lot about it."

The Port Alba Café was on Thompson Street a block below Washington Square Park, next door to a shop where men sat playing chess with each other. It was a tiny café—no more than a dozen tables, all but one of them filled. Young families with small children were eating there. Several couples. One very dignified old man in a white suit who sat alone, sipping an espresso. There was a mural of a fishing village on one wall, a tiny bar with glasses in an overhead rack. The ceiling was of stamped tin. Wonderful smells were coming out of the kitchen.

Des had on a dress for the first time in ages, a sleeveless little yellow knit thing that clung to her hips and bootay for dear life. She wore sandals with it, gold loops in her ears, her grandmother's pearls, a bit of lipstick. She had even painted her toenails, which she almost never did. But this was a special night. She was out on a genuine New York City date with the man she loved.

Mitch wore a white oxford button-down, khakis, and Mephisto walking shoes, which was the same damned thing he always wore. But for this occasion his shirt and trousers were actually pressed and his mop of curly hair combed. He looked positively grown-up.

Tina seated them at the empty table by the window and brought them a bottle of chianti, a loaf of warm, crusty bread, and a platter filled with little plates of antipasti—grilled sardines, white beans in extra-virgin olive oil, marinated calamari salad, fresh buffalo mozzarella with basil leaves and tomatoes. After Tina had poured them each a glass of wine she went to fetch her husband, Ugo, a grave, scrawny little man who was the chef. Ugo solemnly shook hands with Mitch and asked him if he wanted the usual.

"For two," Mitch said, beaming at Des. "If that's okay with you."

"What I've been waiting for, boyfriend."

Ugo disappeared back into the kitchen.

Mitch reached across the table and took her hand. "You are a total hottie, you know that?"

"Um, okay, I'm thinking maybe I should put on a dress more often."

"That's funny, I'm thinking about taking it off of you."

"You're awfully frisky tonight, sir. Happy to get away from Dorset?"

"I'm just excited about spending the night here with you," he said, attacking the grilled sardines.

Des spooned some calamari onto her own plate and dove in. "That was our deal. And a deal's a deal, right?"

"Whatever you say, Master Sergeant."

Des gazed over at the mural of the fishing village, loving it even though she was fully aware that Professor Weiss would pick it to pieces. The proportions, angles, placement of cast shadows—all were wrong, wrong, wrong. "So this was your place, am I right? You and Maisie."

Mitch lowered his eyes, nodding.

"You haven't been back here since she died, have you?"

"No, I haven't." His eyes met hers now. "Is this okay, us coming here?"

"Mitch, it's more than okay. It's an honor."

They had gone through the entire antipasto platter and a half bottle of wine by the time Ugo emerged from the kitchen with a battered copper skillet full of spinach fettuccine. Tina laid warm plates before them and he spooned it out. Ugo had a whole Alfredo thing going on in there with the homemade green pasta and fresh spinach—lots of cream, butter, and melted cheese. Total sin. Especially when Tina was done grating even more cheese onto it.

She hovered there anxiously as Des tasted it. "You like?"

"No, I love." Truly, it was the best pasta Des had ever eaten. It positively melted in her mouth.

Thrilled, Tina left them to it.

"Have you figured out what to do with Tito's script?" she asked Mitch as they ate.

"I'm going to publish it," he replied. "I'll write an introduction that expands on the article I wrote after he died. I'll go into the real deal of what happened to him, complete with the transcript of Will's confession. Esme wants it that way. Whatever money it earns will go into a college scholarship fund for kids in the barrio where Tito grew up. And if someone wants to buy the movie rights, the same deal applies. Sound good?"

"Sounds real good, Mitch."

"Des, what do you think will happen to Dodge?"

"You mean with the law? My guess is he'll cop to malicious mischief, get off with six months probation."

"No jail time?"

"I wouldn't think so. He *is* a pillar of the community, after all," she pointed out dryly.

Mitch sat back from his plate. He had a troubled look on his face. "I'm thinking I don't believe in what I believed in before."

"Which was? . . ."

"Dodge is a really, really bad guy. He's done horrible things to Esme, to other girls, to his business competitors, his friends. He gets a slap on the wrist and is basically free to dust himself off and start all over again. Will, meanwhile, was a decent guy who fell in love with the wrong person, lost his head, and now he, Tito, and Donna are all dead. Where is the justice here?"

Des patted her mouth with her napkin and said, "First of all, you're wrong. Will wasn't a decent guy, he was a stone-cold killer."

"And Dodge?"

"Total human scum, I'll grant you."

"So where's the justice?"

"You don't win them all. That's why I have such a clean kitchen floor."

"Okay, you just lost me."

"Bella gets down on her hands and knees and she scrubs when she's upset. You watch old movies about giant bugs—"

"Not always. Sometimes they're about giant crustaceans."

"And I draw pictures, or at least I used to. I don't know *what* to call the stuff I draw now. Actually, I do—I call it crap. My point is, we all deal in our own way. That's real life."

"Well, it sucks," he grumbled, sipping his wine.

"Sometimes it does. Other times, it can be pretty damned perfect."

"Like when?"

She put her hand over his and squeezed it. "Like right now."

The Tavern was on Horatio and Washington, right around the corner from Mitch's apartment. It had sawdust on the floor and very little in the way of decor. In past days, it had been a saloon favored by the neighborhood's big burly meatpackers. Now it was filled with bright, boisterous young writers, artists, actors and grad students. A lot of them hadn't paired off yet and were assembled in groups. A lot of those groups were mixed. Des saw black faces, Asian faces, all sorts of faces.

It was not, repeat not, a proper dance club. But it was a place he liked and it did have a jukebox. Since he'd insisted on buying dinner she got the drinks while he edged his way warily over to the juke, a look of sheer dread on his face.

She was at the bar fetching them two frosty mugs of New Amsterdam draft when she heard that opening blast of horns—the one that belongs to no other song than "Respect," followed by that slamming guitar riff, and then by the lady herself. And now Aretha was singing about what *she* needed. And Des was gliding her way across the bar toward Mitch, their eyes locked on to each other, and there was no one else in that crowded place, just them. She put their beers down on the juke and raised her arms up high into the air, bumping hips with the boy, feeling the music and the wine and . . . and . . . *Damn,* what *was* he doing with himself? Passing a kidney stone? And where was he going with those two clumsy feet of his? Did he not even *feel* the beat?

But, hey, he was dancing his dance and no one was staring or caring. And he was so damned cute.

Besides, it wasn't long before they were back at his place and they were in each other's arms in his big brass bed. He was still worried about her shoulder but she kept telling him not to be. They made sweet love deep into the night while the sirens and the car alarms serenaded them, and the refrigerator trucks outside the packing houses *beep-beep-beeped* as they backed up and the cabs went *tha-thunk-ker-chunk* over the steel plate Con Ed had put over the hole in the street.

And for some strange reason there was a special urgency that had never been there before for either of them. Together, they found something new and even more fantastic that night in Mitch's bed.

"Now you've felt it," he murmured at her as the early light of dawn approached, Mitch stroking her face gently. Truly, he was the most loving man she'd ever been with.

"Felt what, baby?"

"The energy of the city."

"I thought that was the energy of you and me."

"Maybe we had a little something to do with it," he admitted, immediately falling into a deep sleep with his mouth open.

Des was wide awake herself. Something about being here in his apartment made her feel all wired. She threw on a T-shirt, padded barefoot into the living room and flicked on a lamp, gazing around at his place. She was definitely uneasy here. It was Maisie's place. He'd tried to scour it of her presence after she died. He had told Des this. But there was still a lot that smacked of *her.* Like the exquisite, matching leather loveseat and club chairs positioned just so. And those vintage brass lamps with green glass shades. And the genuine Stickley library table that he used as a desk. Out on Big Sister, the man used an old door on sawhorses. Des's trained eye also caught the small things he had missed, like a fat volume entitled *Simplified Site Engineering* that was shoring up one end of the radiator cover.

Standing there, Des felt a sudden, powerful urge to be somewhere else.

She slipped back into the bedroom for her gym bag. Put on her shorts and running shoes, pocketed Mitch's spare keys and let herself out the door. It was not quite 6:00 A.M. but the cobblestoned street was awake and active. A half dozen meatpackers were going home after their night's work, exhausted but rowdy. An executive type in a spotless seersucker suit was walking his Jack Russell terrier and scanning the *Wall Street Journal*. A young Latino man, stripped to the waist, was working under the hood of his parked car, a sheen of sweat on his bare shoulders, a can of Budweiser within arm's reach. An old lady in the brownstone across the street was watching him from her second-floor window, her arms resting on a cushion on the windowsill, the smoke from her cigarette curling lazily up into the early morning sunlight that slanted low across Gansevoort from the east.

Des found herself lingering there on the stoop of Mitch's building, staring at that lady, that sunlight, that man working on his car. To her surprise, her pulse began to quicken and her fingertips tingled. This was the same sensation she felt whenever she walked into the studio at the art academy—an overwhelming sense of being in a special, hallowed place. Des had never experienced this while standing outside on a street before. Not anywhere.

She headed out, suddenly giddy with excitement. The Chinese laundry down the street was already open. So was the corner grocery store, where a young boy was hosing down the sidewalk and a milk truck was making a delivery. She bought herself a coffee and sipped it as she began walking through the close-knit neighborhood of family-owned brownstones, her eyes open wide, soaking in every detail. The building super who was out bagging the trash, muttering to himself. The housewife in her bathrobe who was moving her car from the no-parking side of the street before she got ticketed. The wasted rock 'n' rollers in black leather climbing out of a cab from their night out, reeking of cigarette smoke and patchouli.

By now it was nearly seven, and some folks were heading off to work. Des followed them, swept along by their urgency. Found herself on Fourteenth Street at the entrance to the subway. Bought a token. Rode the Number 1 train all the way up to Times Square and back, gazing at all of those faces across the car from her, faces representing ten, twenty, thirty different nations and races and ethnic groups. Young faces and old faces, the hopeful and the homeless, students, laborers, and millionaires, all of them standing there shoulder to shoulder, gripping the handrail, clinging to their own individual dreams.

Des was gone for hours. There was a bagel place near Mitch's corner where she bought fresh bagels and two more coffees on her way back. Then she went back down Gansevoort to Mitch's building, the one that had that scrawny London plane tree growing out front in a cutout in the sidewalk. A low iron rail had been positioned around it to keep dogs from peeing on it. It was not an easy life for a tree in the city. As Des started up Mitch's steps she paused, noticing just how tenaciously the plane tree's shallow, exposed roots clung to the soil— exactly like the knuckles of those subway riders she'd just seen— fighting for its place, fighting for its life, fighting for its . . .

And that's when it hit her. Why she hadn't been able to draw them.

Trees weren't things made out of twigs and leaves. They were living, breathing creatures. Their trunks and branches weren't wood, they were muscle and sinew and bone. *That's* what that poor little cedar had been trying to tell her, the one that had been clinging to the side of the cliff at Chapman Falls—until it died saving their lives up there that night.

Trees weren't *things*.

Breathless, she darted inside for her sketch pad, rushed back out and sat down on the stoop, resting it on her bare knees, graphite stick in hand. She started with quick gesture drawings of the plane tree. Except she wasn't drawing a tree anymore—she was drawing a nude figure model who was posed there for her in the morning light, reaching high for the sun. Des drew and she drew, her stick flying across the page.

She barely heard Mitch when he moseyed out and joined her there, yawning and blinking "What time did you get up?"

"Never went to sleep," she replied, as an old lady went by with a grocery cart.

"Morning, Mrs. Fodera," Mitch called to her. "Lovely day."

"Eh," the old lady grunted, waggling a hand.

He sat next to Des on the stoop and opened a coffee, glancing over her shoulder at her pad, not saying another word.

"Do you ever get tired of being so smart?" she asked him.

"Nope, it stays fresh pretty much all the time," he replied, biting into a bagel.

"Mitch, I've been thinking about something. . . ."

"Uh-oh, this sounds serious."

"It is. I'd like to start spending more time in New York than I have been."

"Are you kidding me? I've been begging you to."

"Wait, there's more," she warned him, swallowing. "I'd maybe even, you know, keep a few . . . some of my clothes here. Can you handle that?"

"Would any of these clothes be little yellow dresses?"

Her eyes locked on to his. "I mean it, Mitch. Can you?"

"That all depends," he said gravely. "Would I have to dance in public again?"

"Try that one more time and I'll bust you myself."

"In that case, girlfriend, I think we can work something out."